INTO THE DIAMOND AGE!

This series of the most memorable science fiction stories of past years is rapidly becoming one of Isaac Asimov's master projects. Every reviewer has praised it and every volume has been eagerly sought and added to a growing file of what may eventually become the major encyclopedia of what is worth while in SF short stories and novelettes.

Now we come to 1948, certainly a major year in the dawn of the Diamond Age of Science Fiction. Here you will find H. Beam Piper and Wilmar Shiras, Judith Merril and John D. MacDonald, A.E. Van Vogt and William Tenn, and many more.

Happy reading!

Anthologies from DAW

ASIMOV PRESENTS THE GREAT SF STORIES
The best stories of the last two decades.
Edited by Isaac Asimov and Martin H. Greenberg.

THE ANNUAL WORLD'S BEST SF
The best of the current year.
Edited by Donald A. Wollheim with Arthur W. Saha.

THE YEAR'S BEST HORROR STORIES
An annual of gooseflesh tales.
Edited by Karl Edward Wagner.

THE YEAR'S BEST FANTASY STORIES
An annual of high imagination.
Edited by Arthur W. Saha

TERRA SF
The Best Sf from Western Europe.
Edited by Richard D. Nolane.

HECATE'S CAULDRON
Edited by Susan M. Shwartz

AMAZONS
Edited by Jessica A. Salmonson

WOLLHEIM'S WORLD'S BEST SF
Edited by Donald A. Wollheim

SWORD OF CHAOS
Stories by the Friends of Darkover.
Edited by Marion Zimmer Bradley

ISAAC ASIMOV

Presents

THE GREAT SCIENCE FICTION STORIES

Volume 10, 1948

Edited by Isaac Asimov and Martin H. Greenberg

DAW Books, Inc.

Donald A. Wollheim, Publisher

1633 Broadway, New York, N.Y. 10019

PUBLISHED BY
THE NEW AMERICAN LIBRARY
OF CANADA LIMITED

ACKNOWLEDGMENTS

Table of Contents

Introduction

In the world outside reality, the year began on a bloody note with the assassination of the Indian leader Mahatma Gandhi on January 30. On February 25 a communist coup ended Czechoslovakia's brief moment of post-war democracy as that country fell firmly into the grip of the Soviets. On May 10 the United States Army began to run the U.S. railroad system under orders from President Truman, who moved to head off a threatened strike.

Zionist leader David Ben-Gurion proclaimed the founding of the state of Israel on May 14, the day the British left Palestine. The new country was invaded the following day by the regular armies of five Arab countries, beginning a war that would last into 1949. On June 28 Yugoslavia was expelled from the Cominform, as Marshal Tito insisted on his own form of "national Communism." U.S.-Soviet tension continued to grow throughout the year, formalized by presidential adviser Bernard Baruch's coining of the term "the Cold War." On July 24 Soviet forces began a blockade of all rail and highway movement into the Western sector of Berlin, precipitating the "Berlin Blockade" that would not end until September, 1949. The city was kept alive by a difficult airlift by Western aircraft.

On August 15 the Republic of Korea (South Korea) was established under the rule of President Syngman Rhee; on September 9 the Communists established the Korean People's Democratic Republic (North Korea).

The 1948 U.S. Presidential election was won by Harry Truman in one of the greatest political upsets in American history. Truman won despite challenges from Strom Thurmond's Dixiecrats and Henry Wallace's Progressive Party. On December 15 a federal jury indicted Alger Hiss, a former State Department employee, for perjury, charging that he had lied about passing classified materials to Soviet agents. The indictment was the result of an investigation led by a young California Congressman, Richard M. Nixon.

During 1948 Richard P. Feynman and Julian Schwinger developed a new quantum theory of electrodynamics. Idlewild International Airport (later John F. Kennedy) opened for business in New York. Ferdinand Porsche introduced the car named after him, while Soichiro Honda showed off his new motorcycle. Hench and Kendall synthesized the hormone cortisone. Many people learned the joys of traveling after the introduction of Dramamine. The number of homes with television sets reached 1,000,000.

The Olympic Games, after a long interruption caused by World War II, were held in London. The United States won the most medals, but the powerful Soviet team, competing in the Games for the first time in history, finished a strong second. Leading novels and books included *The Naked and the Dead* by Norman Mailer, *The Heart of the Matter* by Graham Greene, *Intruder in the Dust* by William Faulkner, *The City and the Pillar* by Gore Vidal, and *The Young Lions* by Irwin Shaw. The Cleveland Indians defeated the Boston Braves (remember them?) four games to two in the World Series. Jackson Pollock painted "Composition No. 1." "V-8" cocktail juice was brought out by the Campbell Soup Company.

Top films included *The Treasure of the Sierra Madre*, starring Humphrey Bogart, *The Lady from Shanghai* with Rita Hayworth, *Red River*, with John Wayne, *Portrait of Jennie*, and *Key Largo*, with Lauren Bacall and Humphrey Bogart exchanging knowing glances. Citation won Racing's Triple Crown. The Bell Telephone Laboratories invented the transistor, which would revolutionize electronics and warfare.

Norbert Wiener published *Cybernetics*, while Alfred C. Kinsey published the equally interesting *Sexual Behavior in the Human Male*. "Pogo," *US News and World Report*, and the radial tire made their debuts. Broadway hits included *Mr. Roberts*, *Where's Charley?*, *Summer and Smoke*, *Anne of a Thousand Days* and *Kiss Me Kate*. The world was singing such songs as "Once in Love With Amy," "Tennessee Waltz," "Baby, It's Cold Outside," "I'll Be Home for Christmas," and "Red Roses for a Blue Lady." Three of the top television shows were *Hopalong Cassidy*, *The Ed Sullivan Show*, and

The Original Amateur Hour, with Ted Mack. The McDonald brothers offered franchises to those willing to sell fast food.

Mel Brooks was (probably) still Melvin Kaminsky.

In the real world it was another outstanding year as a large number of excellent science fiction novels and collections were published (many of which had been serialized years before in the magazines), including *Who Goes There?* by John W. Campbell, Jr., *The Sunken World* by Stanton Coblentz, *Divide and Rule* and *The Wheels of If* by L. Sprague de Camp . . . *And Some Were Human* by Lester del Rey, *The Radio Man* by Ralph Milne Farley, *Space Cadet* and *Beyond This Horizon* by Robert A. Heinlein, *The Well of the Unicorn* and *The Carnelian Cube* by Fletcher Pratt (the latter with de Camp), *Walden Two* by B. F. Skinner, *Skylark Three and Triplanetary* by E. E. ("Doc") Smith, *Without Sorcery* by Theodore Sturgeon, *The World of A* by A. E. van Vogt, *The Black Flame* by Stanley G. Weinbaum, and *Darker Than You Think* by Jack Williamson. Many of these books were published by fan publishers whose companies did not last for long. In addition, Groff Conklin published *The Treasury of Science Fiction*, continuing his series of wonderful anthologies that mined the Golden Age.

More wondrous things were happening in the real world as three excellent writers made their maiden voyages into reality: Judith Merril with "That Only a Mother" in June, Charles L. Harness with "Time Tomb" in August, and Peter Phillips with the stunning "Dreams Are Sacred" in September.

The first Westercon was held in September, and the real people gathered together for the sixth time as the World Science Fiction Convention (Torcon in Toronto) moved outside the borders of the United States.

And distant wings were beating as Michael Ashley, Robert P. Holdstock, Jonathan Fast, Vonda McIntyre, Marta Randall, Robert Reginald, Spider Robinson, Pamela Sargent, Brian Stableford, Steven Utley, Joan Vinge, and Laurence Yep were born.

Let us travel back to that honored year of 1948 and enjoy the best stories that the real world bequeathed to us.

DON'T LOOK NOW

by Henry Kuttner (1914—1958)

STARTLING STORIES
March

Henry Kuttner and his wife, C. L. Moore, continued their relative dominance of the second half of the 1940s with this stunning story. Kuttner selected it for My Best Science Fiction Story *(1949), and made the following comment in his introduction: ". . . I can honestly say it is my favorite story because I have reread all my others, on publication, and they disgusted me. For one reason or another, I didn't get around to rereading "Don't Look Now," and can therefore regard it with the unbiased, critical, gemlike eye of the happy creator. . . . Anyway, my wife wrote it."*

Well, the story is wonderful, and it is just possible that Catherine did write it. Two other 1948 stories by Kuttner and/or Moore, "Ex Machina" and "Happy Ending," narrowly missed inclusion in this volume.

(It is a rather sad commentary on humanity that it is always so attractive to think that some small group "controls the Earth"—the Jews, the international bankers, the Communists, the Masons, the Trilateral Commission. Those who believe such things are so sincere, so harried, so paranoid and, if the times are

*bad enough, and if the hunger for a scapegoat is great
enough—so convincing. The Nazis are the most dreadful example in recent history of how far madmen can go
when riding the skeletal horse of paranoia, but their
example has by no means cured the world. Kuttner
satirized this quite effectively in "Don't Look Now"
and the last sentence is one of the classic examples of
what last sentences should be. Personally, I'm almost
relieved that our Mars probes have finally and definitely shown that the Martians—that is, intelligent inhabitants of the planet Mars—do not exist. —For the
sake of our paranoids.—I. A.)*

The man in the brown suit was looking at himself in the mirror
behind the bar. The reflection seemed to interest him even more
deeply than the drink between his hands. He was paying only
perfunctory attention to Lyman's attempts at conversation. This
had been going on for perhaps fifteen minutes before he finally
lifted his glass and took a deep swallow.

"Don't look now," Lyman said.

The brown man slid his eyes sidewise toward Lyman, tilted
his glass higher, and took another swig. Ice cubes slipped down
toward his mouth. He put the glass back on the red-brown wood
and signaled for a refill. Finally he took a deep breath and
looked at Lyman.

"Don't look at what?" he asked.

"There was one sitting right beside you," Lyman said, blinking rather glazed eyes. "He just went out. You mean you
couldn't see him?"

The brown man finished paying for his fresh drink before he
answered. "See who?" he asked, with a fine mixture of boredom,
distaste and reluctant interest. "Who went out?"

"What have I been telling you for the last ten minutes?
Weren't you listening?"

"Certainly I was listening. That is—certainly. You were talking about—bathtubs. Radios. Orson—"

"Not Orson. H. G. Herbert George. With Orson it was just a
gag. H. G. *knew*—or suspected. I wonder if it was simply
intuition with him? He couldn't have had any proof—but he did

stop writing science fiction rather suddenly, didn't he? I'll bet he knew once, though."

"Knew what?"

"About the Martians. All this won't do us a bit of good if you don't listen. It may not anyway. The trick is to jump the gun—with proof. Convincing evidence. Nobody's ever been allowed to produce the evidence before. You *are* a reporter, aren't you?"

Holding his glass, the man in the brown suit nodded reluctantly.

"Then you ought to be taking it all down on a piece of folded paper. I want everybody to know. The whole world. It's important. Terribly important. It explains everything. My life won't be safe unless I can pass along the information and make people believe it."

"Why won't your life be safe?"

"Because of the Martians, you fool. They own the world."

The brown man sighed. "Then they own my newspaper, too," he objected, "so I can't print anything they don't like."

"I never thought of that," Lyman said, considering the bottom of his glass, where two ice cubes had fused into a cold, immutable union. "They're not omnipotent, though. I'm sure they're vulnerable, or why have they always kept under cover? They're afraid of being found out. If the world had convincing evidence—look, people always believe what they read in the newspapers. Couldn't you—"

"Ha," said the brown man with deep significance.

Lyman drummed sadly on the bar and murmured, "There must be some way. Perhaps if I had another drink. . . ."

The brown-suited man tasted his collins, which seemed to stimulate him. "Just what is all this about Martians?" he asked Lyman. "Suppose you start at the beginning and tell me again. Or can't you remember?"

"Of course I can remember. I've got practically total recall. It's something new. Very new. I never could do it before. I can even remember my last conversation with the Martians." Lyman favored the brown man with a glance of triumph.

"When was that?"

"This morning."

"I can even remember conversations I had last week," the brown man said mildly. "So what?"

"You don't understand. They make us forget, you see. They tell us what to do and we forget about the conversation—it's post-hypnotic suggestion, I expect—but we follow their orders just the same. There's the compulsion, though we think we're making our own decisions. Oh, they own the world, all right, but nobody knows it except me."

"And how did you find out?"

"Well, I got my brain scrambled, in a way. I've been fooling around with supersonic detergents, trying to work out something marketable, you know. The gadget went wrong—from some standpoints. High-frequency waves, it was. They went through and through me. Should have been inaudible, but I could hear them, or rather—well, actually I could *see* them. That's what I mean about my brain being scrambled. And after that, I could see and hear the Martians. They've geared themselves so they work efficiently on ordinary brains, and mine isn't ordinary anymore. They can't hypnotize me, either. They can command me, but I needn't obey—now. I hope they don't suspect. Maybe they do. Yes, I guess they do."

"How can you tell?"

"The way they look at me."

"How do they look at you?" asked the brown man, as he began to reach for a pencil and then changed his mind. He took a drink instead. "Well? What are they like?"

"I'm not sure. I can see them, all right, but only when they're dressed up."

"Okay, okay," the brown man said patiently. "How do they look, dressed up?"

"Just like anybody, almost. They dress up in—in human skins. Oh, not real ones, imitations. Like the Katzenjammer Kids zipped into crocodile suits. Undressed—I don't know. I've never seen one. Maybe they're invisible even to me, then, or maybe they're just camouflaged. Ants or owls or rats or bats or—"

"Or anything," the brown man said hastily.

"Thanks. Or anything, of course. But when they're dressed up like humans—like that one who was sitting next to you awhile ago, when I told you not to look—"

"That one was invisible, I gather?"

"Most of the time they are, to everybody. But once in a while, for some reason, they—"

"Wait," the brown man objected. "Make sense, will you? They dress up in human skins and then sit around invisible?"

"Only now and then. The human skins are perfectly good imitations. Nobody can tell the difference. It's that third eye that gives them away. When they keep it closed, you'd never guess it was there. When they want to open it, they go invisible—like *that*. Fast. When I see somebody with a third eye, right in the middle of his forehead, I know he's a Martian and invisible, and I pretend not to notice him.''

"Uh-huh," the brown man said. "Then for all you know, I'm one of your visible Martians."

"Oh, I hope not!" Lyman regarded him anxiously. "Drunk as I am, I don't think so. I've been trailing you all day, making sure. It's a risk I have to take, of course. They'll go to any length—any length at all—to make a man give himself away. I realize that. I can't really trust anybody. But I had to find *someone* to talk to, and I—'' He paused. There was a brief silence. "I could be wrong," Lyman said presently. "When the third eye's closed, I can't tell if it's there. Would you mind opening your third eye for me?" He fixed a dim gaze on the brown man's forehead.

"Sorry," the reporter said. "Some other time. Besides, I don't know you. So you want me to splash this across the front page, I gather? Why didn't you go to see the managing editor? My stories have to get past the desk and rewrite.''

"I want to give my secret to the world," Lyman said stubbornly. "The question is, how far will I get? You'd expect they'd have killed me the minute I opened my mouth to you—except that I didn't say anything while they were here. I don't believe they take us very seriously, you know. This must have been going on since the dawn of history, and by now they've had time to get careless. They let Fort go pretty far before they cracked down on him. But you notice they were careful never to let Ford get hold of genuine proof that would convince people.''

The brown man said something under his breath about a human interest story in a box. He asked, "What do the Martians do, besides hang around bars all dressed up?"

"I'm still working on that," Lyman said. "It isn't easy to understand. They run the world, of course, but why?" He wrinkled his brow and stared appealingly at the brown man. "Why?"

"If they do run it, they've got a lot to explain."

"That's what I mean. From our viewpoint, there's no sense to it. We do things illogically, but only because they tell us to. Everything we do, almost, is pure illogic. Poe's *Imp of the Perverse*—you could give it another name beginning with M. Martian, I mean. It's all very well for psychologists to explain why a murderer wants to confess, but it's still an illogical reaction. Unless a Martian commands him to.''

"You can't be hypnotized into doing anything that violates your moral sense," the brown man said triumphantly.

Lyman frowned. "Not by another human, but you can by a Martian. I expect they got the upper hand when we didn't have more than ape-brains, and they've kept it ever since. They evolved as we did, and kept a step ahead. Like the sparrow on the eagle's back who hitch-hiked till the eagle reached his ceiling, and then took off and broke the altitude record. They conquered the world, but nobody ever knew it. And they've been ruling ever since."

"But—"

"Take houses, for example. Uncomfortable things. Ugly, inconvenient, dirty, everything wrong with them. But when men like Frank Lloyd Wright slip out from under the Martians' thumb long enough to suggest something better, look how the people react. They hate the thought. That's their Martians, giving them orders."

"Look. Why should the Martians care what kind of houses we live in? Tell me that."

Lyman frowned. "I don't like the note of skepticism I detect creeping into this conversation," he announced. "They care, all right. No doubt about it. They *live* in our houses. We don't build for our convenience, we build, under order, for the Martians, the way they want it. They're very much concerned with everything we do. And the more senseless, the more concern.

"Take wars. Wars don't make sense from any human viewpoint. Nobody really wants wars. But we go right on having them. From the Martian viewpoint, they're useful. They give us a spurt in technology, and they reduce the excess population. And there are lots of other results, too. Colonization, for one thing. But mainly technology. In peacetime, if a guy invents jet propulsion, it's too expensive to develop commercially. In wartime, though, it's *got* to be developed. Then the Martians can use it whenever they want. They use us the way they'd use tools or—or limbs. And nobody ever really wins a war—except the Martians."

The man in the brown suit chuckled. "That makes sense," he said. "It must be nice to be a Martian."

"Why not? Up till now, no race ever successfully conquered and ruled another. The underdog could revolt or absorb. If you know you're being ruled, then the ruler's vulnerable. But if the world doesn't know—and it doesn't—

"Take radios," Lyman continued, going off at a tangent. "There's no earthly reason why a sane human should listen to a radio. But the Martians make us do it. They like it. Take bathtubs. Nobody contends bathtubs are comfortable—for us. But they're fine for Martians. All the impractical things we keep on using, even though we know they're impractical—''

"Typewriter ribbons," the brown man said, struck by the thought. "But not even a Martian could enjoy changing a typewriter ribbon."

Lyman seemed to find that flippant. He said that he knew all about the Martians except for one thing—their psychology.

"I don't know *why* they act as they do. It looks illogical sometimes, but I feel perfectly sure they've got sound motives for every move they make. Until I get that worked out I'm pretty much at a standstill. Until I get evidence—proof—and help. I've got to stay under cover till then. And I've been doing that. I do what they tell me, so they won't suspect, and I pretend to forget what they tell me to forget."

"Then you've got nothing much to worry about."

Lyman paid no attention. He was off again on a list of his grievances.

"When I hear the water running in the tub and a Martian splashing around, I pretend I don't hear a thing. My bed's too short and I tried last week to order a special length, but the Martian that sleeps there told me not to. He's a runt, like most of them. That is, I think they're runts. I have to deduce, because you never see them undressed. But it goes on like that constantly. By the way, how's your Martian?"

The man in the brown suit set down his glass rather suddenly. "My Martian?"

"Now listen. I may be just a little bit drunk, but my logic remains unimpaired. I can still put two and two together. Either you know about the Martians, or you don't. If you do, there's no point in giving me that, 'What, *my* Martian?' routine. I know you have a Martian. Your Martian knows you have a Martian. My Martian knows. The point is, do *you* know? Think hard," Lyman urged solicitously.

"No, I haven't got a Martian," the reporter said, taking a quick drink. The edge of the glass clicked against his teeth.

"Nervous, I see," Lyman remarked. "Of course you *have* got a Martian. I suspect you know it."

"What would I be doing with a Martian?" the brown man asked with dogged dogmatism.

"What would you be doing without one? I imagine it's illegal. If they caught you running around without one they'd probably put you in a pound or something until claimed. Oh, you've got one, all right. So have I. So has he, and he, and he—and the bartender." Lyman enumerated the other barflies with a wavering forefinger.

"Of course they have," the brown man said. "But they'll all go back to Mars tomorrow and then you can see a good doctor. You'd better have another dri—"

He was turning toward the bartender when Lyman, apparently by accident, leaned close to him and whispered urgently, *"Don't look now!"*

The brown man glanced at Lyman's white face reflected in the mirror before them.

"It's all right," he said. "There aren't any Mar—"

Lyman gave him a fierce, quick kick under the edge of the bar.

"Shut up! One just came in!"

And then he caught the brown man's gaze and with elaborate unconcern said, "—so naturally, there was nothing for me to do but climb out on the roof after it. Took me ten minutes to get it down the ladder, and just as we reached the bottom it gave one bound, climbed up my face, sprang from the top of my head, and there it was again on the roof, screaming for me to get it down."

"What?" the brown man demanded with pardonable curiosity.

"My cat, of course. What did you think? No, never mind, don't answer that." Lyman's face was turned to the brown man's, but from the corners of his eyes he was watching an invisible progress down the length of the bar toward a booth at the very back.

"Now why did he come in?" he murmured. "I don't like this. Is he anyone you know?"

"Is who—?"

"That Martian. Yours, by any chance? No, I suppose not. Yours was probably the one who went out a while ago. I wonder if he went to make a report, and sent this one in? It's possible. It could be. You can talk now, but keep your voice low, and stop squirming. Want him to notice we can see him?"

"*I* can't see him. Don't drag me into this. You and your Martians can fight it out together. You're making me nervous. I've got to go, anyway." But he didn't move to get off the stool. Across Lyman's shoulder he was stealing glances toward the back of the bar, and now and then he looked at Lyman's face.

"Stop watching me," Lyman said. "Stop watching him. Anybody'd think you were a cat."

"Why a cat? Why should anybody—do I look like a cat?"

"We were talking about cats, weren't we? Cats can see them, quite clearly. Even undressed, I believe. They don't like them."

"Who doesn't like who?"

"Whom. Neither likes the other. Cats can see Martians—sh-h! —but they pretend not to, and that makes the Martians mad. I have a theory that cats ruled the world before Martians came. Never mind. Forget about cats. This may be more serious than you think. I happen to know my Martian's taking tonight off, and I'm pretty sure that was your Martian who went out some time ago. And have you noticed that nobody else in here has his Martian with him? Do you suppose—" His voice sank. "Do you suppose they could be *waiting for us outside?*"

"Oh, Lord," the brown man said. "In the alley with the cats, I suppose."

"Why don't you stop this yammer about cats and be serious for a moment?" Lyman demanded, and then paused, paled, and reeled slightly on his stool. He hastily took a drink to cover his confusion.

"What's the matter now?" the brown man asked.

"Nothing." Gulp. "Nothing. It was just that—he *looked* at me. With—you know."

"Let me get this straight. I take it the Martian is dressed in—is dressed like a human?"

"Naturally."

"But he's invisible to all eyes but yours?"

"Yes. He doesn't want to be visible, just now. Besides—" Lyman paused cunningly. He gave the brown man a furtive glance and then looked quickly down at his drink. "Besides, you know, I rather think you *can* see him—a little, anyway."

The brown man was perfectly silent for about thirty seconds. He sat quite motionless, not even the ice in the drink he held clinking. One might have thought he did not even breathe. Certainly he did not blink.

"What makes you think that?" he asked in a normal voice, after the thirty seconds had run out.

"I—did I say anything? I wasn't listening." Lyman put down his drink abruptly. "I think I'll go now."

"No, you won't," the brown man said, closing his fingers around Lyman's wrist. "Not yet you won't. Come back here. Sit down. Now. What was the idea? Where were you going?"

Lyman nodded dumbly toward the back of the bar, indicating either a juke-box or a door marked MEN.

"I don't feel so good. Maybe I've had too much to drink. I guess I'll—"

"You're all right. I don't trust you back there with that—that invisible man of yours. You'll stay right here until he leaves."

"He's going now," Lyman said brightly. His eyes moved with great briskness along the line of an invisible but rapid progress toward the front door. "See, he's gone. Now let me loose, will you?"

The brown man glanced toward the back booth.

"No," he said, "he isn't gone. Sit right where you are."

It was Lyman's turn to remain quite still, in a stricken sort of way, for a perceptible while. The ice in *his* drink, however, clinked audibly. Presently he spoke. His voice was soft and rather soberer than before.

"You're right. He's still there. You can see him, can't you?"

The brown man said, "Has he got his back to us?"

"You *can* see him, then. Better than I can maybe. Maybe there are more of them here than I thought. They could be anywhere. They could be sitting beside you anywhere you go, and you wouldn't even guess, until—" He shook his head a little. "They'd want to be *sure*," he said, mostly to himself. "They can give you orders and make you forget, but there must be limits to what they can force you to do. They can't make a man betray himself. They'd have to lead him on—until they were sure."

He lifted his drink and tipped it steeply above his face. The ice ran down the slope and bumped coldly against his lip, but he held it until the last of the pale, bubbling amber had drained into his mouth. He set the glass on the bar and faced the brown man.

"Well?" he said.

The brown man looked up and down the bar.

"It's getting late," he said. "Not many people left. We'll wait."

"Wait for what?"

The brown man looked toward the back booth and looked away again quickly.

"I have something to show you. I don't want anyone else to see."

Lyman surveyed the narrow, smoky room. As he looked the last customer beside themselves at the bar began groping in his pocket, tossed some change on the mahogany, and went out slowly.

They sat in silence. The bartender eyed them with stolid disinterest. Presently a couple in the front booth got up and departed, quarreling in undertones.

"Is there anyone left?" the brown man asked in a voice that did not carry down the bar to the man in the apron.

"Only—" Lyman did not finish, but he nodded gently toward the back of the room. "He isn't looking. Let's get this over with. What do you want to show me?"

The brown man took off his wrist watch and pried up the metal case. Two small, glossy photograph prints slid out. The brown man separated them with a finger.

"I just want to make sure of something," he said. "First—why did you pick me out? Quite a while ago, you said you'd been trailing me all day, making sure. I haven't forgotten that. And you knew I was a reporter. Suppose you tell me the truth, now?"

Squirming on his stool, Lyman scowled. "It was the way you looked at things," he murmured. "On the subway this morning—I'd never seen you before in my life, but I kept noticing the way you looked at things—the wrong things, things that weren't there, the way a cat does—and then you'd always look away—I got the idea you could see the Martians too."

"Go on," the brown man said quietly.

"I followed you. All day. I kept hoping you'd turn out to be—somebody I could talk to. Because if I could *know* that I wasn't the only one who could see them, then I'd know there was still some hope left. It's been worse than solitary confinement. I've been able to see them for three years now. Three years. And I've managed to keep my power a secret even from them. And, somehow, I've managed to keep from killing myself, too."

"Three years?" the brown man said. He shivered.

"There was always a little hope. I knew nobody would believe—not without proof. And how can you get proof? It was only that I—I kept telling myself that maybe you could see them too, and if you could, maybe there were others—lots of others—enough so we might get together and work out some way of proving to the world—"

The brown man's fingers were moving. In silence he pushed a photograph across the mahogany. Lyman picked it up unsteadily.

"Moonlight?" he asked after a moment. It was a landscape under a deep, dark sky with white clouds in it. Trees stood white and lacy against the darkness. The grass was white as if with moonlight, and the shadows blurry.

"No, not moonlight," the brown man said. "Infrared. I'm strictly an amateur, but lately I've been experimenting with infrared film. And I got some very odd results."

Lyman stared at the film.

"You see, I live near—" The brown man's finger tapped a certain quite common object that appeared in the photograph. "—and something funny keeps showing up now and then against it. But only with infrared film. Now I know chlorophyll reflects so much infrared light that grass and leaves photograph white. The sky comes out black, like this. There are tricks to using this kind of film. Photograph a tree against a cloud, and you can't tell them apart in the print. But you can photograph through a haze and pick out distant objects the ordinary film wouldn't catch. And sometimes, when you focus on something like this—" He tapped the image of the very common object again. "You get a very odd image on the film. Like that. A man with three eyes."

Lyman held the print up to the light. In silence he took the other one from the bar and studied it. When he laid them down he was smiling.

"You know," Lyman said in a conversational whisper, "a professor of astrophysics at one of the more important universities had a very interesting little item in the *Times* the other Sunday. Name of Spitzer, I think. He said that if there were life on Mars, and if Martians had ever visited earth, there'd be no way to prove it. Nobody would believe the few men who saw them. Not, he said, unless the Martians happened to be photographed. . . ."

Lyman looked at the brown man thoughtfully.

"Well," he said, "it's happened. You've photographed them."

The brown man nodded. He took up the prints and returned them to his watch-case. "I thought so, too. Only until tonight I couldn't be sure. I'd never seen one—fully—as you have. It isn't so much a matter of what you call getting your brain scrambled with supersonics as it is of just knowing where to look. But I've been seeing *part* of them all my life, and so has everybody. It's that little suggestion of movement you never catch except just at the edge of your vision, just out of the corner of your eye. Something that's *almost* there—and when you look fully at it, there's nothing. These photographs showed me the way. It's not easy to learn, but it can be done. We're conditioned to look directly at a thing—the particular thing we want to see clearly, whatever it is. Perhaps the Martians gave us that conditioning. When we see a movement at the edge of our range of vision, it's almost irresistible not to look directly at it. So it vanishes.''

"Then they can be seen—by anybody?"

"I've learned at lot in a few days," the brown man said. "Since I took these photographs. You have to train yourself. It's like seeing a trick picture—one that's really a composite, after you study it. Camouflage. You just have to learn how. Otherwise we can look at them all our lives and never see them.''

"The camera does, though.''

"Yes, the camera does. I've wondered why nobody ever caught them this way before. Once you see them on film, they're unmistakable—that third eye.''

"Infrared film's comparatively new, isn't it? And then I'll bet you have to catch them against that one particular background—you know—or they won't show on the film. Like trees against clouds. It's tricky. You must have had just the right lighting that day, and exactly the right focus, and the lens stopped down just right. A kind of minor miracle. It might never happen again exactly that way. But . . . don't look now.''

They were silent. Furtively, they watched the mirror. Their eyes slid along toward the open door of the tavern.

And then there was a long, breathless silence.

"He looked back at us," Lyman said very quietly. "He looked at us . . . that third eye!''

The brown man was motionless again. When he moved, it was to swallow the rest of his drink.

"I don't think that they're suspicious yet," he said. "The trick will be to keep under cover until we can blow this thing wide open. There's got to be some way to do it—some way that will convince people.''

"There's proof. The photographs. A competent cameraman ought to be able to figure out just how you caught that Martian on film and duplicate the conditions. It's evidence.''

"Evidence can cut both ways," the brown man said. "What I'm hoping is that the Martians don't really like to kill—unless they have to. I'm hoping they won't kill without proof. But—'' He tapped his wrist watch.

"There's two of us now, though," Lyman said. "We've got to stick together. Both of us have broken the big rule—*don't look now*—''

The bartender was at the back, disconnecting the juke box. The brown man said, "We'd better not be seen together unnecessarily. But if we both come to this bar tomorrow night at nine for a drink—that wouldn't look suspicious, even to them.''

"Suppose—'' Lyman hesitated. "May I have one of those photographs?''

"Why?''

"If one of us had—an accident—the other one would still have the proof. Enough, maybe, to convince the right people.''

The brown man hesitated, nodded shortly, and opened his watch case again. He gave Lyman one of the pictures.

"Hide it,'' he said. "It's—evidence. I'll see you here tomorrow. Meanwhile, be careful. Remember to play safe.''

They shook hands firmly, facing each other in an endless second of final, decisive silence. Then the brown man turned abruptly and walked out of the bar.

Lyman sat there. Between two wrinkles in his forehead there was a stir and a flicker of lashes unfurling. The third eye opened slowly and looked after the brown man.

HE WALKED AROUND THE HORSES

by H. Beam Piper (1904—1964)

ASTOUNDING SCIENCE FICTION

April

One of the strangest influences on science fiction writers were the theories of Charles Fort (1874–1932), a writer who spent a considerable portion of his life collecting records of unexplainable events—frogs falling to the earth in droves, the disappearance of people under unusual circumstances, etc. He developed various theories to explain these events, such as the possibility that humans are really the property of unknown aliens. In fact, a Fortean Society was formed to further his investigations. While sf writers did not always share his beliefs, they often used his ideas as the basis of stories, as in "He Walked Around the Horses," which is based on an actual disappearance in 1809. 1948 also saw the first publication of Piper's very popular "Paratime" series in Astounding, *which told of the work of a police force whose major function was to keep people from different time tracks from running into each other. This series was also based on ideas from Fort's books.*

(There are science fiction stories that don't have to be considered science fiction stories. This is one of

*them. It is an "alternate-history" story, a type of story
few are able to handle convincingly. You have to know
the times, and not only be able to present them clearly
and plausibly, but you must trace the consequences of
some small change and make that clear and plausible,
too. Although I've written numerous books of history, I
would have no faith in my own ability to perform the
task, and have never done a story of this kind, nor do I
intend ever to do one. Piper managed, though, and I
have admired this story ever since it was written. And
what I admire most is the final touch of irony (having
nothing to do with the plot itself, but a most delightful
side effect) in the final sentence. If you don't know who
Sir Arthur is, look him up. I. A.)*

In November, 1809, an Englishman named Benjamin Bathurst
vanished, inexplicably and utterly.

He was *en route* to Hamburg from Vienna, where he had been
serving as his Government's envoy to the court of what Napoleon had left of the Austrian Empire. At an inn in Perleburg, in
Prussia, while examining a change of horses for his coach, he
casually stepped out of sight of his secretary and his valet. He
was not seen to leave the inn yard. He was not seen again, ever.

At least, not in this continuum . . .

I

(From Baron Eugen von Krutz, Minister of Police, to His Excellency the Count von Berchtenwald, Chancellor to His Majesty
Freidrich Wilhelm III of Prussia.)

26 November, 1809.

Your Excellency:

A circumstance has come to the notice of this Ministry, the
significance of which I am at a loss to define, but, since it
appears to involve matters of state, both here and abroad, I am
convinced that it is of sufficient importance to be brought to the

personal attention of your Excellency. Frankly, I am unwilling to take any further action in the matter without your Excellency's advice.

Briefly, the situation is this: We are holding, here at the Ministry of Police, a person giving his name as Benjamin Bathurst, who claims to be a British diplomat. This person was taken into custody by the police at Perleburg yesterday, as a result of a disturbance at an inn there; he is being detained on technical charges of causing disorder in a public place, and of being a suspicious person. When arrested, he had in his possession a dispatch-case, containing a number of papers; these are of such an extraordinary nature that the local authorities declined to assume any responsibility beyond having the man sent here to Berlin.

After interviewing this person and examining his papers, I am, I must confess, in much the same position. This is not, I am convinced, any ordinary police matter; there is something very strange and disturbing here. The man's statements, taken alone, are so incredible as to justify the assumption that he is mad. I cannot, however, adopt this theory, in view of his demeanour, which is that of a man of perfect rationality, and because of the existence of these papers. The whole thing is mad; incomprehensible!

The papers in question accompany, along with copies of the various statements taken in Perleburg, and a personal letter to me from my nephew, Lieutenant Rudolph von Tarlburg. This last is deserving of your Excellency's particular attention; Lieutenant von Tarlburg is a very level-headed young officer, not at all inclined to be fanciful or imaginative. It would take a good deal to affect him as he describes.

The man calling himself Benjamin Bathurst is now lodged in an apartment here at the Ministry; he is being treated with every consideration, and, except for freedom of movement, accorded every privilege.

I am, most anxiously awaiting your Excellency's advice, etc., etc.,

KRUTZ.

II

(Report of Traugott Zeller, *Oberwachtmeister, Staatspolizei,* made at Perleburg, 25 November, 1809.)

At about ten minutes past two of the afternoon of Saturday, 25 November, while I was at the police station, there entered a

man known to me as Franz Bauer, an inn servant employed
by Christian Hauck, at the sign of the Sword and Sceptre,
here in Perleburg. This man Franz Bauer made complaint to
Staatspolizeikapitän Ernst Hartenstein, saying that there was a
madman making trouble at the inn where he, Franz Bauer,
worked. I was therefore directed by Staatspolizeikapitän Hartenstein
to go to the Sword and Sceptre Inn, there to act at discretion to
maintain the peace.

Arriving at the inn in company with the said Franz Bauer, I
found a considerable crowd of people in the common-room, and,
in the midst of them, the innkeeper, Christian Hauck, in altercation with a stranger. This stranger was a gentlemanly appearing
person, dressed in travelling clothes, who had under his arm a
small leather dispatch-case. As I entered, I could hear him,
speaking in German with a strong English accent, abusing the
innkeeper, the said Christian Hauck, and accusing him of having
drugged his, the stranger's, wine, and of having stolen his, the
stranger's coach-and-four, and of having abducted his, the stranger's,
secretary and servants. This the said Christian Hauck was loudly
denying, and the other people in the inn were taking the
innkeeper's part, and mocking the stranger for a madman.

On entering, I commanded everyone to be silent, in the King's
name, and then, as he appeared to be the complaining party of
the dispute, I required the foreign gentleman to state to me what
was the trouble. He then repeated his accusations against the
innkeeper, Hauck, saying that Hauck, or rather, another man
who resembled Hauck and who had claimed to be the innkeeper,
had drugged his wine and stolen his coach and made off with his
secretary and his servants. At this point, the innkeeper and the
bystanders all began shouting denials and contradictions, so that I
had to pound on a table with my truncheon to command silence.

I then required the innkeeper, Christian Hauck, to answer the
charges which the stranger had made; this he did with a complete
denial of all of them, saying that the stranger had had no wine in
his inn, and that he had not been inside the inn until a few minutes
before, when he had burst in, shouting accusations, and that
there had been no secretary, and no valet, and no coachman and
no coach-and-four, at the inn, and that the gentleman was raving
mad. To all this, he called the people who were in the common-
room to witness.

I then required the stranger to account for himself. He said
that his name was Benjamin Bathurst, and that he was a British
diplomat, returning to England from Vienna. To prove this, he

produced from his dispatch case sundry papers. One of these was a letter of safe-conduct, issued by the Prussian Chancellery, in which he was named and described as Benjamin Bathurst. The other papers were English, all bearing seals, and appearing to be official documents.

Accordingly, I requested him to accompany me to the police station, and also the innkeeper, and three men whom the innkeeper wanted to bring as witnesses.

TRAUGOTT ZELLER.
Oberwachtmeister.

Report approved,

ERNST HARTENSTEIN.
Staatspolizeikapitän.

III

(Statement of the self-so-called Benjamin Bathurst, taken at the police station at Perleburg, 25 November, 1809.)

My name is Benjamin Bathurst, and I am Envoy Extraordinary and Minister Plenipotentiary of the Government of His Britannic Majesty to the court of His Majesty Franz I, Emperor of Austria, or at least I was until the events following the Austrian surrender made necessary my return to London. I left Vienna on the morning of Monday, the 20th, to go to Hamburg to take ship home; I was travelling in my own coach-and-four, with my secretary, Mr. Bertram Jardine, and my valet, William Small, both British subjects, and a coachman, Josef Bidek, an Austrian subject, whom I had hired for the trip. Because of the presence of French troops, whom I was anxious to avoid, I was forced to make a detour west as far as Salzburg before turning north towards Magdeburg, where I crossed the Elbe. I was unable to get a change of horses for my coach after leaving Gera, until I reached Perleburg, where I stopped at the Sword and Sceptre Inn.

Arriving there, I left my coach in the inn yard, and I and my secretary, Mr. Jardine, went into the inn. A man, not this fellow here, but another rogue, with more beard and less paunch, and more shabbily dressed, but as like him as though he were his brother, represented himself as the innkeeper, and I dealt with him for a change of horses, and ordered a bottle of wine for myself and my secretary, and also a pot of beer apiece for my valet and the coachman, to be taken outside to them. Then Jardine and I sat down to our wine, at a table in the common-room, until the man who claimed to be the innkeeper came back and told us that the fresh horses were harnessed to the coach and ready to go. Then we went outside again.

I looked at the two horses on the off-side, and then walked around in front of the team to look at the two nigh-side horses, and as I did, I felt giddy, as though I were about to fall, and everything went black before my eyes. I thought I was having a fainting spell, something I am not at all subject to, and I put out my hand to grasp the hitching-bar, but could not find it. I am sure, now, that I was unconscious for some time, because when my head cleared, the coach and horses were gone, and in their place was a big farm-wagon, jacked up in front, with the right wheel off, and two peasants were greasing the detached wheel.

I looked at them for a moment, unable to credit my eyes, and then I spoke to them in German, saying, 'Where the devil's my coach-and-four?'

They both straightened, startled; the one who was holding the wheel almost dropped it.

'Pardon, Excellency,' he said. 'There's been no coach-and-four here, all the time we've been here.'

'Yes,' said his mate, 'and we've been here since just after noon.'

I did not attempt to argue with them. It occurred to me—and it is still my opinion—that I was the victim of some plot; that my wine had been drugged, that I had been unconscious for some time during which my coach had been removed and this wagon substituted for it, and that these peasants had been put to work on it and instructed what to say if questioned. If my arrival at the inn had been anticipated, and everything put in readiness, the whole business would not have taken ten minutes.

I therefore entered the inn, determined to have it out with this rascally innkeeper, but when I returned to the common-room, he was nowhere to be seen, and this other fellow, who has also given his name as Christian Hauck, claimed to be the innkeeper and denied knowledge of any of the things I have just stated. Furthermore, there were four cavalrymen, Uhlans, drinking beer and playing cards at the table where Jardine and I had had our wine, and they claimed to have been there for several hours.

I have no idea why such an elaborate prank, involving the participation of many people, should be played on me, except at the instigation of the French. In that case, I cannot understand why Prussian soldiers should lend themselves to it.

BENJAMIN BATHURST.

IV

(Statement of Christian Hauck, innkeeper, taken at the police station at Perleburg, 25 November, 1809.)

May it please your Honour, my name is Christian Hauck, and I keep an inn at the sign of the Sword and Sceptre, and have these past fifteen years, and my father, and his father before him, for the past fifty years, and never has there been a complaint like this against my inn. Your Honour, it is a hard thing for a man who keeps a decent house, and pays his taxes, and obeys the laws, to be accused of crimes of this sort.

I know nothing of this gentleman, nor of his coach nor his secretary nor his servants; I never set eyes on him before he came bursting into the inn from the yard, shouting and raving like a madman, and crying out, 'Where the devil's that rogue of an innkeeper?'

I said to him, 'I am the innkeeper; what cause have you to call me a rogue, sir?'

The stranger replied: 'You're not the innkeeper I did business with a few minutes ago, and he's the rascal I have a row to pick with. I want to know what the devil's been done with my coach, and what's happened to my secretary and my servants.'

I tried to tell him that I knew nothing of what he was talking about, but he would not listen, and gave me the lie, saying that he had been drugged and robbed, and his people kidnapped. He even had the impudence to claim that he and his secretary had been sitting at a table in that room, drinking wine, not fifteen minutes before, when there had been four non-commissioned officers of the Third Uhlans at that table since noon. Everybody in the room spoke up for me, but he would not listen, and was shouting that we were all robbers, kidnappers, and French spies, and I don't know what all, when the police came.

Your Honour, the man is mad. What I have told you about this is the truth, and all that I know about this business, so help me God.

CHRISTIAN HAUCK.

V

(Statement of Franz Bauer, inn-servant, taken at the police station at Perleburg, 25 November, 1809.)

May it please your Honour, my name is Franz Bauer, and I am a servant at the Sword and Sceptre Inn, kept by Christian Hauck.

This afternoon, when I went into the inn yard to empty a bucket of slops on the dung heap by the stables, I heard voices and turned around, to see this gentleman speaking to Wilhelm Beick and Fritz Herzer, who were greasing their wagon in the yard. He had not been in the yard when I had turned around to empty the bucket, and I thought that he must have come in from the street. This gentleman was asking Beick and Herzer where was his coach, and when they told him they didn't know, he turned and ran into the inn.

Of my own knowledge, the man had not been inside the inn before then, nor had there been any coach, or any of the people he spoke of, at the inn, and none of the things he spoke of happened there, for otherwise I would know, since I was at the inn all day.

When I went back inside, I found him in the common-room, shouting at my master, and claiming that he had been drugged and robbed. I saw that he was mad, and was afraid that he would do some mischief, so I went for the police.

FRANZ BAUER
his (X) mark.

VI

(Statements of Wilhelm Beick and Fritz Herzer, peasants, taken at the police station at Perleburg, 25 November, 1809.)

May it please your Honour, my name is Wilhelm Beick, and I am a tenant on the estate of the Baron von Hentig. On this day, I and Fritz Herzer were sent in to Perleburg with a load of potatoes and cabbages which the innkeeper at the Sword and Sceptre had bought from the estate-superintendent. After we had unloaded them, we decided to grease our wagon, which was very dry, before going back, so we unhitched and began working on it. We took about two hours, starting just after we had eaten lunch, and in all that time there was no coach-and-four in the inn yard.

We were just finishing when this gentleman spoke to us, demanding to know where his coach was. We told him that there had been no coach in the yard all the time we had been there, so he turned around and ran into the inn. At the time, I thought that he had come out of the inn before speaking to us, for I know that he could not have come in from the street. Now I do not know where he came from, but I know that I never saw him before that moment.

WILHELM BEICK
his (X) mark.

I have heard the above testimony, and it is true to my own knowledge, and I have nothing to add to it.

FRITZ HERZER
his (X) mark.

VII

(From Staatspolizeikapitän Ernst Hartenstein, to His Excellency, the Baron von Krutz, Minister of Police.)

25 November, 1809.

Your Excellency:

The accompanying copies of statements taken this day will explain how the prisoner, the self-so-called Benjamin Bathurst, came into my custody. I have charged him with causing disorder and being a suspicious person, to hold him until more can be learned about him. However, as he represents himself to be a British diplomat, I am unwilling to assume any further responsibility, and am having him sent to your Excellency, in Berlin.

In the first place, your Excellency, I have the strongest doubts of the man's story. The statement which he made before me, and signed, is bad enough, with a coach-and-four turning into a farm wagon, like Cinderella's coach into a pumpkin, and three people vanishing as though swallowed by the earth. Your Excellency will permit me to doubt that there ever was any such coach, or any such people. But all this is perfectly reasonable and credible, beside the things he said to me, of which no record was made.

Your Excellency will have noticed, in his statement, certain allusions to the Austrian surrender, and to French troops in Austria. After his statement had been taken down, I noticed these allusions, and I inquired, what surrender, and what were

French troops doing in Austria. The man looked at me in a pitying manner, and said:

'News seems to travel slowly, hereabouts; peace was concluded at Vienna on the 14th of last month. And as for what French troops are doing in Austria, they're doing the same things Bonaparte's brigands are doing everywhere in Europe.'

'And who is Bonaparte?' I asked.

He stared at me as though I had asked him, 'Who is the Lord Jehovah?' Then, after a moment, a look of comprehension came into his face.

'So; you Prussians conceded him the title of Emperor, and refer to him as Napoleon,' he said. 'Well, I can assure you that His Britannic Majesty's Government haven't done so, and never will; not so long as one Englishman has a finger left to pull a trigger. General Bonaparte is a usurper; His Britannic Majesty's Government do not recognize any sovereignty in France except the House of Bourbon.' This he said very sternly, as though rebuking me.

It took me a moment or so to digest that, and to appreciate all its implications. Why, this fellow evidently believed, as a matter of fact, that the French Monarchy had been overthrown by some military adventurer named Bonaparte, who was calling himself the Emperor Napoleon, and who had made war on Austria and forced a surrender. I made no attempt to argue with him—one wastes time arguing with madmen—but if this man could believe that, the transformation of a coach-and-four into a cabbage-wagon was a small matter indeed. So, to humour him, I asked him if he thought General Bonaparte's agents were responsible for his trouble at the inn.

'Certainly,' he replied. 'The chances are they didn't know me to see me, and took Jardine for the Minister, and me for the secretary, so they made off with poor Jardine. I wonder, though, that they left me my dispatch case. And that reminds me: I'll want that back. Diplomatic papers, you know.'

I told him, very seriously, that we would have to check his credentials. I promised him I would make every effort to locate his secretary and his servants and his coach, took a complete description of all of them, and persuaded him to go into an upstairs room, where I kept him under guard. I did start inquiries, calling in all my informers and spies, but, as I expected, I could learn nothing. I could not find anybody, even, who had seen him anywhere in Perleburg before he appeared at the Sword and

Sceptre, and that rather surprised me, as somebody should have seen him enter the town, or walk along the street.

In this connection, let me remind your Excellency of the discrepancy in the statements of the servant, Franz Bauer, and of the two peasants. The former is certain the man entered the inn yard from the street; the latter are just as positive that he did not. Your Excellency, I do not like such puzzles, for I am sure that all three were telling the truth to the best of their knowledge. They are ignorant common-folk, I admit, but they should know what they did or did not see.

After I got the prisoner into safe-keeping, I fell to examining his papers, and I can assure your Excellency that they gave me a shock. I had paid little heed to his ravings about the King of France being dethroned, or about this General Bonaparte who called himself the Emperor Napoleon, but I found all these things mentioned in his papers and dispatches, which had every appearance of being official documents. There was repeated mention of the taking, by the French, of Vienna, last May, and of the capitulation of the Austrian Emperor to this General Bonaparte, and of battles being fought all over Europe, and I don't know what other fantastic things. Your Excellency, I have heard of all sorts of madmen—one believing himself to be the Archangel Gabriel, or Mohammed, or a werewolf, and another convinced that his bones are made of glass, or that he is pursued and tormented by devils—but, so help me God, this is the first time I have heard of a madman who had documentary proof for his delusions! Does your Excellency wonder, then, that I want no part of this business?

But the matter of his credentials was even worse. He had papers, sealed with the seal of the British Foreign Office, and to every appearance genuine—but they were signed, as Foreign Minister, by one George Canning, and all the world knows that Lord Castlereagh has been Foreign Minister these last five years. And to cap it all, he had a safe-conduct, sealed with the seal of the Prussian Chancellery—the very seal, for I compared it, under a strong magnifying-glass, with one that I knew to be genuine, and they were identical!—and yet, this letter was signed, as Chancellor, not by Count von Berchtenwald, but by Baron vom und zum Stein, the Minister of Agriculture, and the signature, as far as I could see, appeared to be genuine! This is too much for me, your Excellency; I must ask to be excused from dealing with this matter, before I become as mad as my prisoner!

I made arrangements, accordingly, with Colonel Keitel, of the

Third Uhlans, to furnish an officer to escort this man in to Berlin. The coach in which they come belongs to this police station, and the driver is one of my men. He should be furnished expense money to get back to Perleburg. The guard is a corporal of Uhlans, the orderly of the officer. He will stay with the *Herr Oberleutnant*, and both of them will return here at their own convenience and expense.

I have the honour, your Excellency, to be, etc., etc.,

ERNST HARTENSTEIN.
Staatspolizeikapitän.

VIII

(From Oberleutnant Rudolf von Tarlburg, to Baron Eugen von Krutz.)

26 November, 1809.

Dear Uncle Eugen:

This is in no sense a formal report; I made that at the Ministry, when I turned the Englishman and his papers over to one of your officers—a fellow with red hair and a face like a bulldog. But there are a few things which you should be told, which wouldn't look well in an official report, to let you know just what sort of a rare fish has got into your net.

I had just come in from drilling my platoon, yesterday, when Colonel Keitel's orderly told me that the colonel wanted to see me in his quarters. I found the old fellow in undress in his sitting-room, smoking his big pipe.

'Come in, Lieutenant; come in and sit down, my boy!' he greeted me, in that bluff, hearty manner which he always adopts with his junior officers when he has some particularly nasty job to be done. 'How would you like to take a little trip in to Berlin? I have an errand, which won't take half an hour, and you can stay as long as you like, just so you're back by Thursday, when your turn comes up for road-patrol.'

Well, I thought, this is the bait. I waited to see what the hook would look like, saying that it was entirely agreeable with me, and asking what his errand was.

'Well, it isn't for myself, Tarlburg,' he said. 'It's for this fellow Hartenstein, the *Staatspolizeikapitän* here. He has something he wants done at the Ministry of Police, and I thought of you because I've heard you're related to the Baron von Krutz.

You are, aren't you?' he asked, just as though he didn't know all about who all his officers are related to.

'That's right, Colonel; the Baron is my uncle,' I said. 'What does Hartenstein want done?'

'Why, he has a prisoner whom he wants taken to Berlin and turned over at the Ministry. All you have to do is to take him in, in a coach, and see he doesn't escape on the way, and get a receipt for him, and for some papers. This is a very important prisoner; I don't think Hartenstein has anybody he can trust to handle him. A state prisoner. He claims to be some sort of a British diplomat, and for all Hartenstein knows, maybe he is. Also, he is a madman.'

'A madman?' I echoed.

'Yes, just so. At least, that's what Hartenstein told me. I wanted to know what sort of a madman—there are various kinds of madmen, all of whom must be handled differently—but all Hartenstein would tell me was that he had unrealistic beliefs about the state of affairs in Europe.'

'Ha! What diplomat hasn't?' I asked.

Old Keitel gave a laugh, somewhere between the bark of a dog and the croaking of a raven.

'Yes, naturally! The unrealistic beliefs of diplomats are what soldiers die of,' he said. 'I said as much to Hartenstein, but he wouldn't tell me anything more. He seemed to regret having said even that much. He looked like a man who's seen a particularly terrifying ghost.' The old man puffed hard at his famous pipe for a while, blowing smoke up through his moustache. 'Rudi, Hartenstein has pulled a hot potato out of the ashes, this time, and he wants to toss it to your uncle, before he burns his fingers. I think that's one reason why he got me to furnish an escort for his Englishman. Now, look; you must take this unrealistic diplomat, or this undiplomatic madman, or whatever in blazes he is, in to Berlin. And understand this.' He pointed his pipe at me as though it were a pistol. 'Your orders are to take him there and turn him over at the Ministry of Police. Nothing has been said about whether you turn him over alive or dead, or half one and half the other. I know nothing about this business, and want to know nothing; if Hartenstein wants us to play gaol-warders for him, then, *bei Gott,* he must be satisfied with our way of doing it!'

Well, to cut short the story, I looked at the coach Hartenstein had placed at my disposal, and I decided to chain the left door shut on the outside so that it couldn't be opened from within.

Then, I would put my prisoner on my left, so that the only way out would be past me. I decided not to carry any weapons which he might be able to snatch from me, so I took off my sabre and locked it in the seat-box, along with the dispatch case containing the Englishman's papers. It was cold enough to wear a greatcoat in comfort, so I wore mine, and in the right side pocket, where my prisoner couldn't reach, I put a little leaded bludgeon, and also a brace of pocket-pistols. Hartenstein was going to furnish me a guard as well as a driver, but I said that I would take a servant who could act as guard. The servant, of course, was my orderly, old Johann; I gave him my double hunting-gun to carry, with a big charge of boar-shot in one barrel and an ounce ball in the other.

In addition, I armed myself with a big bottle of cognac. I thought that if I could shoot my prisoner often enough with that, he would give me no trouble.

As it happened, he didn't, and none of my precautions—except the cognac—were needed. The man didn't look like a lunatic to me. He was a rather stout gentleman, of past middle age, with a ruddy complexion and an intelligent face. The only unusual thing about him was his hat, which was a peculiar contraption, looking like the pot out of a close-stool. I put him in the carriage, and then offered him a drink out of my bottle, taking one about half as big myself. He smacked his lips over it and said, 'Well, that's real brandy; whatever we think of their detestable politics, we can't criticize the French for their liquor.' Then, he said, 'I'm glad they're sending me in the custody of a military gentleman, instead of a confounded gendarme. Tell me the truth, Lieutenant: am I under arrest for anything?'

'Why,' I said, 'Captain Hartenstein should have told you about that. All I know is that I have orders to take you to the Ministry of Police, in Berlin, and not to let you escape on the way. These orders I will carry out; I hope you don't hold that against me.'

He assured me that he did not, and we had another drink on it—I made sure, again, that he got twice as much as I did—and then the coachman cracked his whip and we were off for Berlin.

Now, I thought, I am going to see just what sort of a madman this is, and why Hartenstein is making a state affair out of a squabble at an inn. So I decided to explore his unrealistic beliefs about the state of affairs in Europe.

After guiding the conversation to where I wanted it, I asked him:

'What, Herr Bathurst, in your belief, is the real, underlying cause of the present tragic situation in Europe?'

That, I thought, was safe enough. Name me one year, since the days of Julius Caesar, when the situation in Europe hasn't been tragic! And it worked, to perfection.

'In my belief,' says this Englishman, 'the whole damnable mess is the result of the victory of the rebellious colonists in North America, and their blasted republic.'

Well, you can imagine, that gave me a start. All the world knows that the American Patriots lost their war for independence from England; that their army was shattered, that their leaders were either killed or driven into exile. How many times, when I was a little boy, did I not sit up long past my bedtime, when old Baron von Steuben was a guest at Tarlburg-Schloss, listening open-mouthed and wide-eyed to his stories of that gallant lost struggle! How I used to shiver at his tales of the terrible Winter camp, or thrill at the battles, or weep as he told how he held the dying Washington in his arms, and listened to his noble last words, at the Battle of Doylestown! And here, this man was telling me that the Patriots had really won, and set up the republic for which they had fought! I had been prepared for some of what Hartenstein had called unrealistic beliefs, but nothing as fantastic as this.

'I can cut it even finer than that,' Bathurst continued. 'It was the defeat of Burgoyne at Saratoga. We made a good bargain when we got Benedict Arnold to turn his coat, but we didn't do it soon enough. If he hadn't been on the field that day, Burgoyne would have gone through Gates's army like a hot knife through butter.'

But Arnold hadn't been at Saratoga, I know; I have read much of the American War. Arnold was shot dead on New Year's Day of 1776, during the attempted storming of Quebec. And Burgoyne had done just as Bathurst had said: he had gone through Gates like a knife, and down the Hudson to join Howe.

'But, Herr Bathurst,' I asked, 'how could that affect the situation in Europe? America is thousands of miles away, across the ocean.'

'Ideas can cross oceans quicker than armies. When Louis XVI decided to come to the aid of the Americans, he doomed himself and his régime. A successful resistance to royal authority in America was all the French Republicans needed to inspire them. Of course, we have Louis's own weakness to blame, too. If he'd given those rascals a whiff of grapeshot when the mob tried to storm Versailles in 1790 there'd have been no French Revolution.'

But he had. When Louis XVI ordered the howitzers turned on the mob at Versailles, and then sent the dragoons to ride down the survivors, the Republican movement had been broken. That had been when Cardinal Talleyrand, who had then been merely Bishop of Autun, had come to the fore and became the power that he is today in France; the greatest King's Minister since Richelieu.

'And, after that, Louis's death followed as surely as night after day,' Bathurst was saying. 'And because the French had no experience in self-government, their republic was fore-doomed. If Bonaparte hadn't seized power, somebody else would have; when the French murdered their king, they de-livered themselves to dictatorship. And a dictator, unsupported by the prestige of royalty, has no choice but to lead his people into foreign war, to keep them from turning upon him.'

It was like that all the way to Berlin. All these things seem foolish by daylight, but as I sat in the darkness of that swaying coach, I was almost convinced of the reality of what he told me. I tell you, Uncle Eugen, it was fright-ening, as though he were giving me a view of Hell. *Gott in Himmel*, the things that man talked of! Armies swarm-ing over Europe; sack and massacre, and cities burning; block-ades, and starvation; kings deposed, and thrones tumbling like tenpins! Battles in which the soldiers of every nation fought, and in which tens of thousands were mowed down like ripe grain; and, over all, the Satanic figure of a little man in a grey coat, who dictated peace to the Austrian Emperor in Schoenbrunn, and carried the Pope away a prisoner to Savona.

Madman, eh? Unrealistic beliefs, says Hartenstein? Well, give me madmen who drool spittle, and foam at the mouth, and shriek obscene blasphemies. But not this pleasant-seeming gentle-man who sat beside me and talked of horrors in a quiet, cultured voice, while he drank my cognac.

But not all my cognac! If your man at the Ministry—the one with red hair and the bulldog face—tells you that I was drunk when I brought in that Englishman, you had better believe him!

RUDI.

IX

(From Count von Berchtenwald to the British Minister.)

28 November, 1809.

Honoured Sir:

The accompanying *dossier* will acquaint you with the problem confronting this Chancellery, without needless repetition on my part. Please to understand that it is not, and never was, any part of the intentions of the Government of His Majesty Friedrich Wilhelm III to offer any injury or indignity to the Government of His Britannic Majesty George III. We would never contemplate holding in arrest the person, or tampering with the papers, of an accredited envoy of your Government. However, we have the gravest doubt, to make a considerable understatement, that this person who calls himself Benjamin Bathurst is any such envoy, and we do not think that it would be any service to the Government of His Britannic Majesty to allow an impostor to travel about Europe in the guise of a British diplomatic representative. We certainly should not thank the Government of His Britannic Majesty for failing to take steps to deal with some person who, in England, might falsely represent himself to be a Prussian diplomat.

This affair touches us almost as closely as it does your own Government; this man had in his possession a letter of safe conduct, which you will find in the accompanying dispatch-case. It is of the regular form, as issued by this Chancellery, and is sealed with the Chancellery seal, or with a very exact counterfeit of it. However, it has been signed, as Chancellor of Prussia, with a signature indistinguishable from that of the Baron vom und zum Stein, who is the present Minister of Agriculture. Baron Stein was shown the signature, with the rest of the letter covered, and without hesitation acknowledged it for his own writing. However, when the letter was uncovered and shown to him, his surprise and horror were such as would require the pen of a Goethe or a Schiller to describe, and he denied categorically ever having seen the document before.

I have no choice but to believe him. It is impossible to think that a man of Baron Stein's honourable and serious character would be party to the fabrication of a paper of this sort. Even aside from this, I am in the thing as deeply as he; if it is signed with his signature, it is also sealed with my seal, which has not been out of my personal keeping in the ten years that I have been

Chancellor here. In fact, the word 'impossible' can be used to describe the entire business. It was impossible for the man Benjamin Bathurst to have entered the inn yard—yet he did. It was impossible that he should carry papers of the sort found in his dispatch case, or that such papers should exist—yet I am sending them to you with this letter. It is impossible that Baron vom und zum Stein should sign a paper of the sort he did, or that it should be sealed by the Chancellery—yet it bears both Stein's signature and my seal.

You will also find in the dispatch case other credentials ostensibly originating with the British Foreign Office of the same character, being signed by persons having no connection with the Foreign Office, or even with the Government, but being sealed with apparently authentic seals. If you send these papers to London, I fancy you will find that they will there create the same situation as that caused here by this letter of safe-conduct.

I am also sending you a charcoal sketch of the person who calls himself Benjamin Bathurst. This portrait was taken without its subject's knowledge. Baron von Krutz's nephew, Lieutenant von Tarlburg, who is the son of our mutual friend Count von Tarlburg, has a *little friend*, a very clever young lady who is, as you will see, an expert at this sort of work; she was introduced into a room at the Ministry of Police and placed behind a screen, where she could sketch our prisoner's face. If you should send this picture to London, I think that there is a good chance that it might be recognized. I can vouch that it is an excellent likeness.

To tell the truth, we are at our wits' end about this affair. I cannot understand how such excellent imitations of these various seals could be made, and the signature of the Baron vom und zum Stein is the most expert forgery that I have ever seen, in thirty years' experience as a statesman. This would indicate careful and painstaking work on the part of somebody; how, then, do we reconcile this with such clumsy mistakes, recognizable as such by any schoolboy, as signing the name of Baron Stein as Prussian Chancellor, or Mr. George Canning, who is a member of the opposition party and not connected with your Government, as British Foreign Secretary?

These are mistakes which only a madman would make. There are those who think our prisoner is a madman, because of his apparent delusions about the great conqueror, General Bonaparte, *alias* the Emperor Napoleon. Madmen have been known to fabricate evidence to support their delusions, it is true, but I shudder to think of a madman having at his disposal the resources to manufacture the papers you will find in this dispatch case. Moreover, some of our foremost medical men, who have specialized in the disorders of the mind, have interviewed this man Bathurst and say that, save for his fixed belief in a non-existent situation, he is perfectly rational.

Personally, I believe that the whole thing is a gigantic hoax, perpetrated for some hidden and sinister purpose, possibly to create confusion, and undermine the confidence existing between your Government and mine, and to set against one another various persons connected with both Governments, or else as a mask for some other conspiratorial activity. Without specifying any Sovereigns or Governments who might wish to do this, I can think of two groups; namely, the Jesuits, and the outlawed French Republicans, either of whom might conceive such a situation to be to their advantage. Only a few months ago, you will recall, there was a Jacobin plot unmasked at Köln.

But, whatever this business may portend, I do not like it. I want to get to the bottom of it as soon as possible, and I will thank you, my dear Sir, and your Government, for any assistance you may find possible.

I have the honour, Sir, to be, etc., etc., etc.,

BERCHTENWALD.

X

FROM BARON VON KRUTZ, TO THE COUNT VON BERCH-
TENWALD.
MOST URGENT; MOST IMPORTANT.
TO BE DELIVERED IMMEDIATELY AND IN PERSON, RE-
GARDLESS OF CIRCUMSTANCES.

28 November, 1809.

Count von Berchtenwald:

Within the past half-hour, that is, at about eleven o'clock tonight, the man calling himself Benjamin Bathurst was shot and killed by a sentry at the Ministry of Police, while attempting to escape from custody.

A sentry on duty in the rear courtyard of the Ministry observed a man attempting to leave the building in a suspicious and furtive manner. This sentry, who was under the strictest orders to allow no one to enter or leave without written authorization, challenged him; when he attempted to run, the sentry fired his musket at him, bringing him down. At the shot, the Sergeant of the Guard

rushed into the courtyard with his detail, and the man whom the
sentry had shot was found to be the Englishman, Benjamin
Bathurst. He had been hit in the chest with an ounce ball, and
died before the doctor could arrive, and without recovering
consciousness.

An investigation revealed that the prisoner, who was confined
on the third floor of the building, had fashioned a rope from his
bedding, his bed-cord, and the leather strap of his bell-pull; this
rope was only long enough to reach to the window of the office
on the second floor, directly below, but he managed to enter this
by kicking the glass out of the window. I am trying to find out
how he could do this without being heard; I can assure your
Excellency that somebody is going to smart for this night's
work. As for the sentry, he acted within his orders; I have
commended him for doing his duty, and for good shooting, and I
assume full responsibility for the death of the prisoner at his
hands.

I have no idea why the self-so-called Benjamin Bathurst, who,
until now, was well-behaved and seemed to take his confinement philosophically, should suddenly make this rash and fatal
attempt, unless it was because of those infernal dunderheads of
madhouse-doctors who have been bothering him. Only this afternoon, your Excellency, they deliberately handed him a bundle
of newspapers—Prussian, Austrian, French, and English—all
dated within the last month. They wanted, they said, to see how
he would react. Well, God pardon them, they've found out!

What does your Excellency think should be done about giving
the body burial?

                                                    KRUTZ.

(From the British Minister to the Count von Berchtenwald.)

                                          December 20th, 1809.
My dear Count von Berchtenwald:

Reply from London to my letter of the 28th *ult.*, which
accompanied the dispatch case and the other papers, has finally
come to hand. The papers which you wanted returned—the
copies of the statements taken at Perleburg, the letter to the
Baron von Krutz from the police captain, Hartenstein, and the
personal letter of Krutz's nephew, Lieutenant von Tarlburg, and
the letter of safe-conduct found in the dispatch case, accompany
herewith. I don't know what the people at Whitehall did with the
other papers; tossed them into the nearest fire, for my guess.

Were I in your Excellency's place, that's where the papers I am returning would go.

I have heard nothing yet, from my dispatch of the 29th *ult.* concerning the death of the man who called himself Benjamin Bathurst, but I doubt very much if any official notice will ever be taken of it. Your Government had a perfect right to detain the fellow, and, that being the case, he attempted to escape at his own risk. After all, sentries are not required to carry loaded muskets in order to discourage them from putting their hands in their pockets.

To hazard a purely unofficial opinion, I should not imagine that London is very much dissatisfied with this *dénouement*. His Majesty's Government are a hard-headed and matter-of-fact set of gentry who do not relish mysteries, least of all mysteries whose solution may be more disturbing than the original problem.

This is entirely confidential, your Excellency, but those papers which were in that dispatch case kicked up the devil's own row in London, with half the Government bigwigs protesting their innocence to high Heaven, and the rest accusing one another of complicity in the hoax. If that was somebody's intention, it was literally a howling success. For a while, it was even feared that there would be Questions in Parliament, but eventually the whole vexatious business was hushed.

You may tell Count Tarlburg's son that his little friend is a most talented young lady; her sketch was highly commended by no less an authority than Sir Thomas Lawrence, and here, your Excellency, comes the most bedevilling part of a thoroughly bedevilled business. The picture was instantly recognized. It is a very fair likeness of Benjamin Bathurst, or, I should say, Sir Benjamin Bathurst, who is King's Lieutenant-Governor for the Crown Colony of Georgia. As Sir Thomas Lawrence did his portrait a few years back, he is in an excellent position to criticize the work of Lieutenant von Tarlburg's young lady. However, Sir Benjamin Bathurst was known to have been in Savannah, attending to the duties of his office, and in the public eye, all the while that his double was in Prussia. Sir Benjamin does not have a twin brother. It has been suggested that this fellow might be a half-brother, born on the wrong side of the blanket, but, as far as I know, there is no justification for this theory.

The General Bonaparte, alias the Emperor Napoleon, who is given so much mention in the dispatches, seems also to have counterpart in actual life; there is, in the French army, a Colonel of Artillery by that name, a Corsican who Gallicized his original name of Napolione Buonaparte. He is a most brilliant military theoretician; I am sure some of our officers, like General Scharnhorst, could tell you about him. His loyalty to the French Monarchy has never been questioned.

This same correspondence to fact seems to crop up everywhere in that amazing collection of pseudo-dispatches and pseudo-state-papers. The United States of America, you will recall, was the style by which the rebellious colonies referred to themselves, in the Declaration of Philadelphia. The James Madison who is mentioned as the current President of the United States, is now living, in exile, in Switzerland. His alleged predecessor in office, Thomas Jefferson, was the author of the rebel Declaration; after the defeat of the rebels, he escaped to Havana, and died, several years ago, in the Principality of Lichtenstein.

I was quite amused to find our old friend Cardinal Talleyrand—without the ecclesiastical title—cast in the role of chief adviser to the usurper, Bonaparte. His Eminence, I have always thought, is the sort of fellow who would land on his feet on top of any heap, and who would as little scruple to be Prime Minister to His Satanic Majesty as to His Most Christian Majesty.

I was baffled, however, by one name, frequently mentioned in those fantastic papers. This was the English General, Wellington. I haven't the least idea who this person might be.

I have the honour, your Exeellency, etc., etc., etc.,

SIR ARTHUR WELLESLEY.

THE STRANGE CASE OF JOHN KINGMAN

by Murray Leinster
(Will F. Jenkins; 1896—1975)

ASTOUNDING SCIENCE FICTION

May

They called Murray Leinster "The Dean of Science Fiction" and he certainly deserved the title. He sold his first fiction in 1913 and published his last in 1967—fifty-four years of productivity in a variety of genres; a tremendous achievement, made more so by the fact that he was a consistently entertaining and occasionally brilliant craftsman. He left us two clear classics of science fiction—"Sidewise in Time," the first modern parallel world story, and "First Contact" (see our 1945 volume), still the best known story on the subject.

"The Strange Case of John Kingman" is one of his best works, a story that combines (as Everett F. Bleiler and T. E. Dikty have pointed out) elements of the mad scientist, psychology, and Charles Fort.

(One thing that I am particularly equipped to do is to recognize the hidden hand of John Campbell. In my expressionable youth I talked to him a great deal and I was endlessly exposed to his manner of thinking. Will Jenkins was one of Campbell's favorites and he frequently reported on conversations between himself and

Will. I remember vividly one time back in 1941 when he insisted that Will had a very clever chemical method of easily and cheaply separating an element into its isotopes. I was struck dumb with astonishment for I didn't think it was possible—and, of course, it wasn't. In any case, one of Campbell's favorite ideas, in Randall Garrett's phrase, was that "there are supermen among us," and several of his authors chose to (or were bludgeoned into) using the idea. Will did it better than most. Note the very name "king-man."—I. A.)

It started when Dr. Braden took the trouble to look up John Kingman's case-history card. Meadeville Mental Hospital had a beautifully elaborate system of card indexes, because psychiatric research is stressed there. It is the oldest mental institution in the country, having been known as "New Bedlam" when it was founded some years before the Republic of the United States of America. The card-index system was unbelievably perfect. But young Dr. Braden found John Kingman's card remarkably lacking in the usual data.

"Kingman, John," said the card. *"White, male, 5'8", brown-black hair. Note: physical anomaly. Patient has six fingers on each hand, extra digits containing apparently normal bones and being wholly functional. Age . . ."* This was blank. *Race . . ."* This, too, was blank. *"Birthplace . . ."* Considering the other blanks, it was natural for this to be vacant, also. *"Diagnosis: advanced atypical paranoia with pronounced delusions of grandeur apparently unassociated with usual conviction of persecution."* There was a comment here, too. *"Patient apparently understands English very slightly if at all. Does not speak."* Then three more spaces. *"Nearest relative . . ."* It was blank. *"Case history . . ."* It was blank. Then, *"Date of admission . . ."* and it was blank.

The card was notably defective, for the index-card of a patient at Meadeville Mental. A patient's age and race could be unknown if he'd simply been picked up in the street somewhere and never adequately identified. In such an event it was reasonable that his nearest relative and birthplace should be unknown, too. But there should have been some sort of case history—at least of the events leading to his committal to the institution. And certainly, positively, absolutely, the date of his admission should be on the card!

Young Dr. Braden was annoyed. This was at the time when the Jantzen euphoric-shock treatment was first introduced, and young Dr. Braden believed in it. It made sense. He was anxious to attempt it at Meadeville—of course on a patient with no other possible hope of improvement. He handed the card to the clerk in the records department and asked for further data on the case.

Two hours later he smoked comfortably on a very foul pipe, stretched out on grassy sward by the Administration Building. There was a beautifully blue sky overhead, and the shadows of the live oaks reached out in an odd long pattern on the lawn. Young Dr. Braden read meditatively in the *American Journal of Psychiatry*. The article was "Reaction of Ten Paranoid Cases to Euphoric Shock." John Kingman sat in regal dignity on the steps nearby. He wore the nondescript garments of an indigent patient—not supplied with clothing by relatives. He gazed into the distance, to all appearances thinking consciously godlike thoughts and being infinitely superior to mere ordinary humans. He was of an indeterminate age which might be forty or might be sixty or might be anywhere in between. His six-fingered hands lay in studied gracefulness in his lap. He deliberately ignored all of mankind and mankind's doings.

Dr. Braden finished the article. He sucked thoughtfully on the burned-out pipe. Without seeming to do so, he regarded John Kingman again. Mental cases have unpredictable reactions, but as with children and wild animals, much can be done if care is taken not to startle them. Presently young Dr. Braden said meditatively:

"John, I think something can be done for you."

The regal figure turned its eyes. They looked at the younger man. They were aloofly amused at the impertinence of a mere human being addressing John Kingman, who was so much greater than a mere human being that he was not even annoyed at human impertinence. Then John Kingman looked away again.

"I imagine," said Braden, as meditatively as before, "that you're pretty bored. I'm going to see if something can't be done about it. In fact—"

Someone came across the grass toward him. It was the clerk of the records department. He looked very unhappy. He had the card Dr. Braden had turned in with a request for more complete information. Braden waited.

"Er . . . doctor," said the clerk miserably, "there's something wrong! Something terribly wrong! About the records, I mean."

The aloofness of John Kingman had multiplied with the coming of a second, low, human being into his ken. He gazed into the distance in divine indifference to such creatures.

"Well?" said Braden.

"There's no record of his admission!" said the clerk. "Every year there's a complete roster of the patients, you know. I thought I'd just glance back, find out what year his name first appeared, and look in the committal papers for that year. But I went back twenty years, and John Kingman is mentioned every year!"

"Look back thirty, then," said Braden.

"I . . . I did!" said the clerk painfully. "He was a patient here thirty years ago!"

"Forty?" asked Braden.

The clerk gulped.

"Dr. Braden," he said desperately, "I even went to the dead files, where records going back to 1850 are kept. And . . . doctor, he was a patient then!"

Braden got up from the grass and brushed himself off automatically.

"Nonsense!" he said. "That's ninety-eight years ago!"

The clerk looked crushed.

"I know, doctor. There's something terribly wrong! I've never had my records questioned before. I've been here twenty years—"

"I'll come with you and look for myself," said Dr. Braden. "Send an attendant to come here and take him back to his ward."

"Y-yes, doctor," said the clerk, gulping again. "At . . . at once."

He went away at a fast pace between a shuffle and a run. Dr. Braden scowled impatiently.

Then he saw John Kingman looking at him again, and John Kingman was amused. Tolerantly, loftily amused. Amused with a patronizing condescension that would have been infuriating to anyone but a physician trained to regard behavior as symptomatic rather than personal.

"It's absurd," grunted Braden, matter-of-factly treating the patient—as a good psychiatrist does—like a perfectly normal human being. "You haven't been here for ninety-eight years!"

One of the six-fingered hands stirred. While John Kingman

regarded Braden with infinitely superior scorn, six fingers made a gesture as of writing. Then the hand reached out.

Braden put a pencil in it. The other hand reached. Braden fumbled in his pockets and found a scrap of paper. He offered that.

John Kingman looked aloofly into the far distance, not even glancing at what his hands did. But the fingers sketched swiftly, with practiced ease. It took only seconds. Then, negligently, he reached out and returned pencil and paper to Braden. He returned to his godlike indifference to mere mortals. But there was now the faintest possible smile on his face. It was an expression of contemptuous triumph.

Braden glanced at the sketch. There was design there. There was an unbelievable intricacy of relationship between this curved line and that, and between them and the formalized irregular pattern in the center. It was not the drawing of a lunatic. It was cryptic, but it was utterly rational. There is something essentially childish in the background of most forms of insanity. There was nothing childish about this. And it was obscurely, annoyingly familiar. Braden had seen something like it, somewhere, before. It was not in the line of psychiatry, but in some of the physical sciences diagrams like this were used in explanations.

An attendant came to return John Kingman to his ward. Braden folded the paper and put it in his pocket.

"It's not in my line, John," he told John Kingman. "I'll have a check-up made. I think I'm going to be able to do something for you."

John Kingman suffered himself to be led away. Rather, he grandly preceded the attendant, negligently preventing the man from touching him, as if such a touch would be a sacrilege the man was too ignorant to realize.

Braden went to the record office. With the agitated clerk beside him, he traced John Kingman's name to the earliest of the file of dead records. Handwriting succeeded typewriting as he went back through the years. Paper yellowed. Handwriting grew Spencerian. It approached the copperplate. But, in ink turned brown, in yellowed rag paper in the ruled record-books of the Eastern Pennsylvania Asylum—which was Meadeville Mental in 1850—there were the records of a patient named John Kingman for every year. Twice Braden came upon notes alongside the name. One was in 1880. Some staff doctor—there were no psychiatrists in those days— had written, *"High fever."* There was nothing else. In 1853 a neat memo stood beside the name. *"This man has six functioning fingers on each hand."* The memo had been made ninety-five years before.

Dr. Braden looked at the agitated clerk. The record of John Kingman was patently impossible. The clerk read it as a sign of inefficiency in his office and possibly on his part. He would be upset and apprehensive until the source of the error had safely been traced to a predecessor.

"Someone," said Braden dryly—but he did not believe it even then—"forgot to make a note of the explanation. An unknown must have been admitted at some time as John Kingman. In time he died. But somehow the name John Kingman had become a sort of stock name like John Doe, to signify an unidentified patient. Look in the death records for John Kingman. Evidently a John Kingman died, and that same year another unidentified patient was assigned the same name. That's it!"

The clerk almost gasped with relief. He went happily to check. But Braden did not believe it. In 1853 someone had noted that John Kingman had six functioning fingers on each hand. The odds against two patients in one institution having six functioning fingers, even in the same century, would be enormous.

Braden went doggedly to the museum. There the devices used in psychiatric treatments in the days of New Bedlam were preserved, but not displayed. Meadeville Mental had been established in 1776 as New Bedlam. It was the oldest mental institution in the United States, but it was not pleasant to think of the treatment given to patients—then termed "madmen"—in the early days.

The records remained. Calfleather bindings. Thin rag paper. Beautifully shaded writing, done with quill pens. Year after year, Dr. Braden searched. He found John Kingman listed in 1820. In 1801. In 1795. In 1785 the name "John Kingman" was absent from the annual list of patients. Braden found the record of his admission in 1786. On the 21st of May, 1786—ten years after New Bedlam was founded, one hundred and sixty-two years before the time of his search—there was a neat entry:

A poore madman admitted this day has been assigned the name of John Kingman because of his absurdly royal manner and affected dignity. He is five feet eight inches tall, appears to speak no Englishe or any other tongue known to any of the learned men hereabout, and has six fingers on each hand, the extra fingers being perfectly formed and functioning. Dr. Sanforde observed that hee seems to have a high fever. On his left shoulder, when stripped, there appears a curious design which is not tattooing according to any known fashion. His madness appears to be so strong a conviction of his greatness that he will not condescend to notice others as being so much his inferiors, so that if not committed hee would starve. But on three occasions, when being examined by physicians, he put out his hand imperiously for writing instruments and drew very intrikit designs which all agree have no significance. He was committed as a madman by a commission consisting of Drs. Sanforde, Smyth, Hale and Bode.

Young Dr. Braden read the entry a second time. Then a third. He ran his hands through his hair. When the clerk came back to announce distressedly that not in all the long history of the institution had a patient named John Kingman died, Braden was not surprised.

"Quite right," said Braden to the almost hysterical clerk. "He didn't die. But I want John Kingman taken over to the hospital ward. We're going to look him over. He's been rather neglected. Apparently he's had actual medical attention only once in a hundred and sixty-two years. Get out his committal papers for me, will you? He was admitted here May 21st, 1786."

Then Braden left, leaving behind him a clerk practically prostrate with shock. The clerk wildly suspected that Dr. Braden had gone insane. But when he found the committal papers, he decided hysterically that it was he who would shortly be in one of the wards.

John Kingman manifested amusement when he was taken into the hospital laboratory. For a good ten seconds—Braden watched him narrowly—he glanced from one piece of apparatus to another. It was impossible to doubt that after one glance he understood the function and operation of every appliance in the ultramodern, super-scientifically-equipped laboratory of the hospital ward. But he was amused. In particular, he looked at the big X-ray machine and smiled with such contempt that the X-ray technician bristled.

"No paranoid suspicion," said Braden. "Most paranoid patients suspect that they're going to be tortured or killed when they're brought to a place where there's stuff they don't understand."

John Kingman turned his eyes to Braden. He put out his six-fingered hand and made the motion of writing. Braden handed him a pencil and a memo tablet. Negligently, contemptuously, he sketched. He sketched again. He handed the sketches to Braden and retreated into his enormous amused contempt for humanity.

Braden glanced at the scraps of paper. He jerked his head, and the X-ray technician came to his side.

"This," said Braden dryly, "looks like a diagram of an X-ray tube. Is it?"

The technician blinked.

"He don't use the regular symbols," he objected, "but—well— yes. That's what he puts for the target and this's for the cathode— Hm-m-m. Yes—" Then he said suddenly: "Say! This's not right."

He studied the diagram. Then he said in abrupt excitement:

"Look! He's put in a field like in an electron microscope! That's an idea! Do that, and you'd get a straight-line electron flow and a narrower X-ray beam—"

Braden said:

"I wonder! What's this second sketch? Another type of X-ray?"

The X-ray technician studied the second sketch absorbedly. After a time he said dubiously:

"He don't use regular symbols. I don't know. Here's the same sign for the target and that for the cathode.

"This looks like something to . . . hm-m-m . . . accelerate the electrons. Like in a Coolidge tube. Only it's—" He scratched his head. "I see what he's trying to put down. If something like this would work, you could work any tube at any voltage you wanted. Yeah! And all the high EMF would be inside the tube. No danger. Hey! You could work this off dry batteries! A doctor could carry an X-ray outfit in his handbag! And he could get million-volt stuff!"

The technician stared in mounting excitement. Presently he said urgently:

"This is crazy! But . . . look, Doc! Let me have this thing to study over! This is great stuff! This is . . . Gosh! Give me a chance to get this made up and try it out! I don't get it all yet, but—"

Braden took back the sketch and put it in his pocket.

"John Kingman," he observed, "has been a patient here for a hundred and sixty-two years. I think we're going to get some more surprises. Let's get at the job on hand!"

John Kingman was definitely amused. He was amenable, now. His air of pitying condescension, as of a god to imbeciles, under other circumstances would have been infuriating. He permitted himself to be X-rayed as one might allow children to use one as a part of their play. He glanced at the thermometer and smiled contemptuously. He permitted his body temperature to be taken from an armpit. The electrocardiograph aroused just such momentary interest as a child's unfamiliar plaything might cause. With an air of mirth he allowed the tattooed design on his shoulder—it was there—to be photographed. Throughout, he showed such condescending contempt as would explain his failure to be annoyed.

But Braden grew pale as the tests went on. John Kingman's body temperature was 105° F. A "high fever" had been observed in 1850—ninety-eight years before—and in 1786—well over a century and a half previously. But he still appeared to be somewhere between forty and sixty years old. John Kingman's pulse rate was one hundred fifty-seven beats per minute, and the electrocardiograph registered an absolutely preposterous pattern which had no meaning until Braden said curtly: "If he had two hearts, it would look like that!"

When the X-ray plates came out of the fixing-bath, he looked at them with the grim air of someone expecting to see the impossible. And the impossible was there. When John Kingman was admitted to New Bedlam, there were no such things as X-rays on earth. It was natural that he had never been X-rayed before. He had two hearts. He had three extra ribs on each side. He had four more vertebrae than a normal human being. There were distinct oddities in his elbow joints. And his cranial capacity appeared to be something like twelve per cent above that of any but exceptional specimens of humanity. His teeth displayed distinct consistent deviation from the norm in shape.

He regarded Braden with contemptuous triumph when the tests were over. He did not speak. He drew dignity about himself like a garment. He allowed an attendant to dress him again while he looked into the distance, seemingly thinking godlike thoughts. When his toilet was complete he looked again at Braden—with vast condescension—and his six-fingered hands again made a gesture of writing. Braden grew—if possible—slightly paler as he handed over a pencil and pad.

John Kingman actually deigned to glance, once, at the sheet on which he wrote. When he handed it back to Braden and withdrew into magnificently amused aloofness, there were a dozen or more tiny sketches on the sheet. The first was an exact duplicate of the one he had handed Braden before the Administration Building. Beside it was another which was similar but not alike. The third was a specific variation in precise, exact steps until the last pair of sketches divided again into two, of which one—by a perfectly logical extension of the change-pattern—had returned to the original design, while the other was a bewilderingly complex pattern with its formalized central part in two closely-linked sections.

Braden caught his breath. Just as the X-ray man had been puzzled at first by the use of unfamiliar symbols for familiar ideas, so Braden had been puzzled by untraceable familiarity in the first sketch of all. But the last diagram made everything clear. It resembled almost exactly the standard diagrams illustrating fissionable elements as atoms. Once it was granted that John Kingman was no ordinary lunatic, it became clear that here was a diagram of some physical process which began with normal and stable atoms and arrived at an unstable atom—with one of the original atoms returned to its original state. It was, in short, a process of physical catalysis which would produce atomic energy.

Braden raised his eyes to the contemptuous, amused eyes of John Kingman.

"I think you win," he said shakenly. "I still think you're crazy, but maybe we're crazier still."

The commitment papers on John Kingman were a hundred and sixty-two years old. They were yellow and brittle and closely written. John Kingman—said the oddly spelled and sometimes curiously phrased document—was first seen on the morning of April 10, 1786, by a man named Thomas Hawkes, as he drove into Aurora, Pennsylvania, with a load of corn. John Kingman was then clad in very queer garments, not like those of ordinary men. The material looked like silk, save that it seemed also to be metallic. The man Hawkes was astounded, but thought perhaps some strolling player had got drunk and wandered off while wearing his costume for a play or pageant. He obligingly stopped his horse and allowed the stranger to climb in for a ride to town. The stranger was imperious, and scornfully silent. Hawkes asked who he was, and was contemptuously ignored. He asked—seemingly, all the world was talking of such matters then, at least the world about Aurora, Pennsylvania—if the stranger had seen the giant shooting stars of the night before. The stranger ignored him. Arrived in town, the stranger stood in the street with regal dignity, looking contemptuously at the people. A crowd gathered about him but he seemed to feel too superior to notice it. Presently a grave and elderly man—a Mr. Wycherly—appeared and the stranger fixed him with a gesture. He stooped and wrote strange designs in the dust at his feet. When the unintelligible design was meaningless to Mr. Wycherly, the stranger seemed to fly into a very passion of contempt. He spat at the crowd, and the crowd became unruly and constables took him into custody.

Braden waited patiently until both the Director of Meadeville Mental and the man from Washington had finished reading the yellowed papers. Then Braden explained calmly:

"He's insane, of course. It's paranoia. He is as convinced of his superiority to us as—say—Napoleon or Edison would have been convinced of their superiority if they'd suddenly been dumped down among a tribe of Australian bushmen. As a matter of fact, John Kingman may have just as good reason as they would have had to feel his superiority. But if he were sane he would prove it. He would establish it. Instead, he has withdrawn into a remote contemplation of his own greatness. So he is a paranoiac. One may surmise that he was insane when he first appeared. But he doesn't have a delusion of persecution because on the face of it no such theory is needed to account for his present situation."

The Director said in a tolerantly shocked tone:

"Dr. Braden! You speak as if he were not a human being!"

"He isn't," said Braden. "His body temperature is a hundred and five. Human tissues simply would not survive that temperature. He has extra vertebrae and extra ribs. His joints are not quite like ours. He has two hearts. We were able to check his circulatory system just under the skin with infrared lamps, and it is not like ours. And I submit that he has been a patient in this asylum for one hundred and sixty-two years. If he is human, he is at least remarkable!"

The man from Washington said interestedly:

"Where do you think he comes from, Dr. Braden?"

Braden spread out his hands. He said doggedly:

"I make no guesses. But I sent photostats of the sketches he made to the Bureau of Standards. I said that they were made by a patient and appeared to be diagrams of atomic structure. I asked if they indicated a knowledge of physics. You"—He looked at the man from Washington—"turned up thirty-six hours later. I deduce that he has such knowledge."

"He has!" said the man from Washington, mildly. "The X-ray sketches were interesting enough, but the others—apparently he has told us how to get controlled atomic energy out of silicon, which is one of the earth's commonest elements. Where did he come from, Dr. Braden?''

Braden clamped his jaw.

''You noticed that the commitment papers referred to shooting stars then causing much local comment? I looked up the newspapers for about that date. They reported a large shooting star which was observed to descend to the earth. Then, various credible observers claimed that it shot back up to the sky again. Then, some hours afterward, various large shooting stars crossed the sky from horizon to horizon, without ever falling.''

The Director of Meadeville Mental said humorously:

''It's a wonder that New Bedlam—as we were then—was not crowded after such statements!''

The man from Washington did not smile.

''I think,'' he said meditatively, ''that Dr. Braden suggests a spaceship landing to permit John Kingman to get out, and then going away again. And possible pursuit afterward.''

The Director laughed appreciatively at the assumed jest.

''If,'' said the man from Washington, ''John Kingman is not human, and if he comes from somewhere where as much was known about atomic energy almost two centuries ago as he has showed us, and, if he were insane there, he might have seized some sort of vehicle and fled in it because of delusions of persecution. Which in a sense, if he were insane, might be justified. He would have been pursued. With pursuers close behind him he might have landed—here.''

''But the vehicle!'' said the Director. ''Our ancestors would have recorded finishing a spaceship or an airplane.''

''Suppose,'' said the man from Washington, ''that his pursuers had something like . . . say . . . radar. Even we have that! A cunning lunatic would have sent off his vehicle under automatic control to lead his pursuers as long and merry a chase as possible. Perhaps he sent it to dive into the sun. The rising shooting star and the other cruising shooting stars would be accounted for. What do you say, Dr. Braden?''

Braden shrugged.

''There is no evidence. Now he is insane. If we were to cure him—''

''Just how,'' said the man from Washington, ''would you cure him? I thought paranoia was practically hopeless.''

''Not quite,'' Braden told him. ''They've used shock treatment for dementia praecox and schizophrenia, with good results.

Until last year there was nothing of comparable value for paranoia. Then Jantzen suggested euphoric shock. Basically, the idea is to dispel illusions by creating hallucinations.''

The Director fidgeted disapprovingly. The man from Washington waited.

''In euphoric shock,'' said Braden carefully, ''the tensions and anxieties of insane patients are relieved by drugs which produce a sensation of euphoria, or well-being. Jantzen combined hallucination-producing drugs with those. The combination seems to place the patient temporarily in a cosmos in which all delusions are satisfied and all tensions relieved. He has a rest from his struggle against reality. Also he has a sort of super-catharsis, in the convincing realization of all his desires. Quite often he comes out of the first euphoric shock temporarily sane. The percentage of final cures is satisfyingly high.''

The man from Washington said: ''Body chemistry?''

Braden regarded him with new respect. He said:

''I don't know. He's lived on human food for almost two centuries, and in any case it's been proved that the proteins will be identical on all planets, under all suns. But I couldn't be sure about it. There might even be allergies. You say his drawings were very important. It might be wisest to find out everything possible from him before even euphoric shock was tried.''

''Ah, yes!'' said the Director, tolerantly. ''If he has waited a hundred and sixty-two years, a few weeks or months will make no difference. And I would like to watch the experiment, but I am about to start on my vacation—''

''Hardly,'' said the man from Washington.

''I said, I am about to start on my vacation.''

''John Kingman,'' said the man from Washington mildly, ''has been trying for a hundred and sixty-two years to tell us how to have controlled atomic energy, and pocket X-ray machines, and God knows what all else. There may be, somewhere about this institution, drawings of antigravity apparatus, really efficient atomic bombs, spaceship drives or weapons which could depopulate the earth. I'm afraid nobody here is going to communicate with the outside world in any way until the place and all its personnel are gone over . . . ah . . . rather carefully.''

''This,'' said the Director indignantly, ''is preposterous!''

''Quite so. A thousand years of human advance locked in the skull of a lunatic. Nearly two hundred years more of progress and development wasted because he was locked up here. But it would be most preposterous of all to let his information loose to the other lunatics who aren't locked up because they're running governments!''

The Director sat down. The man from Washington said: "Now, Dr. Braden—''

John Kingman spent days on end in scornful, triumphant glee. Braden watched him somberly. Meadeville Mental Hospital was an armed camp with sentries everywhere, and specially about the building in which John Kingman gloated. There were hordes of suitably certified scientists and psychiatrists about him, now, and he was filled with blazing satisfaction.

He sat in regal, triumphant aloofness. He was the greatest, the most important, the most consequential figure on this planet. The stupid creatures who inhabited it—they were only superficially like himself—had at last come to perceive his godliness. Now they clustered about him. In their stupid language which it was beneath his dignity to learn, they addressed him. But they did not grovel. Even groveling would not be sufficiently respectful for such inferior beings when addressing John Kingman. He very probably devised in his own mind the exact etiquette these stupid creatures must practice before he would condescend to notice them.

They made elaborate tests. He ignored their actions. They tried with transparent cunning to trick him into further revelations of the powers he held. Once, in malicious amusement, he drew a sketch of a certain reaction which such inferior minds could not possibly understand. They were vastly excited, and he was enormously amused. When they tried that reaction and square miles turned to incandescent vapor, the survivors would realize that they could not trick or force him into giving them the riches of his godlike mind. They must devise the proper etiquette to appease him. They must abjectly and humbly plead with him and placate him and sacrifice to him. They must deny all other gods but John Kingman. They would realize that he was all wisdom, all power, all greatness when the reaction he had sketched destroyed them by millions.

Braden prevented that from happening. When John Kingman gave a sketch of a new atomic reaction in response to an elaborate trick one of the newcomers had devised, Braden protested grimly.

"The patient," he said doggedly, "is a paranoiac. Suspicion and trickiness are inherent in his mental processes. At any moment, to demonstrate his greatness, he may try to produce unholy destruction. You absolutely cannot trust him! Be careful!''

He hammered the fact home, arguing the sheer flat fact that a paranoiac will do absolutely anything to prove his grandeur.

The new reaction was tried with microscopic quantities of material, and it only destroyed everything within a fifty-yard radius. Which brought the final decision on John Kingman. He was insane. He knew more about one overwhelmingly important subject than all the generations of men. But it was not possible to obtain trustworthy data from him on that subject or any other while he was insane. It was worth while to take the calculated risk of attempting to cure him.

Braden protested again:

''I urged the attempt to cure him,'' he said firmly, ''before I knew he had given the United States several centuries head-start in knowledge of atomic energy. I was thinking of him as a patient. For his own sake, any risk was proper. Since he is not human, I withdraw my urging. I do not know what will happen. Anything could happen.''

His refusal held up treatment for a week. Then a Presidential executive order resolved the matter. The attempt was to be made as a calculated risk. Dr. Braden would make the attempt.

He did. He tested John Kingman for tolerance of euphoric drugs. No unfavorable reaction. He tested him for tolerance of drugs producing hallucination. No unfavorable reaction. Then—

He injected into one of John Kingman's veins a certain quantity of the combination of drugs which on human beings was most effective for euphoric shock, and whose separate constituents had been tested on John Kingman and found harmless. It was not a sufficient dose to produce the full required effect. Braden expected to have to make at least one and probably two additional injections before the requisite euphoria was produced. He was taking no single avoidable chance. He administered first a dosage which should have produced no more than a feeling of mild but definite exhilaration.

And John Kingman went into convulsions. Horrible ones.

There is such a thing as allergy and such a thing as synergy, and nobody understands either. Some patients collapse when given aspirin. Some break out in rashes from penicillin. Some drugs, taken alone, have one effect, and taken together quite another and drastic one. A drug producing euphoria was harmless to John Kingman. A drug producing hallucinations was harmless. But—synergy or allergy or whatever—the two taken together were deadly poison.

He was literally unconscious for three weeks, and in continuous convulsion for two days. He was kept alive by artificial nourishment, glucose, nasal feeding—everything. But his coma was extreme. Four separate times he was believed dead.

But after three weeks he opened his eyes vaguely. In another week he was able to talk. From the first his expression was bewildered. He was no longer proud. He began to learn English. He showed no paranoiac symptoms. He was wholly sane. In fact, his I.Q.—tested later—was ninety, which is well within the range of normal intelligence. He was not overbright, but adequate. And he did not remember who he was. He did not remember anything at all about his life before rousing from coma in the Meadeville Mental Hospital. Not anything at all. It was, apparently, either the price or the cause of his recovery.

Braden considered that it was the means. He urged his views on the frustrated scientists who wanted now to try hypnotism and "truth serum" and other devices for picking the lock of John Kingman's brain.

"As a diagnosis," said Braden, moved past the tendency to be technical, "the poor devil smashed up on something we can't even guess at. His normal personality couldn't take it, whatever it was, so he fled into delusions—into insanity. He lived in that retreat over a century and a half, and then we found him out. And we wouldn't let him keep his beautiful delusions that he was great and godlike and all-powerful. We were merciless. We forced ourselves upon him. We questioned him. We tricked him. In the end, we nearly poisoned him! And his delusions couldn't stand up. He couldn't admit that he was wrong, and he couldn't reconcile such experiences with his delusions. There was only one thing he could do—forget the whole thing in the most literal possible manner. What he's done is to go into what they used to call dementia praecox. Actually, it's infantilism. He's fled back to his childhood. That's why his I.Q. is only ninety, instead of the unholy figure it must have been when he was a normal adult of his race. He's mentally a child. He sleeps, right now, in the foetal position. Which is a warning! One more attempt to tamper with his brain, and he'll go into the only place that's left for him—into the absolute blankness that is the mind of the unborn child!"

He presented evidence. The evidence was overwhelming. In the end, reluctantly, John Kingman was left alone.

He gets along all right, though. He works in the records department of Meadeville Mental now, because there his six-fingered hands won't cause remark. He is remarkably accurate and perfectly happy.

But he is carefully watched. The one question he can answer now is—how long he's going to live. A hundred and sixty-two years is only part of his lifetime. But if you didn't know, you'd swear he wasn't more than fifty.

THAT ONLY A MOTHER

by Judith Merril

ASTOUNDING SCIENCE FICTION
June

Like Peter Phillips' story in this book, "That Only a Mother" is a famous first story. Unlike Phillips' however, this one caused a sensation and was recognized as one of the most important stories of 1948. "Judith Merril" (Josephine Grossman) was an active fan and personality in science fiction before she tried writing it, and she became an influential figure in the field through her work as an editor and anthologist. Her "Best of the Year" series, which appeared from 1956 to 1964, helped to expand the field by drawing attention to excellent stories that were appearing outside of the genre magazines. In addition, she was an influential advocate of the "New Wave" stories being produced in England during the mid-1960s, and her anthology England Swings SF (1968) helped to change the direction of American science fiction.

As a writer, she produced four novels and a brace of fine short stories, all, unfortunately, overshadowed by this powerful one.

(I always think of Judy with a certain amount of sadness. —No, she's alive and well and, as far as I know, happy. That's not it. The point is this—

Some science fiction writers are pertinacious and seemingly endless, to the delight of their readers. As an example, Bob Heinlein, Arthur Clarke, and I (the endlessly cited "Big Three") have been at it for forty years and more now, and show absolutely no signs of any loss in ability. We'll stop when we die, but not short of that, I'm sure. There are others I can name, too. And then there are some who, for several years, blaze across the heavens and then, for some reason, stop. Judy is one of them. She was the morning star predecessor of the great women writers who now are the supernovas of the field; the first to write as well as any man without imitating the characteristic work of men. And then she stopped, which is calamitous. Think of the dozen great novels she might have written in the last thirty years—and did not.—I. A.)

Margaret reached over to the other side of the bed where Hank should have been. Her hand patted the empty pillow, and then she came altogether awake, wondering that the old habit should remain after so many months. She tried to curl up, cat-style, to hoard her own warmth, found she couldn't do it anymore, and climbed out of bed with a pleased awareness of her increasingly clumsy bulkiness.

Morning motions were automatic. On the way through the kitchenette, she pressed the button that would start breakfast cooking—the doctor had said to eat as much breakfast as she could—and tore the paper out of the facsimile machine. She folded the long sheet carefully to the "National News" section, and propped it on the bathroom shelf to scan while she brushed her teeth.

No accidents. No direct hits. At least none that had been officially released for publication. *Now, Maggie, don't get started on that. No accidents. No hits. Take the nice newspaper's word for it.*

The three clear chimes from the kitchen announced that breakfast was ready. She set a bright napkin and cheerful colored dishes on the table in a futile attempt to appeal to a faulty morning appetite. Then, when there was nothing more to prepare, she went for the mail, allowing herself the full pleasure of prolonged anticipation, because today there would *surely* be a letter.

There was. There were. Two bills and a worried note from her mother: "Darling. Why didn't you write and tell me sooner? I'm thrilled, of course, but, well, one hates to mention these things, but are you *certain* the doctor was right? Hank's been around all that uranium or thorium or whatever it is all these years, and I know you say he's a designer, not a technician, and he doesn't get near anything that might be dangerous, but you know he used to, back at Oak Ridge. Don't you think . . . well, of course, I'm just being a foolish old woman, and I don't want you to get upset. You know much more about it than I do, and I'm sure your doctor was right. He *should* know . . ."

Margaret made a face over the excellent coffee, and caught herself refolding the paper to the medical news.

Stop it, Maggie, stop it! The radiologist said Hank's job couldn't have exposed him. And the bombed area we drove past . . . No, no. Stop it, now! Read the social notes or the recipes, Maggie girl.

A well-known geneticist, in the medical news, said that it was possible to tell with absolute certainty, at five months, whether the child would be normal, or at least whether the mutation was likely to produce anything freakish. The worst cases, at any rate, could be prevented. Minor mutations, of course, displacements in facial features, or changes in brain structure could not be detected. And there had been some cases recently, of normal embryos with atrophied limbs that did not develop beyond the seventh or eighth month. But, the doctor concluded cheerfully, the *worst* cases could now be predicted and prevented.

"Predicted and prevented." We predicted it, didn't we? Hank and the others, they predicted it. But we didn't prevent it. We could have stopped it in '46 and '47. Now . . .

Margaret decided against the breakfast. Coffee had been enough for her in the morning for ten years; it would have to do for today. She buttoned herself into interminable folds of material that, the salesgirl had assured her, was the *only* comfortable thing to wear during the last few months. With a surge of pure pleasure, the letter and newspaper forgotten, she realized she was on the next to the last button. It wouldn't be long now.

The city in the early morning had always been a special kind of excitement for her. Last night it had rained, and the sidewalks were still damp-gray instead of dusty. The air smelled the fresher, to a city-bred woman, for the occasional pungency of acrid factory smoke. She walked the six blocks to work, watching the lights go out in the all-night hamburger joints, where the plate-glass walls were already catching the sun, and the lights go on in the dim interiors of cigar stores and drycleaning establishments.

The office was in a new Government building. In the rolovator, on the way up, she felt, as always, like a frankfurter roll in the ascending half of an old-style rotary toasting machine. She abandoned the air-foam cushioning gratefully at the fourteenth floor, and settled down behind her desk, at the rear of a long row of identical desks.

Each morning the pile of papers that greeted her was a little higher. These were, as everyone knew, the decisive months. The war might be won or lost on these calculations as well as any others. The manpower office had switched her here when her old expediter's job got to be too strenuous. The computer was easy to operate, and the work was absorbing, if not as exciting as the old job. But you didn't just stop working these days. Everyone who could do anything at all was needed.

And—she remembered the interview with the psychologist—*I'm probably the unstable type. Wonder what sort of neurosis I'd get sitting home reading that sensational paper . . .*

She plunged into the work without pursuing the thought.

February 18.

Hank darling,

Just a note—from the hospital, no less. I had a dizzy spell at work, and the doctor took it to heart. Blessed if I know what I'll do with myself lying in bed for weeks, just waiting—but Dr. Boyer seems to think it may not be so long.

There are too many newspapers around here. More infanticides all the time, and they can't seem to get a jury to convict any of them. It's the fathers who did it. Lucky thing you're not around, in case—

Oh, darling, that wasn't a very *funny* joke, was it? Write as often as you can, will you? I have too much time to think. But there really isn't anything wrong, and nothing to worry about.

Write often, and remember I love you.

Maggie.

SPECIAL SERVICE TELEGRAM

FEBRUARY 21, 1953
22:04 LK37G

FROM: TECH. LIEUT. H. MARVELL
          X47–016 GCNY
TO: MRS. H. MARVELL
     WOMEN'S HOSPITAL
     NEW YORK CITY

**HAD DOCTOR'S GRAM STOP WILL ARRIVE FOUR OH
TEN STOP SHORT LEAVE STOP YOU DID IT MAGGIE
STOP LOVE HANK**

February 25.

Hank dear,

So you didn't see the baby either? You'd think a place this
size would at lease have visiplates on the incubators, so the
fathers could get a look, even if the poor benighted mommas
can't. They tell me I won't see her for another week, or maybe
more—but of course, mother always warned me if I didn't slow
my pace, I'd probably even have my babies too fast. Why must
she *always* be right?

Did you meet that battle-ax of a nurse they put on here? I
imagine they save her for people who've already had theirs, and
don't let her get too near the prospectives—but a woman like
that simply shouldn't be allowed in a maternity ward. She's
obsessed with mutations, can't seem to talk about anything else.
Oh, well, *ours* is all right, even if it was in an unholy hurry.

I'm tired. They warned me not to sit up so soon, but I *had* to
write you. All my love, darling,

Maggie.

February 29.

Darling,

I finally got to see her! It's all true, what they say about new
babies and the face that only a mother could love—but it's all
there, darling, eyes, ears, and noses—no, only one!—all in the
right places. We're so *lucky*, Hank.

I'm afraid I've been a rambunctious patient. I kept telling that
hatchet-faced female with the mutation mania that I wanted to
see the baby. Finally the doctor came in to "explain" everything

to me, and talking a lot of nonsense, most of which I'm sure no one could have understood, any more than I did. The only thing I got out of it was that she didn't actually *have* to stay in the incubator; they just thought it was "wiser."

I think I got a little hysterical at that point. Guess I was more worried than I was willing to admit, but I threw a small fit about it. The whole business wound up with one of those hushed medical conferences outside the door, and finally the Woman in White said: "Well, we might as well. Maybe it'll work out better that way."

I'd heard about the way doctors and nurses in these places develop a God complex, and believe me it is as true figuratively as it is literally that a mother hasn't got a leg to stand on around here.

I *am* awfully weak, still. I'll write again soon. Love,

Maggie.

March 8.

Dearest Hank,

Well, the nurse was wrong if she told you that. She's an idiot anyhow. It's a girl. It's easier to tell with babies than with cats, and *I know*. How about Henrietta?

I'm home again, and busier than a betatron. They got *everything* mixed up at the hospital, and I had to teach myself how to bathe her and do just about everything else. She's getting prettier, too. When can you get a leave, a *real* leave?

Love,
Maggie.

May 26.

Hank dear,

You should see her now—and you shall. I'm sending along a reel of color movie. My mother sent her those nighties with drawstrings all over. I put one on, and right now she looks like a snow-white potato sack with that beautiful, beautiful flower-face blooming on top. Is that *me* talking? Am I a doting mother? But wait till you *see* her!

July 10.

. . . Believe it or not, as you like, but your daughter can talk, and I don't mean baby talk. Alice discovered it—she's a dental assistant in the WACs, you know—and when she heard the baby giving out what I thought was a string of gibberish, she said the kid knew words and sentences, but couldn't say them clearly because she has no teeth yet. I'm taking her to a speech specialist.

September 13.
. . . We have a prodigy for real! Now that all her front teeth are in, her speech is perfectly clear and—a new talent now—she can sing! I mean really carry a tune! At seven months! Darling, my world would be perfect if you could only get home.

November 19.
. . . At last. The little goon was so busy being clever, it took her all this time to learn to crawl. The doctor says development in these cases is always erratic . . .

SPECIAL SERVICE TELEGRAM

DECEMBER 1, 1953
08:47 LK59F

FROM: TECH. LIEUT. H. MARVELL
X47–016 GCNY
TO: MRS. H. MARVELL
APT. K-17
504 E. 19 St.
N.Y. N.Y.

WEEK'S LEAVE STARTS TOMORROW STOP WILL ARRIVE AIRPORT TEN OH FIVE STOP DON'T MEET ME STOP LOVE LOVE LOVE HANK

Margaret let the water run out of the bathinette until only a few inches were left, and then loosed her hold on the wriggling baby.

"I think it was better when you were retarded, young woman," she informed her daughter happily. "You *can't* crawl in a bathinette, you know."

"Then why can't I go in the bathtub?" Margaret was used to her child's volubility by now, but every now and then it caught her unawares. She swooped the resistant mass of pink flesh into a towel, and began to rub.

"Because you're too little, and your head is very soft, and bathtubs are very hard."

"Oh. Then when can I go in the bathtub?"

"When the outside of your head is as hard as the inside, brainchild." She reached toward a pile of fresh clothing. "I cannot understand," she added, pinning a square of cloth through the nightgown, "why a child of your intelligence can't learn to keep a diaper on the way other babies do. They've been used for centuries, you know, with perfectly satisfactory results."

The child disdained to reply; she had heard it too often. She waited patiently until she had been tucked, clean and sweet-smelling, into a white-painted crib. Then she favored her mother with a smile that inevitably made Margaret think of the first golden edge of the sun bursting into a rosy predawn. She remembered Hank's reaction to the color pictures of his beautiful daughter, and with the thought, realized how late it was.

"Go to sleep, puss. When you wake up, you know, your *daddy* will be here."

"Why?" asked the four-year-old mind, waging a losing battle to keep the ten-month-old body awake.

Margaret went into the kitchenette and set the timer for the roast. She examined the table, and got her clothes from the closet, new dress, new shoes, new slip, new everything, bought weeks before and saved for the day Hank's telegram came. She stopped to pull a paper from the facsimile, and, with clothes and news, went into the bathroom and lowered herself gingerly into the steaming luxury of a scented bath.

She glanced through the paper with indifferent interest. Today at least there was no need to read the national news. There was an article by a geneticist. The same geneticist. Mutations, he said, were increasing disproportionately. It was too soon for recessives; even the first mutants, born near Hiroshima and Nagasaki in 1946 and 1947 were not old enough yet to breed. *But my baby's all right.* Apparently, there was some degree of free radiation from atomic explosions causing the trouble. *My baby's fine. Precocious, but normal.* If more attention had been paid to the first Japanese mutations, he said . . .

There was that little notice in the paper in the spring of '47. That was when Hank quit at Oak Ridge. "Only 2 or 3 percent of those guilty of infanticide are being caught and punished in Japan today . . ." *But* MY BABY'S *all right.*

She was dressed, combed, and ready to the last light brush-on of lip paste, when the door chime sounded. She dashed for the door, and heard for the first time in eighteen months the almost-forgotten sound of a key turning in the lock before the chime had quite died away.

"Hank!"

"Maggie!"

And then there was nothing to say. So many days, so many months of small news piling up, so many things to tell him, and now she just stood there, staring at a khaki uniform and a stranger's pale face. She traced the features with the finger of memory. The same high-bridged nose, wide-set eyes, fine feathery brows; the same long jaw, the hair a little farther back now on the high forehead, the same tilted curve to his mouth. Pale . . . Of course, he'd been underground all this time. And strange, stranger because of lost familiarity than any newcomer's face could be.

She had time to think all that before his hand reached out to touch her, and spanned the gap of eighteen months. Now, again, there was nothing to say, because there was no need. They were together, and for the moment that was enough.

"Where's the baby?"

"Sleeping. She'll be up any minute."

No urgency. Their voices were as casual as though it were a daily exchange, as though war and separation did not exist. Margaret picked up the coat he'd thrown on the chair near the door, and hung it carefully in the hall closet. She went to check the roast, leaving him to wander through the rooms by himself, remembering and coming back. She found him, finally, standing over the baby's crib.

She couldn't see his face, but she had no need to.

"I think we can wake her just this once." Margaret pulled the covers down and lifted the white bundle from the bed. Sleepy lids pulled back heavily from smoky brown eyes.

"Hello." Hank's voice was tentative.

"Hello." The baby's assurance was more pronounced.

He had heard about it, of course, but that wasn't the same as hearing it. He turned eagerly to Margaret. "She really can—?"

"Of course she can, darling. But what's more important, she can even do nice normal things like other babies do, even stupid ones. Watch her crawl!" Margaret set the baby on the big bed.

For a moment young Henrietta lay and eyed her parents dubiously.

"Crawl?" she asked.

"That's the idea. Your daddy is new around here, you know. He wants to see you show off."

"Then put me on my tummy."

"Oh, of course." Margaret obligingly rolled the baby over.

"What's the matter?" Hank's voice was still casual, but an undercurrent in it began to charge the air of the room. "I thought they turned over first."

"This baby"—Margaret would not notice the tension—"*This* baby does things when she wants to."

This baby's father watched with softening eyes while the head advanced and the body hunched up propelling itself across the bed.

"Why, the little rascal." He burst into relieved laughter. "She looks like one of those potato-sack racers they used to have on picnics. Got her arms pulled out of the sleeves already." He reached over and grabbed the knot at the bottom of the long nightie.

"I'll do it, darling." Margaret tried to get there first.

"Don't be silly, Maggie. This may be *your* first baby, but *I* had five kid brothers." He laughed her away, and reached with his other hand for the string that closed one sleeve. He opened the sleeve bow, and groped for an arm.

"The way you wriggle," he addressed his child sternly, as his hand touched a moving knob of flesh at the shoulder, "anyone might think you are a worm, using your tummy to crawl on, instead of your hands and feet."

Margaret stood and watched, smiling. "Wait till you hear her sing, darling—"

His right hand traveled down from the shoulder to where he thought an arm would be, traveled down, and straight down, over firm small muscles that writhed in an attempt to move against the pressure of his hand. He let his fingers drift up again to the shoulder. With infinite care he opened the knot at the bottom of the nightgown. His wife was standing by the bed, saying, "She can do 'Jingle Bells,' and—"

His left hand felt along the soft knitted fabric of the gown, up toward the diaper that folded, flat and smooth, across the bottom end of his child. No wrinkles. No kicking. *No . . .*

"Maggie." He tried to pull his hands from the neat fold in the diaper, from the wriggling body. "Maggie." His throat was dry; words came hard, low and grating. He spoke very slowly, thinking the sound of each word to make himself say it. His head was spinning, but he had to *know* before he let it go. "Maggie, why . . . didn't you . . . tell me?"

"Tell you what, darling?" Margaret's poise was the immemorial patience of woman confronted with man's childish impetuosity.

Her sudden laugh sounded fantastically easy and natural in that room; it was all clear to her now. "Is she wet? I didn't know."

She didn't know. His hands, beyond control, ran up and down the soft-skinned baby body, the sinuous, limbless body. *Oh God, dear God*—his head shook and his muscles contracted in a bitter spasm of hysteria. His fingers tightened on his child— *Oh God, she didn't know . . .*

THE MONSTER

by A. E. van Vogt (1912–   )

ASTOUNDING SCIENCE FICTION

August

1948 was aother banner year for A. E. van Vogt. In addition to the two selections in this book, the year saw the serialization of his The Players A, *a sequel (in many ways a better novel) to his very popular and controversial* The World of A, *and the publication of "The Rull," another installment of an interesting series.*

"The Monster" is a fresh look at a very old science fiction theme—the invaders of Earth story. Here van Vogt speculates on the effects of an invasion of an apparently *lifeless Earth.*

(One of the important corollaries of John Campbell's notion that "there are supermen against us," is that the supermen are human beings, or some human beings, or the descendants of human beings. In fact, I don't think John would consider any story in which human beings were pictured as inferior to other intelligences. This was something I found myself unable to accept, so that I tended to write stories about robots, or about interstellar travel that did not involve extraterrestrial intelligences. In fact, I invented the "all-human Galaxy"

*in order to make an end-run around John Campbell's
convictions. Just the same, by doing this I deprived
myself of the sort of very dramatic situations that A. E.
van Vogt develops in this story—I. A.)*

The great ship poised a quarter of a mile above one of the
cities. Below was a cosmic desolation. As he floated down in his
energy bubble, Enash saw that the buildings were crumbling
with age.

"No signs of war damage!" The bodiless voice touched his
ears momentarily. Enash tuned it out.

On the ground he collapsed his bubble. He found himself in a
walled enclosure overgrown with weeds. Several skeletons lay in
the tall grass beside the rakish building. They were of long,
two-legged, two-armed beings with skulls in each case mounted
at the end of a thin spine. The skeletons, all of adults, seemed in
excellent preservation, but when he bent down and touched one,
a whole section of it crumbled into a fine powder. As he
straightened, he saw that Yoal was floating down nearby. Enash
waited until the historian had stepped out of his bubble, then he
said:

"Do you think we ought to use our method of reviving the
long dead?"

Yoal was thoughtful. "I have been asking questions of the
various people who have landed, and there is something wrong
here. This planet has no surviving life, not even insect life. We'll
have to find out what happened before we risk any colonization."

Enash said nothing. A soft wind was blowing. It rustled
through a clump of trees nearby. He motioned toward the trees.
Yoal nodded and said, "Yes, the plant life has not been harmed,
but plants after all are not affected in the same way as the active
life forms."

There was an interruption. A voice spoke from Yoal's receiver:
"A museum has been found at approximately the center of the
city. A red light has been fixed on the roof."

Enash said, "I'll go with you, Yoal. There might be skeletons
of animals and of the intelligent being in various stages of his
evolution. You didn't answer my question. Are you going to
revive these things?"

Yoal said slowly, "I intend to discuss the matter with the council, but I think there is no doubt. We must know the cause of this disaster." He waved one sucker vaguely to take in half the compass. He added as an afterthought, "We shall proceed cautiously, of course, beginning with an obviously early development. The absence of the skeletons of children indicates that the race had developed personal immortality."

The council came to look at the exhibits. It was, Enash knew, a formal preliminary only. The decision was made. There would be revivals. It was more than that. They were curious. Space was vast, the journeys through it long and lonely, landing always a stimulating experience, with its prospect of new life forms to be seen and studied.

The museum looked ordinary. High-domed ceilings, vast rooms. Plastic models of strange beasts, many artifacts—too many to see and comprehend in so short a time. The life span of a race was imprisoned here in a progressive array of relics. Enash looked with the others, and was glad when they came to the line of skeletons and preserved bodies. He seated himself behind the energy screen, and watched the biological experts take a preserved body out of a stone sarcophagus. It was wrapped in windings of cloth, many of them. The experts did not bother to unravel the rotted material. Their forceps reached through, pinched a piece of skull—that was the accepted procedure. Any part of the skeleton could be used, but the most perfect revivals, the most complete reconstructions resulted when a certain section of the skull was used.

Hamar, the chief biologist, explained the choice of body. "The chemicals used to preserve this mummy show a sketchy knowledge of chemistry. The carvings on the sarcophagus indicate a crude and unmechanical culture. In such a civilization there would not be much development of the potentialities of the nervous system. Our speech experts have been analyzing the recorded voice mechanism which is a part of each exhibit, and though many languages are involved—evidence that the ancient language spoken at the time the body was alive has been reproduced—they found no difficulty in translating the meanings. They have now adapted our universal speech machine, so that anyone who wishes to need only speak into his communicator, and so will have his words translated into the language of the revived person. The reverse, naturally, is also true. Ah, I see we are ready for the first body."

Enash watched intently with the others as the lid was clamped down on the plastic reconstructor, and the growth processes were started. He could feel himself becoming tense. For there was nothing haphazard about what was happening. In a few minutes a full-grown ancient inhabitant of this planet would sit up and stare at them. The science involved was simple and always fully effective.

. . . Out of the shadows of smallness, life grows. The level of beginning and ending, of life and—not life; in that dim region matter oscillates easily between old and new habits. The habit of organic, or the habit of inorganic. Electrons do not have life and un-life values. Atoms form into molecules, there is a step in the process, one tiny step, that is of life—if life begins at all. One step, and then darkness. Or aliveness.

A stone or a living cell. A grain of gold or a blade of grass, the sands of the sea or the equally numerous animalcules inhabiting the endless fishy waters—the difference is there in the twilight zone of matter. Each living cell has in it the whole form. The crab grows a new leg when the old one is torn from its flesh. Both ends of the planarian worm elongate, and soon there are two worms, two identities, two digestive systems, each as greedy as the original, each a whole, unwounded, unharmed by its experience. Each cell can be the whole. Each cell remembers in detail so intricate that no totality of words could ever describe the completeness achieved.

But—paradox—memory is not organic. An ordinary wax record remembers sounds. A wire recorder easily gives up a duplicate of the voice that spoke into it years before. Memory is a physiological impression, a mark on matter, a change in the shape of a molecule, so that when a reaction is desired the *shape* emits the same rhythm of response.

Out of the mummy's skull had come the multi-quadrillion memory shapes from which a response was now being evoked. As ever, the memory held true.

A man blinked, and opened his eyes.

"It is true, then," he said aloud, and the words were translated into the Ganae tongue as he spoke them. "Death is merely an opening into another life—but where are my attendants?" At the end, his voice took on a complaining tone.

He sat up, and climbed out of the case, which had automatically opened as he came to life. He saw his captors. He froze, but only for a moment. He had a pride and a very special arrogant courage, which served him now. Reluctantly, he sank to his knees and made obeisance, but doubt must have been strong in him. "Am I in the presence of the gods of Egypt?" He climbed to his feet. "What nonsense is this? I do not bow to nameless demons."

Captain Gorsid said, "Kill him!"

The two-legged monster dissolved, writhing in the beam of a ray gun.

The second revived man stood up, pale, and trembled with fear. "My God, I swear I won't touch the stuff again. Talk about pink elephants—"

Yoal was curious. "To what *stuff* do you refer, revived one?"

"The old hooch, the poison in the hip pocket flask, the juice they gave me at that speak . . . my lordie!"

Captain Gorsid looked questioningly at Yoal, "Need we linger?"

Yoal hesitated. "I am curious." He addressed the man. "If I were to tell you that we were visitors from another star, what would be your reaction?"

The man stared at him. He was obviously puzzled, but the fear was stronger. "Now, look," he said, "I was driving along, minding my own business. I admit I'd had a shot or two too many, but it's the liquor they serve these days. I swear I didn't see the other car—and if this is some new idea of punishing people who drink and drive, well, you've won. I won't touch another drop as long as I live, so help me."

Yoal said, "He drives a 'car' and thinks nothing of it. Yet we saw no cars. They didn't even bother to preserve them in the museums."

Enash noticed that everyone waited for everyone else to comment. He stirred as he realized the circle of silence would be complete unless he spoke. He said, "Ask him to describe the car. How does it work?"

"Now, you're talking," said the man. "Bring on your line of chalk, and I'll walk it, and ask any questions you please. I may be so tight that I can't see straight, but I can always drive. How does it work? You just put her in gear, and step on the gas."

"Gas," said engineering officer Veed. "The internal combustion engine. That places him."

Captain Gorsid motioned to the guard with the ray gun.

The third man sat up, and looked at them thoughtfully. "From the stars?" he said finally. "Have you a system, or was it blind chance?"

The Ganae councillors in that domed room stirred uneasily in their curved chairs. Enash caught Yoal's eye on him. The shock in the historian's eye alarmed the meteorologist. He thought:

"The two-legged one's adjustment to a new situation, his grasp of realities, was unnormally rapid. No Ganae could have equalled the swiftness of the reaction."

Hamar, the chief biologist, said, "Speed of thought is not necessarily a sign of superiority. The slow, careful thinker has his place in the hierarchy of intellect."

But Enash found himself thinking, it was not the speed; it was the accuracy of the response. He tried to imagine himself being revived from the dead, and understanding instantly the meaning of the presence of aliens from the stars. He couldn't have done it.

He forgot his thought, for the man was out of the case. As Enash watched with the others, he walked briskly over to the window and looked out. One glance, and then he turned back.

"Is it all like this?" he asked.

Once again, the speed of his understanding caused a sensation. It was Yoal who finally replied.

"Yes. Desolation. Death. Ruin. Have you any ideas as to what happened?"

The man came back and stood in front of the energy screen that guarded the Ganae. "May I look over the museum? I have to estimate what age I am in. We had certain possibilities of destruction when I was last alive, but which one was realized depends on the time elapsed."

The councillors looked at Captain Gorsid, who hesitated; then, "Watch him," he said to the guard with the ray gun. He faced the man. "We understand your aspirations fully. You would like to seize control of this situation and ensure your own safety. Let me reassure you. Make no false moves, and all will be well."

Whether or not the man believed the lie, he gave no sign. Nor did he show by a glance or a movement that he had seen the scarred floor where the ray gun had burned his two predecessors into nothingness. He walked curiously to the nearest doorway, studied the other guard who waited there for him, and then, gingerly, stepped through. The first guard followed him, then came the mobile energy screen, and finally, trailing one another, the councillors.

Enash was the third to pass through the doorway. The room contained skeletons and plastic models of animals. The room beyond that was what, for want of a better term, Enash called a culture room. It contained the artifacts from a single period of civilization. It looked very advanced. He had examined some of the machines when they first passed through it, and had thought:

Atomic energy. He was not alone in his recognition. From behind him, Captain Gorsid said to the man:

"You are forbidden to touch anything. A false move will be the signal for the guards to fire."

The man stood at ease in the center of the room. In spite of a curious anxiety, Enash had to admire his calmness. He must have known what his fate would be, but he stood there thoughtfully, and said finally, deliberately, "I do not need to go any farther. Perhaps you will be able to judge better than I of the time that has elapsed since I was born and these machines were built. I see over there an instrument which, according to the sign above it, counts atoms when they explode. As soon as the proper number have exploded it shuts off the power automatically, and for just the right length of time to prevent a chain explosion. In my time we had a thousand crude devices for limiting the size of an atomic reaction, but it required two thousand years to develop those devices from the early beginnings of atomic energy. Can you make a comparison?"

The councillors glanced at Veed. The engineering officer hesitated. At last, reluctantly, he said, "Nine thousand years ago we had a thousand methods of limiting atomic explosions." He paused, then even more slowly, "I have never heard of an instrument that counts out atoms for such a purpose."

"And yet," murmured Shuri, the astronomer, breathlessly, "the race was destroyed."

There was silence. It ended as Gorsid said to the nearest guard, "Kill the monster!"

But it was the guard who went down, bursting into flame. Not just one guard, but the guards! Simultaneously down, burning with a blue flame. The flame licked at the screen, recoiled, and licked more furiously, recoiled and burned brighter. Through a haze of fire, Enash saw that the man had retreated to the far door, and that the machine that counted atoms was glowing with a blue intensity.

Captain Gorsid shouted into his communicator, "Guard all exits with ray guns. Spaceships stand by to kill alien with heavy guns."

Somebody said, "Mental control. Some kind of mental control. What have we run into?"

They were retreating. The blue flame was at the ceiling, struggling to break through the screen. Enash had a last glimpse of the machine. It must still be counting atoms, for it was a hellish blue. Enash raced with the others to the room where the man had been resurrected. There, another energy screen crashed to their rescue. Safe now, they retreated into their separate bubbles and whisked through outer doors and up to the ship. As the great ship soared, an atomic bomb hurtled down from it. The mushroom of flame blotted out the museum and the city below.

"But we still don't know why the race died," Yoal whispered into Enash's ear, after the thunder had died from the heavens behind them.

The pale yellow sun crept over the horizon on the third morning after the bomb was dropped, the eighth day since the landing. Enash floated with the others down on a new city. He had come to argue against any further revival.

"As a meteorologist," he said, "I pronounce this planet safe for Ganae colonization. I cannot see the need for taking any risks. This race has discovered the secrets of its nervous system, and we cannot afford—"

He was interrupted. Hamar, the biologist, said dryly, "If they knew so much why didn't they migrate to other star systems and save themselves?"

"I will concede," said Enash, "that very possibly they had not discovered our system of locating stars with planetary families." He looked earnestly around the circle of his friends. "We have agreed that was a unique accidental discovery. We were lucky, not clever."

He saw by the expressions on their faces that they were mentally refuting his arguments. He felt a helpless sense of imminent catastrophe. For he could see that picture of a great race facing death. It must have come swiftly, but not so swiftly that they didn't know about it. There were too many skeletons in the open, lying in the gardens of magnificent homes, as if each man and his wife had come out to wait for the doom of his kind. He tried to picture it for the council, that last day long, long ago, when a race had calmly met its ending. But his visualization failed somehow, for the others shifted impatiently in the seats that had been set up behind the series of energy screens, and Captain Gorsid said, "Exactly what aroused this intense emotional reaction in you, Enash?"

The question gave Enash pause. He hadn't thought of it as emotional. He hadn't realized the nature of his obsession, so subtly had it stolen upon him. Abruptly now, he realized.

"It was the third one," he said slowly. "I saw him through the haze of energy fire, and he was standing there in the distant doorway watching us curiously, just before we turned to run. His bravery, his calm, the skilful way he had duped us—it all added up."

"Added up to his death!" said Hamar. And everybody laughed.

"Come now, Enash," said Vice-captain Mayad good-humouredly, "you're not going to pretend that this race is braver than our own, or that, with all the precautions we have now taken, we need fear one man?"

Enash was silent, feeling foolish. The discovery that he had had an emotional obsession abashed him. He did not want to appear unreasonable. He made a final protest, "I merely wish to point out," he said doggedly, "that this desire to discover what happened to a dead race does not seem absolutely essential to me."

Captain Gorsid waved at the biologist. "Proceed," he said, "with the revival."

To Enash, he said, "Do we dare return to Gana, and recommend mass migrations—and then admit that we did not actually complete our investigation here? It's impossible, my friend."

It was the old argument, but reluctantly now Enash admitted there was something to be said for that point of view. He forgot that, for the fourth man was stirring.

The man sat up. And vanished.

There was a blank, horrified silence. Then Captain Gorsid said harshly, "He can't get out of there. We know that. He's in there somewhere."

All around Enash, the Ganae were out of their chairs, peering into the energy shell. The guards stood with ray guns held limply in their suckers. Out of the corner of his eye, he saw one of the protective screen technicians beckon to Veed, who went over. He came back grim. He said, "I'm told the needles jumped ten points when he first disappeared. That's on the nucleonic level."

"By ancient Ganae!" Shuri whispered. "We've run into what we've always feared."

Gorsid was shouting into the communicator. "Destroy all the locators on the ship. Destroy them, do you hear!"

He turned with glaring eyes. "Shuri," he bellowed. "They don't seem to understand. Tell those subordinates of yours to act. All locators and reconstructors must be destroyed."

"Hurry, hurry!" said Shuri weakly.

When that was done they breathed more easily. There were grim smiles and a tensed satisfaction. "At least," said Vice-captain Mayad, "he cannot now ever discover Gana. Our great system of locating suns with planets remains our secret. There can be no retaliation for—'' He stopped, said slowly, ''What am I talking about? We haven't done anything. We're not responsible for the disaster that has befallen the inhabitants of this planet.''

But Enash knew what he had meant. The guilt feelings came to the surface at such moments as this—the ghosts of all the races destroyed by the Ganae, the remorseless will that had been in them, when they first landed, to annihilate whatever was here. The dark abyss of voiceless hate and terror that lay behind them; the days on end when they had mercilessly poured poisonous radiation down upon the unsuspecting inhabitants of peaceful planets—all that had been in Mayad's words.

''I still refuse to believe he has escaped.'' That was Captain Gorsid. ''He's in there. He's waiting for us to take down our screens, so he can escape. Well, we won't do it.''

There was silence again as they stared expectantly into the emptiness of the energy shell. The reconstructor rested on metal supports, a glittering affair. But there was nothing else. Not a flicker of unnatural light or shade. The yellow rays of the sun bathed the open spaces with a brilliance that left no room for concealment.

''Guards,'' said Gorsid, ''destroy the reconstructor. I thought he might come back to examine it, but we can't take a chance on that.''

It burned with a white fury. And Enash, who had hoped somehow that the deadly energy would force the two-legged thing into the open, felt his hopes sag within him.

''But where can he have gone?'' Yoal whispered.

Enash turned to discuss the matter. In the act of swinging around, he saw that the monster was standing under a tree a score of feet to one side, watching them. He must have arrived at *that* moment, for there was a collective gasp from the councillors. Everybody drew back. One of the screen technicians, using great presence of mind, jerked up an energy screen between the Ganae and the monster. The creature came forward slowly. He was slim of build, he held his head well back. His eyes shone as from an inner fire.

He stopped as he came to the screen, reached out and touched it with his fingers. It flared, blurred with changing colors. The colors grew brighter, and extended in an intricate pattern all the way from his head to the ground. The blur cleared. The pattern faded into invisibility. The man was through the screen.

He laughed, a soft curious sound; then sobered. "When I first awakened," he said, "I was curious about the situation. The question was, what should I do with you?"

The words had a fateful ring to Enash on the still morning air of that planet of the dead. A voice broke the silence, a voice so strained and unnatural that a moment passed before he recognized it as belonging to Captain Gorsid.

"Kill him!"

When the blasters ceased their effort, the unkillable thing remained standing. He walked slowly forward until he was only a half dozen feet from the nearest Ganae. Enash had a position well to the rear. The man said slowly:

"Two courses suggest themselves, one based on gratitude for reviving me, the other based on reality. I know you for what you are. Yes, *know* you—and that is unfortunate. It is hard to feel merciful. To begin with," he went on, "let us suppose you surrender the secret of the locator. Naturally, now that a system exists, we shall never again be caught as we were."

Enash had been intent, his mind so alive with the potentialities of the disaster that was here that it seemed impossible that he could think of anything else. And yet, a part of his attention was stirred now. "What did happen?" he asked.

The man changed color. The emotions of that far day thickened his voice. "A nucleonic storm. It swept in from outer space. It brushed this edge of our galaxy. It was about ninety light-years in diameter, beyond the farthest limit of our power. There was no escape from it. We had dispensed with spaceships, and had no time to construct any. Castor, the only star with planets ever discovered by us, was also in the path of the storm." He stopped. "The secret?" he said.

Around Enash, the councillors were breathing easier. The fear of race destruction that had come to them was lifting. Enash saw with pride that the first shock was over, and they were not even afraid for themselves.

"Ah," said Yoal softly, "you don't know the secret. In spite of all your great development, we alone can conquer the galaxy." He looked at the others, smiling confidently. "Gentlemen," he said, "our pride in a great Ganae achievement is justified. I suggest we return to our ship. We have no further business on this planet."

There was a confused moment while their bubbles formed, when Enash wondered if the two-legged one would try to stop their departure. But when he looked back, he saw that the man was walking in a leisurely fashion along a street.

That was the memory Enash carried with him, as the ship began to move. That and the fact that the three atomic bombs they dropped, one after the other, failed to explode.

"We will not," said Captain Gorsid, "give up a planet as easily as that. I propose another interview with the creature."

They were floating down again into the city, Enash and Yoal and Veed and the commander. Captain Gorsid's voice tuned in once more:

". . . As I visualize it"—through the mist Enash could see the transparent glint of the other three bubbles around him—"we jumped to conclusions about this creature, not justified by the evidence. For instance, when he awakened, he vanished. Why? Because he was afraid, of course. He wanted to size up the situation. *He* didn't believe he was omnipotent."

It was sound logic. Enash found himself taking heart from it. Suddenly, he was astonished that he had become panicky so easily. He began to see the danger in a new light. Only one man alive on a new planet. If they were determined enough, colonists could be moved in as if he did not exist. It had been done before, he recalled. On several planets, small groups of the original populations had survived the destroying radiation, and taken refuge in remote areas. In almost every case, the new colonists gradually hunted them down. In two instances, however, that Enash remembered, native races were still holding small sections of their planets. In each case, it had been found impractical to destroy them because it would have endangered the Ganae on the planet. So the survivors were tolerated. One man would not take up very much room.

When they found him, he was busily sweeping out the lower floor of a small bungalow. He put the broom aside and stepped on to the terrace outside. He had put on sandals, and he wore a loose-fitting robe made of very shiny material. He eyed them indolently but he said nothing.

It was Captain Gorsid who made the proposition. Enash had to admire the story he told into the language machine. The commander was very frank. That approach had been decided on. He pointed out that the Ganae could not be expected to revive the dead of this planet. Such altruism would be unnatural considering that the ever-growing Ganae hordes had a continual need for new worlds. Each vast new population increment was a problem that could be solved by one method only. In this instance, the colonists would gladly respect the rights of the sole survivor of this world.

It was at this point that the man interrupted. "But what is the purpose of this endless expansion?" He seemed genuinely curious. "What will happen when you finally occupy every planet in this galaxy?"

Captain Gorsid's puzzled eyes met Yoal's, then flashed to Veed, than Enash. Enash shrugged his torso negatively, and felt pity for the creature. The man didn't understand, possibly never could understand. It was the old story of two different viewpoints, the virile and the decadent, the race that aspired to the stars and the race that declined the call of destiny.

"Why not," urged the man, "control the breeding chambers?"

"And have the government overthrown!" said Yoal.

He spoke tolerantly, and Enash saw that the others were smiling at the man's naiveté. He felt the intellectual gulf between them widening. The creature had no comprehension of the natural life forces that were at work. The man spoke again.

"Well, if you don't control them, we will control them for you."

There was silence.

They began to stiffen. Enash felt it in himself, saw the signs of it in the others. His gaze flicked from face to face, then back to the creature in the doorway. Not for the first time, Enash had the thought that their enemy seemed helpless. "Why," he decided, "I could put my suckers around him and crush him."

He wondered if mental control of nucleonic, nuclear, and gravitonic energies included the ability to defend oneself from a macrocosmic attack. He had an idea it did. The exhibition of power two hours before might have had limitations, but if so, it was not apparent. Strength or weakness could make no difference. The threat of threats had been made: "If you don't control—we will."

The words echoed in Enash's brain, and, as the meaning penetrated deeper, his aloofness faded. He had always regarded himself as a spectator. Even when, earlier, he had argued against the revival, he had been aware of a detached part of himself watching the scene rather than being a part of it. He saw with a sharp clarity that that was why he had finally yielded to the conviction of the others. Going back beyond that to remoter days, he saw that he had never quite considered himself a participant in the seizure of the planets of other races. He was the one who looked on, and thought of reality, and speculated on a life that seemed to have no meaning. It was meaningless no longer. He was caught by a tide of irresistible emotion, and swept along. He felt himself sinking, merging with the Ganae mass being. All the strength and all the will of the race surged up in his veins.

He snarled, "Creature, if you have any hopes of reviving your dead race, abandon them now."

The man looked at him, but said nothing. Enash rushed on, "If you could destroy us, you would have done so already. But the truth is that you operate within limitations. Our ship is so built that no conceivable chain reaction could be started in it. For every plate of potential unstable material in it there is a counteracting plate, which prevents the development of a critical pile. You might be able to set off explosions in our engines, but they, too, would be limited, and would merely start the process for which they are intended—confined in their proper space."

He was aware of Yoal touching his arm. "Careful," warned the historian. "Do not in your just anger give away vital information."

Enash shook off the restraining sucker. "Let us not be unrealistic," he said harshly. "This thing has divined most of our racial secrets, apparently merely by looking at our bodies. We would be acting childishly if we assumed that he has not already realized the possibilities of the situation."

"*Enash!*" Captain Gorsid's voice was imperative.

As swiftly as it had come, Enash's rage subsided. He stepped back. "Yes, commander."

"I think I know what you intended to say," said Captain Gorsid. "I assure you I am in full accord, but I believe also that I, as the top Ganae official, should deliver the ultimatum."

He turned. His horny body towered above the man. "You have made the unforgivable threat. You have told us, in effect, that you will attempt to restrict the vaulting Ganae spirit."

"Not the spirit," said the man.

The commander ignored the interruption. "Accordingly, we have no alternative. We are assuming that, given time to locate the materials and develop the tools, you might be able to build a reconstructor. In our opinion it will be at least two years before you can complete it, *even if you know how*. It is an immensely intricate machine, not easily assembled by the lone survivor of a race that gave up its machines millennia before disaster struck.

"You did not have time to build a spaceship. We won't give you time to build a reconstructor.

"Within a few minutes our ship will start dropping bombs. It is possible you will be able to prevent explosions in your vicinity. We will start, accordingly, on the other side of the planet. If you stop us there, then we will assume we need help. In six months of travelling at top acceleration, we can reach a point where the nearest Ganae planet would hear our messages. They will send a fleet so vast that all your powers of resistance will be overcome. By dropping a hundred or a thousand bombs every minute, we will succeed in devastating every city so that not a grain of dust will remain of the skeletons of your people.

"That is our plan. So it shall be. Now, do your worst to us who are at your mercy."

The man shook his head. "I shall do nothing—now!" he said. He paused, then thoughtfully, "Your reasoning is fairly accurate. Fairly. Naturally, I am not all powerful, but it seems to me you have forgotten one little point. I won't tell you what it is. And now," he said, "good day to you. Get back to your ship, and be on your way. I have much to do."

Enash had been standing quietly, aware of the fury building up in him again. Now, with a hiss, he sprang forward, suckers outstretched. They were almost touching the smooth flesh—when something snatched at him.

He was back on the ship.

He had no memory of movement, no sense of being dazed or harmed. He was aware of Veed and Yoal and Captain Gorsid standing near him as astonished as he himself. Enash remained very still, thinking of what the man had said: ". . . *Forgotten one little point.*" Forgotten? That meant they knew. What could it be? He was still pondering about it when Yoal said:

"We can be reasonably certain our bombs alone will not work."

They didn't.

Forty light-years out from Earth, Enash was summoned to the council chambers. Yoal greeted him wanly. "The monster is aboard."

The thunder of that poured through Enash, and with it came a sudden comprehension. "That was what he meant we had forgotten," he said finally, aloud and wonderingly. "That he can travel through space at will within a limit—what was the figure he once used—of ninety light-years."

He sighed. He was not surprised that the Ganae, who had to use ships, would not have thought immediately of such a possibility. Slowly, he began to retreat from the reality. Now that the shock had come, he felt old and weary, a sense of his mind withdrawing again to its earlier state of aloofness. It required a few minutes to get the story. A physicist's assistant, on his way to the storeroom, had caught a glimpse of a man in a lower corridor. In such a heavily manned ship, the wonder was that the intruder had escaped earlier observation. Enash had a thought.

"But after all we are not going all the way to one of our planets. How does he expect to make use of us to locate it if we only use the video—" he stopped. That was it, of course. Directional video beams would have to be used, and the man would travel in the right direction the instant contact was made.

Enash saw the decision in the eyes of his companions, the only possible decision under the circumstances. And yet, it seemed to him they were missing some vital point. He walked slowly to the great video plate at one end of the chamber. There was a picture on it, so sharp, so vivid, so majestic that the unaccustomed mind would have reeled as from a stunning blow. Even to him, who knew the scene, there came a constriction, a sense of unthinkable vastness. It was a video view of a section of the Milky Way. Four hundred *million* stars as seen through telescopes that could pick up the light of a red dwarf at thirty thousand light-years.

The video plate was twenty-five yards in diameter—a scene that had no parallel elsewhere in the plenum. Other galaxies simply did not have that many stars.

Only one in two hundred thousand of those glowing suns had planets.

That was the colossal fact that compelled them now to an irrevocable act. Wearily, Enash looked around him.

"The monster has been very clever," he said quietly. "If we go ahead, he goes with us, obtains a reconstructor, and returns by his method to his planet. If we use the directional beam, he flashes along it, obtains a reconstructor, and again reaches his planet first. In either event, by the time our fleets arrived back here, he would have revived enough of his kind to thwart any attack we could mount."

He shook his torso. The picture was accurate, he felt sure, but it still seemed incomplete. He said slowly, "We have one advantage now. Whatever decision we make, there is no language machine to enable him to learn what it is. We can carry out our plans without his knowing what they will be. He knows that neither he nor we can blow up the ship. That leaves us one real alternative.''

It was Captain Gorsid who broke the silence that followed. ''Well, gentlemen, I see we know our minds. We will set the engines, blow up the controls, and take him with us.''

They looked at each other, race pride in their eyes. Enash touched suckers with each in turn.

An hour later, when the heat was already considerable, Enash had the thought that sent him staggering to the communicator, to call Shuri, the astronomer. ''Shuri,'' he yelled, ''when the monster first awakened—remember Captain Gorsid had difficulty getting your subordinates to destroy the locators. We never thought to ask them what the delay was. Ask them . . . ask them—''

There was a pause, then Shuri's voice came weakly over the roar of the static. ''They . . . couldn't . . . get . . . into the . . . room. The door was locked.''

Enash sagged to the floor. They had missed more than one point, he realized. The man had awakened, realized the situation; and, when he vanished, he had gone to the ship, and there discovered the secret of the locator and possibly the secret of the reconstructor—if he didn't know it previously. By the time he reappeared, he already had from them what he wanted. All the rest must have been designed to lead them to this act of desperation.

In a few moments, now, *he* would be leaving the ship, secure in the knowledge that shortly no alien mind would know his planet existed. Knowing, too, that his race would live again, and this time never die.

Enash staggered to his feet, clawed at the roaring communicator, and shouted his new understanding into it. There was no answer. It clattered with the static of uncontrollable and inconceivable energy. The heat was peeling his armoured hide as he struggled to the matter transmitter. It flashed at him with purple flame. Back to the communicator he ran shouting and screaming.

He was still whimpering into it a few minutes later when the mighty ship plunged into the heart of a blue-white sun.

DREAMS ARE SACRED

by Peter Phillips (1921–   )

ASTOUNDING SCIENCE FICTION
September

Peter Phillips is a British newspaperman who has written only a relatively small number of science fiction stories, all appearing in the 1948–1958 period. His best known story, in addition to the present selection, is the excellent "Lost Memory," which appeared in the May, 1952 issue of Galaxy Science Fiction. *As is the case with several other writers who have appeared in this series, we wish he had written more in the science fiction field.*

"Dreams are Sacred", is one of the very best first stories ever published, a stunning study in paranoia that anticipates the work of such writers as Phillip K. Dick. If you have never read this wonderful story, you are in for a treat.

(It occurs to me that there ought to be a collection of stories in which science fiction/fantasy writers are important characters. I wonder if such stories are ever written by writers who have not themselves written science fiction or fantasy. I can think offhand of one story I have written in which a fantasy writer was the hero. Generally, and this is not surprising, the writers

*tend to be the hero; that was certainly the case in my
own story. Here, however, is a story in which the
science fiction writer is, after a fashion, the menace—
very unusual. Let me point out, by the way, the first
scene, in which people who put ghost stories into the
hands of children are excoriated, while people who put
deadly guns into their hands are pictured as wise and
heroic. Well, I don't have to agree with everything in
these stories that Marty and I select.—I.A.)*

When I was seven, I read a ghost story and babbled of the
consequent nightmare to my father.

"They were coming for me, Pop," I sobbed. "I couldn't run,
and I couldn't stop 'em, great big things with teeth and claws
like the pictures in the book, and I couldn't wake myself up,
Pop, I couldn't come awake."

Pop had a few quiet cuss words for folks who left such things
around for a kid to pick up and read; then he took my hand
gently in his own great paw and led me into the six-acre pasture.

He was wise, with the canny insight into human motives that
the soil gives to a man. He was close to Nature and the hearts
and minds of men, for all men ultimately depend on the good
earth for sustenance and life.

He sat down on a stump and showed me a big gun. I know
now it was a heavy Service Colt .45. To my child eyes, it was
enormous. I had seen shotguns and sporting rifles before, but
this was to be held in one hand and fired. Gosh, it was heavy. It
dragged my thin arm down with its sheer, grim weight when Pop
showed me how to hold it.

Pop said: "It's a killer, Pete. There's nothing in the whole
wide world or out of it that a slug from Billy here won't stop.
It's killed lions and tigers and men. Why, if you aim right, it'll
stop a charging elephant. Believe me, son, there's nothing you
can meet in dreams that Billy here won't stop. And he'll come
into your dreams with you from now on, so there's no call to be
scared of anything."

He drove that deep into my receptive subconscious. At the end
of half an hour, my wrist ached abominably from the kick of that
Colt. But I'd seen heavy slugs tear through two-inch teakwood

and mild steel plating. I'd looked along that barrel, pulled the trigger, felt the recoil rip up my arm and seen the fist-size hole blasted through a sack of wheat.

And that night, I slept with Billy under my pillow. Before I slipped into dreamland, I'd felt again the cool, reassuring butt.

When the Dark Things came again, I was almost glad. I was ready for them. Billy was there, lighter than in my waking hours—or maybe my dream-hand was bigger—but just as powerful. Two of the Dark Things crumpled and fell as Billy roared and kicked, then the others turned and fled.

Then I was chasing them, laughing, and firing from the hip.

Pop was no psychiatrist, but he'd found the perfect antidote to fear—the projection into the subconscious mind of a common-sense concept based on experience.

Twenty years later, the same principle was put into operation scientifically to save the sanity—and perhaps the life—of Marsham Craswell.

"Surely you've heard of him?" said Stephen Blakiston, a college friend of mine who'd majored in psychiatry.

"Vaguely," I said. "Science-fiction, fantasy . . . I've read a little. Screwy."

"Not so. Some good stuff." Steve waved a hand round the bookshelves of his private office in the new Pentagon Mental Therapy Hospital, New York State. I saw multicolored magazine backs, row on row of them. "I'm a fan," he said simply. "Would you call me screwy?"

I backed out of that one. I'm just a sports columnist, but I knew Blakiston was tops in two fields—the psycho stuff and electronic therapy.

Steve said: "Some of it's the old 'peroo, of course, but the level of writing is generally high and the ideas thought-provoking. For ten years, Marsham has been one of the most prolific and best-loved writers in the game.

"Two years ago, he had a serious illness, didn't give himself time to convalesce properly before he waded into writing again. He tried to reach his previous output, tending more and more toward pure fantasy. Beautiful in parts, sheer rubbish sometimes.

"He forced his imagination to work, set himself a wordage routine. The tension became too great. Something snapped. Now he's here."

Steve got up, ushered me out of his office. "I'll take you to see him. He won't see you. Because the thing that snapped was his conscious control over his imagination. It went into high gear, and now instead of writing his stories, he's living them—quite literally, for him.

"Far-off worlds, strange creatures, weird adventures—the detailed phantasmagoria of a brilliant mind driving itself into insanity through the sheer complexity of its own invention. He's escaped from the harsh reality of his strained existence into a dream world. But he may make it real enough to kill himself.

"He's the hero of course," Steve continued, opening the door into a private world. "But even heroes sometimes die. My fear is that his morbidly overactive imagination working through his subconscious mind will evoke in this dream world in which he is living a situation wherein the hero must die.

"You probably know that the sympathetic magic of witchcraft acts largely through the imagination. A person imagines he is being hexed to death—and dies. If Marsham Craswell imagines that one of his fantastic creations kills the hero—himself—then he just won't wake up again.

"Drugs won't touch him. Listen."

Steve looked at me across Marsham's bed. I leaned down to hear the mutterings from the writer's bloodless lips.

". . . . We must search the Plains of Istak for the Diamond. I, Multan, who now have the Sword, will lead thee; for the Snake must die and only in virtue of the Diamond can his death be encompassed. Come."

Craswell's right hand, lying limp on the coverlet, twitched. He was beckoning his followers.

"Still the Snake and the Diamond?" asked Steve. "He's been living that dream for two days. We only know what's happening when he speaks in his role of hero. Often it's quite unintelligible. Sometimes a spark of consciousness filters through, and he fights to wake up. It's pretty horrible to watch him squirming and trying to pull himself back into reality. Have you ever tried to pull yourself out of a nightmare and failed?"

It was then that I remembered Billy, the Colt .45. I told Steve about it, back in his office.

He said: "Sure. Your Pop had the right idea. In fact, I'm hoping to save Marsham by an application of the same principle. To do it, I need the cooperation of someone who combines a lively imagination with a severely practical streak, hoss-sense—and a sense of humor. Yes—you."

"Uh? How can I help? I don't even know the guy."

"You will," said Steve, and the significant way he said it sent a trickle of ice water down my back. "You're going to get closer to Marsham Craswell than one man has ever been to another.

"I'm going to project you—the essential you, that is, your mind and personality—into Craswell's tortured brain."

I made pop-eyes, then thumbed at the magazine-lined wall. "Too much of yonder, brother Steve," I said. "What you need is a drink."

Steve lit his pipe, draped his long legs over the arm of his chair. "Miracles and witchcraft are out. What I propose to do is basically no more miraculous than the way your Pop put that gun into your dreams so you weren't afraid anymore. It's merely more complex scientifically.

"You've heard of the encephalograph? You know it picks up the surface neural currents of the brain, amplifies and records them, showing the degree—or absence—of mental activity. It can't indicate the kind or quality of such activity save in very general terms. By using comparison-graphs and other statistical methods to analyze its data, we can sometimes diagnose incipient insanity, for instance. But that's all—until we started work on it, here at the Pentagon.

"We improved the penetration and induction pickup and needled the selectivity until we could probe any known portion of the brain. What we were looking for was a recognizable pattern among the millions of tiny electric currents that go to make up the imagery of thought, so that if the subject thought of something—a number, maybe—the instruments would react accordingly, give a pattern for it that would be repeated every time he thought of that number.

"We failed, of course. The major part of the brain acts as a unity, no one part being responsible for either simple or complex imagery, but the activity of one portion inducing activity in other portions—with the exception of those parts dealing with automatic impulses. So if we were to get a pattern we should need thousands of pickups—a practical impossibility. It was as if we were trying to divine the pattern of a colored sweater by putting one tiny stitch of it under a microscope.

"Paradoxically, our machine was too selective. We needed, not a probe, but an all-encompassing field, receptive simultaneously to the multitudinous currents that made up a thought pattern.

"We found such a field. But we were no further forward. In a sense, we were back where we started from—because to analyze what the field picked up would have entailed the use of thousands of complex instruments. We had amplified thought, but we could not analyze it.

"There was only one single instrument sufficiently sensitive and complex to do that—another human brain."

I waved for a pause. "I'm home," I said. "You've got a thought-reading machine."

"Much more than that. When we tested it the other day, one of my assistants stepped up the polarity-reversal of the field— that is, the frequency—by accident. I was acting as analyst and the subject was under narcosis.

"Instead of 'hearing' the dull incoherencies of his thoughts, I became part of them. I was inside that man's brain. It was a nightmare world. He wasn't a clear thinker. I was aware of my own individuality. . . . When he came round, he went for me bald-headed. Said I'd been trespassing inside his head.

"With Marsham, it'll be a different matter. The dream world of his coma is detailed, as real as he used to make dream worlds to his readers."

"Hold it," I said. "Why don't you take a peek?"

Steve Blakiston smiled and gave me a high-voltage shot from his big gray eyes. "Three good reasons: I've soaked in the sort of stuff he dreams up, and there's a danger that I would become identified too closely with him. What he needs is a salutary dose of common sense. You're the man for that, you cynical old whisky-hound.

"Secondly, if my mind gave way under the impress of his imagination, I wouldn't be around to treat myself; and thirdly, when—and if—he comes round, he'll want to kill the man who's been heterodyning his dreams. You can scram. But I want to stay and see the results."

"Sorting that out, I gather there's a possibility that I shall wake up as a candidate for a bed in the next ward?"

"Not unless you let your mind go under. And you won't. You've got a cast-iron non-gullibility complex. Just fool around in your usual iconoclastic manner. Your own imagination's pretty good, judging by some of your fight reports lately."

I got up, bowed politely, said: "Thank you, my friend. That reminds me—I'm covering the big fight at the Garden tomorrow night. And I need sleep. It's late. So long."

Steve unfolded and reached the door ahead of me.

"Please," he said, and argued. He can argue. And I couldn't duck those big eyes of his. And he is—or was—my pal. He said it wouldn't take long—(just like a dentist)—and he smacked down every "if" I thought up.

Ten minutes later, I was lying on a twin bed next to that occupied by a silent, white-faced Marsham Craswell. Steve was leaning over the writer adjusting a chrome-steel bowl like a hair-drier over the man's head. An assistant was fixing me up the same way.

Cables ran from the bowls to a movable arm overhead and thence to a wheeled machine that looked like something from the Whacky Science Section of the World's Fair, A.D. 2000.

I was bursting with questions, but the only ones that would come out seemed crazily irrelevant.

"What do I say to this guy? 'Good morning, and how are all your little complexes today?' Do I introduce myself?"

"Just say you're Pete Parnell, and play it off the cuff," said Steve. "You'll see what I mean when you get there."

Get there. That hit me—the idea of making a journey into some nut's nut. My stomach drew itself up to a softball size.

"What's the proper dress for a visit like this? Formal?" I asked. At least, I think I said that. It didn't sound like my voice.

"Wear what you like."

"Uh-huh. And how do I know when to draw my visit to a close?"

Steve came round to my side. "If you haven't snapped Craswell out of it within an hour, I'll turn off the current."

He stepped back to the machine. "Happy dreams."

I groaned.

It was hot. Two high summers rolled into one. No, two suns, blood-red, stark in a brazen sky. Should be cool underfoot—soft green turf, pool table smooth to the far horizon. But it wasn't grass. Dust. Burning green dust—

The gladiator stood ten feet away, eyes glaring in disbelief. All of six-four high, great bronzed arms and legs, knotted muscles, a long shining sword in his right hand.

But his face was unmistakable.

This was where I took a good hold of myself. I wanted to giggle.

"Boy!" I said. "Do you tan quickly! Couple of minutes ago, you were as white as the bed sheet."

The gladiator shaded his eyes from the twin suns. "Is this yet another guise of the magician Garor to drive me insane—an

Earthman here, on the Plains of Istak? Or am I already—mad?'' His voice was deep, smoothly modulated.

My own was perfectly normal. Indeed, after the initial effort, I felt perfectly normal, except for the heat.

I said: ''That's the growing idea where I've just come from—that you're going nuts.''

You know those half-dreams, just on the verge of sleep, in which you can control your own imagery to some extent? That's how I felt. I knew intuitively what Steve was getting at when he said I could play it off the cuff. I looked down. Tweed suit, brogues—naturally. That's what I was wearing when I last looked at myself. I had no reason to think I was wearing—and therefore to be wearing—anything else. But something cooler was indicated in this heat, generated by Marsham Craswell's imagination.

Something like his own gladiator costume, perhaps.

Sandals—fine. There were my feet—in sandals.

Then I laughed. I had nearly fallen into the error of accepting his imagination.

''Do you mind if I switch off one of those suns?'' I asked politely. ''It's a little hot.''

I gave one of the suns a very dirty look. It disappeared.

The gladiator raised his sword. ''You are—Garor!'' he cried. ''But your witchery shall not avail you against the Sword!''

He rushed forward. The shining blade cleaved the air toward my skull.

I thought very, very fast.

The sword clanged, and streaked off at a sharp tangent from my G.I. brain-pan protector. I'd last worn that homely piece of hardware in the Argonne, and I knew it would stop a mere sword. I took it off.

''Now listen to me, Marsham Craswell,'' I said. ''My name's Pete Parnell, of the Sunday *Star*, and—''

Craswell looked up from his sword, chest heaving, startled eyes bright as if with recognition. ''Wait! I know now who you are—Nelpar Retrep, Man of the Seven Moons, come to fight with me against the Snake and his ungodly disciple, magician and sorceress, Garor. Welcome, my friend!''

He held out a huge bronzed hand. I shook it.

It was obvious that, unable to rationalize—or irrationalize—me, he was writing me into the plot of his dream! Right. It had been amusing so far. I'd string along for a while. My imagination hadn't taken a licking—yet.

Craswell said: ''My followers, the great-hearted Dok-men of

the Blue Hills, have just been slain in a gory battle. We were about to brave the many perils of the Plains of Istak in our quest for the Diamond—but all this, of course, you know.''

"Sure," I said. "What now?"

Craswell turned suddenly, pointed. "There," he muttered. "A sight that strikes terror even into my heart—Garor returns to the battle, at the head of her dread Legion of Lakros, beasts of the Overworld, drawn into evil symbiosis with alien intelligences—invulnerable to men, but not to the Sword, or to the mighty weapons of Nelpar of the Seven Moons. We shall fight them alone!''

Racing across the vast plain of green dust toward us was a horde of . . . er . . . creatures. My vocabulary can't cope fully with Craswell's imagination. Gigantic, shimmering things, drooling thick ichor, half-flying, half-lolloping. Enough to say I looked around for a washbasin to spit in. I found one, with soap and towels complete, but I pushed it over, looked at a patch of green dust and thought hard.

The outline of the phone booth wavered a little before I could fix it. I dashed inside, dialed "Police H.Q.? Riot squad here—and quick!''

I stepped outside the booth. Craswell was whirling the Sword round his head, yelling war cries as he faced the onrushing monsters.

From the other direction came the swelling scream of a police siren. Half a dozen good, solid patrol cars screeched to a dust-spurting stop outside the phone booth. I don't have to think hard to get a New York cop car fixed in my mind. These were just right. And the first man out, running to my side and patting his cap on firmly, was just right, too.

Michael O'Faolin, the biggest, toughest, nicest cop I know.

"Mike," I said, pointing. "Fix 'em."

"Shure, an' it's an aisy job f'the bhoys I've brought along," said Mike, hitching his belt.

He deployed his men.

Craswell looked at them fanning out to take the charge, then staggered back toward me, hand over his eyes. "Madness!" he shouted. "What madness is this? What are you doing?"

For a moment, the whole scene wavered. The lone red sun blinked out, the green desert became a murky transparency through which I caught a split-second glimpse of white beds with two figures lying on them. Then Craswell uncovered his eyes.

The monsters began to diminish some twenty yards from the

riot squad. By the time they got to the cops, they were man-size, and very amenable to discipline—enforced by raps over their horny noggins with nightsticks. They were bundled into the squad cars, which set off again over the plains.

Michael O'Faolin remained. I said: "Thanks, Mike. I may have a couple of spare tickets for the big fight tomorrow night. See you later."

"Just what I was wantin', Pete. 'Tis me day off. Now, how do I get home?"

I opened the door of the phone booth. "Right inside." He stepped in. I turned to Craswell.

"Mighty magic, O Nelpar!" he exclaimed. "To creatures of Garor's mind you opposed creatures of your own!"

He'd woven the whole incident into his plot already.

"We must go forward now, Nelpar of the Seven Moons—forward to the Citadel of the Snake, a thousand lokspans over the burning Plains of Istak."

"How about the Diamond?"

"The Diamond—?"

Evidently, he'd run so far ahead of himself getting me fixed into the landscape that he'd forgotten all about the Diamond that could kill the Snake. I didn't remind him.

However, a thousand lokspans over the burning plains sounded a little too far for walking, whatever a lokspan might be.

I said: "Why do you make things tough for yourself, Craswell?"

"The name," he said with tremendous dignity, "is Multan."

"Multan, Sultan, Shashlik, Dikkidam, Hammaneggs or whatever polysyllabic pooh-bah you wish to call yourself—I still ask, why make things tough for yourself when there's plenty of cabs around? Just whistle."

I whistled. The Purple Cab swung in, perfect to the last detail, including a hulking-backed, unshaven driver, dead ringer for the impolite gorilla who'd brought me out to Pentagon that evening.

There is nothing on earth quite so unutterably prosaic as a New York Purple Cab with that sort of driver. The sight upset Craswell, and the green plains wavered again while he struggled to fit the cab into his dream.

"What new magic is this! You are indeed mighty, Nelpar!"

He got in. But he was trembling with the effort to maintain the structure of this world into which he had escaped, against my deliberate attempts to bring it crashing round his ears and restore him to colorless—but sane—normality.

At this stage, I felt curiously sorry for him; but I realized that it might only be by permitting him to reach the heights of creative imagery before dousing him with the sponge from the cold bucket that I could jerk his drifting ego back out of dreamland.

It was dangerous thinking. Dangerous—for me.

Craswell's thousand lokspans appeared to be the equivalent of ten blocks. Or perhaps he wanted to gloss over the mundane near-reality of a cab ride. He pointed forward, past the driver's shoulder: "The Citadel of the Snake!"

To me, it looked remarkably like a wedding cake designed by Dali in red plastic: ten stories high, each story a platter half a mile thick, each platter diminishing in size and offset to the one beneath so that the edifice spiraled toward the glossy sky.

The cab rolled into its vast shadow, stopped beneath the sheer, blank precipice of the base platter, which might have been two miles in diameter. Or three. Or four. What's a mile or two among dreamers?

Craswell hopped out quickly. I got out on the driver's side.

The driver said: "Dollar-fifty."

Square, unshaven jar, low forehead, dirty-red hair straggling under his cap. I said: "Comes high for a short trip."

"Lookit the clock," he growled, squirming his shoulders. "Do I come out and get it?"

I said sweetly: "Go to hell."

Cab and driver shot downward through the green sand with the speed of an express elevator. The hole closed up. The times I've wanted to do just that—

Craswell was regarding me open-mouthed. I said: "Sorry. Now I'm being escapist, too. Get on with the plot."

He muttered something I didn't catch, strode across to the red wall in which a crack, meeting place of mighty gates, had appeared, and raised his sword.

"Open, Garor! Your doom is nigh. Multan and Nelpar are here to brave the terrors of this Citadel and free the world from the tyranny of the Snake!" He hammered at the crack with the sword-hilt.

"Not so loud," I murmured. "You'll wake the neighbors. Why not use the bell-push?" I put my thumb on the button and pressed. The towering gates swung slowly open.

"You . . . you have been here before—"

"Yes—after my last lobster supper." I bowed. "After you."

I followed him into a great, echoing tunnel with fluorescent walls. The gates closed behind us. He paused and looked at me with an odd gleam in his eyes. A gleam of—sanity. And there was anger in the set of his lips. Anger for me, not Garor or the Snake.

It's not nice to have someone trampling all over your ego. Pride is a tiger—even in dreams. The subconscious, as Steve had explained to me, is a function or state of the brain, not a small part of it. In thwarting Craswell, I was disparaging not merely his dream, but his very brain, sneering at his intellectual integrity, at his abilities as an imaginative writer.

In a brief moment of rationality, I believe he was strangely aware of this.

He said quietly: "You have limitations, Nelpar. Your outward-turning eyes are blind to the pain of creation; to you the crystal stars are spangles on the dress of a scarlet woman, and you mock the God-blessed unreason that would make life more than the crawling of an animal from womb to grave. In tearing the veil from mystery, you destroy not mystery—for there are many mysteries, a million veils, world within and beyond worlds—but beauty. And in destroying beauty, you destroy your soul."

These last words, quiet as they sounded, were caught up by the curving walls of the huge tunnel, amplified then diminished in pulsing repetition, loud then soft, a surging hypnotic echo: "Destroy your SOUL, DESTROY your soul. SOUL—"

Craswell pointed with his sword. His voice was exultant. "There is a Veil, Nelpar—and you must tear it lest it become your shroud! The Mist—the Sentient Mist of the Citadel!"

I'll admit that, for a few seconds, he'd had me a little groggy. I felt—subdued. And I understood for the first time his power as a word-spinner.

I knew that it was vital for me to reassert myself.

A thick, gray mist was rolling, wreathing slowly toward us, filling the tunnel to roof-height, puffing out thick, groping tentacles.

"It lives on Life itself," Craswell shouted. "It feeds, not on flesh, but on the vital principle that animates all flesh. I am safe, Nelpar, for I have the Sword. Can your magic save you?"

"Magic!" I said. "There's no gas invented yet that'll get through a Mark 8 mask."

Gas-drill—face-piece first, straps behind the ears. No, I hadn't forgotten the old routine.

I adjusted the mask comfortably. "And if it's not gas," I added, "this will fix it." I felt over my shoulder, unclipped a nozzle, brought it round into the "ready" position.

I had only used a one-man flame-thrower once—in training—but the experience was etched on my memory.

This was a de luxe model. At the first thirty-foot oily, searing blast, the Mist curled in on itself and rolled back the way it had come. Only quicker.

I shucked off the trappings. "You were in the Army for a while, Craswell. Remember?"

The shining translucency of the walls dimmed suddenly, and beyond them I glimpsed, as in a movie close-up through an unfocused projector, the square, intense face of Steve Blakiston.

Then the walls re-formed, and Craswell, still the bronzed, naked-limbed giant of his imagination, was looking at me again, frowning, worried. "Your words are strange, O Nelpar. It seems you are master of mysteries beyond even my knowing."

I put on the sort of face I use when the sports editor queries my expenses, aggrieved, pleading. "Your trouble, Craswell, is that you don't want to know. You just won't remember. That's why you're here. But life isn't bad if you oil it a little. Why not snap out of this and come with me for a drink?"

"I do not understand," he muttered. "But we have a mission to perform. Follow." And he strode off.

Mention of drink reminded me. There was nothing wrong with my memory. And that tunnel was as hot as the green desert. I remembered a very small pub just off the streetcar depot end of Sauchiehall Street, Glasgow, Scotland. A ginger-whiskered ancient, an exile from the Highlands, who'd listened to me enthusing over a certain brand of Scotch. "If ye think that's güid, mon, ye'll no' tasted the brew from ma own private deestillery. Smack yer lips ower this, laddie—" And he'd produced an antique silver flask and poured a generous measure of golden whisky into my glass. I had never tasted such mellow nectar before or since. Until I was walking down the tunnel behind Craswell.

I nearly envisaged the glass, but changed my mind in time to make it the antique flask. I raised it to my lips. Imagination's a wonderful thing.

Craswell was talking. I'd nearly forgotten him.

". . . near the Hall of Madness, where strange music assaults the brain, weird harmonies that enchant, then kill, rupturing the very cells by a mixture of subsonic and supersonic frequencies. Listen!"

We had reached the end of the tunnel and stood at the top of a slope which, broadening, ran gently downward, veiled by a blue haze, like the smoke from fifty million cigarettes, filling a vast circular hall. The haze eddied, moved by vagrant, sluggish currents of air, and revealed on the farther side, dwarfed by distance but obviously enormous, a complex structure of pipes and consoles.

A dozen Mighty Wurlitzers rolled into one would have appeared as a miniature piano at the foot of this towering music-machine.

At its many consoles which, even at that distance, I could see consisted of at least half a dozen manuals each, were multi-limbed creatures—spiders or octopuses or Polilollipops—I didn't ask what Craswell called them—I was listening.

The opening bars were strange enough, but innocuous. Then the multiple tones and harmonies began to swell in volume. I picked out the curious, sweet harshness of oboes and bassoons, the eldritch, rising ululation of a thousand violins, the keen shrilling of a hundred demonic flutes, the sobbing of many cellos. That's enough. Music's my hobby, and I don't want to get carried away in describing how that crazy symphony nearly carried me away.

But if Craswell ever reads this, I'd like him to know that he missed his vocation. He should have been a musician. His dream-music showed an amazing intuitive grasp of orchestration and harmonic theory. If he could do anything like it consciously, he would be a great modern composer.

Yet not too much like it. Because it began to have the effects he had warned about. The insidious rhythm and wild melodies seemed to throb inside my head, setting up a vibration, a burning, in the brain tissue.

Imagine Puccini's "Recondita Armonia" re-orchestrated by Stravinsky then re-arranged by Honegger, played by fifty symphony orchestras in the Hollywood Bowl, and you might begin to get the idea.

I was getting too much of it. Did I say music was my hobby? Certainly—but the only instrument I play is the harmonica. Quite well, too. And with a microphone, I can make lots of nice noise.

A microphone—and plenty of amplifiers. I pulled the harmonica from my pocket, took a deep breath, and whooped into "Tiger Rag," my favorite party-piece.

The stunning blast-wave of jubilant jazz, riffs, tiger-growls and tremolo discords from the tiny mouth organ, crashed into the vast hall from the amplifiers, completely swamping Craswell's mad music.

I heard his agonized shout even above the din. His tastes in music were evidently not as catholic as mine. He didn't like jazz.

The music-machine quavered, the multi-limbed organists, ludicrous in their haste to escape from an unreal doom, shrank, withered to scuttling black beetles; the lighting effects that had sprayed a rich, unearthly effulgence over the consoles died away into pastel, blue gloom; then the great machine itself, caught in swirl upon wave of augmented chords complemented and reinforced by its own outpourings, shivered into fragments, poured in a chaotic stream over the floor of the hall.

I heard Craswll shout again, then the scene changed abruptly. I assumed that, in his desire to blot out the triumphant paean of jazz from his mind, and perhaps in an unconscious attempt to confuse me, he had skipped a part of his plot and, in the opposite of the flashback beloved of screen writers, shot himself forward. We were—somewhere else.

Perhaps it was the inferiority complex I was inducing, or in the transition he had forgotten how tall he was supposed to be, but he was now a mere six feet, nearer my own height.

He was so hoarse, I nearly suggested a gargle. "I . . . I left you in the Hall of Madness. Your magic caused the roof to collapse. I thought you were—killed."

So the flash-forward wasn't just an attempt to confuse me. He'd tried to lose me, write me out of the script altogether.

I shook my head. "Wishful thinking, Craswell old man," I said reproachfully. "You can't kill me off between chapters. You see, I'm not one of your characters at all. Haven't you grasped that yet? The only way you can get rid of me is by waking up."

"Again you speak in riddles," he said, but there was little confidence in his voice.

The place in which we stood was a great, high-vaulted chamber. The lighting effects—as I was coming to expect—were unusual and admirable—many colored shafts of radiance from unseen sources, slowly moving, meeting and merging at the farther end of the chamber in a white, circular blaze which seemed to be suspended over a thronelike structure.

Craswell's size-concepts were stupendous. He'd either studied the biggest cathedrals in Europe, or he was reared inside Grand Central Station. The throne was apparently a good half-mile away, over a completely bare but softly resilient floor. Yet it was coming nearer. We were not walking. I looked at the walls, realized that the floor itself, a gigantic endless belt, was carrying us along.

The slow, inexorable movement was impressive. I was aware

that Craswell was covertly glancing at me. He was anxious that I should be impressed. I replied by speeding up the belt a trifle. He didn't appear to notice.

He said: "We approach the Throne of the Snake, before which, his protector and disciple, stands the female magician and sorceress, Garor. Against her, we shall need all your strange skills, Nelpar, for she stands invulnerable within an invisible shield of pure force.

"You must destroy that barrier, that I may slay her with the Sword. Without her, the Snake, though her master and self-proclaimed master of this world, is powerless, and he will be at our mercy."

The belt came to a halt. We were at the foot of a broad stairway leading to the throne itself, a massive metal platform on which the Snake reposed beneath a brilliant ball of light.

The Snake was—a snake. Coil on coil of overgrown python, with an evil head the size of a football swaying slowly from side to side.

I spent little time looking at it. I've seen snakes before. And there was something worth much more prolonged study standing just below and slightly to one side of the throne.

Craswell's taste in feminine pulchritude was unimpeachable. I had half-expected an ancient, withered horror, but if Flo Ziegfeld had seen this baby, he'd have been scrambling up those steps waving a contract, force-shield or no force-shield, before you could get out the first glissando of a wolf-whistle.

She was a tall, oval-faced, green-eyed brunette, with everything just so, and nothing much in the way of covering—a scanty metal chest-protector and a knee-length, filmy green skirt. She had a tiny, delightful mole on her left cheek.

There was a curious touch of pride in Craswell's voice as he said, rather unnecessarily: "We are here, Garor," and looked at me expectantly.

The girl said: "Insolent fools—you are here to die."

Mm-m-m—that voice, as smooth and rich as a Piatigorski cello note. I was ready to give quite a lot of credit to Craswell's imagination, but I couldn't believe that he'd dreamed up this baby just like that. I guessed that she was modelled on life; someone he knew; someone I'd like to know—someone pulled out of the grab bag of memory in the same way as I had produced Mike O'Faolin and that grubby-chinned cab driver.

"A luscious dish," I said. "Remind me to ask you later for a phone number of the original, Craswell."

Then I said and did something that I have since regretted. It was not the behavior of a gentleman. I said: "But didn't you know they were wearing skirts longer, this season?"

I looked at the skirt. The hem line shot down to her ankles, evening-gown length.

Outraged, Craswell glared at his girlfriend. The skirt became knee-length. I made it fashionable again.

Then that skirt hem was bobbing up and down between her ankles and her knees like a crazy window blind. It was a contest of wills and imaginations, with a very pretty pair of well-covered tibiae as battleground. A fascinating sight, Garor's beautiful eyes blazed with fury. She seemed to be strangely aware of the misbecoming nature of the conflict.

Craswell suddenly uttered a ringing, petulant howl of anger and frustration—a score of lusty-lunged infants whose rattles had been simultaneously snatched from them couldn't have made more noise—and the intriguing scene was erased from view in an eruption of jet-black smoke.

When it cleared, Craswell was still in the same relative position but his sword was gone, his gladiator rig was torn and scorched, and thin trickles of blood streaked his muscular arms.

I didn't like the way he was looking at me. I'd booted his super-ego pretty hard that time.

I said: "So you couldn't take it. You've skipped a chapter again. Wise me up on what I've missed, will you?" Somehow it didn't sound as flippant as I intended.

He spoke incisively. "We have been captured and condemned to die, Nelpar. We are in the Pit of the Beast, and nothing can save us, for I have been deprived of the Sword and you of your magic.

"The ravening jaws of the Beast cannot be stayed. It is the end, Nelpar. The End—"

His eyes, large, faintly luminous, looked into mine. I tried to glance away, failed.

Irritated beyond bearing by my importunate clowning, his affronted ego had assumed the whole power of his brain, to assert itself through his will—to dominate me.

The volition may have been unconscious—he could not know why he hated me—but the effect was damnable.

And for the first time since my brash intrusion into the most private recesses of his mind, I began to doubt whether the whole business was quite—decent.

Sure, I was trying to help the guy, but . . . but dreams are sacred.

Doubt negates confidence. With confidence gone, the gateway is open to fear.

Another voice, sibilant. Steve Blakiston saying, ". . . unless you let your mind go under." My own voice, ". . . wake up as a candidate for a bed in the next ward—" No, not— ". . . not unless you let your mind go under—" And Steve had been scared to do it himself, hadn't he? I'd have something to say to that guy when I got out. If I got out . . . if—

The whole thing just wasn't amusing any more.

"Quit it, Craswell," I said harshly. "Quit making goo-goo eyes, or I'll bat you one—and you'll feel it, coma or no coma."

He said: "What foolish words are these, when we are both so near to death?"

Steve's voice: ". . . sympathetic magic . . . imagination. If he imagines that one of his fantastic creations kills the hero— himself—he just won't wake up again."

That was it. A situation in which the hero must die. And he wanted to envisage my death, too. But he couldn't kill me. Or could he? How could Blakiston know what powers might be unleashed by the concept of death during this ultramundane communion of minds?

Didn't psychiatrists say that the death-urge, the will to die, was buried deep, but potent, in the subconscious minds of men? It was not buried deep here. It was glaring, exultant, starkly displayed in the eyes of Marsham Craswell.

He had escaped from reality into a dream, but it was not far enough. Death was the only full escape—

Perhaps Craswell sensed the confusion of thought and speculation that laid my mind wide open to the suggestions of his rioting, perfervid, death-intent imagination. He waved an arm with the grandiloquent gesture of a Shakespearean Chorus introducing a last act, and brought on his monster.

In detail and vividness it excelled everything that he had dreamed up previously. It was his swan-song as a creator of fantastic forms, and he had wrought well.

I saw, briefly, that we were in the center of an enormous, steep-banked amphitheater. There were no spectators. No crowd scenes for Craswell. He preferred that strange, timeless emptiness which comes from using a minimum number of characters.

Just the two of us, under the blazing rays of great, red suns swinging in a molten sky. I couldn't count them.

I became visually aware only of the Beast.

An ant in the bottom of a washbowl with a dog snuffling at it might feel the same way. If the Beast had been anything like a dog. If it had been anything like *anything*.

It was a mass the size of several elephants. An obscene hulking gob of animated, semi-transparent purple flesh, with a gaping, circular mouth or vent, ringed inside with pointed beslimed tusks, and outside with—eyes.

As a static thing, it would have been a filthy envenomed horror, a thing of surpassing dread in its mere aspect; but the most fearsome thing was its nightmarish mode of progression.

Limbless, it jerked its prodigious bulk forward in a series of heaves—and lubricated its lath with a glaucous, viscid fluid which slopped from its mouth with every jerk.

It was heading for us at an incredible pace. Thirty yards— Twenty—

The rigidity of utter fear gripped my limbs. This was true nightmare. I tried desperately to think . . . flame-thrower . . . how . . . I couldn't remember . . . my mind was slipping away from me in face of the onward surging of that protoplasmic juggernaut . . . the slime first, then the mouth, closing . . . my thoughts were a screaming turmoil—

Another voice, a deep, drawling, kindly voice, from an unforgettable hour in childhood—"There's nothing in the whole wide world or out of it that a slug from Billy here won't stop. There's nothing you can meet in dreams that Billy here won't stop. He'll come into your dreams with you from now on. There's no call to be scared of anything." Then the cool, hard butt in my hand, the recoil, the whining irresistible chunk of hot, heavy metal—deep in my subconscious.

"Pop!" I gasped. "Thanks, Pop."

The Beast was looming over me. But Billy was in my hand, pointing into the mouth. I fired.

The Beast jerked back on its slimy trail, began to dwindle, fold in on itself. I fired again and again.

I became aware once more of Craswell beside me. He looked at the dying Beast, still huge, but rapidly diminishing, then at the dull metal of the old Colt in my hand, the wisp of blue smoke from its uptilted barrel.

And then he began to laugh.

Great, gusty laughter, but with a touch of hysteria.

And as he laughed, he began to fade from view. The red suns

sped away into the sky, became pin points; and the sky was white and clean and blank—like a ceiling.

In fact—what beautiful words are "In fact"—In fact, in sweet reality, it *was* a ceiling.

Then Steve Blakiston was peering down, easing the chromium bowl off the rubber pads round my head.

"Thanks, Pete," he said. "Half an hour to the minute. You worked on him quicker than an insulin shock."

I sat up, adjusting myself mentally. He pinched my arm. "Sure—you're awake. I'd like you to tell me just what you did—but not now. I'll ring you at your office."

I saw an assistant taking the bowl off Craswell's head.

Craswell blinked, turned his head, saw me. Half a dozen expressions, none of them pleasant, chased over his face.

He heaved upright, pushed aside the assistant.

"You lousy bum," he shouted. "I'll murder you!"

I just got clear before Steve and one of the others grabbed his arms.

"Let me get at him—I'll tear him open!"

"I warned you," Steve panted. "Get out, quick."

I was on my way. Marsham Craswell in a nightshirt may not have been quite so impressive physically as the bronzed gladiator of his dreams, but he was still passably muscular.

That was last night. Steve rang this morning.

"Cured," he said triumphantly. "Sane as you are. Said he realized he'd been overworking, and he's going to take things easier—give himself a rest from fantasy and write something else. He doesn't remember a thing about his dream-coma—but he had a curious feeling that he'd still like to do something unpleasant to a certain guy who was in the next bed to him when he woke up. He doesn't know why, and I haven't told him. But better keep clear."

"The feeling is mutual," I said. "I don't like his line in monsters. What's he going to write now—love stories?"

Steve laughed. "No. He's got a sudden craze for Westerns. Started talking this morning about the sociological and historical significance of the Colt revolver. He jotted down the title of his first yarn—'Six-Gun Rule.' Hey—is that based on something you pulled on him in his dream?"

I told him.

* * *

So Marsham Craswell's as sane as me, huh? I wouldn't take bets.

Three hours ago, I was on my way to the latest heavyweight match at Madison Square Garden when I was buttonholed by an off-duty policeman.

Michael O'Faolin, the biggest, toughest, nicest cop I know.

"Pete, m'boy," he said. "I had the strangest dream last night. I was helpin' yez out of a bit of a hole, and when it was all over, you said, in gratitude it may have been, that yez might have a couple of spare tickets f'the fight this very night, and I was wondering whether it could have been a sort of tellypathy like, and—"

I grabbed the corner of the bar doorway to steady myself. Mike was still jabbering on when I fumbled for my own tickets and said: "I'm not feeling too well, Mike. You go. I'll pick my stuff up from the other sheets. Don't think about it, Mike. Just put it down to the luck of the Irish."

I went back to the bar and thought hard into a large whisky, which is the next best thing to a crystal ball for providing a focus of concentration.

"Tellypathy, huh?"

No, said the whisky. Coincidence. Forget it.

Yet there's something in telepathy. Subconscious telepathy— two dreaming minds in rapport. But I wasn't dreaming. I was just tagging along in someone else's dream. Minds are particularly receptive in sleep. Premonitions and what-have-you. But I wasn't sleeping either. Six and four makes minus ten, strike three—you're out. You're nuts, said the whisky.

I decided to find myself a better quality crystal ball. A Scotch in a crystal glass at Cevali's club.

So I hailed a Purple Cab. There was something reminiscent about the back of the driver's head. I refused to think about it. Until the payoff.

"Dollar-fifty," he growled, then leaned out. "Say—ain't I seen you some place?"

"I'm around," I said, in a voice that squeezed with reluctance past my larynx. "Didn't you drive me out to Pentagon yesterday?"

"Yeah, that's it," he said. Square unshaven jaw, low forehead, dirty red hair straggling under his cap. "Yeah—but there's something else about your pan. I took a sleep between cruises last night and had a daffy dream. You seemed to come into it. And I got the screwiest idea you already owe me a dollar-fifty."

For a moment, I toyed with the idea of telling him to go to hell. But the roadway wasn't green sand. It looked too solid to open up. So I said, "Here's five," and staggered into Cevali's.

I looked into a whisky glass until my brain began to clear, then I phoned Steve Blakiston and talked. "It's the implications," I said finally. "I'm driving myself bats trying to figure out what would have happened if I'd conjured up a few score of my acquaintances. Would they all have dreamed the same dream if they'd been asleep?"

"Too diffuse," said Steve, apparently through a mouthful of sandwich. "That would be like trying to broadcast on dozens of wavelengths simultaneously with the same transmitter. Your brain was an integral part of that machine, occupying the same position in the circuit as a complexus of recording instruments, keyed in place with Craswell's brain—until the pick-up frequency was raised. What happened then I imagined purely as an induction process. It was—as far as the Craswell hook-up was concerned, but—"

I couldn't stand the juicy champing noises any longer, and said: "Swallow it before you choke." The guy lives on sandwiches.

His voice cleared. "Don't you see what we've got? During the amplification of the cerebral currents, there was a backsurge through the tubes and the machine became a transmitter. These two guys were sleeping, their unconscious minds wide open and acting as receivers; you'd seen them during the day, envisaged them vividly—and got tuned in, disturbing their minds and giving them dreams. Ever heard of sympathetic dreams? Ever dreamed of someone you haven't seen for years, and the next day he looks you up? Now we can do it deliberately—mechanically assisted dream telepathy, the waves reinforced and transmitted electronically! Come on over. We've got to experiment some more."

"Sometimes," I said, "I sleep. That's what I intend to do now—without mechanical assistance. So long."

A nightcap was indicated. I wandered back to the club bar. I should have gone home.

She hipped her way to the microphone in front of the band, five-foot ten of dream wrapped up in a white, glove-tight gown. An oval-faced, green-eyed brunette with a tiny, delightful mole on her left cheek. The gown was a little exiguous about the upper regions, perhaps, but not as whistle-worthy as the outfit Craswell had dreamed on her.

Backstage, I got a double shot of ice from those green eyes. Yes, she knew Mr. Craswell slightly. No, she wasn't asleep around midnight last night. And would I be so good as to inform her what business it was of mine? College type, ultra. How they do drift into the entertainment business. Not that I mind.

When I asked about the refrigeration, she said: "It's merely that I have no particular desire to know you, Mr. Parnell."

"Why?"

"I'm hardly accountable to you for my preferences." She frowned as if trying to recall something, added: "In any case—I don't know. I just don't like you. Now if you'll pardon me, I have another number to sing—"

"But, please . . . let me explain—"

"Explain what?"

She had me there. I stumble-tongued, and got a back view of the gown.

How can you apologize to a girl when she doesn't even know that you owe her an apology? She hadn't been asleep, so she couldn't have dreamed about the skirt incident. And if she had—she was Craswell's dream, not mine. But through some aberration a trickle of thought waves from Blakiston's machine had planted an unreasonable antipathy to me in her subconscious mind. And it would need a psychiatrist to dig it out. Or—

I phoned Steve from the club office. He was still chewing. I said: "I've got some intensive thinking to do—into that machine of yours. I'll be right over."

She was leaving the microphone as I passed the band on my way out. I looked at her as she came up, getting every detail fixed.

"What time do you go to bed?" I asked.

I saw the slap coming and ducked.

I said: "I can wait. I'll be seeing you. Happy dreams."

MARS IS HEAVEN!

by Ray Bradbury (1920–   )

PLANET STORIES

Fall

"Mars is Heaven" is one of the most famous stories that form a part of The Martian Chronicles, *one of the cornerstones of modern science fiction. Tremendously moving, it is at the same time a terrifying story, for it concerns people confronted by* shape-changers, *creatures that look like something they are not. The concept of the shape-changer seems to tap into the psyche of human beings—they (and their close relation the* possessor) *always seem to frighten us, as the commercial success of the movie* The Thing *(1982) testifies.*

Bradbury's skill is so great that the obvious impossibilities of his Martian landscape do not really bother us.

(It seems to me that when I was young, the stories I read were populated exclusively by people who either lived in small towns [preferably midwestern] or who lived in big cities and were spiritually lost and longed to return to the small towns from which they had come. That made me worry about myself. I was indeed born in a small town, but not in the United States, and I arrived in New York City at such a young age that I

remember nothing else. What's more, I love New York City and don't want to live in a small town. They make me feel rather an outsider. Even in science fiction, which we ordinarily think of as future-oriented and technophilic, we have the small-town syndrome with Ray Bradbury and Clifford Simak as the most skillful exploiters thereof. My favorite science-fictional small town, however, is by all odds the one in "Mars is Heaven!" That is how small towns ought to be [in my own prejudiced mind].—I.A.)

The ship came down from space. It came down from the stars and the black velocities, and the shining movements and the silent gulfs of space. It was a new ship, the only one of its kind, it had fire in its belly and men in its body, and it moved with clean silence, fiery and hot. In it were seventeen men, including a captain. A crowd had gathered at the New York tarmac and shouted and waved their hands up into the sunlight, and the rocket had jerked up, bloomed out great flowers of heat and color, and run away into space on the first voyage to Mars!

Now it was decelerating with metal efficiency in the upper zones of Martian atmosphere. It was still a thing of beauty and strength. It had shorn through meteor streams, it had moved in the majestic black midnight waters of space like a pale sea leviathan, it had passed the sickly, pocked mass of the ancient moon, and thrown itself onward into one nothingness following another. The men within it had been battered, thrown about, sickened, made well again, scarred, made pale, flushed, each in his turn. One man had died after a fall, but now, seventeen of the original eighteen with their eyes clear in their heads and their faces pressed to the thick glass ports of the rocket, were watching Mars swing up under them.

"Mars! Mars! Good old Mars, here we are!" cried Navigator Lustig.

"Good old Mars!" said Samuel Hinkston, archaeologist.

"Well," said Captain John Black.

The ship landed softly on a lawn of green grass. Outside, upon the lawn, stood an iron deer. Farther up the lawn, a tall brown Victorian house sat in the quiet sunlight, all covered with scrolls and rococo, its windows made of blue and pink and yellow and green colored glass. Upon the porch were hairy geraniums and an old swing which was hooked into the porch ceiling and which now swung back and forth, back and forth, in a little breeze. At the top of the house was a cupola with diamond, leaded-glass windows, and a dunce-cap roof! Through the front window you could see an ancient piano with yellow keys and a piece of music titled *Beautiful Ohio* sitting on the music rest.

Around the rocket in four directions spread the little town, green and motionless in the Martian spring. There were white houses and red brick ones, and tall elm trees blowing in the wind, and tall maples and horse chestnuts. And church steeples with golden bells silent in them.

The men in the rocket looked out and saw this. Then they looked at one another and then they looked out again. They held on to each other's elbows, suddenly unable to breathe, it seemed. Their faces grew pale and they blinked constantly, running from glass port to glass port of the ship.

"I'll be damned," whispered Lustig, rubbing his face with his numb fingers, his eyes wet. "I'll be damned, damned, damned."

"It can't be, it just can't be," said Samuel Hinkston.

"Lord," said Captain John Black.

There was a call from the chemist. "Sir, the atmosphere is fine for breathing, sir."

Black turned slowly. "Are you sure?"

"No doubt of it, sir."

"Then we'll go out," said Lustig.

"Lord, yes," said Samuel Hinkston.

"Hold on," said Captain John Black. "Just a moment. Nobody gave any orders."

"But, sir—"

"Sir, nothing. How do we know what this is?"

"We know what it is, sir," said the chemist. "It's a small town with good air in it, sir."

"And it's a small town the like of Earth towns," said Samuel Hinkston, the archaeologist. "Incredible. It can't be, but it is."

Captain John Black looked at him, idly. "Do you think that the civilizations of two planets can progress at the same rate and evolve in the same way, Hinkston?"

"I wouldn't have thought so, sir."

Captain Black stood by the port. "Look out there. The geraniums. A specialized plant. That specific variety has only

been known on Earth for fifty years. Think of the thousands of
years of time it takes to evolve plants. Then tell me if it is logical
that the Martians should have: one, leaded glass windows; two,
cupolas; three, porch swings; four, an instrument that looks like
a piano and probably is a piano; and, five, if you look closely, if
a Martian composer would have published a piece of music
titled, strangely enough, *Beautiful Ohio*. All of which means that
we have an Ohio River here on Mars!"

"It is quite strange, sir."

"Strange, hell, it's absolutely impossible, and I suspect the
whole bloody shooting setup. Something's wrong here, and I'm
not leaving the ship until I know what it is."

"Oh, sir," said Lustig.

"Darn it," said Samuel Hinkston. "Sir, I want to investigate
this at first hand. It may be that there are similar patterns of thought,
movement, civilization on *every* planet in our system. We may
be on the threshold of the great psychological and metaphysical
discovery in our time, sir, don't you think?"

"I'm willing to wait a moment," said Captain John Black.

"It may be, sir, that we are looking upon a phenomenon that,
for the first time, would absolutely prove the existence of a God,
sir."

"There are many people who are of good faith without such
proof, Mr. Hinkston."

"I'm one myself, sir. But certainly a thing like this, out
there," said Hinkston, "could not occur without divine inter-
vention, sir. It fills me with such terror and elation I don't know
whether to laugh or cry, sir."

"Do neither, then, until we know what we're up against."

"Up against, sir?" inquired Lustig. "I see that we're up
against nothing. It's a good quiet, green town, much like the one
I was born in, and I like the looks of it."

"When were you born, Lustig?"

"In 1910, sir."

"That makes you fifty years old now, doesn't it?"

"This being 1960, yes, sir."

"And you, Hinkston?"

"1920, sir. In Illinois. And this looks swell to me, sir."

"This couldn't be Heaven," said the captain, ironically.
"Though, I must admit, it looks peaceful and cool, and pretty
much like Green Bluff, where I was born, in 1915." He looked
at the chemist. "The air's all right, is it?"

"Yes, sir."

"Well, then, tell you what we'll do. Lustig, you and Hinkston and I will fetch ourselves out to look this town over. The other 14 men will stay aboard ship. If anything untoward happens, lift the ship and get the hell out, do you hear what I say, Craner?"

"Yes, sir. The hell out we'll go, sir. Leaving *you*?"

"A loss of three men's better than a whole ship. If something bad happens get back to Earth and warn the next Rocket, that's Lingle's Rocket, I think, which will be completed and ready to take off some time around next Christmas, what he has to meet up with. If there's something hostile about Mars we certainly want the next expedition to be well armed."

"So are we, sir. We've got a regular arsenal with us."

"Tell the men to stand by the guns, then, as Lustig and Hinkston and I go out."

"Right, sir."

"Come along, Lustig, Hinkston."

The three men walked together, down through the levels of the ship.

It was a beautiful spring day. A robin sat on a blossoming apple tree and sang continuously. Showers of petal snow sifted down when the wind touched the apple tree, and the blossom smell drifted upon the air. Somewhere in the town, somebody was playing the piano and the music came and went, came and went, softly, drowsily. The song was *Beautiful Dreamer*. Somewhere else, a phonograph, scratchy and faded, was hissing out a record of *Roamin' In The Gloamin'*, sung by Harry Lauder.

The three men stood outside the ship. The port closed behind them. At every window, a face pressed, looking out. The large metal guns pointed this way and that, ready.

Now the phonograph record being played was:

> "Oh give me a June night
> The moonlight and you—"

Lustig began to tremble. Samuel Hinkston did likewise.

Hinkston's voice was so feeble and uneven that the captain had to ask him to repeat what he had said. "I said, sir, that I think I have solved this, all of this, sir!"

"And what is the solution, Hinkston?"

The soft wind blew. The sky was serene and quiet and somewhere a stream of water ran through the cool caverns and tree shadings of a ravine. Somewhere a horse and wagon trotted and rolled by, bumping.

"Sir, it must be, it has to be, this is the *only* solution! Rocket travel began to Mars in the years before the first World War, sir!"

The captain stared at his archaeologist. "No!"

"But, yes, sir! You must admit, look at all of this! How else explain it, the houses, the lawns, the iron deer, the flowers, the pianos, the music!"

"Hinkston, Hinkston, oh," and the captain put his hand to his face, shaking his head, his hand shaking now, his lips blue.

"Sir, listen to me." Hinkston took his elbow persuasively and looked up into the captain's face, pleading. "Say that there were some people in the year 1905, perhaps, who hated wars and wanted to get away from Earth and they got together, some scientists, in secret, and built a rocket and came out here to Mars."

"No, no, Hinkston."

"Why not? The world was a different place in 1905, they could have kept it a secret much more easily."

"But the work, Hinkston, the work of building a complex thing like a rocket, oh, no, no." The captain looked at his shoes, looked at his hands, looked at the houses, and then at Hinkston.

"And they came up here, and naturally the houses they built were similar to Earth houses because they brought the cultural architecture with them, and here it is!"

"And they've lived here all these years?" said the captain.

"In peace and quiet, sir, yes. Maybe they made a few trips, to bring enough people here for one small town, and then stopped, for fear of being discovered. That's why the town seems so old-fashioned. I don't see a thing, myself, that is older than the year 1927, do you?"

"No, frankly, I don't, Hinkston."

"These are *our* people, sir. This is an American city; it's definitely not European!"

"That—that's right, too, Hinkston."

"Or maybe, just maybe, sir, rocket travel is older than we think. Perhaps it started in some part of the world hundreds of years ago, was discovered and kept secret by a small number of men, and they came to Mars, with only occasional visits to Earth over the centuries."

"You make it sound almost reasonable."

"It is, sir. It has to be. We have the proof here before us, all we have to do now, is find some people and verify it!"

"You're right there, of course. We can't just stand here and talk. Did you bring your gun?"

"Yes, but we won't need it."

"We'll see about it. Come along, we'll ring that doorbell and see if anyone is home."

Their boots were deadened of all sound in the thick green grass. It smelled from a fresh mowing. In spite of himself, Captain John Black felt a great peace come over him. It had been thirty years since he had been in a small town, and the buzzing of spring bees on the air lulled and quieted him, and the fresh look of things was a balm to the soul.

Hollow echoes sounded from under the boards as they walked across the porch and stood before the screen door. Inside, they could see a bead curtain hung across the hall entry, and a crystal chandelier and a Maxfield Parrish painting framed on one wall over a comfortable Morris Chair. The house smelled old, and of the attic, and infinitely comfortable. You could hear the tinkle of ice rattling in a lemonade pitcher. In a distant kitchen, because of the heat of the day, someone was preparing a soft, lemon drink.

Captain John Black rang the bell.

Footsteps, dainty and thin, came along the hall and a kind-faced lady of some forty years, dressed in the sort of dress you might expect in the year 1909, peered out at them.

"Can I help you?" she asked.

"Beg your pardon," said Captain Black, uncertainly. "But we're looking for, that is, could you help us, I mean." He stopped. She looked out at him with dark wondering eyes.

"If you're selling something," she said. "I'm much too busy and I haven't time." She turned to go.

"No, *wait*," he cried, bewilderedly. "What town is this?"

She looked him up and down as if he were crazy. "What do you mean, what town is it? How could you be in a town and not know what town it was?"

The captain looked as if he wanted to go sit under a shady apple tree. "I beg your pardon," he said. "But we're strangers here. We're from Earth, and we want to know how this town got here and you got here."

"Are you census takers?" she asked.

"No," he said.

"What do you want then?" she demanded.

"Well," said the captain.

"Well?" she asked.

"How long has this town been here?" he wondered.

"It was built in 1868," she snapped at them. "Is this a game?"

"No, not a game," cried the captain. "Oh, God," he said. "Look here. We're from Earth!"

"From *where*?" she said.

"From Earth!" he said.

"Where's that?" she said.

"From Earth," he cried.

"Out of the ground, do you mean?"

"No, from the planet Earth!" he almost shouted. "Here," he insisted, "come out on the porch and I'll show you."

"No," she said, "I won't come out there, you are all evidently quite mad from the sun."

Lustig and Hinkston stood behind the captain. Hinkston now spoke up. "Mrs.," he said. "We came in a flying ship across space, among the stars. We came from the third planet from the sun, Earth, to this planet, which is Mars. *Now* do you understand, Mrs.?"

"Mad from the sun," she said, taking hold of the door. "Go away now, before I call my husband who's upstairs taking a nap, and he'll beat you all with his fists."

"But—" said Hinkston. "This is Mars, is it not?"

"This," explained the woman, as if she were addressing a child, "is Green Lake, Wisconsin, on the continent of America, surrounded by the Pacific and Atlantic Oceans, on a place called the world, or sometimes, the Earth. Go away now. Good-bye!"

She slammed the door.

The three men stood before the door with their hands up in the air toward it, as if pleading with her to open it once more.

They looked at one another.

"Let's knock the door down," said Lustig.

"We can't," sighed the captain.

"Why not?"

"She didn't do anything bad, did she? We're the strangers here. This is private property. Good God, Hinkston!" He went and sat down on the porchstep.

"What, sir?"

"Did it ever strike you, that maybe we got ourselves, somehow, some way, fouled up. And, by accident, came back and landed on Earth!''

"Oh, sir, oh, sir, oh oh, sir." And Hinkston sat down numbly and thought about it.

Lustig stood up in the sunlight. "How could we have done that?"

"I don't know, just let me think."

Hinkston said, "But we checked every mile of the way, and we saw Mars and our chronometers said so many miles gone, and we went past the moon and out into space and here we are, on Mars. I'm sure we're on Mars, sir."

Lustig said, "But, suppose, just suppose that, by accident, in space, in time, or something, we landed on a planet in space, in another time. Suppose this is Earth, thirty or fifty years ago? Maybe we got lost in the dimensions, do you think?"

"Oh, go away, Lustig."

"Are the men in the ship keeping an eye on us, Hinkston?"

"At their guns, sir."

Lustig went to the door, rang the bell. When the door opened again, he asked, "What year is this?"

"1926, of course!" cried the woman, furiously, and slammed the door again.

"Did you hear that?" Lustig ran back to them, wildly. "She said 1926! We *have* gone back in time! This *is* Earth!"

Lustig sat down and the three men let the wonder and terror of the thought afflict them. Their hands stirred fitfully on their knees. The wind blew, nodding the locks of hair on their heads.

The captain stood up, brushing off his pants. "I never thought it would be like this. It scares the hell out of me. How can a thing like this happen?"

"Will anybody in the whole town believe us?" wondered Hinkston. "Are we playing around with something dangerous? Time, I mean. Shouldn't we just take off and go home?"

"No. We'll try another house."

They walked three houses down to a little white cottage under an oak tree. "I like to be as logical as I can get," said the captain. He nodded at the town. "How does this sound to you, Hinkston? Suppose, as you said originally, that rocket travel occurred years ago. And when the Earth people had lived here a number of years they began to get homesick for Earth. First a mild neurosis about it, then a full-fledged psychosis. Then, threatened insanity. What would you do, as a psychiatrist, if faced with such a problem?''

Hinkston thought. ''Well, I think I'd re-arrange the civilization on Mars so it resembled Earth more and more each day. If there was any way of reproducing every plant, every road and every lake, and even an ocean, I would do so. Then I would, by some vast crowd hypnosis, theoretically anyway, convince everyone in a town this size that this really *was* Earth, not Mars at all.''

''Good enough, Hinkston. I think we're on the right track now. That woman in that house back there, just *thinks* she's living on Earth. It protects her sanity. She and all the others in this town are the patients of the greatest experiment in migration and hypnosis you will ever lay your eyes on in your life.''

''That's it, sir!'' cried Lustig.

''Well,'' the captain sighed. ''Now we're getting somewhere. I feel better. It all sounds a bit more logical now. This talk about time and going back and forth and traveling in time turns my stomach upside down. But, *this* way—'' He actually smiled for the first time in a month. ''Well. It looks as if we'll be fairly welcome here.''

''Or, will we, sir?'' said Lustig. ''After all, like the Pilgrims, these people came here to escape Earth. Maybe they won't be too happy to see us, sir. Maybe they'll try to drive us out or kill us?''

''We have superior weapons if that should happen. Anyway, all we can do is try. This next house now. Up we go.''

But they had hardly crossed the lawn when Lustig stopped and looked off across the town, down the quiet, dreaming afternoon street. ''Sir,'' he said.

''What is it, Lustig?'' asked the captain.

''Oh, sir, *sir*, what I see, what I do see now before me, oh, oh—'' said Lustig, and he began to cry. His fingers came up, twisting and trembling, and his face was all wonder and joy and incredulity. He sounded as if any moment he might go quite insane with happiness. He looked down the street and he began to run, stumbling, awkwardly, falling, picking himself up, and running on. ''Oh, God, God, thank you, God! Thank you!''

''Don't let him get away!'' The captain broke into a run.

Now Lustig was running at full speed, shouting. He turned into a yard halfway down the little shady side street and leaped up upon the porch of a large green house with an iron rooster on the roof.

He was beating upon the door, shouting and hollering and crying when Hinkston and the captain ran up and stood in the yard.

The door opened. Lustig yanked the screen wide and in a high wail of discovery and happiness, cried out, "Grandma! Grandpa!"

Two old people stood in the doorway, their faces lighting up.

"Albert!" Their voices piped and they rushed out to embrace and pat him on the back and move around him. "Albert, oh, Albert, it's been so many years! How you've grown, boy, how big you are, boy, oh, Albert boy, how are you!"

"Grandma, Grandpa!" sobbed Albert Lustig. "Good to see you! You look fine, fine! Oh, fine!" He held them, turned them, kissed them, hugged them, cried on them, held them out again, blinked at the little old people. The sun was in the sky, the wind blew, the grass was green, the screen door stood open.

"Come in, lad, come in, there's lemonade for you, fresh, lots of it!"

"Grandma, Grandpa, good to see you! I've got friends down here! Here!" Lustig turned and waved wildly at the captain and Hinkston, who, all during the adventure on the porch, had stood in the shade of a tree, holding onto each other. "Captain, captain, come up, come up, I want you to meet my grandfolks!"

"Howdy," said the folks. "Any friend of Albert's is ours, too! Don't stand there with your mouth open! Come on!"

In the living room of the old house it was cool and a grandfather clock ticked high and long and bronzed in one corner. There were soft pillows on large couches and walls filled with books and a rug cut in a thick rose pattern and antimacassars pinned to furniture, and lemonade in the hand, sweating, and cool on the thirsty tongue.

"Here's to our health." Grandma tipped her glass to her porcelain teeth.

"How long you *been* here, Grandma?" said Lustig.

"A good many years," she said tartly. "Ever since we died."

"Ever since you what?" asked Captain John Black, putting his drink down.

"Oh, yes," Lustig looked at his captain. "They've been dead thirty years."

"And you *sit* there, calmly!" cried the captain.

"Tush," said the old woman, and winked glitteringly at John Black. "Who are we to question what happens? Here we are. What's life, anyways? Who does what for why and where? All we know is here we are, alive again, and no questions asked. A

second chance.'' She toddled over and held out her thin wrist to
Captain John Black. ''Feel.'' He felt. ''Solid, ain't I?'' she
asked. He nodded. ''You hear my voice, don't you?'' she inquired.
Yes, he did. ''Well, then,'' she said in triumph, ''why go
around questioning?''

''Well,'' said the captain, ''it's simply that we never thought
we'd find a thing like this on Mars.''

''And now you've found it. I dare say there's lots on every
planet that'll show you God's infinite ways.''

''Is this Heaven?'' asked Hinkston.

''Nonsense, no. It's a world and we get a second chance.
Nobody told us why. But then nobody told us why we were on
Earth, either. That *other* Earth, I mean. The one you came from.
How do we know there wasn't *another* before *that* one?''

''A good question,'' said the captain.

The captain stood up and slapped his hand on his leg in an
off-hand fashion. ''We've got to be going. It's been nice. Thank
you for the drinks.''

He stopped. He turned and looked toward the door, startled.

Far away, in the sunlight, there was a sound of voices, a
crowd, a shouting and a great hello.

''What's that?'' asked Hinkston.

''We'll soon find out!'' And Captain John Black was out the
front door abruptly, jolting across the green lawn and into the
street of the Martian town.

He stood looking at the ship. The ports were open and his
crew were streaming out, waving their hands. A crowd of people
had gathered and in and through and among these people the
members of the crew were running, talking, laughing, shaking
hands. People did little dances. People swarmed. The rocket lay
empty and abandoned.

A brass band exploded in the sunlight, flinging off a gay tune
from upraised tubas and trumpets. There was a bang of drums
and a shrill of fifes. Little girls with golden hair jumped up
and down. Little boys shouted, ''Hooray!'' And fat men passed
around ten-cent cigars. The mayor of the town made a speech.
Then, each member of the crew with a mother on one arm, a
father or sister on the other, was spirited off down the street, into
little cottages or big mansions and doors slammed shut.

The wind rose in the clear spring sky and all was silent. The
brass band had banged off around a corner leaving the rocket to
shine and dazzle alone in the sunlight.

"Abandoned!" cried the captain. "Abandoned the ship, they did! I'll have their skins, by God! They had orders!"

"Sir," said Lustig. "Don't be too hard on them. Those were all old relatives and friends."

"That's no excuse!"

"Think how they felt, captain, seeing familiar faces outside the ship!"

"I would have obeyed orders! I would have—" The captain's mouth remained open.

Striding along the sidewalk under the Martian sun, tall, smiling, eyes blue, face tan, came a young man of some twenty-six years.

"John!" the man cried, and broke into a run.

"What?" said Captain John Black. He swayed.

"John, you old beggar, you!"

The man ran up and gripped his hand and slapped him on the back.

"It's you," said John Black.

"Of course, who'd you *think* it was!"

"Edward!" The captain appealed now to Lustig and Hinkston, holding the stranger's hand. "This is my brother Edward. Ed, meet my men, Lustig, Hinkston! My brother!"

They tugged at each other's hands and arms and then finally embraced. "Ed!" "John, you old bum, you!" "You're looking fine, Ed, but, Ed, what is this? You haven't changed over the years. You died, I remember, when you were twenty-six, and I was nineteen, oh God, so many years ago, and here you are, and, Lord, what goes on, what goes on?"

Edward Black gave him a brotherly knock on the chin. "Mom's waiting," he said.

"Mom?"

"And Dad, too."

"And Dad?" The captain almost fell to earth as if hit upon the chest with a mighty weapon. He walked stiffly and awkwardly, out of coordination. He stuttered and whispered and talked only one or two words at a time. "Mom alive? Dad? Where?"

"At the old house on Oak Knoll Avenue."

"The old house." The captain stared in delighted amazement. "Did you *hear* that, Lustig, Hinkston?"

"I know it's hard for you to believe."

"But alive. Real."

"Don't I *feel* real?" The strong arm, the firm grip, the white smile. The light, curling hair.

Hinkston was gone. He had seen his own house down the

street and was running for it. Lustig was grinning. "Now you understand, sir, what happened to everybody on the ship. They couldn't help themselves."

"Yes. Yes," said the captain, eyes shut. "Yes." He put out his hand. "When I open my eyes, you'll be gone." He opened his eyes. "You're still here. God, Edward, you look fine!"

"Come along, lunch is waiting for you. I told Mom."

Lustig said, "Sir, I'll be with my grandfolks if you want me."

"What? Oh fine, Lustig. Later, then."

Edward grabbed his arm and marched him. "You need support."

"I do. My knees, all funny. My stomach, loose. God."

"There's the house. Remember it?"

"Remember it? Hell! I bet I can beat you to the front porch!"

They ran. The wind roared over Captain John Black's ears. The earth roared under his feet. He saw the golden figure of Edward Black pull ahead of him in the amazing dream of reality. He saw the house rush forward, the door open, the screen swing back. "Beat you!" cried Edward, bounding up the steps. "I'm an old man," panted the captain, "and you're still young. But, then, you *always* beat me, I remember!"

In the doorway, Mom, pink and plump and bright. And behind her, pepper grey, Dad, with his pipe in his hand.

"Mom, Dad!"

He ran up the steps like a child, to meet them.

It was a fine long afternoon. They finished lunch and they sat in the living room and he told them all about his rocket and his being captain and they nodded and smiled upon him and Mother was just the same, and Dad bit the end off a cigar and lighted it in his old fashion. Mom brought in some iced tea in the middle of the afternoon. Then, there was a big turkey dinner at night and time flowing on. When the drumsticks were sucked clean and lay brittle upon the plates, the captain leaned back in his chair and exhaled his deep contentment. Dad poured him a small glass of dry sherry. It was seven-thirty in the evening. Night was in all the trees and coloring the sky, and the lamps were halos of dim light in the gentle house. From all the other houses down the streets came sounds of music, pianos playing, laughter.

Mom put a record on the victrola and she and Captain John Black had a dance. She was wearing the same perfume he remembered from the summer when she and Dad had been killed in the train accident. She was very real in his arms as they danced lightly to the music.

"I'll wake in the morning," said the captain. "And I'll be in my rocket in space, and all this will be gone."

"No, no, don't think that," she cried softly, pleadingly. "We're here. Don't question. God is good to us. Let's be happy."

The record ended with a circular hissing.

"You're tired, son," said Dad. He waved his pipe. "You and Ed go on upstairs. Your old bedroom is waiting for you."

"The old one?"

"The brass bed and all," laughed Edward.

"But I should report my men in."

"Why?" Mother was logical.

"Why? Well, I don't know. No reason, I guess. No, none at all. What's the difference?" He shook his head. "I'm not being very logical these days."

"Good night, son." She kissed his cheek.

" 'Night, Mom."

"Sleep tight, son." Dad shook his hand.

"Same to you, Pop."

"It's good to have you home."

"It's good to *be* home."

He left the land of cigar smoke and perfume and books and gentle light and ascended the stairs, talking, talking with Edward. Edward pushed a door open and there was the yellow brass bed and the old semaphore banners from college days and a very musty raccoon coat which he petted with strange, muted affection. "It's too much," he said faintly. "Like being in a thunder shower without an umbrella. I'm soaked to the skin with emotion. I'm numb. I'm tired."

"A night's sleep between cool clean sheets for you, my bucko." Edward slapped wide the snowy linens and flounced the pillows. Then he put up a window and let the night-blooming jasmine float in. There was moonlight and the sound of distant dancing and whispering.

"So this is Mars," said the captain undressing.

"So this is Mars." Edward undressed in idle, leisurely moves, drawing his shirt off over his head, revealing golden shoulders and the good muscular neck.

The lights were out, they were into bed, side by side, as in the days, how many decades ago? The captain lolled and was nourished by the night wind pushing the lace curtains out upon the dark room air. Among the trees, upon a lawn, someone had cranked up a portable phonograph and now it was playing softly, "I'll be loving you, always, with a love that's true, always."

The thought of Anna came to his mind. "Is Anna here?"

His brother, lying straight out in the moonlight from the window, waited and then said, "Yes. She's out of town. But she'll be here in the morning."

The captain shut his eyes. "I want to see Anna very much."

The room was square and quiet except for their breathing. "Good night, Ed."

A pause. "Good night, John."

He lay peacefully, letting his thoughts float. For the first time the stress of the day was moved aside, all of the excitement was calmed. He could think logically now. It had all been emotion. The bands playing, the sight of familiar faces, the sick pounding of your heart. But—now . . .

How? He thought. How was all this made? And why? For what purpose? Out of the goodness of some kind God? Was God, then, really that fine and thoughtful of His children? How and why and what for?

He thought of the various theories advanced in the first heat of the afternoon by Hinkston and Lustig. He let all kinds of new theories drop in lazy pebbles down through his mind, as through a dark water, now, turning, throwing out dull flashes of white light. Mars. Earth. Mom. Dad. Edward. Mars. Martians.

Who had lived here a thousand years ago on Mars? Martians? Or had this always been like this? Martians. He repeated the word quietly, inwardly.

He laughed out loud, almost. He had the most ridiculous theory, all of a sudden. It gave him a kind of chilled feeling. It was really nothing to think of, of course. Highly improbable. Silly. Forget it. Ridiculous.

But, he thought, just suppose. Just *suppose* now, that there were Martians living on Mars and they saw our ship coming and saw us inside our ship and hated us. Suppose, now, just for the hell of it, that they wanted to destroy us, as invaders, as un- wanted ones, and they wanted to do it in a very clever way, so that we would be taken off guard. Well, what would the best weapon be that a Martian could use against Earthmen with atom weapons?

The answer was interesting. Telepathy, hypnosis, memory and imagination.

Suppose all these houses weren't real at all, this bed not real, but only figments of my own imagination, given substance by telepathy and hypnosis by the Martians.

Suppose these houses are really some other shape, a Martian shape, but, by playing on my desires and wants, these Martians have made this seem like my old home town, my old house, to lull me out of my suspicions? What better way to fool a man, than by his own emotions.

And suppose those two people in the next room, asleep, are not my mother and father at all. But two Martians, incredibly brilliant, with the ability to keep me under this dreaming hypnosis all of the time?

And that brass band, today? What a clever plan it would be. First, fool Lustig, then fool Hinkston, then gather a crowd around the rocket ship and wave. And all the men in the ship, seeing mothers, aunts, uncles, sweethearts dead ten, twenty years ago, naturally, disregarding orders, would rush out and abandon the ship. What more natural? What more unsuspecting? What more simple? A man doesn't ask too many questions when his mother is suddenly brought back to life; he's much too happy. And the brass band played and everybody was taken off to private homes. And here we all are, tonight, in various houses, in various beds, with no weapons to protect us, and the rocket lies in the moonlight, empty. And wouldn't it be horrible and terrifying to discover that all of this was part of some great clever plan by the Martians to divide and conquer us, and kill us. Some time during the night, perhaps, my brother here on this bed, will change form, melt, shift, and become a one-eyed, green-and-yellow-toothed Martian. It would be very simple for him just to turn over in bed and put a knife into my heart. And in all those other houses down the street a dozen other brothers or fathers suddenly melting away and taking out knives and doing things to the unsuspecting, sleeping men of Earth.

His hands were shaking under the covers. His body was cold. Suddenly it was not a theory. Suddenly he was very afraid. He lifted himself in bed and listened. The night was very quiet. The music had stopped. The wind had died. His brother (?) lay sleeping beside him.

Very carefully he lifted the sheets, rolled them back. He slipped from bed and was walking softly across the room when his brother's voice said, ''Where are you going?''

''What?''

His brother's voice was quite cold. "I said, where do you think you're going?"

"For a drink of water."

"But you're not thirsty."

"Yes, yes, I am."

"No, you're not."

Captain John Black broke and ran across the room. He screamed. He screamed twice.

He never reached the door.

In the morning, the brass band played a mournful dirge. From every house in the street came little solemn processions bearing long boxes and along the sun-filled street, weeping and changing, came the grandmas and grandfathers and mothers and sisters and brothers, walking to the churchyard, where there were open holes dug freshly and new tombstones installed. Seventeen holes in all, and seventeen tombstones. Three of the tombstones said, CAPTAIN JOHN BLACK, ALBERT LUSTIG, and SAMUEL HINKSTON.

The mayor made a little sad speech, his face sometimes looking like the mayor, sometimes looking like something else.

Mother and Father Black were there, with Brother Edward, and they cried, their faces melting now from a familiar face into something else.

Grandpa and Grandma Lustig were there, weeping, their faces also shifting like wax, shivering as a thing does in waves of heat on a summer day.

The coffins were lowered. Somebody murmured about "the unexpected and sudden deaths of seventeen fine men during the night—"

Earth was shoveled in on the coffin tops.

After the funeral the brass band slammed and banged back into town and the crowd stood around and waved and shouted as the rocket was torn to pieces and strewn about and blown up.

THANG

by Martin Gardner (1914—)

COMMENT

Fall

Martin Gardner is an excellent science writer whose humorous and challenging puzzle stories appear regularly in Isaac Asimov's Science Fiction Magazine. *He is also the author of such outstanding books as* Fads and Fallacies in the Name of Science *(1957),* The Annotated Alice *(1960),* The Ambidextrous Universe *(1964), and many others. In addition, he has written the* Mathematical Games *feature in* Scientific American *for many years.*

"Thang" is the best of his too few science fiction stories.

(The first time I ever met Martin Gardner, I said to him, "Mr. Gardner, I've got every one of your books that I could find and I am such an admirer of your style that I do my best to imitate it." And he replied to me, "Isn't that strange? I do my best to imitate yours."

Some years later, I nominated him for membership in "The Trap Door Spiders," a small grouping of highly intelligent and articulate people who find no music more enticing and compelling than the sounds of each other's voices, and who each makes sense out of the cacophony by listening only to his own. Why Martin should enjoy the group when he is so quiet himself, I don't know, but enjoy it, he did, and we enjoyed him, until he decided to retire and move to North Carolina, something for which I will never forgive him. I miss him so badly.—I.A.)

The Earth had completed another turn about the sun, whirling slowly and silently as it always whirled. The East had experienced a record-breaking crop of yellow rice and yellow children, larger stockpiles of atomic weapons were accumulating in certain strategic centers, and the sages of the University of Chicago were uttering words of profound wisdom, when Thang reached down and picked up the Earth between his thumb and finger.

Thang had been sleeping. When he finally awoke and blinked his six opulent eyes at the blinding light (for the light of our stars when viewed in their totality is no thing of dimness) he had become uncomfortably aware of an empty feeling near the pit of his stomach. How long he had been sleeping even he did not know exactly, for in the mind of Thang time is a term of no significance. Although the ways of Thang are beyond the ways of men, and the thoughts of Thang scarcely conceivable by our thoughts; still—stating the matter roughly and in the language we know— the ways of Thang are this: When Thang is not asleep, he hungers.

After blinking his opulent eyes (in a specific consecutive order which had long been his habit) and stretching forth a long arm to sweep aside the closer suns, Thang squinted into the deep. The riper planets were near the center and usually could be recognized by surface texture; but frequently Thang had to thump them with his middle finger. It was some time until he found a piece that suited him. He picked it up with his right hand and shook off most of the adhering salty moisture. Other fingers scaled away thin flakes of bluish ice that had caked on opposite sides. Finally, he dried the ball completely by rubbing it on his chest.

He bit into it. It was soft and juicy, neither unpleasantly hot nor freezing to the tongue; and Thang, who always ate the entire planet, core and all, lay back contentedly, chewing slowly and permitting his thoughts to dwell idly on trivial matters, when he felt himself picked up suddenly by the back of the neck.

He was jerked upward and backward by an arm of tremendous bulk (an arm covered with greyish hair and exuding a foul smell). Then he was lowered even more rapidly. He looked down in time to see an enormous mouth—red and gaping and watering around the edges—then the blackness closed over him with a slurp like a clap of thunder.

For there are other gods than Thang.

BROOKLYN PROJECT

by William Tenn (Philip Klass; 1920–   )

PLANET STORIES
Fall

One of the most interesting of the several types of time travel story are those that suggest that a tiny change in some seeming minor aspect of the past might result in tremendous changes in the present. Perhaps the most famous story of this type is Ray Bradbury's "A Sound of Thunder" (1952). Here, the witty and urbane Professor Klass turns his attention to this concept, with entertaining and chilling effect.

(Every once in a while, I amuse myself with thoughts of the unknowable:

1) You know what your senses tell you; but how can you find out what other peoples' senses tell them? X and Y both agree that a rose is something each calls "red," but what does "red" look like to X and Y? The same?

2) Suppose the Universe is expanding steadily and rapidly, everything in it—everything including you and every part of you and all the atoms that make up you and everything else. Could you tell? Would it matter? Or suppose everything was contracting—or sometimes contracting or expanding?

3) Suppose the Earth and the Universe were created 6,000 years ago, with all the fossils in place, with the light from the stars en route to us, and all the evidence pointing to a big bang having taken place 15 billion years ago. How could we tell? For that matter, suppose it were all created one second ago, with each of us at our present age and created with all our present memories? How could we tell?

4) Suppose every once in a while, people traveled into the past and changed everything radically and that all of us exist now because such a change has just taken place————

Oh, well, you see what I mean.—I. A.)

The gleaming bowls of light set in the creamy ceiling dulled when the huge, circular door at the back of the booth opened. They returned to white brilliance as the chubby man in the severe black jumper swung the door shut behind him and dogged it down again.

Twelve reporters of both sexes exhaled very loudly as he sauntered to the front of the booth and turned his back to the semi-opaque screen stretching across it. Then they all rose in deference to the cheerful custom of standing whenever a security official of the government was in the room.

He smiled pleasantly, waved at them and scratched his nose with a wad of mimeographed papers. His nose was large and it seemed to give added presence to his person. "Sit down, ladies and gentlemen, do sit down. We have no official fol-de-rol in the Brooklyn Project. I am your guide, as you might say, for the duration of this experiment: the acting secretary to the executive assistant on press relations. My name is not important. Please pass these among you."

They each took one of the mimeographed sheets and passed the rest on. Leaning back in the metal bucket-seats, they tried to make themselves comfortable. Their host squinted through the heavy screen and up at the wall clock which had one slowly revolving hand. He patted his black garment jovially where it was tight around the middle.

"To business. In a few moments, man's first large-scale

excursion into time will begin. Not by humans, but with the aid of a photographic and recording device which will bring us incalculably rich data on the past. With this experiment, the Brooklyn Project justifies ten billion dollars and over eight years of scientific development; it shows the validity not merely of a new method of investigation, but of a weapon which will make our glorious country even more secure, a weapon which our enemies may justifiably dread.

"Let me caution you, first, not to attempt the taking of notes even if you have been able to smuggle pens and pencils through Security. Your stories will be written entirely from memory. You all have a copy of the Security Code with the latest additions as well as a pamphlet referring specifically to Brooklyn Project regulations. The sheets you have just received provide you with the required lead for your story; they also contain suggestions as to treatment and coloring. Beyond that—so long as you stay within the framework of the documents mentioned— you are entirely free to write your stories in your own variously original ways. The press, ladies and gentlemen, must remain untouched and uncontaminated by government control. Now, any questions?"

The twelve reporters looked at the floor. Five of them began reading from their sheets. The paper rustled noisily.

"What, no questions? Surely there must be more interest than this in a project which has broken the last possible frontier—the fourth dimension, Time. Come now, you are the representatives of the nation's curiosity—you must have questions. Bradley, you look doubtful. What's bothering you? I assure you, Bradley, that I don't bite."

They all laughed and grinned at each other.

Bradley half-rose and pointed at the screen. "Why does it have to be so thick? I'm not the slightest bit interested in finding out how chronar works, but all we can see from here is a greyed and blurry picture of men dragging apparatus around on the floor. And why does the clock only have one hand?"

"A good question," the acting secretary said. His large nose seemed to glow. "A very good question. First, the clock has but one hand, because, after all, Bradley, this is an experiment in Time, and Security feels that the time of the experiment itself may, through some unfortunate combination of information leakage and foreign correlation—in short, a clue might be needlessly exposed. It is sufficient to know that when the hand points to the red dot, the experiment will begin. The screen is translucent and the scene below somewhat blurry for the same reason: camouflage of detail and adjustment. I *am* empowered to inform you that the *details* of the apparatus are—uh, very significant. Any other questions? Culpepper? Culpepper of Consolidated, isn't it?''

"Yes, sir. Consolidated News Service. Our readers are very curious about that incident of the Federation of Chronar Scientists. Of course, they have no respect or pity for them—the way they acted and all—but just what did they mean by saying that this experiment was dangerous because of insufficient data? And that fellow, Dr. Shayson, their president, do you know if he'll be shot?''

The man in black pulled at his nose and paraded before them thoughtfully. "I must confess that I find the views of the Federation of Chronar Scientists—or the federation of *chronic sighers,* as we at Pike's Peak prefer to call them—are a trifle too exotic for my tastes; I rarely bother with weighing the opinions of a traitor in any case. Shayson himself may or may not have incurred the death penalty for revealing the nature of the work with which he was entrusted. On the other hand, he—uh, *may not* or *may* have. That is all I can say about him for reasons of security.''

Reasons of security. At mention of the dread phrase, every reporter had straightened against the hard back of his chair. Culpepper's face had lost its pinkness in favor of a glossy white. They can't consider the part about Shayson a leading question, he thought desperately. But I shouldn't have cracked about that damned federation!

Culpepper lowered his eyes and tried to looked as ashamed of the vicious idiots as he possibly could. He hoped the acting secretary to the executive assistant on press relations would notice his horror.

The clock began ticking very loudly. Its hand was now only one-fourth of an arc from the red dot at the top. Down on the floor of the immense laboratory, activity had stopped. All of the seemingly tiny men were clustered around two great spheres of shining metal resting against each other. Most of them were watching dials and switchboards intently; a few, their tasks completed, chatted with the circle of black-jumpered Security guards.

"We are almost ready to begin Operation Periscope. Operation Periscope, of course, because we are, in a sense, extending a periscope into the past—a periscope which will take pictures and record events of various periods ranging from fifteen thousand years to four billion years ago. We felt that in view of the various critical circumstances attending this experiment—international, scientific—a more fitting title would be Operation Crossroads. Unfortunately, that title has been—uh, preempted.''

Everyone tried to look as innocent of the nature of that other experiment as years of staring at locked library shelves would permit.

''No matter. I will now give you a brief background in chronar practice as cleared by Brooklyn Project Security. Yes, Bradley?''

Bradley again got partly out of his seat. ''I was wondering—we know there has been a Manhattan Project, a Long Island Project, a Westchester Project and now a Brooklyn Project. Has there ever been a Bronx Project? I come from the Bronx; you know, civic pride.''

''Quite. Very understandable. However, if there is a Bronx Project you may be assured that until its work has been successfully completed, the only individuals outside of it who will know of its existence are the President and the Secretary of Security. If—*if*, I say—there is such an institution, the world will learn of it with the same shattering suddenness that it learned of the Westchester Project. I don't think that the world will soon forget *that*.''

He chuckled in recollection and Culpepper echoed him a bit louder than the rest. The clock's hand was close to the red mark.

''Yes, the Westchester Project and now this; our nation shall yet be secure! Do you realize what a magnificent weapon chronar places in our democratic hands? To examine only one aspect— consider what happened to the Coney Island and Flatbush Subprojects (the events are mentioned in those sheets you've received) before the uses of chronar were fully appreciated.

''It was not yet known in those first experiments that Newton's third law of motion—action equalling reaction—held for time as well as it did for the other three dimensions of space. When the first chronar was excited backwards into time for the length of a ninth of a second, the entire laboratory was propelled into the future for a like period and returned in an—uh, unrecognizable condition. That fact, by the by, has prevented excursions into the future: the equipment seems to suffer amazing alterations and no human could survive them. But do you realize what we could do to an enemy by virtue of that property alone? Sending an adequate mass of chronar into the past while it is adjacent to a hostile nation would force that nation into the future—all of it simultaneously—a future from which it would return populated only with corpses!''

He glanced down, placed his hands behind his back and teetered on his heels. ''That is why you see two spheres on the floor. Only one of them, the ball on the right, is equipped with chronar. The other is a dummy, matching the other's mass perfectly and serving as a counterbalance. When the chronar is excited, it will plunge four billion years into our past and take photographs of an earth that was still a half-liquid, partly gaseous mass solidifying rapidly in a somewhat inchoate solar system.

''At the same time, the dummy will be propelled four billion years into the future, from whence it will return much changed but for reasons we don't completely understand. They will strike each other at what is to us *now* and bounce off again to approximately half the chronological distance of the first trip, where our chronar apparatus will record data of an almost solid planet, plagued by earthquakes and possibly holding forms of sub-life in the manner of certain complex molecules.

''After each collision, the chronar will return roughly half the number of years covered before, automatically gathering information each time. The geological and historical periods we expect it to touch are listed from I to XXV in your sheets; there will be more than twenty-five, naturally, before both balls come to rest, but scientists feel that all periods after that number will be touched for such a short while as to be unproductive of photographs and other material. Remember, at the end, the balls will be doing little more than throbbing in place before coming to rest, so that even though they still ricochet centuries on either side of the present, it will be almost unnoticeable. A question, I see.''

The thin woman in gray tweeds beside Culpepper got to her feet. ''I—I know this is irrelevant,'' she began, ''but I haven't been able to introduce my question into the discussion at any pertinent moment. Mr. Secretary—''

''Acting secretary,'' the chubby little man in the black suit told her genially. ''I'm only the acting secretary. Go on.''

''Well, I want to say—Mr. Secretary, is there any way at all that our post-experimental examination time may be reduced? Two years is a very long time to spend inside Pike's Peak simply out of fear that one of us may have seen enough and be unpatriotic enough to be dangerous to the nation. Once our stories have passed the censors, it seems to me that we could be allowed to return to our homes after a safety period of say, three months. I have two small children and there are others here—''

''Speak for yourself, Mrs. Bryant!'' the man from Security roared. ''It *is* Mrs. Bryant, isn't it? Mrs. Bryant of the Women's Magazine Syndicate? Mrs. *Alexis* Bryant.'' He seemed to be making minute pencil notes across his brain.

Mrs. Bryant sat down beside Culpepper again, clutching her copy of the amended Security Code, the special pamphlet on the Brooklyn Project and the thin mimeographed sheet of paper very close to her breast. Culpepper moved hard against the opposite arm of his chair. Why did everything have to happen to him? Then, to make matters worse, the crazy woman looked tearfully at him as if expecting sympathy. Culpepper stared across the booth and crossed his legs.

''You must remain within the jurisdiction of the Brooklyn Project because that is the only way that Security can be *certain* that no important information leakage will occur before the apparatus has changed beyond your present recognition of it. You didn't have to come, Mrs. Bryant—you volunteered. You all volunteered. After your editors had designated you as their choices for covering this experiment, you all had the peculiarly democratic privilege of refusing. None of you did. You recognized that to refuse this unusual honor would have shown you incapable of thinking in terms of National Security, would have, in fact, implied a criticism of the Security Code itself from the standpoint of the usual two-year examination time. And now this! For someone who had hitherto been thought as able and trustworthy as yourself, Mrs. Bryant, to emerge at this late hour with such a request makes me, why it,'' the little man's voice dropped to a whisper, ''—it almost makes me doubt the effectiveness of our security screening methods.''

Culpepper nodded angry affirmation at Mrs. Bryant who was bitting her lips and trying to show a tremendous interest in the activities on the laboratory floor.

''The question *was* irrelevant. Highly irrelevant. It took up time which I had intended to devote to a more detailed discussion of the popular aspects of chronar and its possible uses in industry. But Mrs. Bryant must have her little feminine outburst: it makes no difference to Mrs. Bryant that our nation is daily surrounded by more and more hostility, more and more danger. These things matter not in the slightest to Mrs. Bryant. All she is concerned with are the two years of her life that her country asks her to surrender so that the future of her own children may be more secure.''

The acting secretary smoothed his black jumper and became calmer. Tension in the booth decreased.

''Activation will occur at any moment now, so I will briefly touch upon those most interesting periods which the chronar will record for us and from which we expect the most useful data. I and II, of course, since they are the periods at which the earth was forming into its present shape. Then III, the Pre-Cambrian Period of the Proterozoic, one billion years ago, the first era in which we find distinct records of life—crustaceans and algae for the most part. VI, a hundred twenty-five million years in the past, covers the Middle Jurassic of the Mesozoic. This excursion into the so-called ''Age of Reptiles'' may provide us with photographs of dinosaurs and solve the old riddle of their coloring, as well as photographs, if we are fortunate, of the first appearance of mammals and birds. Finally, VIII and IX, the Oligocene and Miocene Epochs of the Tertiary Period, mark the emergence of man's earliest ancestors. Unfortunately, the chronar will be oscillating back and forth so rapidly by that time that the chance of any decent recording—''

A gong sounded. The hand of the clock touched the red mark. Five of the technicians below pulled switches and, almost before the journalists could lean forward, the two spheres were no longer visible through the heavy plastic screen. Their places were empty.

''The chronar has begun its journey to four billion years in the past! Ladies and gentlemen, an historic moment—a profoundly historic moment! It will not return for a little while; I shall use the time in pointing up and exposing the fallacies of the—ah, *federation of chronic sighers!*''

Nervous laughter rippled at the acting secretary to the executive assistant on press relations. The twelve journalists settled down to hearing the ridiculous ideas torn apart.

''As you know, one of the fears entertained about travel to the past was that the most innocent-seeming acts would cause cataclysmic changes in the present. You are probably familiar with the fantasy in its most currently popular form; if Hitler had been killed in 1930, he would not have forced scientists in Germany and later occupied countries to emigrate, this nation might not have had the atomic bomb, thus no third atomic war, and Australia would still be above the Pacific.

''The traitorous Shayson and his illegal federation extended this hypothesis to include much more detailed and minor acts such as shifting a molecule of hydrogen that in our past really was never shifted.

"At the time of the first experiment at the Coney Island Sub-project, when the chronar was sent back for one-ninth of a second, a dozen different laboratories checked through every device imaginable, searched carefully for any conceivable change. There were none! Government officials concluded that the time stream was a rigid affair, past, present and future, and nothing in it could be altered. But Shayson and his cohorts were not satisfied, they—"

> *I. Four billion years ago. The chronar floated in a cloud-let of silicon dioxide above the boiling earth and languidly collected its data with automatically operating instruments. The vapor it had displaced condensed and fell in great, shining drops.*

"—insisted that we should do no further experimenting until we had checked the mathematical aspects of the problem yet again. They went so far as to state that it was possible that if changes occurred we would not notice them, that no instruments imaginable could detect them. They said that we would accept these changes as things that had always existed. Well! This at a time when our country—and theirs, ladies and gentlemen of the press, *theirs*, too—was in greater danger than ever. Can you—"

Words failed him. He walked up and down the booth, shaking his head. All the reporters on the long, wooden bench shook their heads with him in sympathy.

There was another gong. The two dull spheres appeared briefly, clanged against each other and ricocheted off into opposite chrono-logical directions.

"There you are." The government official waved his arms at the transparent laboratory floor above them. "The first oscilla-tion has been completed; has anything changed? Isn't everything the same? But the dissidents would maintain that alterations have occurred and we haven't noticed them. With such faith-based, unscientific viewpoints, there can be no argument. People like these—"

> *II. Two billion years ago. The great ball clicked its photo-graphs of the fiery, erupting ground below. Some red-hot crusts rattled off its sides. Five or six thousand complex molecules lost their basic structure as they impinged against it. A hundred didn't.*

"—will labor thirty hours a day out of thirty-three to convince you that black isn't white, that we have seven moons instead of two. They are especially dangerous—"

A long, muted note as the apparatus collided with itself. The warm orange of the corner lights brightened as it started out again.

"—because of their learning, because they are looked to for guidance in better ways of vegetation." The government official was slithering up and down rapidly now, gesturing with all of his pseudopods. "We are faced with a very difficult problem, at present—"

III. One billion years ago. The primitive triple trilobite the machine had destroyed when it materialized began drifting down wetly.

"—a *very* difficult problem. The question before us: should we *shllk* or shouldn't we *shllk?*" He was hardly speaking English now; in fact, for some time, he hadn't been speaking at all. He had been stating his thoughts by slapping one pseudopod against the other—as he always had. . . .

IV. A half-billion years ago. Many different kinds of bacteria died as the water changed temperature slightly.

"This, then, is no time for half-measures. If we can reproduce well enough—"

V. Two hundred fifty million years ago. VI. One hundred twenty-five million years ago.

"to satisfy the Five Who Spiral, we have—"

VII. Sixty-two million years. VIII. Thirty-one million. IX. Fifteen million. X. Seven and a half million.

"—spared all attainable virtue. Then—"

XI. XII. XIII. XIV. XV. XVI. XVII. XVIII. XIX. Bong—bong—bong bongbongbongongongngngng . . .

"—we are indeed ready for refraction. And that, I tell you is good enough for those who billow and those who snap. But those who billow will be proven wrong as always, for in the snapping is the rolling and in the rolling is only truth. There need be no change merely because of sodden cilia. The apparatus has rested at last in the fractional conveyance; shall we view it subtly?"

They all agreed, and their bloated purpled bodies dissolved into liquid and flowed up and around to the apparatus. When they reached its four square blocks, now no longer shrilling mechanically, they rose, solidified and regained their slime-washed forms.

"See," cried the thing that had been the acting secretary to the executive assistant on press relations. "See, no matter how subtly! Those who billow were wrong: we haven't changed." He extended fifteen purple blobs triumphantly. "Nothing has changed!"

RING AROUND THE REDHEAD

by John D. MacDonald (1916—   )

STARTLING STORIES

November

*John D. MacDonald is the best-selling mystery and suspense writer whose novels starring Travis McGee are read all over the world. He began his writing career after service in World War II with a veritable flood of stories in almost all the pulp magazines still in existence, and he wrote in all genres: mystery, sports, fantasy, Western, and science fiction. His total output in sf was only some fifty stories and three novels—*Wine of the Dreamers *(1951),* Ballroom of the Skies *(1952), and* The Girl, The Gold Watch, and Everything *(1962). The best of his science fiction short stories can be found in* Other Times, Other Days *(1978). His success in other fields deprived sf of a great talent, as the two selections in this book demonstrate.*

(When things are new in science, they are grist for the science fiction writer's mill; they could be given all kinds of magical powers. I remember when heavy water was made magical in science fiction; and before my time, radium was.

In the first few years after Hiroshima, nuclear explosions could be held accountable for anything. They made it possible to reach into other dimensions or to travel in time. My first book, Pebble in the Sky, *began with precisely such a device, intended to get the plot going. Of course, although it was published in 1950, the first version of* Pebble *was written in 1947.*

"Ring Around the Redhead" also starts with the mysterious effect of a nuclear explosion—but you're allowed one assumption in a science fiction story. After that, the story moves along with inevitability.—I. A.)

The prosecuting attorney was a lean specimen named Amery Heater. The buildup given the murder trial by the newspapers had resulted in a welter of open-mouthed citizens who jammed the golden oak courtroom.

Bill Maloney, the defendant, was sleepy and bored. He knew he had no business being bored. Not with twelve righteous citizens who, under the spell of Amery Heater's quiet, confidential oratory were beginning to look at Maloney as though he were a fiend among fiends.

The August heat was intense and flies buzzed around the upper sashes of the dusty windows. The city sounds drifted in the open windows, making it necessary for Amery Heater to raise his voice now and again.

But though Bill Maloney was bored, he was also restless and worried. Mostly he was worried about Justin Marks, his own lawyer.

Marks cared but little for this case. But, being Bill Maloney's best friend, he couldn't very well refuse to handle it. Justin Marks was a proper young man with a Dewey mustache and frequent daydreams about Justice Marks of the Supreme Court. He somehow didn't feel that the Maloney case was going to help him very much.

Particularly with the very able Amery Heater intent on getting the death penalty.

The judge was a puffy old citizen with signs of many good years at the brandy bottle, the hundreds of gallons of which surprisingly had done nothing to dim the keenness of eye or brain.

Bill Maloney was a muscular young man with a round face, a

round chin and a look of sleepy skepticism. A sheaf of his coarse, corn-colored hair jutted out over his forehead. His eyes were clear, deep blue.

He stifled a yawn, remembering what Justin Marks had told him about making a good impression on the jury. He singled out a plump lady juror in the front row and winked solemnly at her. She lifted her chin with an audible sniff.

No dice there. Might as well listen to Amery Heater.

"... and we, the prosecution, intend to prove that on the evening of July tenth, William Howard Maloney did murderously attack his neighbor, James Finch and did kill James Finch by crushing his skull. We intend to prove there was a serious dispute between these men, a dispute that had continued for some time. We further intend to prove that the cause of this dispute was the dissolute life being led by the defendant."

Amery Heater droned on and on. The room was too hot. Bill Maloney slouched in his chair and yawned. He jumped when Justin Marks hissed at him. Then he remembered that he had yawned and he smiled placatingly at the jury. Several of them looked away, hurriedly.

Fat little Doctor Koobie took the stand. He was sworn in and Amery Heater, polite and respectful, asked questions which established Koobie's name, profession and presence at the scene of the "murder" some fifty minutes after it had taken place.

"And now, Dr. Koobie, would you please describe in your own words exactly what you found."

Koobie hitched himself in his chair, pulled his trousers up a little over his chubby knees and said, "No need to make this technical. I was standing out by the hedge between the two houses. I was on Jim Finch's side of the hedge. There was a big smear of blood around. Some of it was spattered on the hedge. Barberry, I think. On the ground there was some hunks of brain tissue, none of them bigger than a dime. Also a piece of scalp maybe two inches square. Had Jim's hair on it all right. Proved that in the lab. Also found some pieces of bone. Not many." He smiled peacefully. "Guess old Jim is dead all right. No question of that. Blood was his and the hair was his."

Three jurors swallowed visibly and a fourth began to fan himself vigorously.

Koobie answered a few other questions and then Justin Marks took over the cross-examination.

"What would you say killed Jim Finch?"

Many people gasped at the question, having assumed that the defense would be that, lacking a body, there was no murder.

Koobie put a fat finger in the corner of his mouth, took it out again. "Couldn't rightly say."

"Could a blow from a club or similar weapon have done it?"

"Good Lord, no! Man's head is a pretty durable thing. You'd have to back him up against a solid concrete wall and bust him with a full swing with a baseball bat and you still wouldn't do that much hurt. Jim was standing right out in the open."

"Dr. Koobie, imagine a pair of pliers ten feet long and proportionately thick. If a pair of pliers like that were to have grabbed Mr. Finch by the head, smashing it like a nut in a nutcracker, could it have done that much damage?"

Koobie pulled his nose, tugged on his ear, frowned, and said, "Why, if it clamped down real sudden like, I imagine it could. But where'd Jim go?"

"That's all, thank you," Justin Marks said.

Amery Heater called other witnesses. One of them was Anita Hempflet.

Amery said, "You live across the road from the defendant?"

Miss Anita Hempflet was fiftyish, big-boned, and of the same general consistency as the dried beef recommended for Canadian canoe trips. Her voice sounded like fingernails on the third grade blackboard.

"Yes I do. I've lived there thirty-five years. That Maloney person, him sitting right over there, moved in two years ago, and I must say that I . . ."

"You are able to see Mr. Maloney's house from your windows?"

"Certainly!"

"Now tell the court when it was that you first saw the red-headed woman."

She licked her lips. "I first saw that . . . that woman in May. A right pleasant morning it was, too. Or it was until I saw her. About ten o'clock, I'd say. She was right there in Maloney's front yard, as bold as brass. Had on some sort of shiny silver thing. You couldn't call it a dress. Too short for that. Didn't half cover her the way a lady ought to be covered. Not by half. She was . . ."

"What was she doing?"

"Well, she come out of the house and she stopped and looked around as though she was surprised at where she was. My eyes are good. I could see her face. She looked all around. Then she sort of slouched, like she was going to keel over or something. She walked real slow down toward the gate. Mr. Maloney came running out of the house and I heard him yell to her. She stopped. Then he was making signs to her, for her to go back into the house. Just like she was deaf or something. After a while she went back in. I guessed she probably was made deaf by that awful bomb thing the government lost control of near town three days before that.''

"You didn't see her again?"

"Oh, I saw her plenty of times. But after that she was always dressed more like a girl should be dressed. Far as I could figure out, Mr. Maloney was buying her clothes in town. It wasn't right that anything like that should be going on in a nice neighborhood. Mr. Finch didn't think it was right either. Runs down property values, you know.''

"In your knowledge, Miss Hempflet, did Mr. Maloney and the deceased ever quarrel?"

"They started quarreling a few days after that woman showed up. Yelling at each other across the hedge. Mr. Finch was always scared of burglars. He had that house fixed up so nobody could get in if he didn't want them in. A couple of times I saw Bill Maloney pounding on his door and rapping on the windows. Jim wouldn't pay any attention.''

Justin cross-examined.

"You say, Miss Hempflet, that the defendant was going down and shopping for this woman, buying her clothes. In your knowledge, did he buy her anything else?"

Anita Hempflet sniggered. "Say so! Guess she must of been feeble minded. I asked around and found out he bought a blackboard and chalk and some kids' books.''

"Did you make any attempt to find out where this woman came from, this woman who was staying with Mr. Maloney?"

"Should say I did! I know for sure that she didn't come in on the train or Dave Wattle would've seen her. If she'd come by bus, Myrtle Gisco would have known it. Johnny Farness didn't drive her in from the airport. I figure that any woman who'd live openly with a man like Maloney must have hitchhiked into town. She didn't come any other way.''

"That's all, thank you," Justin Marks said.

Maloney sighed. He couldn't understand why Justin was looking so worried. Everything was going fine. According to plan. He saw the black looks the jury was giving him, but he wasn't worried. Why, as soon as they found out what had actually happened, they'd be all for him. Justin Marks seemed to be sweating.

He came back to the table and whispered to Bill, "How about temporary insanity?"

"I guess it's okay if you like that sort of thing."

"No. I mean as a plea!"

Maloney stared at him. "Justy, old boy. Are you nuts? All we have to do is tell the truth."

Justin Marks rubbed his mustache with his knuckle and made a small bleating sound that acquired him a black look from the judge.

Amery Heater built his case up very cleverly and very thoroughly. In fact, the jury had Bill Maloney so definitely electrocuted that they were beginning to give him sad looks—full of pity.

It took Amery Heater two days to complete his case. When it was done, it was a solid and shining structure, every discrepancy explained—everything pinned down. Motive. Opportunity. Everything.

On the morning of the third day, the court was tense with expectancy. The defense was about to present its case. No one knew what the case was, except, of course, Bill Maloney, Justin Marks, and the unworldly redhead who called herself Rejapachalandakeena. Bill called her Keena. She hadn't appeared in court.

Justin Marks stood up and said to the hushed court, "Your Honor. Rather than summarize my defense at this point, I would like to put William Maloney on the stand first and let him tell the story in his own words."

The court buzzed. Putting Maloney on the stand would give Amery Heater a chance to cross-examine. Heater would rip Maloney to tiny shreds. The audience licked its collective chops.

"Your name?"

"William Maloney, 12 Braydon Road."

"And your occupation?"

"Tinkering. Research, if you want a fancy name."

"Where do you get your income?"

"I've got a few gimmicks patented. The royalties come in."

"Please tell the court all you know about this crime of which you are accused. Start at the beginning, please."

Bill Maloney shoved the blond hair back off his forehead with a square, mechanic's hand and smiled cheerfully at the jury. Some of them, before they realized it, had smiled back. They felt the smiles on their lips and sobered instantly. It wasn't good form to smile at a vicious murderer.

Bill slouched in the witness chair and laced his fingers across his stomach.

"It all started," he said, "the day the army let that rocket get out of hand on the seventh of May. I've got my shop in my cellar. Spend most of my time down there.

"That rocket had an atomic warhead, you know. I guess they've busted fifteen generals over that affair so far. It exploded in the hills forty miles from town. The jar upset some of my apparatus and stuff. Put it out of kilter. I was sore.

"I turned around, cussing away to myself, and where my coal bin used to be, there was a room. The arch leading into the room was wide and I could see in. I tell you, it really shook me up to see that room there. I wondered for a minute if the bomb hadn't given me delusions.

"The room I saw didn't have any furniture in it. Not like furniture we know. It had some big cubes of dull silvery metal, and some smaller cubes. I couldn't figure out the lighting.

"Being a curious cuss, I walked right through the arch and looked around. I'm a great one to handle things. The only thing in the room I could pick up was a gadget on top of the biggest cube. It hardly weighed a thing.

"In order to picture it, you've got to imagine a child's hoop made of silvery wire. Then right across the wire imagine the blackest night you've ever seen, rolled out into a thin sheet and stretched tight like a drumhead on that wire hoop.

"As I was looking at it I heard some sort of deep vibration and there I was, stumbling around in my coal bin. The room was gone. But I had that darn hoop in my hand. That hoop with the midnight stretched across it.

"I took it back across to my workbench where the light was better. I held it in one hand and poked a finger at that black stuff. My finger went right through. I didn't feel a thing. With my finger still sticking through it, I looked on the other side.

"It was right there that I named the darn thing. I said, 'Gawk!' And that's what I've called it ever since. The Gawk. My finger didn't come through on the other side. I stuck my whole arm through. No arm. I pulled it back out. Quick. Arm was okay. Somehow it seemed warm on the other side of the gawk.

"Well, you can imagine what it was like for me, a tinkerer, to get my hands on a thing like that. I forgot all about meals and so on. I had to find out what it was and why. I couldn't see my own hand on the other side of it. I put it right up in front of my face, reached through from the back and tried to touch my nose. I couldn't do it. I reached so deep that without the gawk there, my arm would have been halfway through my head . . ."

"Objection!" Amery Heater said. "All this has nothing to do with the fact . . ."

"My client," Justin said, "is giving the incidents leading up to the alleged murder."

"Overruled," the judge said.

Maloney said, "Thanks. I decided that my arm had to be someplace when I stuffed it through the gawk. And it wasn't in this dimension. Maybe not even in this time. But it had to be someplace. That meant that I had to find out what was on the other side of the gawk. I could use touch, sight. Maybe I could climb through. It intrigued me, you might say.

"I started with touch. I put my hand through, held it in front of me and walked. I walked five feet before my hand rammed up against something. I felt it. It seemed to be a smooth wall. There wasn't such a wall in my cellar.

"There has to be some caution in science. I didn't stuff my head through. I couldn't risk it. I had the hunch there might be something unfriendly on the other side of the gawk. I turned the thing around and stuck my hand through from the other side. No wall. There was a terrible pain. I yanked my hand back. A lot of little bloodvessels near the surface had broken. I dropped the gawk and jumped around for a while. Found out I had a bad case of frostbite. The broken blood vessels indicated that I had stuffed my hand into a vacuum. Frostbite in a fraction of a second indicated nearly absolute zero. It seemed that maybe I had put my hand into space. It made me glad it had been my hand instead of my head.

"I propped the thing up on my bench and shoved lots of things through, holding them a while and bringing them back out. Made a lot of notes on the effect of absolute zero on various materials.

"By that time I was bushed. I went up to bed. Next day I had some coffee and then built myself a little periscope. Shoved it through. Couldn't see a thing. I switched the gawk, tested with a thermometer, put my hand through. Warm enough. But the periscope didn't show me a thing. I wondered if maybe something happened to light rays when they went through that blackness. Turns out that I was right.

"By about noon I had found out another thing about it. Every time I turned it around I was able to reach through into a separate and distinct environment. I tested that with the thermometer. One of the environments I tested slammed the mercury right out through the top of the glass and broke the glass and burned my hand. I was glad I hadn't hit that one the first time. It would have burned my hand off at the wrist.

"I began to keep a journal of each turn of the gawk, and what seemed to be on the other side of it. I rigged up a jig on my workbench and began to grope through the gawk with my fire-place tongs.

"Once I jabbed something that seemed to be soft and alive. Those tongs were snatched right through the gawk. Completely gone. It gave me the shudders, believe me. If it had been my hand instead of the tongs, I wouldn't be here. I have a hunch that whatever snatched those tongs would have been glad to eat me.

"I rigged up some grappling hooks and went to work. Couldn't get anything. I put a lead weight on some cord and lowered it through. Had some grease on the end of the weight. When the cord slacked off, I pulled it back up. There was fine yellow sand on the bottom of the weight. And I had lowered it thirty-eight feet before I hit sand.

"On try number two hundred and eight, I brought an object back through the gawk. Justy has it right there in his bag. Show it to the people, Justy."

Justin looked annoyed at the informal request, but he unstrapped the bag and took out an object. He passed it up to the judge who looked at it with great interest. Then it was passed through the jury. It ended up on the table in front of the bench, tagged as an exhibit.

"You can see, folks, that such an object didn't come out of our civilization."

"Objection!" Heater yelled. "The defendant could have made it."

"Hush up!" the judge said.

"Thanks. As you can see that object is a big crystal. That thing in the crystal is a golden scorpion, about five times life size. The corner is sawed off there because Jim Finch sawed it off. You notice that he sawed off a big enough piece to get a hunk of the scorpion's leg. Jim told me that leg was solid gold. That whole bug is solid gold. I guess it was an ornament in some other civilization.

"Now that gets me around to Jim Finch. As you all know, Jim

retired from the jewelry business about five years ago. Jim was a pretty sharp trader. You know how he parlayed his savings across the board so that he owned a little hunk of just about everything in town. He was always after me to let him in on my next gimmick. I guess those royalty checks made his mouth water. We weren't what you'd call friends. I passed the time of day with him, but he wasn't a friendly man.

"Anyway, when I grabbed this bug out of the gawk, I thought of Jim Finch. I wanted to know if such a thing could be made by a jeweler. Jim was home and his eyes popped when he saw it. You know how he kept that little shop in his garage and made presents for people? Well, he cut off a section with a saw. Then he said that he'd never seen anything like it and he didn't know how on earth it was put together. I told him that it probably wasn't put together on earth. That teased him a little and he kept after me until I told him the whole story. He didn't believe it. That made me mad. I took him over into my cellar and showed him a few things. I set the gawk between two boxes so it was parallel to the floor, then dropped my grapples down into it. In about three minutes I caught something and brought it up. It seemed to be squirming."

Maloney drew a deep breath.

"That made me a shade cautious. I brought it up slow. The head of the thing came out. It was like a small bear—but more like a bear that had been made into a rug. Flat like a leech, and instead of front legs it just seemed to have a million little sucker disks around the flat edge. It screamed so hard, with such a high note, that it hurt my ears. I dropped it back through.

"When I looked around, old Jim was backed up against the cellar wall, mumbling. Then he got down on his hands and knees and patted the floor under the gawk. He kept right on mumbling. Pretty soon he asked me how that bear-leech and that golden bug could be in the same place. I explained how I had switched the gawk. We played around for a while and then came up with a bunch of stones. Jim handled them, and his eyes started to pop out again. He began to shake. He told me that one of the stones was an uncut ruby. You couldn't prove it by me. It would've made you sick to see the way old Jim started to drool. He talked so fast I could hardly understand him. Finally I got the drift. He wanted us to go in business and rig up some big machinery so we could dig through the gawk and come back with all kinds of things. He wanted bushels of rubies and a few tons of gold.

"I told him I wasn't interested. He got so mad he jumped up and down. I told him I was going to fool around with the thing for a while and then I was going to turn it over to some scientific foundation so the boys could go at it in the right way.

"He looked mad enough to kill me. He told me we could have castles and cars and yachts and a million bucks each. I told him that the money was coming in faster than I could spend it already and all I wanted was to stay in my cellar and tinker.

"I told him that I guessed the atomic explosion had dislocated something, and the end product belonged to science. I also told him very politely to get the devil home and stop bothering me.

"He did, but he sure hated to leave. Well, by the morning of the tenth, I had pretty well worn myself out. I was bushed and jittery from no sleep. I had made twenty spins in a row without getting anything, and I had begun to think I had run out of new worlds on the other side of the gawk.

"Like a darn fool, I yanked it off the jig, took it like a hoop and scaled it across the cellar. It went high, then dropped lightly, spinning.

"And right there in my cellar was this beautiful redhead. She was dressed in a shiny silver thing. Justy's got that silver thing in his bag. Show it to the people. You can see that it's made out of some sort of metal mesh, but it isn't cold like metal would be. It seems to hold heat and radiate it."

The metal garment was duly passed around. Everybody felt of it, exclaimed over it. This was better than a movie. Maloney could see from Amery Heater's face that the man wanted to claim the metal garment was also made in the Maloney cellar.

Bill winked at him. Amery Heater flushed a dull red.

"Well, she stood there, right in the middle of the gawk which was flat against the floor. She had a dazed look on her face. I asked her where she had come from. She gave me a blank look and a stream of her own language. She seemed mad about something. And pretty upset.

"Now what I should have done was pick up that gawk and lift it back up over her head. That would have put her back in her own world. But she stepped out of it, and like a darn fool, I stood and held it and spun it, nervous like. In spinning it, I spun her own world off into some mathematical equation I couldn't figure.

"It was by the worst or the best kind of luck, depending on how you look at it, that I made a ringer on her when I tossed the gawk across the cellar. Her makeup startled me a little. No lipstick. Tiny crimson beads on the end of each eyelash. Tiny emerald green triangles painted on each tooth in some sort of enamel. Nicely centered. Her hairdo wasn't any wackier than some you see every day.

"Well, she saw the gawk in my hands and she wasn't dumb at all. She came at me, her lips trembling, her eyes pleading, and tried to step into it. I shook my head, hard, and pushed her back and set it back in the jig. I shoved a steel rod through, holding it in asbestos mittens. The heat beyond the blackness turned the whole rod cherry red in seconds. I shoved it on through the rest of the way, then showed her the darkened mitten. She was quick. She got the most horrified look on her face.

"Then she ran upstairs, thinking it was some sort of joke, I guess. I noticed that she slammed right into the door, as though she expected it to open for her. By the time I got to her, she had figured out the knob. She went down the walk toward the gate.

"That's when nosy Anita must have seen her. I shouted and she turned around and the tears were running right down her face. I made soothing noises and she let me lead her back into the house. I've never seen a prettier girl or one stacked any . . . I mean her skin is translucent, sort of. Her eyes are enormous. And her hair is a shade of red that you never see.

"She had no place to go and she was my responsibility. I certainly didn't feel like turning her over to the welfare people. I fixed her up a place to sleep in my spare room and I had to show her everything. How to turn on a faucet. How to turn the lights off and on.

"She didn't do anything except cry for four days. I gave her food that she didn't eat. She was a mess. Worried me sick. I didn't have any idea how to find her world again. No idea at all. Of course, I could have popped her into any old world, but it didn't seem right.

"On the fourth day I came up out of the cellar and found her sitting in a chair looking at a copy of See Magazine. She seemed very much interested in the pictures of the women. She looked up at me and smiled. That was the day I went into town and came back with a mess of clothes for her. I had to show her how a zipper worked, and how to button a button."

He looked as if that might have been fun.

"After she got all dressed up, she smiled some more and that evening she ate well. I kept pointing to things and saying the right name for them.

"I tell you, once she heard the name for something, she didn't forget it. It stayed right with her. Nouns were easy. The other words were tough. About ten that night I finally caught her name. It was Rejapachalandakeena. She seemed to like to have me call her Keena. The first sentence she said was, 'Where is Keena?'

"That is one tough question. Where is here and now? Where is this world, anyway? On what side of what dimension? In which end of space? On what twisted convolution of the time stream? What good is it to say 'This is the world'? It just happens to be our world. Now I know that there are plenty of others.

"Writing came tougher for her than the sounds of the words. She showed me her writing. She took a piece of paper, held the pencil pointing straight up and put the paper on top of the rug. Then she worked that pencil like a pneumatic hammer, starting at the top right corner and going down the page. I couldn't figure it until she read it over, and made a correction by sticking in one extra hole in the paper. I saw then that the pattern of holes was very precise—like notes on a sheet of music.

"She went through the grade school readers like a flash. I was buying her some arithmetic books one day, and when I got back she said, 'Man here while Billy gone.' She was calling me Billy. 'Keena hide,' she said.

"Well, the only thing missing was the gawk, and with it, Keena's chance to make a return to her own people. I thought immediately of Jim Finch. I ran over and pounded on his door. He undid the chain so he could talk to me through a five-inch crack, but I couldn't get in. I asked him if he had stolen the little item. He told me that I'd better run to the police and tell them exactly what it was that I had lost, and then I could tell the police exactly how I got it. I could tell by the look of naked triumph in his eyes that he had it. And there wasn't a thing I could do about it.

"Keena's English improved by leaps and bounds and pretty soon she was dipping into my texts on chemistry and physics. She seemed puzzled. She told me that we were like her people a few thousand years back. Primitives. She told me a lot about her world. No cities. The houses are far apart. No work. Everyone is assigned to a certain cultural pursuit, depending on basic ability. She was a designer. In order to train herself, she had had to learn the composition of all fabricated materials used in her world.

"I took notes while she talked. When I get out of this jam,

I'm going to revolutionize the plastics industry. She seemed bright enough to be able to take in the story of how she suddenly appeared in my cellar. I gave it to her slow and easy.

"When I was through, she sat very still for a long time. Then she told me that some of the most brilliant men of her world had long ago found methods of seeing into other worlds beyond their own. They had borrowed things from worlds more advanced than their own, and had thus been able to avoid mistakes in the administration of their own world. She told me that it was impossible that her departure should go unnoticed. She said that probably at the moment of her disappearance, all the resources of a great people were being concentrated on that spot where she had been standing talking to some friends. She told me that some trace of the method would be found and that they would then scan this world, locate her and take her back.

"I asked her if it would be easier if we had the gawk, and she said that it wasn't necessary, and that if it was, she would merely go next door and see Jim Finch face to face. She said she had a way, once she looked into his eyes, of taking over the control of his involuntary muscles and stopping his heartbeat.

"I gasped, and she smiled sweetly and said that she had very nearly done it to me when I had kept her from climbing back through the gawk. She said that everybody in her world knew how to do that. She also said that most adults knew how to create, out of imagination, images that would respond to physical tests. To prove it she stared at the table. In a few seconds a little black box slowly appeared out of misty nothingness. She told me to look at it. I picked it up. It was latched. I opened it. Her picture smiled out at me. She was standing before the entrance of a white castle that seemed to reach to the clouds.

"Suddenly it was gone. She explained that when she stopped thinking of it, it naturally disappeared, because that was what had caused it. Her thinking. I asked her why she didn't think up a doorway to her own world and then step through it while she was still thinking about it. She said that she could only think up things by starting with their basic physical properties and working up from there, like a potter starts with clay.

"So I stopped heckling Jim Finch at about that time. I was sorry, because I wanted the gawk back. Best toy I'd ever had. Once I got a look in Jim's garage window. He'd forgot to pull the shade down all the way. He had the gawk rigged up on a stand, and had a big arm, like the bucket on a steam shovel rigged up, only just big enough to fit through the hoop. He wasn't working it when I saw him. He was digging up the concrete in the corner of his cellar. He was using a pick and he had a shovel handy. He was pale as death. I saw then that he had a human arm in there on the floor and blood all over. The bucket was rigged with jagged teeth. It didn't take much imagination to figure out what Jim had done.

"Some poor innocent character in one of those other worlds had had a massive contraption come out of nowhere and chaw his arm off. I thought of going to the police, and then I thought of how easy it would be for Jim Finch to get me stuck away in a padded cell, while he stayed on the outside, all set to pull more arms off more people."

Heater glanced uneasily at the jury. They were drinking it in.

"I told Keena about it and she smiled. She told me that Jim was digging into many worlds and that some of them were pretty advanced. I gradually got the idea that old Jim was engaging in as healthy an occupation as a small boy climbing between the bars and tickling the tigers. I began to worry about old Jim a little. You all know about that couple of bushels of precious stones that were found in his house. That's what made him tickle the tigers. But the cops didn't find that arm. I guess that after he got the hole dug, Jim got over his panic and realized that all he had to do was switch the gawk around and toss the arm through. Best place for old razor blades I ever heard of.

"Well, as May turned into June and June went by, Keena got more and more confident of her eventual rescue. As I learned more about her world, I got confident of it too. In a few thousand years we may be as bright as those people. I hope we are. No wars, no disease.

"And the longer she stayed with me, the more upset I got about her leaving me. But it was what she wanted. I guess it's what I'd want, if somebody shoved me back a thousand years B.C. I'd want to get home, but quick.

"On the tenth of July, I got a phone call from Jim Finch. His voice was all quavery like a little old lady. He said, 'Maloney, I want to give that thing back to you. Right away.' Anything Jim Finch gave anybody was a spavined gift horse. I guessed that the gobblies were after him like Keena had hinted.

"So I just laughed at him. Maybe I laughed to cover up the fact that I was a little scared, too. What if some world he messed with dropped a future type atomic bomb back through the gawk into his lap? I told him to burn it up if he was tired of it.

"I didn't know Jim could cuss like that. He said that it wouldn't burn and he couldn't break it or destroy it anyway. He said that he was coming out and throw it across the hedge into my yard right away.

"As I got to my front door, he came running out of his house. He carried the thing like it was going to blow up.

"Just as he got to the hedge, I saw a misty circle in the air over his head. Only it was about ten feet across. A pair of dark blue shiny pliers with jaws as big as the judge's desk there swooped down and caught him by the head. The jaws snapped shut so hard that I could hear sort of a thick, wet, popping sound as all the bones in old Jim's head gave way all at once.

"He dropped the gawk and hung limp in those closed jaws for a moment, then he was yanked up through that misty circle into nothingness. Gone. Right before my eyes. The misty circle drifted down to grass level, and then faded away. The gawk faded right away with it. You know what it made me think of? Of a picnic where you're trying to eat and a bug gets on your arm and bothers you. You pinch it between your thumb and forefinger, roll it once and throw it away. Old Jim was just about as important to those blue steel jaws as a hungry red ant is to you or me. You could call those gems he got crumbs, I guess.

"I was just getting over being sick in my own front yard when Timmy came running over, took one look at the blood and ran back. The police came next. That's all there is to tell. Keena is still around and Justy will bring her in to testify tomorrow."

Bill Maloney yawned and smiled at the jury.

Amery Heater got up, stuck his thumbs inside his belt and walked slowly and heavily over to Bill.

He stared into Bill's smiling face for ten long seconds. Bill shuffled his feet and began to look uncomfortable.

In a low bitter tone, Amery Heater said, "Gawks! Golden scorpions! Tangential worlds! Blue jaws!" He sighed heavily, pointed to the jury and said, "Those are intelligent people, Maloney. No questions!"

The judge had to pound with his gavel to quiet the court. As soon as the room was quiet, he called an adjournment until ten the following morning.

When Bill Maloney was brought out of his cell into court the next morning, the jurors gave each other wise looks. It was obvious that the young man had spent a bad night. There were puffy areas under his eyes. He scuffed his heels as he walked, sat down heavily and buried his face in his hands. They wondered why his shoulders seemed to shake.

Justin Marks looked just as bad. Or worse.

Bill was sunk in a dull lethargy, in an apathy so deep that he didn't know where he was, and cared less.

Justin Marks stood up and said, "Your Honor, we request an adjournment of the case for twenty-four hours."

"For what reason?"

"Your Honor, I intended to call the woman known as Keena to the stand this morning. She was in a room at the Hotel Hollyfield. Last night she went up to her room at eleven after I talked with her in the lounge. She hasn't been seen since. Her room is empty. All her possessions are there, but she is gone. I would like time to locate her, your Honor."

The judge looked extremely disappointed.

He pursed his lips and said, in a sweet tone, "You are sure that such a woman actually exists, counsellor?"

Justin Marks turned pale and Amery Heater chuckled.

"Of course, your Honor! Why, only last night . . ."

"Her people came and got her," Bill Maloney said heavily. He didn't look up. The jury shifted restlessly. They had expected to be entertained by a gorgeous redhead. Without her testimony, the story related by Maloney seemed even more absurd than it had seemed when they had heard it. Of course, it would be a shame to electrocute a nice clean young man like that, but really you can't have people going about killing their neighbors and then concocting such a fantasy about it . . .

"What's that?" the judge asked suddenly.

It began as a hum, so low as to be more of a vibration than a sound. A throb that seemed to come from the bowels of the earth. Slowly it increased in pitch and in violence, and if the judge had any more to say on the subject, no one heard him. He appeared to be trying to beat the top of his desk in with the gavel. But the noise couldn't be heard.

Slowly climbing up the audible range, it filled the court. As it passed the index of vibration of the windows, they shattered, but the falling glass couldn't be heard. A man who had been wearing glasses stared through empty frames.

The sound passed beyond the upper limits of the human ear, became hypersonic, and every person in the courtroom was suddenly afflicted with a blinding headache.

It stopped as abruptly as a scream in the night.

For a moment there was a misty arch in the solid wall. Beyond it was the startling vagueness of a line of blue hills. Hills that didn't belong there.

She came quickly through the arch. It faded. She was not tall, but gave the impression of tallness. Her hair was the startling red of port wine, her skin so translucent as to seem faintly bluish. Her eyes were halfway between sherry and honey. Tiny crimson beads were on the tip of each eyelash. Her warm full lips were parted, and they could all see the little green enameled triangles on her white teeth. Her single garment was like the silver metallic garment they had touched. But it was golden. Without any apparent means of support, it clung to her lovely body, following each line and curve.

She looked around the court. Maloney's eyes were warm blue fire. "Keena!" he gasped. She ran to him, threw herself on him, her arms around his neck, her face hidden in the line of jaw, throat and shoulder. He murmured things to her that the jury strained to hear.

Amery Heater, feeling his case fade away, was the first to recover.

"Hypnotism!" he roared.

It took the judge a full minute of steady pounding to silence the spectators. "One more disturbance like this, and I'll clear the court," he said.

Maloney had come to life. She sat on his lap and they could hear her say, "What are they trying to do to you?"

He smiled peacefully. "They want to kill me, honey. They say I killed Jim Finch."

She turned and her eyes shriveled the jury and the judge.

"Stupid!" she hissed.

There was a little difficulty swearing her in. Justin Marks, his confidence regained, thoroughly astonished at finding that Bill Maloney had been telling the truth all along, questioned Keena masterfully. She backed up Maloney's story in every particular. Maloney couldn't keep his eyes off her. Her accent was odd, and her voice had a peculiar husky and yet liquid quality.

Justin Marks knuckled his mustache proudly, bowed to Amery Heater and said, "Do you wish to cross-examine?"

Heater nodded, stood up, and walked slowly over. He gave Keena a long and careful look. "Young woman, I congratulate you on your acting ability. Where did you get your training? Surely you've been on the stage."

"Stage?"

"Oh, come now! All this has been very interesting, but now we must discard this dream world and get down to facts. What is your real name?"

"Rejapachalandakeena."

Heater sighed heavily. "I see that you are determined to maintain your silly little fiction. That entrance of yours was somehow engineered by the defendant, I am sure." He turned and smiled at the jury—the smile of a fellow conspirator.

"Miss So-and-so, the defense has all been based on the idea that you come from some other world, or some hidden corner of time, or out of the woodwork. I think that what you had better do is just prove to us that you do come from some other world." His voice dripped with sarcasm. "Just do one or two things for us that we common mortals can't do, please."

Keena frowned, propped her chin on her fist. After a few moments she said, "I do not know completely what you are able to do. Many primitive peoples have learned through a sort of intuition. Am I right in thinking that those people behind that little fence are the ones who decide whether my Billy is to be killed?"

"Correct."

She turned and stared at the jury for a long time. Her eyes passed from face to face, slowly. The jurors were oddly uncomfortable.

She said, "It is very odd. That woman in the second row. The second one from the left. It is odd that she should be there. Not very long ago she gave a poison, some sort of vegetable base poison, to her husband. He was sick for a long time and he died. Is that not against your silly laws?"

The woman in question turned pale green, put her hands to her throat, rolled her eyes up and slid quietly off the chair. No one made a move to help her. All eyes were on Keena.

Some woman back in the courtroom said shrilly, "I knew there was something funny about the way Dave died! I knew it! Arrest Mrs. Watson immediately!"

Keena's eyes turned toward the woman who had spoken. The woman sat down suddenly.

Keena said, "This man you call Dave. His wife killed him because of you. I can read that in your eyes."

Amery Heater chuckled. "A very good trick, but pure imagination. I rather guess you have been prepared for this situation, and my opponent has briefed you on what to do should I call on you in this way."

Keena's eyes flashed. She said, "You are a most offensive person."

She stared steadily at Amery Heater. He began to sweat. Suddenly he screamed and began to dance about. Smoke poured from his pockets. Blistering his fingers, he threw pocketknife, change, moneyclip on the floor. They glowed dull red, and the smell of scorching wood filled the air.

A wisp of smoke rose from his tie clip, and he tore that off, sucking his blistered fingers. The belt buckle was next. By then the silver coins had melted against the wooden floor. But there was one last thing he had to remove. His shoes. The eyelets were metal. They began to burn the leather.

At last, panting and moaning he stood, surrounded by the cherry red pieces of metal on the floor.

Keena smiled and said softly, "Ah, you have no more metal on you. Would you like to have further proof?"

Amery Heater swallowed hard. He looked up at the open-mouthed judge. He glanced at the jury.

"The prosecution withdraws," he said hoarsely.

The judge managed to close his mouth.

"Case dismissed," he said. "Young woman, I suggest you go back wherever you came from."

She smiled blandly up at him. "Oh, no! I can't go back. I went back once and found that my world was very empty. They laughed at my new clothes. I said I wanted Billy. They said they would transport him to my world. But Billy wouldn't be happy there. So I came back."

Maloney stood up, yawned and stretched. He smiled at the jury. Two men were helping the woman back up into her chair. She was still green.

He winked at Keena and said, "Come on home, honey."

They walked down the aisle together and out the golden oak doors. Nobody made a sound, or a move to stop them.

Anita Hempflet, extremely conscious of the fact that the man who had left her waiting at the altar thirty-one years before was buried just beyond the corn hills in her vegetable garden, forced her razor lips into a broad smile, beamed around at the people sitting near her and said, in her high, sharp voice:

"Well! That girl is going to make a lovely neighbor! If you folks will excuse me, I'm going to take her over some fresh strawberry preserves."

PERIOD PIECE

by J. J. "Coupling" (John R. Pierce; 1910—)

ASTOUNDING SCIENCE FICTION

November

Dr. John R. Pierce was one of the most distinguished scientists to publish regularly in the science fiction magazines. Before becoming a Professor of Engineering at the California Institute of Technology, he served as an administrator and researcher with the Bell Telephone Laboratories. He is the author of many notable scientific works, including Theory and Design of Electron Beams. *His crisp short stories appeared mostly in* Astounding, *under his own name and as by "Coupling."*

"Period Piece" is an outstanding cyborg story, and one of the first to focus on the alienation of an individual who is part machine and part something else.

(Consider one clause in the story: "Eddington's idea that the known universe is merely what man is able to perceive and measure." It seems to me [with the clarity of hindsight] that this is an obvious tautology. The known universe is the knowable universe. We know about the universe only what we can know, and anything we can't know is not part of it. So what else is knew?

Are there things about the Universe that we cannot

know in the usual way of observing and measuring, but that we can know in some other way—intuition, revelation, mad insight? If so, how can you know that what you know in these non-knowing ways is really so. Anything you know without knowing, others can know only on your flat statement without any proof other than "I know!"

All this leads to such madness that I, for one, am content with the knowable. That is enough to know. And somehow all this, I think, has something to do with the story—I. A.)

It was at that particular party of Cordoban's that he began actually to have doubts—real doubts. Before, there had been puzzlement and some confusion. But now, among these splendid people, in this finely appointed apartment, he wondered who he was, and where he was.

After his friend—or, his keeper?—Gavin had introduced him to his host, there had been a brief conversation about the twentieth century. Cordoban, a graying man with both dignity and alertness, asked the usual questions, always addressing Smith with the antique title, Mister, which he seemed to relish as an oddity. To Smith it seemed that Cordoban received the answers with the sort of rapt attention a child might give to a clever mechanical toy.

"Tell me, Mr. Smith," Cordoban said, "some of the scientists of your day must have been philosophers as well, were they not?"

Smith could not remember having been asked just this question before. For a moment he could think of nothing. Then, suddenly, as always, the knowledge flooded into his mind. He found himself making a neat little three-minute speech almost automatically. The material seemed to arrange itself as he spoke, telling how Einstein forced an abandonment of the idea of simultaneity, of Eddington's idea that the known universe is merely what man is able to perceive and measure, of Milne's two time scales, and of the strange ideas of Rhine and Dunne concerning precognition. He had always been a clever speaker, ever since high school, he thought.

"Of course," he found himself concluding, "it was not until later in the century that Chandra Bhopal demonstrated the absurdity of time travel."

Cordoban stared at him queerly. For a moment Smith was scarcely conscious of what he had said. Then he formulated his thoughts.

"But time travel must be possible," he said, "for I'm a twentieth century man, and I'm here in the thirty-first century."

He looked about the pleasant room, softly lighted, with deep recesses of color, for assurance, and at the handsome people, grouped standing or sitting in glowing pools of pearly illumination.

"Of course you're here, fellow," Cordoban said, reassuringly.

The remark was so true and so banal that Smith scarcely heard it. His thoughts were groping. Slowly, he was piecing together an argument.

"But time travel *is* absurd," he said.

Cordoban looked a little annoyed and made a nod with his head which Smith did not quite follow.

"It was shown in the twentieth century to be absurd," Smith said.

But, had it been shown in his part of the twentieth century, he wondered?

Cordoban glanced to his left.

"We know very little about the twentieth century," he said.

Gavin knows about the twentieth century, Smith thought.

Then, following Cordoban's glance, he saw that a young woman had detached herself from a group and was moving toward them. A segment of the pearly illumination followed her, making her a radiant creature indeed.

"Myria," Cordoban said, smiling, "you particularly wanted to meet Mr. Smith."

Myria smiled at Smith.

"Indeed, yes," she said. "I've always been curious about the twentieth century. And you must tell me about your music."

Cordoban bowed slightly and withdrew, the light which had been playing on him, seemingly from nowhere, detaching itself from the pool about Myria and Smith. And Smith's doubts fled to the back of his mind, crowded out, almost, by a flood of thoughts about music. And Myria was an enchanting creature.

Smith felt very chipper the next morning as he rose and bathed. The twentieth century had nothing like this to offer, he reflected. He knit his brows for a moment, trying to remember just what his room had been like, but at that moment the cupboard softly buzzed and he withdrew the glass of bland liquid which was his breakfast. His mind wandered while he sipped it. It wasn't until he walked down the corridor and sat in the office opposite Gavin that his doubts at Cordoban's returned to his mind.

Gavin was droning out the schedule. "We have a pretty full day, Smith," he said. "First, a couple of hours at the Lollards' country estate. We can stop by the Primus's on the way back. Then, a full afternoon at a party given by the decorators' council. In the evening—"

"Gavin," Smith said, "why do we see all these people?"

"Why," Gavin answered, a little taken aback, "everyone wants to see a man from the twentieth century."

"But why these people?" Smith persisted. "They all ask the same questions. And I never see them again. I just go on repeating myself."

"Are we too frivolous by twentieth century standards?" Gavin asked, smiling and leaning back in his chair.

Smith smiled back. Then his thoughts troubled him again. Cordoban hadn't been frivolous.

"How much do *you* know about the twentieth century, Gavin?" he asked, keeping his tone light.

"Pretty much what you do," Gavin replied.

But this couldn't be! Gavin appeared to be a kind of social tutor and arranger of things. As far as Smith could remember, mostly, information had passed from Gavin to him, not from him to Gavin. He decided to pursue the matter further, and as Gavin leaned forward to glance at the schedule again, Smith spoke once more.

"By the way, Gavin," he asked, "who is Cordoban?"

"Director of the Historical Institute, of course. I told you before we went there," Gavin replied.

"Who is Myria?" Smith asked.

"One of his secretaries," Gavin said. "A man of his position always has one on call."

"Cordoban said that not much was known about the twentieth century," Smith remarked mildly.

Gavin started up as if he had been stung. Then he sank back and opened his mouth. It was a moment before he found the words.

"Directors—" he said, and waved his hand as if brushing

the matter aside. Smith was really puzzled now. "Gavin," he said, "is time travel possible?"

If Gavin had been startled, he was at his ease now.

"You're here," he said, "not in the twentieth century."

Gavin spoke in so charming and persuasive a manner that Smith felt like a fool for a moment. His thoughts were slipping back toward the schedule when he realized, that wasn't an answer. It wasn't even couched as one. But this was silly, too. If it wasn't an answer, it was just what one would say.

Still, he'd try again.

"Gavin," he said, "Cordoban—"

"Look," Gavin said with a smile, "you'll get used to us in time. We'll keep the Lollards and their guests waiting if we don't start now. It isn't asking too much of you to see them now, is it? And you'll like it. They have a lovely fifteenth-century Chinese garden, with a dragon in a cave."

After all, Smith thought, he did owe his collective hosts of the thirty-first century something. And it was amusing.

The Lollards' garden was amusing, and so was the dragon, which breathed out smoke and roared. Primus's was dull, but the decorators' council had a most unusual display of fabrics which tinkled when they were touched, and of individual lighting in color. The evening was equally diverting, and delightful but strange people asked the same frivolous questions. Smith was diverted enough so that his doubts did not return until late that night.

But when Gavin left him at the door, Smith did not go to his bed and his usual dreamless sleep. Instead, he sat down in a chair, closed his eyes, and thought.

What did these people know about the twentieth century? Gavin had said, what he, Smith, knew. But that must be a great deal. An adult man, he, for instance, had a huge store of memories, accumulated over all his years. The human brain, he found himself thinking, has around ten billion nerve cells. If these were used to store words on a binary basis, they would hold some four hundred million words—a prodigious amount of learning. Tokayuki had, in 2117—

Strange, but he didn't remember talking with Gavin or anyone else about Tokayuki! And he could not have remembered about a man who had lived a century after his. But he could pursue this later.

Getting back to the gist of the matter, Cordoban had said that he knew little about the twentieth century. Yet Cordoban had not seemed anxious to question him at length. A few words about the philosophy of science, a dry enough subject, and he had called his secretary Myria—yes, Smith now saw, Cordoban had called Myria to relieve himself of Smith's presence. Here was an obviously astute man, and an historian, foregoing an opportunity to learn about an era of which he professed ignorance.

Well, I suppose one untrained man doesn't know much about an era, even his own, Smith thought. That is, not by thirty-first century standards. But, then, how do they know what I know? he wondered. Nobody has asked me any very searching questions.

Gavin and his schedules, now! All the occasions were purely social. That was strange! Most of the people weren't those likely to have much detailed interest in another era. Decorators, some, like the Lollards, apparently entirely idle-retired, perhaps. Anyway, the conversation was so much social chitchat.

Cordoban, now, had been an historian, even though he hadn't been curious. But that, too, was a purely social occasion. And Gavin himself! Just a sort of guide to a man from another age. Certainly not a curious man. Why not? Were men of the twentieth century so common here? But certainly he would have been brought into contact with others. Besides, time traveling was absurd!

But that was getting off the track. He *was* here. He didn't need Cordoban or Gavin to assure him of that. Being here, he would expect serious questioning by a small group—not all these frivolous, if delightful, parties. Surely he could tell them a great deal they had not asked.

Well, for instance, what could he tell them? His own personal experiences. What had happened day by day. But what had happened day by day? His schooling, for one thing. High school, in particular. As he thought about high schools, there quickly rose in his mind a sequence of facts about their organization and curriculum. It was as if he were reviewing a syllabus on the subject.

The three-minute talks were getting him, he decided. He was so used to these impersonal summaries that they came to his mind automatically. Right now, he must be tired. He would spend more time thinking in the morning.

So Smith went to bed, thought about the events of the day a little, including the Lollards' amusing fire-breathing dragon, and was quickly asleep.

* * *

The following morning Smith did not feel chipper. He rose and bathed out of a sense of duty and routine. But then he sat down and ignored the buzzing of the cupboard which announced his breakfast. A pattern had crystallized in his mind over night. His thoughts in their uncertainty had paved the way for this, no doubt. But what was in his mind was no uncertain conclusion.

He, Smith, was no man of the twentieth century! He had carefully implanted memories, factual theses concerning his past, summaries of twentieth century history. But no real past! The little details that made a past were missing. Time travel was absurd. He was a fraud! An impostor!

But whom was he fooling? Not Gavin, he saw now. Not men like Cordoban. Was he fooling anyone? All of the people seemed eager to talk with him. Cordoban himself had been eager to talk with him. Cordoban had not been feigning. Cordoban had not been fooled. It seemed likely that Smith himself was the only one fooled.

But why? It was a stupid trick for people so obviously intelligent. What did they get out of this silly game? It could hardly be any personal quality of his—any charm. They were all so charming themselves.

Myria, Cordoban's secretary, for instance. A lovely woman. Handsome, poised, beautifully dressed. Suddenly a little three-minute talk about women in the twentieth century formed in Smith's mind. In part of his mind, that is. In a way, he watched it unfold. And with surprise.

He had thought of Myria as merely handsome and handsomely dressed. But even across the centuries—no, he must remember that he was not from the twentieth century. Across whatever gulf there was, there could have been more than this. Just how did he, Smith, differ from other men?

Well, what did he know of mankind? He reviewed matters in his mind, and went through little summaries on psychology, anthropology, and physiology. It was in the midst of this last that he felt a horrible conviction which changed his course from thought to action.

His first action was to wind a small gold chain which was a part of his clothing tightly around the tip of his index finger. The tip remained smooth and brown.

Dropping the chain, he dug the sharp point of a writing

instrument into his fingertip, ignoring the pain. The point passed into the rubbery flesh. There was no blood! But there was a little flash and a puff of vapor, and the finger went numb.

He was a cleverly constructed period piece, like the Lollards' dragon! Like a clockwork nightingale! That was why these people admired him briefly, for what he was—a charming mechanical toy!

Smith scarcely thought. The little review of twentieth century psychology returned to his mind, and automatically he opened the door onto the balcony and stepped over the railing. Consistent to the last, he thought in dull pain as he fell toward the ground twenty stories below.

But it wasn't the last. There was a terrible wrenching shock, a clashing noise, and confusion. Afterwards, there were still vision and hearing. True, the world stood at an odd angle. He saw the building leaning crazily into the sky. From the brief synopsis of physiology he gleaned that his psycho-kinetic sense was gone. He no longer felt which way his head and eyes were turned. Other senses than sight and sound were gone as well, and when he tried he found that he could not move. Junk, lying here, he thought bitterly. Not even release! But now he could see Gavin bending over him, and another man who looked as if he might be a mechanic.

"Junk," the mechanic said. "It's lucky we couldn't put the brain in that, or it would be gone, too. Making a new body won't be so bad," he added.

"I suppose we'll have to turn off the brain and reform the patterns," Gavin mused.

"You'd have had to, anyway," the mechanic said. "You must have put in something inconsistent or we wouldn't have had this failure."

"It's a shame, though," Gavin said. "I got to like him. Silly, isn't it? But he seemed so nearly alive. We spent a lot of time together. Now everything that happened, everything he learned, will have to be wiped out."

"You know," the mechanic said, "it gives me the creeps, sometimes. I mean, thinking, if I were just a body, connected by a tight beam to a brain off somewhere. And if, when the body was destroyed, the brain—"

"Nonsense," said Gavin.

He gestured toward Smith's crumpled body, and then up toward the building where, presumably, was Smith's brain.

"You'll be thinking that that thing was conscious, next," he said. "Come on, let's turn the brain off."

Smith stared numbly at the crazily leaning building, waiting for them to turn off his brain.

DORMANT

by A. E. van Vogt

STARTLING STORIES
November

A. E. van Vogt's second contribution to the best of 1948 is one of the author's major themes—power and its uses—a subject that is a constant through his work, sometimes obliquely, sometimes overtly, as in his Weapons Shop stories. "Dormant" was chosen for inclusion in The Best From Startling Stories *(1953) by Samuel Mines, himself a most underrated and capable editor.*

(I've spent my life as a writer without looking too closely at what it was I did while I was writing. Since I didn't pay any attention to subtleties I gradually learned to write directly, and with as little elaboration as I could possibly manage.

For instance, I would simply never start a story with the sentence "Old was that island." If I wanted to start a story with that notion I would surely phrase it as follows: "The island was old." If emphasis were wanted, I might add an exclamation mark. The reason for my choice would be that it was the simplest way of expressing the thought. Van Vogt's way would seem to my ears to be a kind of psuedo-archaism; an attempt at poetic inversion when none was necessary.

However, "Old was that island," emphasizes "old."
That is the first word of the story and, what do you
know, it has significance. See what I miss by avoiding
subtleties.—I. A.)

Old was that island. Even the thing that lay in the outer channel exposed to the rude wash of the open sea had never guessed, when it was alive a million years before, that here was a protuberance of primeval earth itself.

The island was roughly three miles long and, at its widest, half a mile across. It curved tensely around a blue lagoon and the thin shape of its rocky, foam-ridden arms and hands came down toward the toe of the island—like a gigantic man bending over, striving to reach his feet and not quite making it.

Through the channel made by that gap between the toes and the fingers came the sea.

The water resented the channel. With an endless patience it fought to break the wall of rock, and the tumult of the waters was a special sound—a blend of all that was raucous and unseemly in the eternal quarrel between resisting land and encroaching wave.

At the very hub of the screaming waters lay Iilah, dead now almost forever, forgotten by time and the universe.

Early in 1941 Japanese ships came and ran the gauntlet of dangerous waters into the quiet lagoon. From the deck of one of the ships a pair of curious eyes pondered the thing, where it lay in the path of the rushing sea. But the owner of those eyes was the servant of a government that frowned on extra-military ventures of its personnel.

And so engineer Taku Onilo merely noted in his report that, "At the mouth of this channel there lies a solid shape of glittery rocklike substance about four hundred feet long and ninety feet wide."

The little yellow men built their underground gas and oil tanks and departed toward the setting sun. The water rose and fell, rose and fell again. The days and the years drifted by, and the hand of time was heavy. The seasonal rains arrived on their rough schedule and washed away the marks of man. Green growth sprouted where machines had exposed the raw earth.

The war ended. The underground tanks sagged a little in their beds of earth and cracks appeared in several main pipes. Slowly the oil drained off and for years a yellow-green oil slick brightened the gleam of the lagoon waters.

In the reaches of Bikini Atoll, hundreds of miles away, first one explosion, then another, started in motion an intricate pattern of radioactivated waters. The first seepage of that potent energy reached the island in the early fall of 1946.

It was about six months later that a patient clerk, ransacking the records of the Imperial Japanese Navy in Tokyo, reported the existence of the oil tanks. In due time—1948—the destroyer *Coulson* set forth on its routine voyage of examination.

The time of the nightmare was come.

Lieutenant Keith Maynard, a masochist of long experience, peered gloomily through his binoculars at the island. He was prepared to find something wrong but he expected a distracting monotony of sameness, not something radically different.

"Usual undergrowth," he muttered, "and a backbone of semi-mountain, running like a framework the length of the island, trees—"

He stopped there.

A broad swath had been cut through the palms on the near shoreline. They were not just down—they were crushed deep into a furrow that was already alive with grass and small growth. The furrow, which looked about a hundred feet wide, led upward from the beach to the side of a hill, to where a large rock lay half buried near the top of the hill.

Puzzled, Maynard glanced down at the Japanese photographs of the island. Involuntarily, he turned toward his executive officer, Lieutenant Gerson.

"Good lord!" he said, "how did that rock get up *there?* It's not on any photographs."

The moment he had spoken he regretted it. Gerson looked at him, with his usual faint antagonism, shrugged and said, "Maybe we've got the wrong island."

Maynard did not answer that. He considered Gerson a queer character. The man's tongue dripped ceaselessly with irony.

"I'd say it weighs about two million tons. The Japs probably dragged it up there to confuse us."

Maynard said nothing. He was annoyed that he had ever made a comment—and particularly annoyed because, for a moment, he had actually thought of the Japs in connection with the rock. The weight estimate, which he instantly recognized as fairly accurate, ended all his wilder thoughts.

If the Japs could move a rock weighing two million tons they had also won the war. Still, it was very curious and deserved investigation—afterward.

They ran the channel without incident. It was wider and deeper than Maynard had understood from the Jap accounts, which made everything easy. Their midday meal was eaten in the shelter of the lagoon. Maynard noted the oil on the water and issued immediate warnings against throwing matches overboard. After a brief talk with the other officers, he decided that they would set fire to the oil as soon as they had accomplished their mission and were out of the lagoon.

About one-thirty boats were lowered and they made shore in quick order. In an hour, with the aid of transcribed Japanese blueprints, they located the four buried tanks. It took somewhat longer to assess the dimensions of the tanks and to discover that three of them were empty.

Only the smallest contained high-octane gasoline, not worth the attention of the larger navy tankers that were still cruising around, picking up odd lots of Japanese and American matériel.

Maynard presumed that a lighter would eventually be dispatched for the gasoline, but that was none of his business.

In spite of the speed with which his job had been accomplished, Maynard climbed wearily up to the deck just as darkness was falling.

He must have overdone it a little because Gerson said too loudly, "Worn out, sir?"

Maynard stiffened. And it was that comment rather than any inclination that decided him not to postpone his exploration of the rock. As soon as possible after the evening meal he called for volunteers.

It was pitch dark as the boat, with seven men and Bosun's Mate Yewell and himself, was beached on the sands under the towering palms.

The party headed inland.

There was no moon and the stars were scattered among remnant clouds of the rainy season just past. They walked in the furrow, where the trees had been literally plowed into the ground. In the pale light of the flashlights the spectacle of numerous trees, burned and planed into a smoothed levelness with the soil, was unnatural.

Maynard heard one of the men mumble, "Must have been some freak of a typhoon did that."

Not only a typhoon, Maynard decided, but a ravenous fire followed by a monstrous wind, so monstrous that—his brain paused. He couldn't imagine any storm big enough to lift a two-million-ton rock to the side of a hill a quarter of a mile long and four hundred feet above sea level.

From nearby, the rock looked like nothing more than rough granite. In the beam of the flashlights it glinted with innumerable streaks of pink. Maynard led his party alongside it and the vastness of it grew upon him as he climbed past its four hundred feet of length and peered up at gleaming walls, like cliffs looming above him.

The upper end, buried though it was deeper into the ground, rose at least fifty feet above his head.

The night had grown uncomfortably warm. Maynard was perspiring freely. He enjoyed a moment of weary pleasure in the thought that he was doing his duty under unpleasant circumstances. He stood uncertain, gloomily savoring the intense primitive silence of the night.

"Break off some samples here and there," he said finally. "Those pink streaks look interesting."

It was a few seconds later that a man's scream of agony broke through the thrall of darkness.

Flashlights blinked on. They showed Seaman Hicks twisting on the ground beside the rock. In the bright flame of the lights, the man's wrists showed as a smoldering, blackened husk with the entire hand completely burned off.

He had touched Iilah.

Maynard gave the miserable wretch morphine and they rushed him back to the ship. Radio contact was established with base and a consulting surgeon gave cut-by-cut instructions on the operation. It was agreed that a hospital plane would be dispatched for the patient.

There must have been some puzzlement at headquarters as to how the accident had occurred, because "further information" was requested about the "hot" rock. By morning the people at the other end were calling it a meteorite. Maynard, who did not normally question opinions offered by his superiors, frowned over the identification and pointed out that this meteorite weighed two million tons and rested on the surface of the island.

"I'll send the assistant engineer officer to take its temperature," he said.

An engine-room thermometer registered the rock's surface temperature at eight-hundred-odd degrees Fahrenheit. The answer to that was a question that shocked Maynard.

"Why, yes," he replied, "we're getting mild radioactive reactions from the water but nothing else. And nothing serious. Under the circumstances we'll withdraw from the lagoon at once and await the ships with the scientists."

He ended that conversation, pale and shaken. Nine men, including himself, had walked along within a few yards of the rock, well within the deadly danger zone. In fact, even the *Coulson*, more than half a mile away, would have been affected.

But the gold leaves of the electroscope stood out stiff and the Geiger-Mueller counter clucked only when placed in the water and then only at long intervals.

Relieved, Maynard went down to have another look at Seaman Hicks. The injured man slept uneasily but he was not dead, which was a good sign. When the hospital plane arrived there was a doctor aboard, who attended Hicks and then gave everyone on the destroyer a blood-count test. He came up on deck, a cheerful young man, and reported to Maynard.

"Well, it can't be what they suspect," he said. "Everybody's okay, even Hicks, except for his hand. That burned awfully quick, if you ask me, for a temperature of only eight hundred."

"I think his hand stuck," said Maynard. And he shuddered. In his fashion he had mentally experienced the entire accident.

"So that's the rock," said Dr. Clason. "Does seem odd how it got there."

They were still standing there five minutes later when a hideous screaming from below deck made a discordant sound on the still air of that remote island lagoon.

Something stirred in the depths of Iilah's awareness of himself, something that he had intended to do—he couldn't remember what.

That was the first real thought he had in late 1946, when he felt the impact of outside energy. And stirred with returning life.

The outside flow waxed and waned. It was abnormally, abysmally dim. The crust of the planet that he knew had palpitated with the ebbing but potent energies of a world not yet cooled from its sun state.

It was only slowly that Iilah realized the extent of the disaster that was his environment. At first he was inwardly inclined, too pallidly alive to be interested in externals.

He forced himself to become more conscious of his environment. He looked forth with his radar vision out upon a strange world.

He was lying on a shallow plateau near the top of a mountain. The scene was desolate beyond his memory. There was not a glint nor pressure of atomic fire—not a bubble of boiling rock nor a swirl of energy heaved skyward by some vast interior explosion.

He did not think of what he saw as an island surrounded by an apparently limitless ocean. He saw the land below the water as well as above it.

His vision, based as it was on ultra-ultra short waves, could not see water.

He recognized that he was on an old and dying planet, where life had long since become extinct.

Alone and dying on a forgotten planet—if he could only find the source of the energy that had revived him.

By a process of simple logic he started down the mountain in the direction from which the current of atomic energy seemed to be coming. Somehow he found himself below it and had to levitate himself heavily, back up. Once started upward, he headed for the nearest peak, with the intention of seeing what was on the other side.

As he propelled himself out of the invisible, unsensed waters of the lagoon, two diametrically opposite phenomena affected him. He lost all contact with the water-borne current of atomic energy. And, simultaneously, the water ceased to inhibit the neutron and deuteron activity of his body.

His life took on an increased intensity. The tendency to slow stiflement ended. His great form became a self-sustaining pile, capable of surviving for the normal radioactive lifespan of the elements that composed it—still on an immensely less-than-normal activity level for him.

Iilah thought, "There was something I was going to do."

The flow of electrons through a score of gigantic cells as he strained to remember increased, then slowed gradually when no memory came.

The fractional increase of his life energy brought with it a wider, more exact understanding of his situation. Wave on wave of perceptive radaric forces flowed from him to the Moon, to Mars, to all the planets of the solar system—and the echoes that came back were examined with an alarmed awareness that out there, too, were dead bodies.

He was caught in the confines of a dead system, prisoned until the relentless exhaustion of his material structure brought him once more to rapport with the dead mass of the planet on which he was marooned.

He realized now that he had been dead. Just how it had happened he could not recall, except that explosively violent, frustrating substance had belched around him, buried him, and snuffed out his life processes. The atomic chemistry involved must eventually have converted the stuff into a harmless form, no longer capable of hindering him. But he was dead by then.

Now he was alive again, but in so dim a fashion that there was nothing to do but wait for the end. He waited. . . .

In 1948 he watched the destroyer float toward him through the sky. Long before it slowed and stopped just below him, he had discovered that it was not a life form related to him. It manufactured a dull internal heat and, through its exterior walls, he could see the vague glow of fires.

All that first day Iilah waited for the creature to show awareness of him. But not a wave of life emanated from it. And yet it floated in the sky above the plateau, an impossible phenomenon, utterly outside all his experience.

To Iilah, who had no means of sensing water, who could not even imagine air, and whose ultra waves passed through human beings as if they did not exist, the reaction could only mean one thing—here was an alien life form that had adapted itself to the dead world around him.

Gradually Iilah grew excited. The thing could move freely above the surface of the planet. It would know if any source of atomic energy remained anywhere. The problem was to get into communication with it.

The sun was high on the meridian of another day when Iilah directed the first questioning pattern of thought toward the destroyer. He aimed straight at the vaguely glowing fires in the engine room, where, he reasoned, would be the intelligence of the alien creature.

The thirty-four men who died in the spaces in and around the engine room and the fire room were buried on shore. Their surviving comrades, including all officers, moved half a mile up the east coast. And at first they expected to stay there until the abandoned *Coulson* ceased to give off dangerous radioactive energies.

On the seventh day, when transport planes were already dumping scientific equipment and personnel, three of the men fell sick and their blood count showed a fateful decrease in the number of red corpuscles. Although no orders had arrived, Maynard took alarm and ordered the entire crew shipped for observation to Hawaii.

He allowed the officers to make their own choice, but advised the second engineer officer, the first gunnery officer, and several ensigns who had helped hoist the dead men up to deck, to take no chances, but to grab space on the first planes.

Although all were ordered to leave, several crew members asked permission to remain. And, after a careful questioning by Gerson, a dozen men who could prove that they had not been near the affected area were finally permitted to stay.

Maynard would have preferred to see Gerson himself depart, but in this he was disappointed. Of the officers who had been aboard the destroyer at the time of the disaster, Lieutenants Gerson, Lausson, and Haury, the latter two being gunnery officers, and Ensigns McPelty, Roberts, and Manchioff, remained on the beach.

Among the higher ratings remaining behind were the chief commissary steward, Jenkins, and chief bosun's mate Yewell.

The navy group was ignored except that several times requests were made that they move their tents out of the way. Finally, when it seemed evident that they would be crowded out once more, Maynard in annoyance ordered the canvas moved well down the coast, where the palms opened up to form a grassy meadow.

Maynard grew puzzled, then grim, as the weeks passed and no orders arrived concerning the disposal of his command. In one of the Stateside papers that began to follow the scientists, the bulldozers and cement mixers onto the island he read an item in an "inside" column that gave him his first inkling.

According to the columnist, there had been a squabble between navy bigwigs and the civilian members of the Atomic Control Board over control of the investigation. With the result that the navy had been ordered to "stay out."

Maynard read the account with mixed feelings and a dawning understanding that he was *the* navy representative on the island. The realization included a thrilling mental visualization of himself rising to the rank of admiral—if he handled the situation right. Just what would be right, aside from keeping a sharp eye on everything, he couldn't decide.

It was an especially exquisite form of self-torture.

He couldn't sleep. He spent his days wandering as unobtrusively as possible through the ever vaster encampment of the army of scientists and their assistants. At night he had several hiding places from which he watched the brilliantly lighted beach.

It was a fabulous oasis of brightness in the dark vaulting vastness of a Pacific night. For a full mile string upon string of lights spread along the whispering waters. They silhouetted and spotlighted the long, thick, back-curving, cement-like walls that reared up eerily, starting at the rim of the hill. Protective walls were already soaring up around the rock itself, striving to block it off from all outside contact.

Always, at midnight, the bulldozers ceased their roarings, the cement-mixing trucks dumped their last loads and scurried down the makeshift beach road and so to silence. The entire, already intricate organization settled into an uneasy slumber—and Maynard waited with the painful patience of a man doing more than his duty, usually until around one o'clock, when he, too, would make his way to his bed.

The secret habit paid off. He was the only man who actually witnessed the rock climb to the top of the hill.

It was a stupendous event. The time was about a quarter to one and Maynard was on the point of calling it a day when he heard the sound. It was like a truck emptying a load of gravel. For a bare moment he thought of it entirely in relation to his hiding place.

His night-spying activities were going to be found out.

An instant after that the rock reared up into the brilliance of the lights.

There was a roaring now of cement barriers, crumbling before that irresistible movement. Fifty, sixty, then ninety feet of monster rock loomed up above the hill and slid with a heavy power over the crown.

And stopped.

For two months Iilah had watched the freighters breast the channel. Just why they followed that route interested him. And he wondered if there was some limitation on them, that kept them at such an exact level.

What was more interesting by far, however, was that in every case the aliens would slide around the island and disappear behind a high promontory that was the beginning of the east shore. In every case, after they had been gone for a few days, they would slide into view again, glide through the channel, and gradually move off through the sky.

During those months Iilah caught tantalizing glimpses of small but much faster winged ships that shot down from a great height—and disappeared behind the crest of the hill to the east.

Always to the east. His curiosity grew enormous, but he was reluctant to waste energy. And it was not until he grew aware of a nighttime haze of lights that brightened the eastern sky at night, that he finally set off the more violent explosions on his lower surface that made directive motion possible.

He climbed the last seventy or so feet to the top of the hill. And regretted it immediately.

One ship lay a short distance offshore. The haze of light along the eastern slope seemed to have no source. As he watched, scores of trucks and bulldozers raced around, some of them coming quite close to him.

Just what they wanted, or what they were doing he could not make out. He sent several questioning thought waves at various of the objects, but there was no response.

He gave it up as a bad job.

The rock was still resting on the top of the hill the next morning, poised so that both sides of the island were threatened by the stray bursts of energy which it gave off so erratically.

Maynard heard his first account of the damage done from Jenkins, the chief commissary steward. Seven truck-drivers and two bulldozer men dead, a dozen men suffering from glancing burns—and two months' labor wrecked.

There must have been a conference among the scientists, for, shortly after noon, trucks and bulldozers, loaded with equipment, began to stream past the navy camp. A seaman, dispatched to follow them, reported that they were setting up camp on the point at the lower end of the island.

Just before dark a notable event took place in the social history of the island. The director of the project, together with four executive scientists, walked into the lighted area and asked for Maynard.

The group was smiling and friendly. There was handshaking all around. Maynard introduced Gerson, who unfortunately (so far as Maynard was concerned) was in the camp at the moment. And then the visiting delegation got down to business.

"As you know," said the director, "the *Coulson* is only partially radioactive. The rear gun turret is quite unaffected, and we accordingly request that you cooperate with us and fire on the rock until it is broken into sections."

"Huh!" said Maynard.

It took only a moment for him to recover from his astonishment and to know what he would answer to that.

At no time, during the next few days, did Maynard question the belief of the scientists that the rock should be broken up and so rendered harmless. He refused their request and then doggedly continued to refuse it.

It was not until the third day that he thought of a reason.

"Your precautions, gentlemen," he said, "are not sufficient. I do not consider that moving the camp out to the point is a sufficient safeguard in the event that the rock should blow up. Now, of course, if I should receive a command from a naval authority to do as you wish. . . ."

He left that sentence dangling—and saw from their disappointed faces that there must have been a feverish exchange of radio messages with their own headquarters. The arrival of a Kwajalein paper on the fourth day quoted a "high" Washington naval officer as saying that, "any such decisions must be left to the judgment of the naval commander on the island."

And that, if a properly channeled request was made, the navy would be glad to send an atomic expert of its own to the scene.

It was obvious to Maynard that he was handling the situation exactly as his superiors desired. The only thing was that, even as he finished reading the account, the silence was broken by the unmistakable bark of a destroyer's five-inch guns, that sharpest of all gunfire sounds.

Unsteadily Maynard climbed to his feet. An awful suspicion was on him. A swift glance around the camp showed that Gerson and his crony, gunnery officer Haury, were nowhere in sight.

His anger was instantly personal. He began to climb to the nearest height. Before he reached it the second shattering roar came from the other side of the lagoon, and once again an ear-splitting explosion echoed from the vicinity of the rock.

Maynard reached his vantage point and, through his binoculars, saw about a dozen men scurrying over the aft deck in and about the rear gun turret. It was impossible to make out if Gerson and Haury were among those aboard. There seemed to be no uniforms.

His first terrible suspicion faded. A new and grimmer fury came, this time against the camp director, and a determination to assure himself that every man assisting on the destroyer was arrested for malicious and dangerous trespass.

A vague thought came that it was a sorry day indeed when interbureau squabbles could cause such open defiance of the armed forces, as if nothing more were involved than a struggle for power. But that thought faded as swiftly as it came.

He waited for the third firing, then hurried down the hill to his camp. Swift commands to the men and officers sent eight of them to positions along the shore of the island, where they could watch boats trying to land.

With the rest Maynard headed toward the nearest navy boat. He had to take the long way around, by way of the point, and there must have been radio communication between the point and those on the ship, for a motor boat was just disappearing around the far end of the island when Maynard approached the now silent and deserted *Coulson*.

He hesitated. Should he give chase? A careful study of the rock proved it to be apparently unbroken. The failure cheered him, but it also made him cautious. It wouldn't do for his superiors to discover that he had not taken the necessary precautions to prevent the destroyer being boarded.

He was still pondering the problem when Iilah started down the hill, straight toward the destroyer.

Iilah saw the first bright puff from the destroyer's guns. And then he had a moment during which he observed an object flash toward him. In the old, old times he had developed defenses against hurtling objects. Quite automatically now, he tensed for the blow of this one.

The object, instead of merely striking him with its hardness, exploded. The impact was stupendous. His protective crust cracked. The concussion blurred and distorted the flow from every electronic plate in his great mass.

Instantly the automatic stabilizing "tubes" sent off balancing impulses. The hot, internal, partly rigid, partly fluid matter that made up the greater portion of his body, grew hotter, more fluidic.

The weaknesses induced by that tremendous concussion accepted the natural union of a liquid—and hardened instantly under enormous pressure.

Sane again, Iilah considered what had happened. An attempt at communication?

The possibility excited him. Instead of closing the gap in his outer wall he hardened the matter immediately behind it, thus cutting off wasteful radiation.

He waited.

Again the hurtling object and the enormously potent blow, as

struck him. . . . After a dozen blows, each with its resulting
disaster to his protective shell, Iilah writhed with doubts.

If these were messages he could not receive them or understand.
He began reluctantly to allow the chemical reactions that sealed
the protective barrier. Faster than he could seal the holes, the
hurtling objects breached his defenses.

And still he did not think of what had happened as an attack.

In all his previous existence he had never been attacked in
such a fashion. Just what methods had been used against him,
Iilah could not remember. But certainly nothing so purely
molecular.

The conviction that it was an attack came reluctantly and he
felt no anger. The reflex of defense in him was logical, not
emotional. He studied the destroyer and it seemed to him that his
purpose must be to drive it away.

And he must drive away every similar creature that tried to
come near him. All the scurrying objects he had seen when he
mounted the crest of the hill—all that must depart. Everything
eventually, but first the destroyer.

He started down the hill.

The creature floating above the plateau had ceased exuding
flame. As Iilah eased himself near it, the only sign of life was a
smaller object that darted alongside it.

There was a moment then when Iilah entered the water. That
was a shock. He had almost forgotten that there was a level of
his desolate mountain below which his life forces were affected.

He hesitated.

Then, slowly, he slid farther down the depressing area, conscious that he had attained a level of strength that he could
maintain against such a purely negative pressure.

The destroyer began to fire at him. The shells, delivered at
point-blank range, poked deep holes into the ninety-foot cliff
with which Iilah faced his enemy.

As that wall of rock touched the destroyer the firing stopped.
Maynard and his men, having defended the *Coulson* as long as
possible, tumbled over the far side into their boat and raced away
as fast as possible.)

Iilah shoved. The pain that he felt from those titanic blows
was the pain that comes to all living creatures experiencing
partial dissolution.

Laboriously his body repaired itself. And with anger and
hatred and fear now he shoved. In a few minutes he had tangled
the curiously unwieldy structure in the rocks that rose up to form

the edge of the plateau. Beyond was the sharp declining slope of the mountain.

A curious thing happened. Once among the rocks the creature started to shudder and shake, as if caught by some inner destructive force. It fell over on its side and lay there like some wounded thing, quivering and breaking up.

It was an amazing spectacle. Iilah withdrew from the water, reclimbed the mountain, and plunged down into the sea on the other side, where a freighter was just getting under way. It swung around the promontory and successfully floated through the channel and out, coasting along high above the bleak valley that fell away beyond the breakers. It moved along for several miles, then slowed and stopped.

Iilah would have liked to chase it further, but he was limited to ground movement. And so, the moment the freighter had stopped, he turned and headed toward the point, where all the small objects were cluttered.

He did not notice the men who plunged into the shallows near the shore and from that comparative safety watched the destruction of their equipment. Iilah left a wake of burning and crushed vehicles. The few drivers who tried to get their machines away became splotches of flesh and blood inside and on the metal of their machines.

There was a fantastic amount of stupidity and panic. Iilah moved at a speed of about eight miles an hour. Three hundred and seventeen men were caught in scores of individual traps and crushed by a monster that did not even know they existed.

Each man must have felt himself personally pursued.

Afterward Iilah climbed to the nearest peak and studied the sky for further interlopers.

Only the freighter remained, a shadowy threat some four miles away.

Darkness cloaked the island, slowly. Maynard moved cautiously through the grass, flashing his flashlight directly in front of him on a sharp downward slant.

Every little while he called out, "Anybody around?"

It had been like that four hours now. Through the fading day they had searched for survivors, each time loading them aboard their boat and ferrying them through the channel and out to where the freighter waited.

The orders had come through by radio. They had forty-eight hours to get clear of the island. After that the bomb run would be made by a drone plane.

Maynard pictured himself walking along on this monster-inhabited, night-enveloped island. And the shuddery thrill that came was almost pure unadulterated pleasure. He felt himself pale with a joyous terror.

It was like the time when his ship had been among those shelling a Jap-held beach. He had been gloomy until, suddenly, he had pictured himself out there on the beach at the receiving end of the shells.

He began to torture himself with the possibility that, somehow, he might be left behind when the freighter finally withdrew.

A moan from the near darkness ended that thought. In the glow of the flashlight Maynard saw a vaguely familiar face. The man had been smashed by a falling tree.

As Executive Officer Gerson came forward and administered morphine, Maynard bent closer to the injured man and peered at him anxiously.

It was one of the world-famous scientists on the island. Ever since the disaster the radio messages had been asking for him. There was not a scientific body on the globe that cared to commit itself to the navy bombing plan until he had given his opinion.

"Sir," began Maynard, "what do you think about—"

He stopped. He settled mentally back on his heels.

Just for a moment he had forgotten that the naval authorities had already ordered the atomic bomb dropped, after being given governmental authority to do as they saw fit.

The scientist stirred. "Maynard," he croaked, "there's something funny about that creature. Don't let them do any—"

His eyes grew bright with pain. His voice trailed.

It was time to push questions. The great man would soon be deep in a doped sleep and he would be kept that way. In a moment it would be too late.

The moment passed.

Lieutenant Gerson climbed to his feet. "There, that ought to do it, Captain." He turned to the seamen carrying the stretchers. "Two of you take this man back to the boat. Careful. I've put him to sleep."

Maynard followed the stretcher without a word. He had a sense of having been saved from the necessity of making a decision rather than of having made one.

The night dragged on.

The morning dawned grayly. Shortly after the sun came up a tropical shower stormed across the island and rushed off eastward.

The sky grew amazingly blue and the world of water all around seemed motionless, so calm did the sea become.

Out of the blue distance, casting a swiftly moving shadow on that still ocean, flew the drone plane.

Long before it came in sight, Iilah sensed the load it carried. He quivered through his mass. Enormous electron tubes waxed and waned with expectancy and, for a brief while, he thought it was one of his own kind coming near.

As the plane drew closer he sent cautious thoughts toward it. Several planes, to which he had directed his thought waves, had twisted jerkily in midair and tumbled down out of control.

This one did not deviate from its course. When it was almost directly overhead a large object dropped from it, turned lazily over and over as it curved toward Iilah. It was set to explode about a hundred feet above the target.

The timing was perfect, the explosion titanic.

As soon as the blurring effects of so much new energy had passed, the now fully alive Iilah thought in a quiet though rather startled comprehension, "Why, of course, that's what I was trying to remember. That's what I was supposed to do."

He was puzzled that he could have forgotten. He had been sent during the course of an interstellar war—which apparently was still going on. He had been dropped on the planet under enormous difficulties and had been instantly snuffed out by enemy frustrators.

Now, he was ready to do his job.

He took test sightings on the sun and on the planets that were within reach of his radar signals. Then he set in motion an orderly process that would dissolve all the shields inside his own body.

He gathered his pressure forces for the final thrust that would bring the vital elements hard together at exactly the calculated moment.

The explosion that knocked a planet out of its orbit was recorded on every seismograph on the globe.

It would be some time, however, before astronomers would discover that earth was falling into the sun.

And no man would live to see Sol flare into nova brightness and burn up the solar system before gradually sinking back into a dim G state.

Even if Iilah had known that it was not the same war that had raged ten thousand million centuries before, he would have had no choice but to do as he did.

Robot atom bombs do not make up their own minds.

IN HIDING

by Wilmar H. Shiras (1908—   )

ASTOUNDING SCIENCE FICTION

November

It is safe to say that this story caught the science fiction readership of the time by surprise. Readers had not heard of the author, and few knew that she was a woman. The story made a tremendous impact, led to four other connecting novelettes, and was finally published in book form as Children of the Atom *(1953). The central idea is an old one in science fiction, dating back at least to Stapledon's* Odd John *and somewhat reminiscent of A. E. van Vogt's* Slain. *The mutated, exceptional child was and still is popular; perhaps some of the science fiction readership see themselves in this way or would like to think so.*

In any event, "In Hiding" is an excellent story, in spite of the fact that we now know that the type and cause of the mutation is impossible. Ms. Shiras is still writing and still publishing in the science fiction field, although her output over the years has been small.

("There are supermen among us," remember? They could be our children. —Except that I never believed it. That's not the way mutations take place. Besides, I was a bright child once, and I made people uneasy. My

father was convinced there was something odd about me, and John Campbell actually tried to tell me once that I might be a mutation. [I shouldn't have laughed.] The trouble was that I was quite sure that my bright- ness was well within the normal variation of the human species and was balanced by an abysmal capacity for various kinds of stupidities that were also [thank good- ness] within the normal variation of the species. I've known lots of bright people who had, in their time, been frighteningly bright children [some of them, I reluctantly admit, manifestly brighter than I am, or was] and all of them show plenty of capacity for non- brightness too. To expect anything else is to expect a chimpanzee to give birth to a young chimpanzee which, for some reason, is as bright as an ordinary human child. —But who cares about that. Read the story, and please don't bother to remind me that I, too, in some of my stories have used mutations to good effect. I know!—I.A.)

Peter Welles, psychiatrist, eyed the boy thoughtfully. Why had Timothy Paul's teacher sent him for examination?

"I don't know, myself, that there's really anything wrong with Tim," Miss Page had told Dr. Welles. "He seems perfectly normal. He's rather quiet as a rule, doesn't volunteer answers in class or anything of that sort. He gets along well enough with other boys and seems reasonably popular, although he has no special friends. His grades are satisfactory—he gets B faithfully in all his work. But when you've been teaching as long as I have, Peter, you get a feeling about certain ones. There is a tension about him—a look in his eyes sometimes—and he is very absentminded."

"What would your guess be?" Welles had asked. Sometimes these hunches were very valuable. Miss Page had taught school for thirty-odd years; she had been Peter's teacher in the past, and he thought highly of her opinion.

"I ought not to say," she answered. "There's nothing to go on—yet. But he might be starting something, and if it could be headed off—"

"Physicians are often called before the symptoms are sufficiently marked for the doctor to be able to see them," said Welles. "A patient, or the mother of a child, or any practiced observer, can often see that something is going to be wrong. But it's hard for the doctor in such cases. Tell me what you think I should look for."

"You won't pay too much attention to me? It's just what occurred to me, Peter; I know I'm not a trained psychiatrist. But it could be delusions of grandeur. Or it could be a withdrawing from the society of others. I always have to speak to him twice to get his attention in class—and he has no real chums."

Welles had agreed to see what he could find, and promised not to be too much influenced by what Miss Page herself called "an old woman's notions."

Timothy, when he presented himself for examination, seemed like an ordinary boy. He was perhaps a little small for his age, he had big dark eyes and close-cropped dark curls, thin sensitive fingers and—yes, a decided air of tension. But many boys were nervous on their first visit to the—psychiatrist. Peter often wished that he was able to concentrate on one or two schools, and spend a day a week or so getting acquainted with all the youngsters.

In response to Welles' preliminary questioning, Tim replied in a clear, low voice, politely and without wasting words. He was thirteen years old, and lived with his grandparents. His mother and father had died when he was a baby, and he did not remember them. He said that he was happy at home, and that he liked school "pretty well," that he liked to play with other boys. He named several boys when asked who his friends were.

"What lessons do you like at school?"

Tim hesitated, then said: "English, and arithmetic . . . and history . . . and geography," he finished thoughtfully. Then he looked up, and there was something odd in the glance.

"What do you like to do for fun?"

"Read, and play games."

"What games?"

"Ball games . . . and marbles . . . and things like that. I like to play with other boys," he added, after a barely perceptible pause, "anything they play."

"Do they play at your house?"

"No; we play on the school grounds. My grandmother doesn't like noise."

Was that the reason? When a quiet boy offers explanations, they may not be the right ones.

"What do you like to read?"

But about his reading Timothy was vague. He liked, he said, to read "boys' books," but could not name any.

Welles gave the boy the usual intelligence tests. Tim seemed willing, but his replies were slow in coming. *Perhaps,* Welles thought, I'm imagining this, but he is too careful—too *cautious.* Without taking time to figure exactly, Welles knew what Tim's I.Q. would be—about 120.

"What do you do outside of school?" asked the psychiatrist.

"I play with the other boys. After supper, I study my lessons."

"What did you do yesterday?"

"We played ball on the school playground."

Welles waited a while to see whether Tim would say anything of his own accord. The seconds stretched into minutes.

"Is that all?" said the boy finally. "May I go now?"

"No; there's one more test I'd like to give you today. A game, really. How's your imagination?"

"I don't know."

"Cracks on the ceiling—like those over there—do they look like anything to you? Faces, animals, or anything?"

Tim looked.

"Sometimes. And clouds, too. Bob saw a cloud last week that was like a hippo." Again the last sentence sounded like something tacked on at the last moment, a careful addition made for a reason.

Welles got out the Rorschach cards. But at the sight of them, his patient's tension increased, his wariness became unmistakably evident. The first time they went through the cards, the boy could scarcely be persuaded to say anything but, "I don't know."

"You can do better than this," said Welles. "We're going through them again. If you don't see anything in these pictures, I'll have to mark you a failure," he explained. "That won't do. You did all right on the other things. And maybe next time we'll do a game you'll like better."

"I don't feel like playing this game now. Can't we do it again next time?"

"May as well get it done now. It's not only a game, you know, Tim; it's a test. Try harder, and be a good sport."

So Tim, this time, told what he saw in the ink blots. They went through the cards slowly, and the test showed Tim's fear, and that there was something he was hiding; it showed his caution, a lack of trust, and an unnaturally high emotional self-control.

Miss Page had been right; the boy needed help.

"Now," said Welles cheerfully, "that's all over. We'll just run through them again quickly and I'll tell you what other people have seen in them."

A flash of genuine interest appeared on the boy's face for a moment.

Welles went through the cards slowly, seeing that Tim was attentive to every word. When he first said, "And some see what you saw here," the boy's relief was evident. Tim began to relax, and even to volunteer some remarks. When they had finished he ventured to ask a question.

"Dr. Welles, could you tell me the name of this test?"

"It's sometimes called the Rorschach test, after the man who worked it out."

"Would you mind spelling that?"

Welles spelled it, and added: "Sometimes it's called the ink-blot test."

Tim gave a start of surprise, and then relaxed again with a visible effort.

"What's the matter? You jumped."

"Nothing."

"Oh, come on! Let's have it," and Welles waited.

"Only that I thought about the ink-pool in the Kipling stories," said Tim, after a minute's reflection. "This is different."

"Yes, very different," laughed Welles. "I've never tried that. Would you like to?"

"Oh, no, sir," cried Tim earnestly.

"You're a little jumpy today," said Welles. "We've time for some more talk, if you are not too tired."

"No, I'm not very tired," said the boy warily.

Welles went to a drawer and chose a hypodermic needle. It wasn't usual, but perhaps—"I'll just give you a little shot to relax your nerves, shall I? Then we'd get on better."

When he turned around, the stark terror on the child's face stopped Welles in his tracks.

"Oh, no! Don't! Please, please, don't!"

Welles replaced the needle and shut the drawer before he said a word.

"I won't," he said, quietly. "I didn't know you didn't like shots. I won't give you any, Tim."

The boy, fighting for self-control, gulped and said nothing.

"It's all right," said Welles, lighting a cigarette and pretending to watch the smoke rise. Anything rather than appear to be watching the badly shaken small boy shivering in the chair opposite him. "Sorry. You didn't tell me about the things you don't like, the things you're afraid of."

The words hung in the silence.

"Yes," said Timothy slowly. "I'm afraid of shots. I hate needles. It's just one of those things." He tried to smile.

"We'll do without them, then. You've passed all the tests, Tim, and I'd like to walk home with you and tell your grandmother about it. Is that all right with you?"

"Yes, sir."

"We'll stop for something to eat," Welles went on, opening the door for his patient. "Ice cream, or a hot dog."

They went out together.

Timothy Paul's grandparents, Mr. and Mrs. Herbert Davis, lived in a large old-fashioned house that spelled money and position. The grounds were large, fenced, and bordered with shrubbery. Inside the house there was little that was new, everything was well-kept. Timothy led the psychiatrist to Mr. Davis's library, and then went in search of his grandmother.

When Welles saw Mrs. Davis, he thought he had some of the explanation. Some grandmothers are easy-going, jolly, comparatively young. This grandmother was, as it soon became apparent, quite different.

"Yes, Timothy is a pretty good boy," she said, smiling on her grandson. "We have always been strict with him, Dr. Welles, but I believe it pays. Even when he was a mere baby, we tried to teach him right ways. For example, when he was barely three I read him some little stories. And a few days later he was trying to tell us, if you will believe it, that he could read! Perhaps he was too young to know the nature of a lie, but I felt it my duty to make him understand. When he insisted, I spanked him. The child had a remarkable memory, and perhaps he thought that was all there was to reading. Well! I don't mean to brag of my brutality," said Mrs. Davis, with a charming smile. "I assure you, Dr. Welles, it was a painful experience for me. We've had very little occasion for punishments. Timothy is a good boy."

Welles murmured that he was sure of it.

"Timothy, you may deliver your papers now," said Mrs. Davis. "I am sure Dr. Welles will excuse you." And she settled herself for a good long talk about her grandson.

Timothy, it seemed, was the apple of her eye. He was a quiet boy, an obedient boy, and a bright boy.

"We have our rules, of course. I have never allowed Timothy

to forget that children should be seen and not heard, as the good old-fashioned saying is. When he first learned to turn somersaults, when he was three or four years old, he kept coming to me and saying, 'Grandmother, see me!' I simply had to be firm with him. 'Timothy,' I said, 'let us have no more of this! It is simply showing off. If it amuses you to turn somersaults, well and good. But it doesn't amuse me to watch you endlessly doing it. Play if you like, but do not demand admiration.' "

"Did you never play with him?"

"Certainly I played with him. And it was a pleasure to me also. We—Mr. Davis and I—taught him a great many games, and many kinds of handicraft. We read stories to him and taught him rhymes and songs. I took a special course in kindergarten craft, to amuse the child—and I must admit that it amused me also!" added Tim's grandmother, smiling reminiscently. "We made houses of toothpicks, with balls of clay at the corners. His grandfather took him for walks and drives. We no longer have a car, since my husband's sight has begun to fail him slightly, so now the garage is Timothy's workshop. We had windows cut in it, and a door, and nailed the large doors shut."

It soon became clear that Tim's life was not all strictures by any means. He had a workshop of his own, and upstairs beside his bedroom was his own library and study.

"He keeps his books and treasures there," said his grandmother, "his own little radio, and his schoolbooks, and his typewriter. When he was only seven years old, he asked us for a typewriter. But he is a careful child, Dr. Welles, not at all destructive, and I had read that in many schools they make use of typewriters in teaching young children to read and write and to spell. The words look the same as in printed books, you see; and less muscular effort is involved. So his grandfather got him a very nice noiseless typewriter, and he loved it dearly. I often hear it purring away as I pass through the hall. Timothy keeps his own rooms in good order, and his shop also. It is his own wish. You know how boys are—they do not wish others to meddle with their belongings. 'Very well, Timothy,' I told him, 'if a glance shows me that you can do it yourself properly, nobody will go into your rooms; but they must be kept neat.' And he has done so for several years. A very neat boy, Timothy."

"Timothy didn't mention his paper route," remarked Welles. "He said only that he plays with other boys after school."

"Oh, but he does," said Mrs. Davis. "He plays until five o'clock, and then he delivers his papers. If he is late, his grandfather walks down and calls him. The school is not very far from here, and Mr. Davis frequently walks down and watches the boys at their play. The paper route is Timothy's way of earning money to feed his cats. Do you care for cats, Dr. Welles?''

"Yes, I like cats very much," said the psychiatrist. "Many boys like dogs better."

"Timothy had a dog when he was a baby—a collie." Her eyes grew moist. "We all loved Ruff dearly. But I am no longer young, and the care and training of a dog is difficult. Timothy is at school or at the Boy Scout camp or something of the sort a great part of the time, and I thought it best that he should not have another dog. But you wanted to know about our cats, Dr. Welles. I raise Siamese cats."

"Interesting pets," said Welles cordially. "My aunt raised them at one time."

"Timothy is very fond of them. But three years ago he asked me if he could have a pair of black Persians. At first I thought not; but we like to please the child, and he promised to build their cages himself. He had taken a course in carpentry at vacation school. So he was allowed to have a pair of beautiful black Persians. But the very first litter turned out to be short-haired, and Timothy confessed that he had mated his queen to my Siamese tom, to see what would happen. Worse yet, he had mated his tom to one of my Siamese queens. I really was tempted to punish him. But, after all, I could see that he was curious as to the outcome of such crossbreeding. Of course I said the kittens must be destroyed. The second litter was exactly like the first—all black, with short hair. But you know what children are. Timothy begged me to let them live, and they were his first kittens. Three in one litter, two in the other. He might keep them, I said, if he would take full care of them and be responsible for all the expense. He mowed lawns and ran errands and made little footstools and bookcases to sell, and did all sorts of things, and probably used his allowance, too. But he kept the kittens and has a whole row of cages in the yard beside his workshop.''

"And their offspring?" inquired Welles, who could not see what all this had to do with the main question, but was willing to listen to anything that might lead to information.

"Some of the kittens appear to be pure Persian, and others pure Siamese. These he insisted on keeping, although, as I have explained to him, it would be dishonest to sell them, since they are not pure-bred. A good many of the kittens are black short-haired and these we destroy. But enough of cats, Dr. Welles. And I am afraid I am talking too much about my grandson.''

''I can understand that you are very proud of him,'' said Welles.

''I must confess that we are. And he is a bright boy. When he and his grandfather talk together, and with me also, he asks very intelligent questions. We do not encourage him to voice his opinions—I detest the smart-Aleck type of small boy—and yet I believe they would be quite good opinions for a child of his age.''

''Has his health always been good?'' asked Welles.

''On the whole, very good. I have taught him the value of exercise, play, wholesome food and suitable rest. He has had a few of the usual childish ailments, not seriously. And he never has colds. But, of course, he takes his cold shots twice a year when we do.''

''Does he mind the shots?'' asked Welles, as casually as he could.

''Not at all. I always say that he, though so young, sets an example I find hard to follow. I still flinch, and really rather dread the ordeal.''

Welles looked toward the door at a sudden, slight sound.

Timothy stood there, and he had heard. Again, fear was stamped on his face and terror looked out of his eyes.

''Timothy,'' said his grandmother, ''don't stare.''

''Sorry, sir,'' the boy managed to say.

''Are your papers all delivered? I did not realize we had been talking for an hour, Dr. Welles. Would you like to see Timothy's cats?'' Mrs. Davis inquired graciously. ''Timothy, take Dr. Welles to see your pets. We have had quite a talk about them.''

Welles got Tim out of the room as fast as he could. The boy led the way around the house and into the side yard where the former garage stood.

There the man stopped.

''Tim,'' he said, ''you don't have to show me the cats if you don't want to.''

''Oh, that's all right.''

''Is that part of what you are hiding? If it is, I don't want to see it until you are ready to show me.''

Tim looked up at him then.

"Thanks," he said. "I don't mind about the cats. Not if you like cats really."

"I really do. But, Tim, this I would like to know: You're not afraid of the needle. Could you tell me why you were afraid . . . why you said you were afraid . . . of my shot? The one I promised not to give you after all?"

Their eyes met.

"You won't tell?" asked Tim.

"I won't tell."

"Because it was pentothal. Wasn't it?"

Welles gave himself a slight pinch. Yes, he was awake. Yes, this was a little boy asking him about pentothal. A boy who— yes, certainly, a boy who knew about it.

"Yes, it was," said Welles. "A very small dose. You know what it is?"

"Yes, sir. I . . . I read about it somewhere. In the papers."

"Never mind that. You have a secret—something you want to hide. That's what you are afraid about, isn't it?"

The boy nodded dumbly.

"If it's anything wrong, or that might be wrong, perhaps I could help you. You'll want to know me better, first. You'll want to be sure you can trust me. But I'll be glad to help, any time you say the word, Tim. Or I might stumble on to things the way I did just now. One thing though—I never tell secrets."

"Never?"

"Never. Doctors and priests don't betray secrets. Doctors seldom, priests never. I guess I am more like a priest, because of the kind of doctoring I do."

He looked down at the boy's bowed head.

"Helping fellows who are scared sick," said the psychiatrist very gently. "Helping fellows in trouble, getting things straight again, fixing things up, unsnarling tangles. When I can, that's what I do. And I don't tell anything to anybody. It's just between that one fellow and me."

But, he added to himself, *I'll have to find out. I'll have to find out what ails this child. Miss Page is right—he needs me.*

They went to see the cats.

There were the Siamese in their cages, and the Persians in their cages, and there, in several small cages, the short-haired black cats and their hybrid offspring. "We take them into the house, or let them into this big cage, for exercise," explained Tim. "I take mine into my shop sometimes. These are all mine. Grandmother keeps hers on the sun porch."

"You'd never know these were not all pure-bred," observed Welles. "Which did you say were the full Persians? Any of their kittens here?"

"No; I sold them."

"I'd like to buy one. But these look just the same—it wouldn't make any difference to me. I want a pet, and wouldn't use it for breeding stock. Would you sell me one of these?"

Timothy shook his head.

"I'm sorry. I never sell any but the pure-breds."

It was then that Welles began to see what problem he faced. Very dimly he saw it, with joy, relief, hope and wild enthusiasm.

"Why not?" urged Welles. "I can wait for a pure-bred, if you'd rather, but why not one of these? They look just the same. Perhaps they'd be more interesting."

Tim looked at Welles for a long, long minute.

"I'll show you," he said. "Promise to wait here? No, I'll let you come into the workroom. Wait a minute, please."

The boy drew a key from under his blouse, where it had hung suspended from a chain, and unlocked the door of his shop. He went inside, closed the door, and Welles could hear him moving about for a few moments. Then he came to the door and beckoned.

"Don't tell grandmother," said Tim. "I haven't told her yet. If it lives, I'll tell her next week."

In the corner of the shop under a table there was a box, and in the box there was a Siamese cat. When she saw a stranger she tried to hide her kittens; but Tim lifted her gently, and then Welles saw. Two of the kittens looked like little white rats with stringy tails and smudgy paws, ears and noses. But the third— yes, it was going to be a different sight. It was going to be a beautiful cat if it lived. It had long, silky white hair like the finest Persian, and the Siamese markings were showing up plainly.

Welles caught his breath.

"Congratulations, old man! Haven't you told anyone yet?"

"She's not ready to show. She's not a week old."

"But you're going to show her?"

"Oh, yes, grandmother will be thrilled. She'll love her. Maybe there'll be more."

"You knew this would happen. You made it happen. You planned it all from the start," accused Welles.

"Yes," admitted the boy.

"How did you know?"

The boy turned away.

"I read it somewhere," said Tim.

The cat jumped back into the box and began to nurse her babies. Welles felt as if he could endure no more. Without a glance at anything else in the room—and everything else was hidden under tarpaulins and newspapers—he went to the door.

"Thanks for showing me, Tim," he said. "And when you have any to sell, remember me. I'll wait. I want one like that."

The boy followed him out and locked the door carefully.

"But Tim," said the psychiatrist, "that's not what you were afraid I'd find out. I wouldn't need a drug to get you to tell me this, would I?"

Tim replied carefully, "I didn't want to tell this until I was ready. Grandmother really ought to know first. But you made me tell you."

"Tim," said Peter Welles earnestly, "I'll see you again. Whatever you are afraid of, don't be afraid of me. I often guess secrets. I'm on the way to guessing yours already. But nobody else need ever know."

He walked rapidly home, whistling to himself from time to time. Perhaps he, Peter Welles, was the luckiest man in the world.

He had scarcely begun to talk to Timothy on the boy's next appearance at the office, when the phone in the hall rang. On his return, when he opened the door he saw a book in Tim's hands. The boy made a move as if to hide it, and thought better of it.

Welles took the book and looked at it.

"Want to know more about Rorschach, eh?" he asked.

"I saw it on the shelf. I—"

"Oh, that's all right," said Welles, who had purposely left the book near the chair Tim would occupy. "But what's the matter with the library?"

"They've got some books about it, but they're on the closed shelves. I couldn't get them." Tim spoke without thinking first, and then caught his breath.

But Welles replied calmly: "I'll get it out for you. I'll have it next time you come. Take this one along today when you go. Tim, I mean it—you can trust me."

"I can't tell you anything," said the boy. "You've found out some things. I wish . . . oh, I don't know what I wish! But I'd rather be let alone. I don't need help. Maybe I never will. If I do, can't I come to you then?"

Welles pulled out his chair and sat down slowly.

"Perhaps that would be the best way, Tim. But why wait for the ax to fall? I might be able to help you ward it off—what you're afraid of. You can kid people along about the cats; tell them you were fooling around to see what would happen. But you can't fool all of the people all of the time, they tell me. Maybe with me to help, you could. Or with me to back you up, the blowup would be easier. Easier on your grandparents, too."

"I haven't done anything wrong!"

"I'm beginning to be sure of that. But things you try to keep hidden may come to light. The kitten—you could hide it, but you don't want to. You've got to risk something to show it."

"I'll tell them I read it somewhere."

"That wasn't true, then. I thought not. You figured it out."

There was silence.

Then Timothy Paul said: "Yes, I figured it out. But that's my secret."

"It's safe with me."

But the boy did not trust him yet. Welles soon learned that he had been tested. Tim took the book home, and returned it, took the library books which Welles got for him, and in due course returned them also. But he talked little and was still wary. Welles could talk all he liked, but he got little or nothing out of Tim. Tim had told all he was going to tell. He would talk about nothing except what any boy would talk about.

After two months of this, during which Welles saw Tim officially once a week and unofficially several times—showing up at the school playground to watch games, or meeting Tim on the paper route and treating him to a soda after it was finished— Welles had learned very little more. He tried again. He had probed no more during the two months, respected the boy's silence, trying to give him time to get to know and trust him.

But one day he asked: "What are you going to do when you grow up, Tim? Breed cats?"

Tim laughed a denial.

"I don't know what, yet. Sometimes I think one thing, sometimes another."

This was a typical boy answer. Welles disregarded it.

"What would you like to do best of all?" he asked.

Tim leaned forward eagerly. "What you do!" he cried.

"You've been reading up on it, I suppose," said Welles, as casually as he could. "Then you know, perhaps, that before anyone can do what I do, he must go through it himself, like a patient. He must also study medicine and be a full-fledged doctor, of course. You can't do that yet. But you can have the works now, like a patient.''

''Why? For the experience?''

''Yes. And for the cure. You'll have to face that fear and lick it. You'll have to straighten out a lot of other things, or at least face them.''

''My fear will be gone when I'm grown up,'' said Timothy. ''I think it will. I hope it will.''

''Can you be sure?''

''No,'' admitted the boy. ''I don't know exactly why I'm afraid. I just know I *must* hide things. Is that bad, too?''

''Dangerous, perhaps.''

Timothy thought a while in silence. Welles smoked three cigarettes and yearned to pace the floor, but dared not move.

''What would it be like?'' asked Tim finally.

''You'd tell me about yourself. What you remember. Your childhood—the way your grandmother runs on when she talks about you.''

''She sent me out of the room. I'm not supposed to think I'm bright,'' said Tim, with one of his rare grins.

''And you're not supposed to know how well she reared you?''

''She did fine,'' said Tim. ''She taught me all the wisest things I ever knew.''

''Such as what?''

''Such as shutting up. Not telling all you know. Not showing off.''

''I see what you mean,'' said Welles. ''Have you heard the story of St. Thomas Aquinas?''

''No.''

''When he was a student in Paris, he never spoke out in class, and the others thought him stupid. One of them kindly offered to help him, and went over all the work very patiently to make him understand it. And then one day they came to a place where the other student got all mixed up and had to admit he didn't understand. Then Thomas suggested a solution and it was the right one. He knew more than any of the others all the time; but they called him the Dumb Ox.''

Tim nodded gravely.

''And when he grew up?'' asked the boy.

''He was the greatest thinker of all time,'' said Welles. ''A fourteenth-century super-brain. He did more original work than any other ten great men; and he died young.''

After that, it was easier.

"How do I begin?'' asked Timothy.

"You'd better begin at the beginning. Tell me all you can remember about your early childhood, before you went to school.''

Tim gave this his consideration.

"I'll have to go forward and backward a lot," he said. "I couldn't put it all in order.''

"That's all right. Just tell me today all you can remember about that time of your life. By next week you'll have remembered more. As we go on to later periods of your life, you may remember things that belonged to an earlier time; tell them then. We'll make some sort of order out of it.''

Welles listened to the boy's revelations with growing excitement. He found it difficult to keep outwardly calm.

"When did you begin to read?'' Welles asked.

"I don't know when it was. My grandmother read me some stories, and somehow I got the idea about the words. But when I tried to tell her I could read, she spanked me. She kept saying I couldn't, and I kept saying I could, until she spanked me. For a while I had a dreadful time, because I didn't know any word she hadn't read to me—I guess I sat beside her and watched, or else I remembered and then went over it by myself right after. I must have learned as soon as I got the idea that each group of letters on the page was a word.''

"The word-unit method,'' Welles commented. "Most self-taught readers learned like that.''

"Yes. I have read about it since. And Macaulay could read when he was three, but only upside-down, because of standing opposite when his father read the Bible to the family.''

"There are many cases of children who learned to read as you did, and surprised their parents. Well? How did you get on?''

"One day I noticed that two words looked almost alike and sounded almost alike. They were 'can' and 'man.' I remember staring at them and then it was like something beautiful boiling up in me. I began to look carefully at the words, but in a crazy excitement. I was a long while at it, because when I put down the book and tried to stand up I was stiff all over. But I had the idea, and after that it wasn't hard to figure out almost any words. The really hard words are the common ones that you get all the

time in easy books. Other words are pronounced the way they
are spelled.''

"And nobody knew you could read?''

"No. Grandmother told me not to say I could, so I didn't. She
read to me often, and that helped. We had a great many books,
of course. I liked those with pictures. Once or twice they caught
me with a book that had no pictures, and then they'd take it
away and say, 'I'll find a book for a little boy.' ''

"Do you remember what books you liked then?''

"Books about animals, I remember. And geographies. It was
funny about animals—''

Once you got Timothy started, thought Welles, it wasn't hard
to get him to go on talking.

"One day I was at the Zoo,'' said Tim, "and by the cages
alone. Grandmother was resting on a bench and she let me walk
along by myself. People were talking about the animals and I
began to tell them all I knew. It must have been funny in a way,
because I had read a lot of words I couldn't pronounce correctly,
words I had never heard spoken. They listened and asked me
questions and I thought I was just like grandfather, teaching
them the way he sometimes taught me. And then they called
another man to come, and said, 'Listen to this kid; he's a
scream!' and I saw they were all laughing at me.''

Timothy's face was redder than usual, but he tried to smile as
he added, "I can see now how it must have sounded funny. And
unexpected, too; that's a big point in humor. But my little
feelings were so dreadfully hurt that I ran back to my grandmother crying, and she couldn't find out why. But it served me
right for disobeying her. She always told me not to tell people
things; she said a child had nothing to teach its elders.''

"Not in that way, perhaps—at that age.''

"But, honestly, some grown people don't know very much,''
said Tim. "When we went on the train last year, a woman came
up and sat beside me and started to tell me things a little boy
should know about California. I told her I'd lived here all my
life, but I guess she didn't even know we are taught things in
school, and she tried to tell me things, and almost everything
was wrong.''

"Such as what?'' asked Welles, who had also suffered from
tourists.

"We . . . she said so many things . . . but I thought this was
the funniest: She said all the Missions were so old and interesting,
and I said yes, and she said, 'You know, they were all built long

before Columbus discovered America,' and I thought she meant it for a joke, so I laughed. She looked very serious and said, 'Yes, those people all come up here from Mexico.' I suppose she thought they were Aztec temples.''

Welles, shaking with laughter, could not but agree that many adults were sadly lacking in the rudiments of knowledge.

''After that Zoo experience, and a few others like it, I began to get wise to myself,'' continued Tim. ''People who knew things didn't want to hear me repeating them, and people who didn't know, wouldn't be taught by a four-year-old baby. I guess I was four when I began to write.''

''How?''

''Oh, I just thought if I couldn't say anything to anybody at any time, I'd burst. So I began to put it down—in printing, like in books. Then I found out about writing, and we had some old-fashioned schoolbooks that taught how to write. I'm left-handed. When I went to school, I had to use my right hand. But by then I had learned how to pretend that I didn't know things. I watched the others and did as they did. My grandmother told me to do that.''

''I wonder why she said that,'' marveled Welles.

''She knew I wasn't used to other children, she said, and it was the first time she had left me to anyone else's care. So, she told me to do what the others did and what my teacher said,'' explained Tim simply, ''and I followed her advice literally. I pretended I didn't know anything, until the others began to know it, too. Lucky I was so shy. But there were things to learn, all right. Do you know, when I was first sent to school, I was disappointed because the teacher dressed like other women. The only picture of teachers I had noticed were those in an old Mother Goose book, and I thought that all teachers wore hoop skirts. But as soon as I saw her, after the little shock of surprise, I knew it was silly, and I never told.''

The psychiatrist and the boy laughed together.

''We played games. I had to learn to play with children, and not be surprised when they slapped or pushed me. I just couldn't figure out why they'd do that, or what good it did them. But if it was to surprise me, I'd say 'Boo' and surprise them some time later; and if they were mad because I had taken a ball or something they wanted, I'd play with them.''

''Anybody ever try to beat you up?''

''Oh, yes. But I had a book about boxing—with pictures. You

can't learn much from pictures, but I got some practice too, and that helped. I didn't want to win, anyway. That's what I like about games of strength or skill—I'm fairly matched, and I don't have to be always watching in case I might show off or try to boss somebody around.''

''You must have tried bossing sometimes.''

''In books, they all cluster around the boy who can teach new games and think up new things to play. But I found out that doesn't work. They just want to do the same thing all the time—like hide and seek. It's no fun if the first one to be caught is 'it' next time. The rest just walk in any old way and don't try to hide or even to run, because it doesn't matter whether they are caught. But you can't get the boys to see that, and play right, so the last one caught is 'it'.''

Timothy looked at his watch.

''Time to go,'' he said. ''I've enjoyed talking to you, Dr. Welles. I hope I haven't bored you too much.''

Welles recognized the echo and smiled appreciatively at the small boy.

''You didn't tell me about the writing. Did you start to keep a diary?''

''No. It was a newspaper. One page a day, no more and no less. I still keep it,'' confided Tim. ''But I get more on the page now. I type it.''

''And you write with either hand now?''

''My left hand is my own secret writing. For school and things like that I use my right hand.''

When Timothy had left, Welles congratulated himself. But for the next month he got no more. Tim would not reveal a single significant fact. He talked about ball-playing, he described his grandmother's astonished delight over the beautiful kitten, he told of its growth and the tricks it played. He gravely related such enthralling facts as that he liked to ride on trains, that his favorite wild animal was the lion, and that he greatly desired to see snow falling. But not a word of what Welles wanted to hear. The psychiatrist, knowing that he was again being tested, waited patiently.

Then one afternoon when Welles, fortunately unoccupied with a patient, was smoking a pipe on his front porch, Timothy Paul strode into the yard.

''Yesterday Miss Page asked me if I was seeing you and I said yes. She said she hoped my grandparents didn't find it too expensive, because you had told her I was all right and didn't need to have her worrying about me. And then I said to grandma, was it expensive for you to talk to me, and she said, 'Oh no, dear; the school pays for that. It was your teacher's idea that you have a few talks with Dr. Welles.' ''

"I'm glad you came to me, Tim, and I'm sure you didn't give me away to either of them. Nobody's paying me. The school pays for my services if a child is in a bad way and his parents are poor. It's a new service, since 1956. Many maladjusted children can be helped—much more cheaply to the state than the cost of having them go crazy or become criminals or something. You understand all that. But—sit down, Tim!—I can't charge the state for you, and I can't charge your grandparents. You're adjusted marvelously well in every way, as far as I can see; and when I see the rest, I'll be even more sure of it.''

"Well—gosh! I wouldn't have come—'' Tim was stammering in confusion. "You ought to be paid. I take up so much of your time. Maybe I'd better not come any more.''

"I think you'd better. Don't you?''

"Why are you doing it for nothing, Dr. Welles?''

"I think you know why.''

The boy sat down in the glider and pushed himself meditatively back and forth. The glider squeaked.

"You're interested. You're curious,'' he said.

"That's not all, Tim.''

Squeak-squeak. Squeak-squeak.

"I know,'' said Timothy. "I believe it. Look, is it all right if I call you Peter? Since we're friends.''

At their next meeting, Timothy went into details about his newspaper. He had kept all the copies, from the first smudged, awkwardly printed pencil issues to the very latest neatly typed ones. But he would not show Welles any of them.

"I just put down every day the things I most wanted to say, the news or information or opinion I had to swallow unsaid. So it's a wild medley. The earlier copies are awfully funny. Sometimes I guess what they were all about, what made me write them. Sometimes I remember. I put down the books I read too, and mark them like school grades, on two points—how I liked the book, and whether it was good. And whether I had read it before, too.''

"How many books do you read? What's your reading speed?''

It proved that Timothy's reading speed on new books of adult

level varied from eight hundred to nine hundred fifty words a
minute. The average murder mystery—he loved them—took him
a little less than an hour. A year's homework in history Tim
performed easily by reading his textbook through three or four
times during the year. He apologized for that, but explained that
he had to know what was in the book so as not to reveal in
examinations too much that he had learned from other sources.
Evenings, when his grandparents believed him to be doing homework he spent his time reading other books, or writing his
newspaper, "or something." As Welles had already guessed,
Tim had read everything in his grandfather's library, everything
of interest in the public library that was not on the closed
shelves, and everything he could order from the state library.

"What do the librarians say?"

"They think the books are for my grandfather. I tell them that,
if they ask what a little boy wants with such a big book. Peter,
telling so many lies is what gets me down. I have to do it, don't
I?"

"As far as I can see, you do," agreed Welles. "But here's
material for a while in my library. There'll have to be a closed
shelf here, too, though, Tim."

"Could you tell me why? I know about the library books.
Some of them might scare people, and some are—"

"Some of my books might scare you too, Tim. I'll tell you a
little about abnormal psychology if you like, one of these days,
and then I think you'll see that until you're actually trained to
deal with such cases, you'd be better off not knowing too much
about them."

"I don't want to be morbid," agreed Tim. "All right. I'll read
only what you give me. And from now on I'll tell you things.
There was more than the newspaper, you know."

"I thought as much. Do you want to go on with your tale?"

"It started when I first wrote a letter to a newspaper—of
course, under a pen name. They printed it. For a while I had a
high old time of it—a letter almost every day, using all sorts of
pen names. Then I branched out to magazines, letters to the
editor again. And stories—I tried stories."

He looked a little doubtfully at Welles, who said only: "How
old were you when you sold the first story?"

"Eight," said Timothy. "And when the check came, with my
name on it, 'T. Paul,' I didn't know what in the world to do."

"That's a thought. What did you do?"

"There was a sign in the window of the bank. I always read

signs, and that one came back to my mind. 'Banking By Mail.' You can see I was pretty desperate. So I got the name of a bank across the Bay and I wrote them—on my typewriter—and said I wanted to start an account, and here was a check to start it with. Oh, I was scared stiff, and had to keep saying to myself that, after all, nobody could do much to me. It was my own money. But you don't know what it's like to be only a small boy! They sent the check back to me and I died ten deaths when I saw it. But the letter explained. I hadn't endorsed it. They sent me a blank to fill out about myself. I didn't know how many lies I dared to tell. But it was my money and I had to get it. If I could get it into the bank, then some day I could get it out. I gave my business as 'author' and I gave my age as twenty-four. I thought that was awfully old.''

"I'd like to see the story. Do you have a copy of the magazine around?''

"Yes," said Tim. "But nobody noticed it—I mean, 'T. Paul' could be anybody. And when I saw magazines for writers on the newsstands and bought them, I got on to the way to use a pen name on the story and my own name and address up in the corner. Before that I used a pen name and sometimes never got the things back or heard about them. Sometimes I did, though.''

"What then?''

"Oh, then I'd endorse the check payable to me and sign the pen name, and then sign my own name under it. Was I scared to do that! But it was my money.''

"Only stories?''

"Articles, too. And things. That's enough of that for today. Only—I just wanted to say—a while ago, T. Paul told the bank he wanted to switch some of the money over to a checking account. To buy books by mail, and such. So, I could pay you, Dr. Welles—'' with sudden formality.

"No, Tim," said Peter Welles firmly. "The pleasure is all mine. What I want is to see the story that was published when you were eight. And some of the other things that made T. Paul rich enough to keep a consulting psychiatrist on the payroll. And, for the love of Pete, will you tell me how all this goes on without your grandparents' knowing a thing about it?''

"Grandmother thinks I send in box tops and fill out coupons," said Tim. "She doesn't bring in the mail. She says her little boy gets such a big bang out of that little chore. Anyway that's what she said when I was eight. I played mailman. And there were box tops—I showed them to her, until she said, about the third time, that really she wasn't greatly interested in such matters. By now she has the habit of waiting for me to bring in the mail.''

Peter Welles thought that was quite a day of revelation. He spent a quiet evening at home, holding his head and groaning, trying to take it all in.

And that I.Q.—120, nonsense! The boy had been holding out on him. Tim's reading had obviously included enough about I. Q. tests, enough puzzles and oddments in magazines and such, to enable him to stall successfully. What could he do if he would cooperate?

Welles made up his mind to find out.

He didn't find out. Timothy Paul went swiftly through the whole range of Superior Adult tests without a failure of any sort. There were no tests yet devised that could measure his intelligence. While he was still writing his age with one figure, Timothy Paul had faced alone, and solved alone, problems that would have baffled the average adult. He had adjusted to the hardest task of all—that of appearing to be a fairly normal, B-average small boy.

And it must be that there was more to find out about him. What did he write? And what did he do besides read and write, learn carpentry and breed cats and magnificently fool his whole world?

When Peter Welles had read some of Tim's writings, he was surprised to find that the stories the boy had written were vividly human, the product of close observation of human nature. The articles, on the other hand, were closely reasoned and showed thorough study and research. Apparently Tim read every word o' several newspapers and a score or more of periodicals.

"Oh, sure," said Tim, when questioned. "I read everything. I go back once in a while and review old ones, too."

"If you can write like this," demanded Welles, indicating a magazine in which a staid and scholarly article had appeared, "and this"—this was a man-to-man political article giving the arguments for and against a change in the whole Congressional system—"then why do you always talk to me in the language of an ordinary stupid schoolboy?"

"Because I'm only a boy," replied Timothy. "What would happen if I went around talking like that?"

"You might risk it with me. You've showed me these things."

"I'd never dare to risk talking like that. I might forget and do it again before others. Besides, I can't pronounce half the words."

"What!"

"I never look up a pronunciation," explained Timothy. "In case I do slip and use a word beyond the average, I can anyway hope I didn't say it right."

Welles shouted with laughter, but was sober again as he realized the implications back of that thoughtfulness.

"You're just like an explorer living among savages," said the psychiatrist. "You have studied the savages carefully and tried to imitate them so they won't know there are differences."

"Something like that," acknowledged Tim.

"That's why your stories are so human," said Welles. "That one about the awful little girl—"

They both chuckled.

"Yes, that was my first story," said Tim. "I was almost eight, and there was a boy in my class who had a brother, and the boy next door was the other one, the one who was picked on."

"How much of the story was true?"

"The first part. I used to see, when I went over there, how that girl picked on Bill's brother's friend, Steve. She wanted to play with Steve all the time herself and whenever he had boys over, she'd do something awful. And Steve's folks were like I said—they wouldn't let Steve do anything to a girl. When she threw all the watermelon rinds over the fence into his yard, he just had to pick them all up and say nothing back; and she'd laugh at him over the fence. She got him blamed for things he never did, and when he had work to do in the yard she'd hang out of her window and scream at him and make fun. I thought first, what made her act like that, and then I made up a way for him to get even with her, and wrote it out the way it might have happened."

"Didn't you pass the idea on to Steve and let him try it?"

"Gosh, no! I was only a little boy. Kids seven don't give ideas to kids ten. That's the first thing I had to learn—to be always the one that kept quiet, especially if there was any older boy or girl around, even only a year or two older. I had to learn to look blank and let my mouth hang open and say, 'I don't get it,' to almost everything."

"And Miss Page thought it was odd that you had no close friends of your own age," said Welles. "You must be the loneliest boy that ever walked this earth, Tim. You've lived in hiding like a criminal. But tell me, what are you afraid of?"

"I'm afraid of being found out, of course. The only way I can live in this world is in disguise—until I'm grown up, at any rate. At first it was just my grandparents' scolding me and telling me not to show off, and the way people laughed if I tried to talk to them. Then I saw how people hate anyone who is better or brighter or luckier. Some people sort of trade off; if you're bad at one thing you're good at another, but they'll forgive you for being good at some things, if you're not good at others so they can balance it off. They can beat you at something. You have to strike a balance. A child has no chance at all. No grownup can stand it to have a child know anything he doesn't. Oh, a little thing if it amuses them. But not much of anything. There's an old story about a man who found himself in a country where everyone else was blind. I'm like that—but they shan't put out my eyes. I'll never let them know I can see anything.''

"Do you see things that no grown person can see?"

Tim waved his hand towards the magazines.

"Only like that, I meant. I hear people talking in street cars and stores, and while they work, and around. I read about the way they act—in the news. I'm like them, just like them, only I seem about a hundred years older—more matured.''

"Do you mean that none of them have much sense?''

"I don't mean that exactly. I mean that so few of them have any, or show it if they do have. They don't even seem to want to. They're good people in their way, but what could they make of me? Even when I was seven, I could understand their motives, but they couldn't understand their own motives. And they're so lazy—they don't seem to want to know or to understand. When I first went to the library for books, the books I learned from were seldom touched by any of the grown people. But they were meant for ordinary grown people. But the grown people didn't want to know things—they only wanted to fool around. I feel about most people the way my grandmother feels about babies and puppies. Only she doesn't have to pretend to be a puppy all the time,'' Tim added, with a little bitterness.

"You have a friend now, in me.''

"Yes, Peter,'' said Tim, brightening up. "And I have pen friends, too. People like what I write, because they can't see I'm only a little boy. When I grow up—''

Tim did not finish that sentence. Welles understood, now, some of the fears that Tim had not dared to put into words at all. When he grew up, would he be as far beyond all other grownups as he had, all his life, been above his contemporaries? The adult friends whom he now met on fairly equal terms—would they then, too, seem like babies or puppies?

Peter did not dare to voice the thought, either. Still less did he venture to hint at another thought. Tim, so far, had no great interest in girls; they existed for him as part of the human race, but there would come a time when Tim would be a grown man and would wish to marry. And where among the puppies could he find a mate?

"When you're grown up, we'll still be friends," said Peter. "And who are the others?"

It turned out that Tim had pen friends all over the world. He played chess by correspondence—a game he never dared to play in person, except when he forced himself to move the pieces about idly and let his opponent win at least half the time. He had, also, many friends who had read something he had written, and had written to him about it, thus starting a correspondence-friendship. After the first two or three of these, he had started some on his own account, always with people who lived at a great distance. To most of these he gave a name which, although not false, looked it. That was Paul T. Lawrence. Lawrence was his middle name; and with a comma after the Paul, it was actually his own name. He had a post office box under that name, for which T. Paul of the large bank account was his reference.

"Pen friends abroad? Do you know languages?"

Yes, Tim did. He had studied by correspondence, also; many universities gave extension courses in that manner, and lent the student records to play so that he could learn the correct pronunciation. Tim had taken several such courses, and learned other languages from books. He kept all these languages in practice by means of the letters to other lands and the replies which came to him.

"I'd buy a dictionary, and then I'd write to the mayor of some town, or to a foreign newspaper, and ask them to advertise for some pen friends to help me learn the language. We'd exchange souvenirs and things."

Nor was Welles in the least surprised to find that Timothy had also taken other courses by correspondence. He had completed, within three years, more than half the subjects offered by four separate universities, and several other courses, the most recent being Architecture. The boy, not yet fourteen, had completed a full course in that subject, and had he been able to disguise himself as a full-grown man, could have gone out at once and built almost anything you'd like to name, for he also knew much of the trades involved.

"It always said how long an average student took, and I'd take that long," said Tim, "so, of course, I had to be working several schools at the same time."

"And carpentry at the playground summer school?"

"Oh, yes. But there I couldn't do too much, because people could see me. But I learned how, and it made a good coverup, so I could make cages for the cats, and all that sort of thing. And many boys are good with their hands. I like to work with my hands. I built my own radio, too—it gets all the foreign stations, and that helps me with my languages."

"How did you figure it out about the cats?" said Welles.

"Oh, there had to be recessives, that's all. The Siamese coloring was a recessive, and it had to be mated with another recessive. Black was one possibility, and white was another, but I started with black because I liked it better. I might try white too, but I have so much else on my mind—"

He broke off suddenly and would say no more.

Their next meeting was by prearrangement at Tim's workshop. Welles met the boy after school and they walked to Tim's home together; there the boy unlocked his door and snapped on the lights.

Welles looked around with interest. There was a bench, a tool chest. Cabinets, padlocked. A radio, clearly not store-purchased. A file cabinet, locked. Something on a table, covered with a cloth. A box in the corner—no, two boxes in two corners. In each of them was a mother cat with kittens. Both mothers were black Persians.

"This one must be all black Persian," Tim explained. "Her third litter and never a Siamese marking. But this one carries both recessives in her. Last time she had a Siamese short-haired kitten. This morning—I had to go to school. Let's see."

They bent over the box where the newborn kittens lay. One kitten was like the mother. The other two were Siamese-Persian; a male and a female.

"You've done it again, Tim!" shouted Welles. "Congratulations!"

They shook hands in jubilation.

"I'll write it in the record," said the boy blissfully.

In a nickel book marked "compositions" Tim's left hand

added the entries. He had used the correct symbols—F_1, F_2, F_3; Ss, Bl.

"The dominants in capitals," he explained, "B for black, and S for short hair; the recessives in small letters—s for Siamese, l for long hair. Wonderful to write ll or ss again, Peter! Twice more. And the other kitten is carrying the Siamese marking as a recessive."

He closed the book in triumph.

"Now," and he marched to the covered thing on the table, "my latest big secret."

Tim lifted the cloth carefully and displayed a beautifully built doll house. No, a model house—Welles corrected himself swiftly. A beautiful model, and—yes, built to scale.

"The roof comes off. See, it has a big storage room and a room for a play room or a maid or something. Then I lift off the attic—"

"Good heavens!" cried Peter Welles. "Any little girl would give her soul for this!"

"I used fancy wrapping papers for the wallpapers. I wove the rugs on a little hand loom," gloated Timothy. "The furniture's just like real, isn't it? Some I bought; that's plastic. Some I made of construction paper and things. The curtains were the hardest; but I couldn't ask grandmother to sew them—"

"Why not?" the amazed doctor managed to ask.

"She might recognize this afterwards," said Tim, and he lifted off the upstairs floor.

"Recognize it? You haven't showed it to her? Then when would she see it?"

"She might not," admitted Tim. "But I don't like to take some risks."

"That's a very livable floor plan you've used," said Welles, bending closer to examine the house in detail.

"Yes, I thought so. It's awful how many house plans leave no clear wall space for books or pictures. Some of them have doors placed so you have to detour around the dining room table every time you go from the living room to the kitchen, or so that a whole corner of a room is good for nothing, with doors at all angles. Now, I designed this house to—"

"You designed it, Tim!"

"Why, sure. Oh, I see—you thought I built it from blueprints I'd bought. My first model home, I did, but the architecture courses gave me so many ideas that I wanted to see how they would look. Now, the cellar and game room—"

* * *

Welles came to himself an hour later, and gasped when he looked at his watch.

"It's too late. My patient has gone home again by this time. I may as well stay—how about the paper route?"

"I gave that up. Grandmother offered to feed the cats as soon as I gave her the kitten. And I wanted the time for this. Here are the pictures of the house."

The color prints were very good.

"I'm sending them and an article to the magazines," said Tim. "This time I'm T. L. Paul. Sometimes I used to pretend all the different people I am were talking together—but now I talk to you instead, Peter."

"Will it bother the cats if I smoke? Thanks. Nothing I'm likely to set on fire, I hope? Put the house together and let me sit here and look at it. I want to look in through the windows. Put its lights on. There."

The young architect beamed, and snapped on the little lights.

"Nobody can see in here. I got Venetian blinds; and when I work in here, I even shut them sometimes."

"If I'm to know all about you, I'll have to go through the alphabet from A to Z," said Peter Welles. "This is Architecture. What else in the A's?"

"Astronomy. I showed you those articles. My calculations proved correct. Astrophysics—I got A in the course, but haven't done anything original so far. Art, no. I can't paint or draw very well, except mechanical drawing. I've done all the Merit Badge work in scouting, all through the alphabet."

"Darned if I can see you as a Boy Scout," protested Welles.

"I'm a very good Scout. I have almost as many badges as any other boy my age in the troop. And at camp I do as well as most city boys."

"Do you do a good turn every day?"

"Yes," said Timothy. "Started that when I first read about Scouting—I was a Scout at heart before I was old enough to be a Cub. You know, Peter, when you're very young, you take all that seriously about the good deed every day, and the good habits and ideals and all that. And then you get older and it begins to seem funny and childish and posed and artificial, and you smile in a superior way and make jokes. But there is a third step, too, when you take it all seriously again. People who make fun of the Scout Law are doing the boys a lot of harm; but those who believe in things like that don't know how to say so, without sounding priggish and platitudinous. I'm going to do an article on it before long.''

"Is the Scout Law your religion—if I may put it that way?"

"No," said Timothy. "But 'a Scout is Reverent.' Once I tried to study the churches and find out what was the truth. I wrote letters to pastors of all denominations—all those in the phone book and the newspaper—when I was on a vacation in the East, I got the names, and then wrote after I got back. I couldn't write to people here in the city. I said I wanted to know which church was true, and expected them to write to me and tell me about theirs, and argue with me, you know. I could read library books, and all they had to do was recommend some, I told them, and then correspond with me a little about them.''

"Did they?"

"Some of them answered," said Tim, "but nearly all of them told me to go to somebody near me. Several said they were very busy men. Some gave me the name of a few books, but none of them told me to write again, and . . . and I was only a little boy. Nine years old, so I couldn't talk to anybody. When I thought it over, I knew that I couldn't very well join any church so young, unless it was my grandparents' church. I keep on going there—it is a good church and it teaches a great deal of truth, I am sure. I'm reading all I can find, so when I am old enough I'll know what I must do. How old would you say I should be, Peter?''

"College age," replied Welles. "You are going to college? By then, any of the pastors would talk to you—except those that are too busy!''

"It's a moral problem, really. Have I the right to wait? But I have to wait. It's like telling lies—I have to tell some lies, but I hate to. If I have a moral obligation to join the true church as soon as I find it, well, what then? I can't until I'm eighteen or twenty?''

"If you can't, you can't. I should think that settles it. You are legally a minor, under the control of your grandparents, and while you might claim the right to go where your conscience leads you, it would be impossible to justify and explain your choice without giving yourself away entirely—just as you are obliged to go to school until you are at least eighteen, even though you know more than most Ph.D's. It's all part of the game, and He who made you must understand that.''

"I'll never tell you any lies," said Tim. "I was getting so desperately lonely—my pen pals didn't know anything about me really. I told them only what was right for them to know. Little kids are satisfied to be with other people, but when you get a little older you have to make friends, really."

"Yes, that's a part of growing up. You have to reach out to others and share thoughts with them. You've kept to yourself too long as it is."

"It wasn't that I wanted to. But without a real friend, it was only pretense, and I never could let my playmates know anything about me. I studied them and wrote stories about them and it was all of them, but it was only a tiny part of me."

"I'm proud to be your friend, Tim. Every man needs a friend. I'm proud that you trust me."

Tim patted the cat a moment in silence and then looked up with a grin.

"How would you like to hear my favorite joke?" he asked.

"Very much," said the psychiatrist, bracing himself for almost any major shock.

"It's records. I recorded this from a radio program."

Welles listened. He knew little of music, but the symphony which he heard pleased him. The announcer praised it highly in little speeches before and after each movement. Timothy giggled.

"Like it?"

"Very much. I don't see the joke."

"I wrote it."

"Tim, you're beyond me! But I still don't get the joke."

"The joke is that I did it by mathematics. I calculated what ought to sound like joy, grief, hope, triumph, and all the rest, and—it was just after I had studied harmony; you know how mathematical that is."

Speechless, Welles nodded.

"I worked out the rhythms from different metabolisms—the way you function when under the influences of these emotions; the way your metabolic rate varies, your heartbeats and respiration and things. I sent it to the director of that orchestra, and he didn't get the idea that it was a joke—of course I didn't explain—he produced the music. I get nice royalties from it, too."

"You'll be the death of me yet," said Welles in deep sincerity. "Don't tell me anything more today; I couldn't take it. I'm going home. Maybe by tomorrow I'll see the joke and come back to laugh. Tim, did you ever fail at anything?"

"There are two cabinets full of articles and stories that didn't sell. Some of them I feel bad about. There was the chess story. You know, in 'Through the Looking Glass,' it wasn't a very good game, and you couldn't see the relation of the moves to the story very well.''

"I never could see it at all."

"I thought it would be fun to take a championship game and write a fantasy about it, as if it were a war between two little old countries, with knights and foot-soldiers, and fortified walls in charge of captains, and the bishops couldn't fight like warriors, and, of course, the queens were women—people don't kill them, not in hand-to-hand fighting and . . . well, you see? I wanted to make up the attacks and captures, and keep the people alive, a fairytale war you see, and make the strategy of the game and the strategy of the war coincide, and have everything fit. It took me ever so long to work it out and write it. To understand the game as a chess game and then to translate it into human actions and motives, and put speeches to it to fit different kinds of people. I'll show it to you. I loved it. But nobody would print it. Chess players don't like fantasy, and nobody else likes chess. You have to have a very special kind of mind to like both. But it was a disappointment. I hoped it would be published, because the few people who like that sort of thing would like it *very* much.''

"I'm sure I'll like it."

"Well, if you do like that sort of thing, it's what you've been waiting all your life in vain for. Nobody else has done it." Tim stopped, and blushed as red as a beet. "I see what grandmother means. Once you get started bragging, there's no end to it. I'm sorry, Peter."

"Give me the story. I don't mind, Tim—brag all you like to me; I understand. You might blow up if you never expressed any of your legitimate pride and pleasure in such achievements. What I don't understand is how you have kept it all under for so long."

"I had to," said Tim.

The story was all its young author had claimed. Welles chuckled as he read it, that evening. He read it again, and checked all the moves and the strategy of them. It was really a fine piece of work. Then he thought of the symphony, and this time he was able to laugh. He sat up until after midnight, thinking about the boy. Then he took a sleeping pill and went to bed.

The next day he went to see Tim's grandmother. Mrs. Davis received him graciously.

"Your grandson is a very interesting boy," said Peter Welles carefully. "I'm asking a favor of you. I am making a study of various boys and girls in this district, their abilities and backgrounds and environment and character traits and things like that. No names will ever be mentioned, of course, but a statistical report will be kept, for ten years or longer, and some case histories might later be published. Could Timothy be included?"

"Timothy is such a good, normal little boy, I fail to see what would be the purpose of including him in such a survey."

"That is just the point. We are not interested in maladjusted persons in this study. We eliminate all psychotic boys and girls. We are interested in boys and girls who succeed in facing their youthful problems and making satisfactory adjustments to life. If we could study a selected group of such children, and follow their progress for the next ten years at least—and then publish a summary of the findings, with no names used—"

"In that case, I see no objection," said Mrs. Davis.

"If you'd tell me, then, something about Timothy's parents—their history?"

Mrs. Davis settled herself for a good long talk.

"Timothy's mother, my only daughter, Emily," she began, "was a lovely girl. So talented. She played the violin charmingly. Timothy is like her, in the face, but has his father's dark hair and eyes. Edwin had very fine eyes."

"Edwin was Timothy's father?"

"Yes. The young people met while Emily was at college in the East. Edwin was studying atomics there."

"Your daughter was studying music?"

"No; Emily was taking the regular liberal arts course. I can tell you little about Edwin's work, but after their marriage he returned to it and . . . you understand, it is painful for me to recall this, but their deaths were such a blow to me. They were so young."

Welles held his pencil ready to write.

"Timothy has never been told. After all, he must grow up in this world, and how dreadfully the world has changed in the past thirty years, Dr. Welles! But you would not remember the day before 1945. You have heard, no doubt, of the terrible explosion in the atomic plant, when they were trying to make a new type of bomb? At the time, none of the workers seemed to be injured. They believed the protection was adequate. But two years later they were all dead or dying."

Mrs. Davis shook her head sadly. Welles held his breath, bent his head, scribbled.

"Tim was born just fourteen months after the explosion, fourteen months to the day. Everyone still thought that no harm had been done. But the radiation had some effect which was very slow—I do not understand such things—Edwin died, and then Emily came home to us with the boy. In a few months she, too, was gone.

"Oh, but we do not sorrow as those who have no hope. It is hard to have lost her, Dr. Welles, but Mr. Davis and I have reached the time of life when we can look forward to seeing her again. Our hope is to live until Timothy is old enough to fend for himself. We were so anxious about him; but you see he is perfectly normal in every way."

"Yes."

"The specialists made all sorts of tests. But nothing is wrong with Timothy."

The psychiatrist stayed a little longer, took a few more notes, and made his escape as soon as he could. Going straight to the school, he had a few words with Miss Page and then took Tim to his office, where he told him what he had learned.

"You mean—I'm a mutation?"

"A mutant. Yes, very likely you are. I don't know. But I had to tell you at once."

"Must be a dominant, too," said Tim, "coming out this way in the first generation. You mean—there may be more? I'm not the only one?" he added in great excitement. "Oh, Peter, even if I grow up past you I won't have to be lonely?"

There. He had said it.

"It could be, Tim. There's nothing else in your family that could account for you."

"But I have never found anyone at all like me. I would have known. Another boy or girl my age—like me—I would have known."

"You came West with your mother. Where did the others go, if they existed? The parents must have scattered everywhere, back to their homes all over the country, all over the world. We can trace them, though. And, Tim, haven't you thought it's just a little bit strange that with all your pen names and various contacts, people don't insist more on meeting you? Everything gets done by mail? It's almost as if the editors are used to people who hide. It's almost as if people are used to architects and astronomers and composers whom nobody ever sees, who are only names in care of other names at post office boxes. There's a chance—just a chance, mind you—that there are others. If there are, we'll find them."

"I'll work out a code they will understand," said Tim, his

face screwed up in concentration. "In articles—I'll do it—several magazines and in letters I can enclose copies—some of my pen friends may be the ones—"

"I'll hunt up the records—they must be on file somewhere—psychologists and psychiatrists know all kinds of tricks—we can make some excuse to trace them all—the birth records—"

Both of them were talking at once, but all the while Peter Welles was thinking sadly, perhaps he had lost Tim now. If they did find those others, those to whom Tim rightfully belonged, where would poor Peter be? Outside, among the puppies—

Timothy Paul looked up and saw Peter Welles's eyes on him. He smiled.

"You were my first friend, Peter, and you shall be forever," said Tim. "No matter what, no matter who."

"But we must look for the others," said Peter.

"I'll never forget who helped me," said Tim.

An ordinary boy of thirteen may say such a thing sincerely, and a week later have forgotten all about it. But Peter Welles was content. Tim would never forget. Tim would be his friend always. Even when Timothy Paul and those like him should unite in a maturity undreamed of, to control the world if they chose, Peter Welles would be Tim's friend—not a puppy, but a beloved friend—as a loyal dog loved by a good master, is never cast out.

KNOCK

by Fredric Brown (1906—1972)

THRILLING WONDER STORIES
December

Fredric Brown, an old friend of this series, returns with one of his best and most famous stories. Its subject matter, the last man on Earth, has become somewhat of a cliché in science fiction since it is one of the oldest themes, going back (at least) to Mary Shelley's The Last Man *in the early 19th century. However, in the capable hands of Fredric Brown a simple idea becomes an ironic masterpiece of sf.*

(This is one of those stories that once read is never forgotten. Or, perhaps I ought to say, more cautiously, it is one of those stories that, once I read it, I never forget. I would, however, like to make a point about the story that I've never seen made. It illuminates with absolute clarity the sexist nature of our language. Ask yourself: What does "man" mean?

Now ask yourself: If you didn't think of "man" in a peculiarly unfair way, would that two-sentence horror story at the beginning be a horror story and would you need Fred to point it out to you?—I.A.)

There is a sweet little horror story that is only two sentences long:

"The last man on Earth sat alone in a room. There was a knock on the door . . ."

Two sentences and an ellipsis of three dots. The horror, of course, isn't in the two sentences at all; it's in the ellipsis, the implication: *what* knocked at the door? Faced with the unknown, the human mind supplies something vaguely horrible.

But it wasn't horrible, really.

The last man on Earth—or in the universe, for that matter—*sat alone in a room*. It was a rather peculiar room. He'd just noticed how peculiar it was and he'd been studying out the reason for its peculiarity. His conclusion didn't horrify him, but it annoyed him.

Walter Phelan, who had been associate professor of anthropology at Nathan University up until the time two days ago when Nathan University had ceased to exist, was not a man who horrified easily. Not that Walter Phelan was a heroic figure, by any wild stretch of the imagination. He was slight of stature and mild of disposition. He wasn't much to look at, and he knew it.

Not that his appearance worried him now. Right now, in fact, there wasn't much feeling in him. Abstractedly, he knew that two days ago, within the space of an hour, the human race had been destroyed, except for him and, somewhere, a woman—one woman. And that was a fact which didn't concern Walter Phelan in the slightest degree. He'd probably never see her and didn't care too much if he didn't.

Women just hadn't been a factor in Walter's life since Martha had died a year and a half ago. Not that Martha hadn't been a good wife—albeit a bit on the bossy side. Yes, he'd loved Martha, in a deep, quiet way. He was only forty now, and he'd been only thirty-eight when Martha had died, but—well—he just hadn't thought about women since then. His life had been his books, the ones he read and the ones he wrote. Now there wasn't any point in writing books, but he had the rest of his life to spend in reading them.

True, company would be nice, but he'd get along without it. Maybe after a while, he'd get so he'd enjoy the occasional company of one of the Zan, although that was a bit difficult to imagine. Their thinking was so alien to his that there seemed no common ground for discussion, intelligent though they were, in a way.

An ant is intelligent, in a way, but no man ever established communication with an ant. He thought of the Zan, somehow, as super-ants, although they didn't look like ants, and he had a hunch that the Zan regarded the human race as the human race had regarded ordinary ants. Certainly what they'd done to Earth had been what men did to ant hills—and it had been done much more efficiently.

But they had given him plenty of books. They'd been nice about that, as soon as he had told them what he wanted, and he had told them that the moment he had learned that he was destined to spend the rest of his life alone in this room. The rest of his life, or as the Zan had quaintly expressed it, for-ev-er. Even a brilliant mind—and the Zan obviously had brilliant minds—has its idiosyncrasies. The Zan had learned to speak Terrestrial English in a matter of hours but they persisted in separating syllables. But we digress.

There was a knock on the door.

You've got it all now, except the three dots, the ellipsis, and I'm going to fill that in and show you that it wasn't horrible at all.

Walter Phelan called out, ''Come in,'' and the door opened. It was, of course, only a Zan. It looked exactly like the other Zan; if there was any way of telling one of them from another, Walter hadn't found it. It was about four feet tall and it looked like nothing on Earth—nothing, that is, that had been on Earth until the Zan came there.

Walter said, ''Hello, George.'' When he'd learned that none of them had names he decided to call them all George, and the Zan didn't seem to mind.

This one said, ''Hel-lo, Wal-ter.'' That was ritual; the knock on the door and the greetings. Walter waited.

''Point one,'' said the Zan. ''You will please henceforth sit with your chair turned the other way.''

Walter said, ''I thought so, George. That plain wall is transparent from the other side, isn't it?''

''It is trans-par-ent.''

''Just what I thought. I'm in a zoo. Right?''

''That is right.''

Walter sighed. ''I knew it. That plain, blank wall, without a single piece of furniture against it. And made of something different from the other walls. If I persist in sitting with my back to it, what then? You will kill me? I ask hopefully.''

''We will take a-way your books.''

''You've got me there, George. All right, I'll face the other

way when I sit and read. How many other animals besides me
are in this zoo of yours?''

"Two hun-dred and six-teen.''

Walter shook his head. "Not complete, George. Even a bush
league zoo can beat that—*could* beat that, I mean, if there were
any bush league zoos left. Did you just pick at random?''

"Ran-dom sam-ples, yes. All spe-cies would have been too
many. Male and fe-male each of one hun-dred and eight kinds.''

"What do you feed them? The carnivorous ones, I mean.''

"We make food. Syn-thet-ic.''

"Smart,'' said Walter. "And the flora? You got a collection
of that, too?''

"Flo-ra was not hurt by vi-bra-tions. It is all still grow-ing.''

"Nice for the flora,'' said Walter. "You weren't as hard on it,
then, as you were on the fauna. Well, George, you started out
with 'point one'. I deduce there is a point two kicking around
somewhere. What is it?''

"Some-thing we do not un-der-stand. Two of the o-ther a-ni-
mals sleep and do not wake? They are cold.''

"It happens in the best regulated zoos, George,'' Walter
Phelan said. "Probably not a thing wrong with them except that
they're dead.''

"Dead? That means stopped. But noth-ing stopped them.
Each was a-lone.''

Walter stared at the Zan. "Do you mean, George, you don't
know what natural death is?''

"Death is when a be-ing is killed, stopped from liv-ing.''

Walter Phelan blinked. "How old are you, George?'' he
asked.

"Six-teen—you would not know the word. Your pla-net went
a-round your sun a-bout sev-en thou-sand times. I am still young.''

Walter whistled softly. "A babe in arms,'' he said. He thought
hard a moment. "Look, George,'' he said, "you've got something to learn about this planet you're on. There's a guy here
who doesn't hang around where you come from. An old man
with a beard and a scythe and an hourglass. Your vibrations
didn't kill him.''

"What is he?''

"Call him the Grim Reaper, George. Old Man Death. Our
people and animals live until somebody—Old Man Death—*stops*
them ticking.''

"He stopped the two crea-tures? He will stop more?''

*   *   *

Walter opened his mouth to answer, and then closed it again. Something in the Zan's voice indicated that there would be a worried frown on his face, if he had had a face recognizable as such.

"How about taking me to these animals who won't wake up?" Walter asked. "Is that against the rules?"

"Come," said the Zan.

That had been the afternoon of the second day. It was the next morning that the Zan came back, several of them. They began to move Walter Phelan's books and furniture. When they'd finished that, they moved him. He found himself in a much larger room a hundred yards away.

He sat and waited and this time, too, when there was a knock on the door, he knew what was coming and politely stood up. A Zan opened the door and stood aside. A woman entered.

Walter bowed slightly. "Walter Phelan," he said, "in case George didn't tell you my name. George tries to be polite, but he doesn't know all of our ways."

The woman seemed calm; he was glad to notice that. She said, "My name is Grace Evans, Mr. Phelan. What's this all about? Why did they bring me here?"

Walter was studying her as she talked. She was tall, fully as tall as he, and well-proportioned. She looked to be somewhere in her early thirties, about the age Martha had been. She had the same calm confidence about her that he'd always liked about Martha, even though it had contrasted with his own easy-going informality. In fact, he thought she looked quite a bit like Martha.

"I think I know why they brought you here, but let's go back a bit," he said. "Do you know just what has happened otherwise?"

"You mean that they've—killed everyone?"

"Yes. Please sit down. You know how they accomplished it?"

She sank into a comfortable chair nearby. "No," she said. "I don't know just how. Not that it matters, does it?"

"Not a lot. But here's the story—what I know of it, from getting one of them to talk, and from piecing things together. There isn't a great number of them—here, anyway. I don't know how numerous a race they are where they came from and I don't know where that is, but I'd guess it's outside the Solar System. You've seen the space ship they came in?"

"Yes. It's as big as a mountain."

"Almost. Well, it has equipment for emitting some sort of a

vibration—they call it that, in our language, but I imagine it's more like a radio wave than a sound vibration—that destroys all animal life. It—the ship itself—is insulated against the vibration. I don't know whether its range is big enough to kill off the whole planet at once, or whether they flew in circles around the earth, sending out the vibratory waves. But it killed everybody and everything instantly and, I hope, painlessly. The only reason we, and the other two-hundred-odd animals in this zoo, weren't killed was because we were inside the ship. We'd been picked up as specimens. You do know this is a zoo, don't you?''

"I—I suspected it.''

"The front walls are transparent from the outside. The Zan were pretty clever at fixing up the inside of each cubicle to match the natural habitat of the creature it contains. These cubicles, such as the one we're in, are of plastic, and they've got a machine that makes one in about ten minutes. If Earth had had a machine and a process like that, there wouldn't have been any housing shortage. Well, there isn't any housing shortage now, anyway. And I imagine that the human race—specifically you and I—can stop worrying about the A-bomb and the next war. The Zan certainly solved a lot of problems for us.''

Grace Evans smiled faintly. "Another case where the operation was successful, but the patient died. Things *were* in an awful mess. Do you remember being captured? I don't. I went to sleep one night and woke up in a cage on the space ship.''

"I don't remember either,'' Walter said. "My hunch is that they used the vibratory waves at low intensity first, just enough to knock us all out. Then they cruised around, picking up samples more or less at random for their zoo. After they had as many as they wanted, or as many as they had space in the ship to hold, they turned on the juice all the way. And that was that. It wasn't until yesterday they knew they'd made a mistake and had underestimated us. They thought we were immortal, as they are.''

"That we were—what?''

"They can be killed, but they don't know what natural death is. They didn't, anyway, until yesterday. Two of us died yesterday.''

"Two of—Oh!''

"Yes, two of us animals in their zoo. One was a snake and one was a duck. Two species gone irrevocably. And by the Zan's way of figuring time, the remaining member of each species is going to live only a few minutes, anyway. They figured they had permanent specimens."

"You mean they didn't realize what short-lived creatures we are?"

"That's right," Walter said. "One of them is young at seven thousand years, he told me. They're bisexual themselves, incidentally, but they probably breed once every ten thousand years or thereabouts. When they learned yesterday how ridiculously short a life expectancy we terrestrial animals have, they were probably shocked to the core—if they have cores. At any rate they decided to reorganize their zoo—two by two instead of one by one. They figure we'll last longer collectively if not individually."

"Oh!" Grace Evans stood up, and there was a faint flush on her face. "If you think—if they think—" She turned toward the door.

"It'll be locked," Walter Phelan said calmly. "But don't worry. Maybe they think, but I *don't* think. You needn't even tell me you wouldn't have me if I were the last man on Earth; it would be corny under the circumstances."

"But are they going to keep us locked up together in this one little room?"

"It isn't so little; we'll get by. I can sleep quite comfortably in one of these overstuffed chairs. And don't think I don't agree with you perfectly, my dear. All personal considerations aside, the least favor we can do the human race is to let it end with us and not be perpetuated for exhibition in a zoo."

She said, "Thank you," almost inaudibly, and the flush receded from her cheeks. There was anger in her eyes, but Walter knew that it wasn't anger at him. With her eyes sparkling like that, she looked a lot like Martha, he thought.

He smiled at her and said, "Otherwise—"

She started out of her chair, and for an instant he thought she was going to come over and slap him. Then she sank back wearily. "If you were a *man*, you'd be thinking of some way to—They can be killed, you said?" Her voice was bitter.

"Oh, certainly. I've been studying them. They look horribly different from us, but I think they have about the same metabolism we have, the same type of circulatory system, and probably the same type of digestive system. I think that anything that would kill one of us would kill one of them."

"But you said—"

"Oh, there are differences, of course. Whatever factor it is in man that ages him, they don't have. Or else they have some gland that man doesn't have, something that renews cells."

She had forgotten her anger now. She leaned forward eagerly. She said, "I think that's right. And I don't think they feel pain."

"I was hoping that. But what makes you think so, my dear?"

"I stretched a piece of wire that I found in the desk on my cubicle across the door so my Zan would fall over it. He did, and the wire cut his leg."

"Did he bleed red?"

"Yes, but it didn't seem to annoy him. He didn't get mad about it; didn't even mention it. When he came back the next time, a few hours later, the cut was gone. Well, almost gone. I could see just enough of a trace of it to be sure it was the same Zan."

Walter Phelan nodded slowly.

"He wouldn't get angry, of course," he said. "They're emotionless. Maybe, if we killed one, they wouldn't even punish us. But it wouldn't do any good. They'd just give us our food through a trap door and treat us as men would have treated a zoo animal that had killed a keeper. They'd just see that he didn't have a crack at any more keepers."

"How many of them are there?" she asked.

"About two hundred, I think, in this particular space ship. But undoubtedly there are many more where they came from. I have a hunch this is just an advance guard, sent to clear off this planet and make it safe for Zan occupancy."

"They did a good—"

There was a knock at the door, and Walter Phelan called out, "Come in." A Zan stood in the doorway.

"Hello, George," said Walter.

"Hel-lo, Wal-ter," said the Zan.

It may or may not have been the same Zan, but it was always the same ritual.

"What's on your mind?" Walter asked.

"An-oth-er crea-ture sleeps and will not wake. A small fur-ry one called a wea-sel."

Walter shrugged.

"It happens, George. Old Man Death. I told you about him."

"And worse. A Zan has died. This morning."

"Is that worse?" Walter looked at him blandly. "Well, George, you'll have to get used to it, if you're going to stay around here.''

The Zan said nothing. It stood there.

Finally Walter said, ''Well?''

''About wea-sel. You ad-vise the same?''

Walter shrugged again. ''Probably won't do any good. But sure, why not?''

The Zan left.

Walter could hear his footsteps dying away outside. He grinned. ''It might work, Martha,'' he said.

''Mar—My name is Grace, Mr. Phelan. What might work?''

''My name is Walter, Grace. You might as well get used to it. You know, Grace, you do remind me a lot of Martha. She was my wife. She died a couple of years ago.''

''I'm sorry,'' said Grace. ''But what might work? What were you talking about to the Zan?''

''We'll know tomorrow,'' Walter said. And she couldn't get another word out of him.

That was the fourth day of the stay of the Zan.

The next was the last.

It was nearly noon when one of the Zan came. After the ritual, he stood in the doorway, looking more alien than ever. It would be interesting to describe him for you, but there aren't words.

He said, ''We go. Our coun-cil met and de-ci-ded.''

''Another of you died?''

''Last night. This is a pla-net of death.''

Walter nodded. ''You did your share. You're leaving two hundred and thirteen creatures alive, out of quite a few billion. Don't hurry back.''

''Is there a-ny-thing we can do?''

''Yes. You can hurry. And you can leave our door unlocked, but not the others. We'll take care of the others.''

Something clicked on the door; the Zan left.

Grace Evans was standing, her eyes shining.

She asked, ''What—? How—?''

''Wait,'' cautioned Walter. ''Let's hear them blast off. It's a sound I want to remember.''

The sound came within minutes, and Walter Phelan, realizing how rigidly he'd been holding himself, relaxed in his chair.

''There was a snake in the Garden of Eden, too, Grace, and it got us in trouble,'' he said musingly. ''But this one made up for it. I mean the mate of the snake that died day before yesterday. It was a rattlesnake.''

"You mean it killed the two Zan who died? But—"

Walter nodded. "They were babes in the woods here. When they took me to look at the first creatures who 'were asleep and wouldn't wake up,' and I saw that one of them was a rattler, I had an idea, Grace. Just maybe, I thought, poison creatures were a development peculiar to Earth and the Zan wouldn't know about them. And, too, maybe their metabolism was enough like ours so that the poison would kill them. Anyway, I had nothing to lose trying. And both maybes turned out to be right."

"How did you get the snake to—"

Walter Phelan grinned. He said, "I told them what affection was. They didn't know. They were interested, I found, in preserving the remaining one of each species as long as possible, to study the picture and record it before it died. I told them it would die immediately because of the loss of its mate, unless it had affection and petting—constantly. I showed them how with the duck. Luckily it was a tame one, and I held it against my chest and petted it a while to show them. Then I let them take over with it—and the rattlesnake."

He stood up and stretched, and then sat down again more comfortably.

"Well, we've got a world to plan," he said. "We'll have to let the animals out of the ark, and that will take some thinking and deciding. The herbivorous wild ones we can let go right away. The domestic ones, we'll do better to keep and take charge of; we'll need them. But the carnivora—Well, we'll have to decide. But I'm afraid it's got to be thumbs down."

He looked at her. "And the human race. We've got to make a decision about that. A pretty important one."

Her face was getting a little pink again, as it had yesterday; she sat rigidly in her chair.

"*No!*" she said.

He didn't seem to have heard her. "It's been a nice race, even if nobody won it," he said. "It'll be starting over again now, and it may go backward for a while until it gets its breath, but we can gather books for it and keep most of its knowledge intact, the important things anyway. We can—"

He broke off as she got up and started for the door. Just the way his Martha would have acted, he thought, back in the days when he was courting her, before they were married.

He said, "Think it over, my dear, and take your time. But come back."

The door slammed. He sat waiting, thinking out all the things there were to do, once he started, but in no hurry to start them; and after a while he heard her hesitant footsteps coming back.

He smiled a little. See? It wasn't horrible, really.

The last man on Earth sat alone in a room. There was a knock on the door . . .

A CHILD IS CRYING

by John D. MacDonald

THRILLING WONDER STORIES

December

John D. MacDonald's second contribution to the best of 1948 is a moving story that can best be described as a "pre-holocaust" tale. The effects of Hiroshima on science fiction writers and their work were still being felt in 1948 (indeed, are still being felt today), and "A Child is Crying" is one of the finest stories of its kind.

This story is also the fifth and last in this book that first appeared in Thrilling Wonder Stories or its sister magazine, Startling Stories, and points up the fact that John Campbell and his Astounding Science Fiction did not have a death grip on the sf market in the second half of the 1940s.

(One value of this series of volumes, by the way, is that we are able to look over the work of a given year with the perspective of a generation's advance. This is the fifth story in this volume which deals with one aspect or another of the influence of the nuclear bomb. There were simply dozens of stories published in the late 1940s that were not [in our opinion] good enough to include in these volumes. We see, though, that they *were all wrong. The nuclear bomb had no mysterious, science-fictional consequences as far as we can tell. The only thing it does is what we knew all along it would do—destroy! It can smash civilization, kill billions of people, damage the Earth to the point where it might not recover for millions of years, if at all—but the scientists who witnessed the Alamogordo explosion knew that, and many tried to prevent Hiroshima for that reason. Science fiction has not accurately predicted anything beyond this.—I. A.)*

His mother, who was brought to New York with him, said, at the press conference, ''Billy is a very bright boy. There isn't anything else we can teach him.''

The school teacher, back in Albuquerque, shuddered delicately, looking at the distant stars, her head on the broad shoulder of the manual training teacher. She said, ''I'm sorry, Joe, if I talk about him too much. It seems as if everywhere I go and everything I do, I can feel those eyes of his watching me.''

Bain, the notorious pseudo-psychiatrist, wrote an article loaded with clichés in which he said, ''Obviously the child is a mutation. It remains to be seen whether or not his peculiar talents are inheritable.'' Bain mentioned the proximity of Billy's birthplace to atomic experimentation.

Emanuel Gardensteen was enticed out of his New Jersey study where he was putting on paper his newest theories in symbolic logic and mathematical physics. Gardensteen spent five hours in a locked room with Billy. At the end of the interview Gardensteen emerged, biting his thin lips. He returned to New Jersey, locked his house, and took a job as a section hand repairing track on the Pennsy Railroad. He refused to make a statement to the press.

John Folmer spent four days getting permission to go ninety feet down the corridor of the Pentagon Building to talk to a man who was entitled to wear five stars on his uniform.

''Sit down, Folmer,'' the general said. ''All this is slightly irregular.''

''It's an irregular situation,'' Folmer retorted. ''I couldn't trust Garrity and Hoskins to relay my idea to you in its original form.''

The lean little man behind the mammoth desk licked his lips slowly. "You infer that my subordinates are either stupid or self-seeking?"

Folmer lit a cigarette, keeping his movements slow and unhurried. He grinned at the little gray man. "Sir, suppose you let me tell you what I'm thinking, and after you have the story, then you can assess any blame you feel is due."

"Go ahead."

"You have read about Billy Massner, General?"

The gray man snorted. "Read about him! I've read about him, listened to newscasts about him, watched his monstrous little face in the newsreels. The devil with him! A confounded freak."

"But is he?" Folmer queried, his eyes fixed on the general's face.

"What do you mean, Folmer. Get to the point."

"Certainly. It is of no interest to you or to me, General, to determine the reason for the kid's talents. What do we know about those talents? Just this. The kid could read and write and carry on a conversation when he was thirteen months old. At two and a half he was doing quadratic equations. At four, completely on his own, he worked out theories regarding non-Euclidian geometry and theories of relativity that parallel the work of Einstein. Now he is seven. You read the Beach Report after the psychologists got through with him. He can carry a conversation on mathematical concepts right on over the heads of our best men who have given their life to such things.

"The thing that happened to Gardensteen is an example. The Beach Report states that William Massner, age 7, is the most completely rational being ever tested. The factor of imagination is so small as not to respond to any known test. The kid gets his results by taking known and observed data and extrapolating from that point, proving his theories by exhaustive cross checks."

"So what, Folmer? So what?" the general snapped.

"What is our weapon of war, General? The top weapon?" Folmer asked meaningly.

"The atom bomb, of course!"

"And the atom bomb was made possible by the work of physicists in the realm of pure theory. The men who made the first bomb compare to Billy Massner the way you and I compare to those men."

"What are you getting at?" The general's tone showed curiosity and a little uneasiness.

"Just this, General. Billy Massner is a national resource. He is our primary weapon of offense and defense. As soon as our enemy realize what we have in this kid, I have a hunch they'll have him killed. Inside that head of his is our success in the war that's coming up one of these days."

The general placed his small hard palm on a yellow octagonal pencil and rolled it back and forth on the surface of his huge desk. The wrinkles between his eyebrows deepened. He said gently, "Folmer, I'm sort of out of my depth on this atomic business. To me it's just a new explosive—more effective than those in use up to this time."

"And it will be continually improved," Folmer asserted. "You know what a very small portion of the available energy is released right now. I'll bet you this kid can point out the way to release all the potential energy."

"Why haven't you talked this over with the head physicist?"

"But I have! He sneered at the kid at first. I managed to get him an interview with Billy. Now he's on my side. He's too impressed to be envious. The kid fed him a production shortcut."

The general shrugged in a tired way. "What do we have to do?"

"I've talked to the boy's mother and last week I flew out and saw the father. They only pretend to love the kid. He isn't exactly the sort of person you can love. They'll be willing to let me adopt him. They'll sign him over. It will cost enough dough out of the special fund to give them a life income of a thousand a month."

"And then what?" the general wanted to know.

"The kid is rational. I explain to him what we want. If he does what we want him to do, he gets anything in the world *he* wants. Simple."

The general straightened his shoulders. "Okay, Folmer," he snapped. "Get under way. And make sure this monster of yours is protected until we can get him behind wire."

Folmer stood up and smiled. "I took the liberty of putting a guard on him, sir."

"Good work! I'll be available to iron out any trouble you run into. I'll have a copy disc of this conversation cut for your file. . . ."

In spite of the general's choice of words, William Massner was not a monster. He was slightly smaller than average for his age, fine-boned and with dark hair and fair skin. His knuckles had the usual grubby childhood look about them. At casual glance he seemed a normal, decent-looking youngster. The difference was in the absolute immobility of his face. His eyes were gray and level. He had never been known, since the age of six months, to show fear, anger, surprise or joy.

After the brief ten minutes in court, John Folmer brought Billy Massner to his hotel room. Folmer sat on the bed and Billy sat on a chair by the windows. John Folmer was a slightly florid man of thirty, with pale thinning hair and a soft bulge at the waistline. His hands were pink and well-kept. Though he had conducted all manner of odd negotiations with the confidence of an imaginative and thorough-going bureaucrat, the quiet gray-eyed child gave him a feeling of awe.

"Bill," he said, "are you disappointed in your parents for signing you away?"

"I made them uncomfortable. Their affection was a pretense. It was an obvious move for them to trade me for financial security." The boy's voice had the flat precision of a slide rule.

Folmer tried to smile warmly. "Well, Bill, at least the sideshow is over. We've gotten you away from all the publicity agents. You must have been getting sick of that."

"If you hadn't stopped it, I would have," the boy stated.

Folmer stared. "How would you do that?"

"I have observed average children. I would become an average child. They would no longer be interested."

"You could fake possessing their mentality?"

"It wouldn't be difficult," the boy said. "At the present time I am faking an intelligence level as much lower than my true level as the deviation between a normal child and the level I am faking."

Folmer uncomfortably avoided the level gray eyes. He said heartily, "We'll admit you're pretty . . . unusual, Bill. All the head doctors have been trying to find out why and how. But nobody has ever asked you for your opinion. Why are you such a . . . deviation from the norm, Bill?"

The boy looked at him for several motionless seconds. "There is nothing to be gained by giving you that information, Folmer."

Folmer stood up and walked over to the boy. He glared down at him, his arm half lifted. "Don't get snippy with me, you little freak!"

The level gray eyes met his. Folmer took three jerky steps backward and sat down awkwardly on the bed. "How did you do that?" he gasped.

"I suggested it to you."

"But—"

"I could just as well have suggested that you open the window and step out." And the child added tonelessly, "We're on the twenty-first floor."

Folmer got out a cigarette with shaking hands and lit it, sucking the smoke deep into his lungs. He tried to laugh. "Then why didn't you?"

"I don't like unnecessary effort. I have made a series of time-rhythm extrapolations. Even though you are an unimportant man, your death now would upset the rhythm of one of the current inevitabilities, changing the end result. With your death I would be forced to isolate once again all variables and re-establish the new time-rhythm to determine one segment of the future."

Folmer's eyes bulged. "You can tell what will happen in the future?"

"Of course. A variation of the statement that the end pre-exists in the means. The future pre-exists in the present, with all variables subject to their own cyclical rhythm."

"And my going out the window would change the future?"

"One segment of it," the boy replied.

Folmer's hands shook. He looked down at them. "Do—do you know when I'm supposed to die?"

"If I tell you, the fact of your knowledge will make as serious an upset in time-rhythm as the fact of your stepping out the window. Your probable future actions would be conditioned by your knowledge."

Folmer smiled tightly. "You're hedging. You don't know the future."

"You called me up here to tell me that we are taking a plane today or tomorrow to a secret research laboratory in Texas. We will take that plane. In Texas the head physicist at the laboratory will set up a morning conference system whereby each staff member will bring current research problems to a roundtable meeting. I will answer the questions they put to me. No more than that. I will not indicate any original line of research, even though I will be asked to do so."

"And why not?"

"For the same reason that you are not now dead on the pavement two hundred feet below that window. Any interference with time-rhythm means laborious re-calculations. Since by a process of extrapolation I can determine the future, my efforts would be conditioned by my knowledge of that future."

Folmer tried to keep his voice steady as he asked, "You could foresee military attacks?"

"Of course," the child said.

"Do you know of any?"

"I do."

"You will advise us of them so that we can prepare, so that we can strike first?" In spite of himself Folmer sounded eager.

"I will not. . . ."

Folmer took William Massner to Texas. They landed at San Antonio where an army light plane took them a hundred miles northwest to the underground laboratories of the government where able men kept themselves from thinking of the probable results of their work. They were keen and sensitive men, the best that the civilized world had yet produced—but they worked with death, with the musty odor of the grave like a gentle touch against their lips. And they didn't stop to think. It was impossible to think of consequences. Think of the job at hand. Think of CM. Think in terms of unbelievable temperatures, of the grotesque silhouette of a man baked into the asphalt of Hiroshima. . . .

Billy was given a private suite, his needs attended to by two WAC corporals who had been given extensive security checks. The two girls were frightened of the small boy. They were frightened because he spent one full hour each day doing a series of odd physical exercises which he had worked out for himself. But that didn't frighten them as much as the fact that during the rest of his free time he sat absolutely motionless in a chair, his eyes half closed, gazing at a blank wall a few feet in front of him. At times he seemed to be watching something, some image against the flat white wall.

Folmer was unable to sleep. He didn't eat properly. He had told no one of his talk with Billy at the New York hotel. His knowledge ate at him. As his cheeks sagged and turned sallow, as his plump body seemed to wither, the fear in his eyes became deeper and more set.

The research staff made more progress during the first month of roundtable meetings than they had during the entire previous year. The younger men went about with an air of excitement thinly covered by a rigid control. The older men seemed to sink more deeply into fortified battlements of the mind. William Massner's slow and deliberate answers to involved questions resulted in the scrapping of two complete lines of research and a tremendous spurt of progress in other lines.

Folmer could not forget the attack which Billy had spoken of and, moreover, could not forget the fact that Billy knew when the attack would occur. As Folmer lay rigid and unsleeping during the long hours of night, he felt that the silver snouts of mighty rockets were screaming through the stratosphere, arching and falling toward him, reaching out to explode each separate molecule of his body into a hot whiteness.

On the twenty-third of October, after William Massner had been at the Research Center for almost seven weeks, Folmer, made bold by stiff drinks, sought out Burton Janks, the Security Control Officer. They went together to a small soundproofed storeroom and closed the door behind them. Janks was a slim, tanned man with pale milky eyes, dry brown hair and muscular hands. He listened to Folmer's story without any change in expression.

When Folmer had finished, Janks said, "I'm turning you over to Robertson for a psycho."

"Don't be a fool, Burt! Give me a chance to prove it first!" Folmer pleaded.

"Prove that nonsense! How?"

"Will you grant that if any part of my story is true, all of it is true?"

Janks shrugged. "Sure."

"Then do this one thing, Burt. The kid'll be coming out of conference in about ten minutes. He'll go along the big corridor and take the elevator up to his apartment level. Meet him in the corridor, walk up to him and pretend that you are going to slap him. Your guards will be with you. You're the only man who could try such a thing and get away with it."

Janks stretched lazily. "I'd enjoy batting the little jerk's ears back. Maybe I won't pretend."

Ten minutes later Janks stood beside Folmer. They leaned against the wall of the corridor. The door at the end opened and Billy came out, closely followed by the two young guards who were always with him whenever he was out of his apartment. Billy walked slowly and steadily, no expression on his small-boy face, no glint of light in his ancient gray eyes.

Janks said, "Here goes," and walked out to intercept them. He nodded at the guards, drew one hand back as though to strike the boy. For a second Janks stood motionless. Then he went

backward with odd, wooden steps, his back slamming against
the corridor wall with a force that nearly knocked him off his
feet. Billy stared at him for a moment without expression before
continuing toward his apartment. The two guards stood with
their mouths open, staring at Janks, and then hurried to their
proper position a few feet behind William Massner.

Janks was pale. He looked toward the small figure of Billy
turned to Folmer and said, "Come on. We'll report to W. W.
Gates."

Gates was an unhappy man. He had been a reasonably competent physicist, blessed with a charming personality and an ability
to handle administrative details. As a consequence, he was no
longer permitted to do research, but had become the buffer
between the military and the research staff. His nominal position
was head of research, but his time was spent on reports in
quadruplicate and in soothing the battered sensibilities of the
research staff. Gates loved his profession and continually told
himself that he was helping it more by staying out of it. His
rationalization didn't make him feel any better. He looked like a
bald John L. Lewis without the eyebrows. And without the
voice. Gates talked in a plaintive squeak.

He sat very still and listened while Folmer told the complete
story and Janks substantiated it. Little beads of sweat appeared on
Gates' upper lip in spite of the air-conditioning.

He said slowly, "If I had never sat in on the conferences, I
wouldn't believe it. Science has believed that the future is the
result of an infinite progression of possibilities and probabilities
with a factor of complete randomness. If you quoted him properly,
Folmer, this time-rhythm he spoke of indicates some kind of a
pattern in the randomness, so that if you can isolate all the
possibilities and probabilities and determine the past rhythm, you
can extend that pattern. It's sort of a statistical approach to
metaphysics and quite beyond our current science. I wish you
hadn't told me."

"I've got an idea, sir," Folmer said. Both men looked at him.
"I've spent a long time watching the kid. This reading the future
is okay for big stuff, but little things fool him. Once he stumbled
and fell against a door. Another time one of the men accidentally
tramped on his foot. It hurt the kid."

"What does that mean?" Janks said.

"It means that the kid can avoid big stuff if he wants to, but
not minor accidents. I don't think we can carry this much
further. The three of us right here are carrying the ball. It's up to

us. The future is locked up in the kid's mind. Now, here's what we do. . . . ''

Corporal Alice Dentro was nervous. She knew that she had to forget her personal fears and carry out her orders. An order was an order, wasn't it? She was in the army, wasn't she? After all, her superiors must know what they're doing.

She aimlessly dusted the furniture and glanced toward the chair where William Massner sat motionless, staring at a blank wall. Her lips were tight, and little droplets of cold sweat trickled down her body. She moved constantly closer to the boy. Five feet from him, she reached into her blouse pocket and pulled out the hypodermic. It slid easily out of the aseptic plastic case. Quickly she held it up to the light, depressed the plunger until a drop of the clear liquid appeared at the needly tip.

A few feet closer. Now she could reach out and touch him. He didn't move. She held herself very still, the needle poised. A quick thrust. The boy jumped as the needle slid through the fabric of his sleeve and penetrated the smooth skin. She pushed the plunger before he twisted away. She backed across the room, dropping the hypodermic. It glistened against the thick pile of the rug. She stood with her back against the door. Billy tried to stand, but slumped back. In a few seconds his chin dropped on his chest, and he began to snore softly.

She glanced at her watch. With a trembling hand she unlocked the door. Gates, Janks and Folmer came in quickly and quietly. With them was Dr. Badloe from the infirmary. He carried a small black case. Janks nodded at Alice Dentro. She slipped out into the corridor and walked quickly away, her shoulders squared. Behind her she heard the click of the lock on the steel door.

As the results of the first drug went away, Billy was given small increments of a derivative of scopolamine. They had turned his chair around, loosened his clothing. Only one light shone in the apartment. It was directed at his face. Dr. Badloe sat near him, fingers on the boy's pulse. Janks, Gates and Folmer stood just outside the circle of light.

"He's ready now," Badloe said. "Just one of you ask the questions."

Both Janks and Folmer looked at Gates. He nodded. In his thin, high voice he said, "Billy, is it true that you can read the future?"

The small lips twitched. In a small, sleepy voice Billy said, "Yes. Not every aspect of the future. Merely those segments of it which interest me. The method is subject to a standard margin of error.''

''Can you explain that margin of error?'' Gates asked.

''Yes. One segment of the future concerns my relationship with this organization. My study of the future indicated that Folmer, knowing my ability to read the future, would interest others and that a successful attempt would be made to render me powerless to keep my readings to myself.''

The three men stared at each other in sudden shock. Gates, with a quaver in his voice said, ''Then you knew that we would—do this thing?''

''Yes?''

''Why didn't you anticipate it and avoid it?''

''To do so would have been to alter the future,'' the sleepy voice responded.

''Are you a mutation caused by atomic radiation?''

''No.''

''What are you?''

''A direct evolutionary product. There are precedents in history. The man who devised the bow and arrow is a case in point. He was necessary to humanity because otherwise humanity would not have survived. He was more capable than his fellows.'' The boy's droning voice halted.

''Are we to assume then that your existence is necessary to the survival of humanity?'' Gates questioned.

''Yes. The factor missing from man's intellect is the ability to read the future. To do so requires a more lucid mind than has hitherto existed. The use of atomic energy makes a knowledge of the future indispensable to survival. Thus evolution has provided humanity with a new species of man able to anticipate the results of his own actions.''

''Will we be attacked?''

''Of course. And you will counterattack again and again. As a result of this plan of yours, you hope to be able to attack first, but your military won't credit my ability to see into the future.''

''When will the attack come?'' Gates prodded.

''No less than forty, not more than fifty-two days from today. Minor variables that cannot be properly estimated give that margin for error.''

''Who will win?''

''Win? There will be no victory. That is the essential point. In the past the wars between city states ceased because the city states became too small as social units in a shrinking world

Today a country is too small a social unit. This war will be the terminal point for inter-country warfare, as it will dissolve all financial, linguistic and religious barriers.''

''What will the population of the world be when this war is over?'' was Gates' next question.

''Between fifty and a hundred and fifty millions. There will be an additional fifty per cent shrinkage due to disease before population begins to climb again.''

There was silence in the darkened room. The boy sat motionless, awaiting the next query. Badloe had taken his fingers from the boy's pulse and sat with his face in his hands.

Gates said slowly, ''I don't understand. You spoke as though your type of individual has come into the world as an evolutionary answer to atomics. If this war will happen, in what sense are you saving mankind?''

''My influence is zero at this point,'' was the boy's answer. ''I will be ready when the war is over. I will survive it, because I can anticipate the precautions to be taken. After it is over the ability to read the future will keep mankind from branching off into a repetition of militarism and fear. I have no part in this conflict.''

''But you have improved our techniques!'' Gates protested.

''I have increased your ability to destroy,'' Billy corrected him. ''Were I to increase it further, you would be enabled to make the earth completely uninhabitable.''

''Then your work is through?''

''Obviously. The result of the drug you have administered to me will be to impair the use of my intellect. I will be sent away. My abilities will return in sufficient time to enable me to survive.''

Gates' voice became a whisper. ''Are there others like you?''

''I estimate that there are at least twenty in the world today. Obviously many have managed to conceal their gifts. The oldest should be not more than nine. They are scattered all over the earth. They all have an excellent chance of survival. Thirty years from now there will be more than a thousand of us.''

Gates glanced over at Janks, saw the fear and the obvious question. Folmer had the same expression on his face. With a voice that had in it a small touch of madness, Gates said, ''What is the future of those of us in this room? Will we survive?''

''I have not explored the related probabilities. I knew in New York that it was necessary for Folmer to survive to bring me here and to tell you of my abilities. It can be calculated.''

"Now?"

"Give me thirty seconds."

Again the room the room was silent. Badloe had lifted his face, his eyes naked with fear. Janks shifted uneasily. Folmer stood, barely breathing. Gates twisted his fingers together. The seconds ticked by. Four men waited for the word of death or life.

Billy Massner licked his lips. "Not one of you will live more than three months from this date." It was a flat, calm statement. Badloe made a sound in his throat.

"He's crazy!" Janks snarled.

They wanted to believe Janks. They had to believe the boy.

Gates whispered, "How will we die?"

They watched the small-boy face. Slowly the impassivity of it melted away. The gray eyes opened and they were not the dead gray eyes the men had grown accustomed to. They were the frightened eyes of boyhood. There was fear on the small face. Fear and indecision.

The voice had lost its flat and deadly calm.

"Who are you?" the boy asked, close to tears. "What do you want? What are you doing to me? I want to go home!"

In the darkened room four men stood and watched a small boy cry.

LATE NIGHT FINAL

by Eric Frank Russell (1905–1978)

ASTOUNDING SCIENCE FICTION

December

Eric Frank Russell returns with his third appearance in this series (see Volumes 5 and 9) and with one of his best stories. "Late Night Final" is a culture confrontation story, a type that has a long and honorable history in science fiction. Russell here posits rigidity vs. flexibility and force vs. seeming passivity in a story that anticipates his wonderful "And Then There Were None" of 1951, which is the much better known story.

Isaac, the more I reread Russell the more convinced I am that he was one of the finest sf writers of his time. And although he was reasonably well known (he won a Hugo Award in 1955), it is sad that his work is almost entirely out of print. Publishers, please take note—there is a gold mine of wonderful writing waiting to come back into print.

(Campbell always enjoyed stories in which apparently superior aliens, were beaten by the apparently weak people they were trying to conquer. That is, he enjoyed them when the apparently weak people were Earthpeople—and no one wrote this kind of story more plausibly than Russell. Of course, if we restrict it to

Earthpeople as a whole then it is the apparently weak Americans who cannot be conquered by apparently superior foreigners ["Hogan's Heroes" on television is the best-known example of this.]

Somehow, I feel that Campbell would no longer enjoy this kind of story nor encourage it to be written for his magazine, if he were still alive. You see, a very powerful army came to this backward nation inhabited by primitive, inferior people and fought them for ten years and lost, and with the Vietnam War this whole notion has been stood on its head. Maybe we should all of us forget this business of conquest altogether. Where's the fun? This is exactly what Russell implies, I think. —I.A.)

Commander Cruin went down the extending metal ladder, paused a rung from the bottom, placed one important foot on the new territory, and then the other. That made him the first of his kind on an unknown world.

He posed there in the sunlight, a big bull of a man meticulously attired for the occasion. Not a spot marred his faultlessly cut uniform of gray-green on which jeweled orders of merit sparkled and flashed. His jack boots glistened as they had never done since the day of launching from the home planet. The golden bells of his rank tinkled on his heelhooks as he shifted his feet slightly. In the deep shadow beneath the visor of his ornate helmet his hard eyes held a glow of self-satisfaction.

A microphone came swinging down to him from the air lock he'd just left. Taking it in a huge left hand, he looked straight ahead with the blank intentness of one who sees long visions of the past and longer visions of the future. Indeed, this was as visionary a moment as any there had been in his world's history.

"In the name of Huld and the people of Huld," he enunciated officiously, "I take this planet." Then he saluted swiftly, slickly, like an automaton.

Facing him, twenty-two long, black spaceships simultaneously thrust from their forward ports their glorypoles ringed with the red-black-gold colors of Huld. Inside the vessels twenty-two crews of seventy men apiece stood rigidly erect, saluted, broke into well-drilled song, "Oh, heavenly fatherland of Huld."

When they had finished, Commander Cruin saluted again. The crews repeated their salute. The glorypoles were drawn in. Cruin mounted the ladder, entered his flagship. All locks were closed. Along the valley the twenty-two invaders lay in military formation, spaced equidistantly, noses and tails dead in line.

On a low hill a mile to the east a fire sent up a column of thick smoke. It spat and blazed amid the remnants of what had been the twenty-third vessel—and the eighth successive loss since the fleet had set forth three years ago. Thirty then. Twenty-two now.

The price of empire.

Reaching his cabin, Commander Cruin lowered his bulk into the seat behind his desk, took off his heavy helmet, adjusted an order of merit which was hiding modestly behind its neighbor.

"Step four," he commented with satisfaction.

Second Commander Jusik nodded respectfully. He handed the other a book. Opening it, Cruin meditated aloud.

"Step one: Check planet's certain suitability for our form of life." He rubbed his big jowls. "We know it's suitable."

"Yes, sir. This is a great triumph for you."

"Thank you, Jusik." A craggy smile played momentarily on one side of Cruin's broad face. "Step two: Remain in planetary shadow at distance of not less than one diameter while scout boats survey world for evidence of superior life forms. Three: Select landing place far from largest sources of possible resistance but adjacent to a source small enough to be mastered. Four: Declare Huld's claim ceremoniously, as prescribed in manual on procedure and discipline." He worked his jowls again. "We've done all that."

The smile returned, and he glanced with satisfaction out of the small port near his chair. The port framed the smoke column on the hill. His expression changed to a scowl, and his jaw muscles jumped.

"Fully trained and completely qualified," he growled sardonically. "Yet he had to smash up. Another ship and crew lost in the very moment we reach our goal. The eighth such loss. There will be a purge in the astronautical training center when I return."

"Yes, sir," approved Jusik, dutifully. "There is no excuse for it."

"There are no excuses for anything," Cruin retorted.

"No, sir."

Snorting his contempt, Cruin looked at his book. "Step five
Make all protective preparations as detailed in defense manual."
He glanced up into Jusik's lean, clearcut features. "Every cap
tain has been issued with a defense manual. Are they carryin
out its orders?"

"Yes, sir. They have started already."

"They better had! I shall arrange a demotion of the slowest."
Wetting a large thumb, he flipped a page over. "Step six: I
planet does hold life forms of suspected intelligence, obtai
specimens." Lying back in his seat he mused a moment, the
barked: "Well, for what are you waiting?"

"I beg your pardon, sir?"

"Get some examples," roared Cruin.

"Very well, sir." Without blinking, Jusik saluted, marche
out.

The self-closer swung the door behind him. Cruin surveyed
with a jaundiced eye.

"Curse the training center," he rumbled. "It has deteriorate
since I was there."

Putting his feet on the desk, he waggled his heels to make th
bells tinkle while he waited for the examples.

Three specimens turned up of their own accord. They wer
seen standing wide-eyed in a row near the prow of numbe
twenty-two, the endmost ship of the line. Captain Somir brough
them along personally.

"Step six calls for specimens, sir," he explained to Com
mander Cruin. "I know that you require ones better than these
but I found these under our nose."

"Under your nose? You land and within short time other lif
forms are sightseeing around your vessel? What about you
protective precautions?"

"They are not completed yet, sir. They take some time."

"What were your lookouts doing—sleeping?"

"No, sir," assured Somir desperately. "They did not think
necessary to sound a general alarm for such as these."

Reluctantly, Cruin granted the point. His gaze ran contemptu
ously over the trio. Three kids. One was a boy, knee-high
snubnosed, chewing at a chubby fist. The next, a skinny-legged
pigtailed girl obviously older than the boy. The third, was anothe
girl almost as tall as Somir, somewhat skinny, but with a hint c
coming shapeliness hiding in her thin attire. All three wer
freckled, all had violently red hair.

The tall girl said to Cruin: "I'm Marva—Marva Meredith." She indicated her companions. "This is Sue and this is Sam. We live over there, in Williamsville." She smiled at him and suddenly he noticed that her eyes were a rich and startling green. "We were looking for blueberries when we saw you come down."

Cruin grunted, rested his hands on his paunch. The fact that this planet's life manifestly was of his own shape and form impressed him not at all. It had never occurred to him that it could have proved otherwise. In Huldian thought, all superior life must be humanoid and no exploration had yet provided evidence to the contrary.

"I don't understand her alien gabble and she doesn't understand Huldian," he complained to Somir. "She must be dull-witted to waste her breath thus."

"Yes, sir," agreed Somir. "Do you wish me to hand them over to the tutors?"

"No. They're not worth it." He eyed the small boy's freckles with distaste, never having seen such a phenomenon before. "They are badly spotted and may be diseased. *Pfaugh!*" He grimaced with disgust. "Did they pass through the ray-sterilizing chamber as they came in?"

"Certainly, sir. I was most careful about that."

"Be equally careful about any more you may encounter." Slowly, his authoritative stare went from the boy to the pigtailed girl and finally to the tall one. He didn't want to look at her, yet knew that he was going to. Her cool green eyes held something that made him vaguely uncomfortable. Unwillingly he met those eyes. She smiled again, with little dimples. "Kick 'em out!" he rapped at Somir.

"As you order, sir."

Nudging them, Somir gestured toward the door. The three took hold of each other's hands, filed out.

"Bye!" chirped the boy, solemnly.

"Bye!" said pigtails, shyly.

The tall girl turned in the doorway. "Good-bye!"

Gazing at her uncomprehendingly, Cruin fidgeted in his chair. She dimpled at him, then the door swung to.

"Good-bye." He mouthed the strange word to himself. Considering the circumstances in which it had been uttered, evidently it meant farewell. Already he had picked up one word of their language.

"Step seven: Gain communication by tutoring specimens until they are proficient in Huldian."

Teach them. Do not let them teach you—teach *them*. The slaves must learn from the masters, not the masters from the slaves.

"Good-bye." He repeated it with savage self-accusation. A minor matter, but still an infringement of the book of rules. There are no excuses for anything.

Teach them.

The slaves—

Rockets rumbled and blasted deafeningly as ships maneuvered themselves into the positions laid down in the manual of defense. Several hours of careful belly-edging were required for this. In the end, the line had reshaped itself into two groups of eleven-pointed stars, noses at the centers, tails outward. Ash of blast-destroyed grasses, shrubs and trees covered a wide area beyond the two menacing rings of main propulsion tubes which could incinerate anything within one mile.

This done, perspiring, dirt-coated crews lugged out their forward armaments, remounted them pointing outward in the spaces between the vessels' splayed tails. Rear armaments still aboard already were directed upward and outward. Armaments plus tubes now provided a formidable field of fire completely surrounding the double encampment. It was the Huldian master plan conceived by Huldian master planners. In other more alien estimation, it was the old covered-wagon technique, so incredibly ancient that it had been forgotten by all but most earnest students of the past. But none of the invaders knew that.

Around the perimeter they stacked the small, fast, well-armed scouts of which there were two per ship. Noses outward, tails inward, in readiness for quick take-off, they were paired just beyond the parent vessels, below the propulsion tubes, and out of line of the remounted batteries. There was a lot of moving around to get the scouts positioned at precisely the same distances apart and making precisely the same angles. The whole arrangement had that geometrical exactness beloved of the military mind.

Pacing the narrow catwalk running along the top surface of his flagship, Commander Cruin observed his toiling crews with satisfaction. Organization, discipline, energy, unquestioning obedience—those were the prime essentials of efficiency. On such had Huld grown great. On such would Huld grow greater.

Reaching the tail-end, he leaned on the stop-rail, gazed down upon the concentric rings of wide, stubby venturis. His own crew were checking the angles of their two scouts already positioned. Four guards, heavily armed, came marching through the ash with Jusik in the lead. They had six prisoners.

Seeing him, Jusik bawled: "Halt!" Guard and guarded stopped with a thud of boots and a rise of dust. Looking up, Jusik saluted.

"Six specimens, sir."

Cruin eyed them indifferently. Half a dozen middle-aged men in drab, sloppily fitting clothes. He would not have given a snap of the fingers for six thousand of them.

The biggest of the captives, the one second from the left, had red hair and was sucking something that gave off smoke. His shoulders were wider than Cruin's own though he didn't look half the weight. Idly, the commander wondered whether the fellow had green eyes; he couldn't tell that from where he was standing.

Calmly surveying Cruin, this prisoner took the smoke-thing from his mouth and said, tonelessly: "By hokey, a brasshat!" Then he shoved the thing back between his lips and dribbled blue vapor.

The others looked doubtful, as if either they did not comprehend or found it past belief.

"Jeepers, *no*!" said the one on the right, a gaunt individual with thin, saturnine features.

"I'm telling you," assured Redhead in the same flat voice.

"Shall I take them to the tutors, sir?" asked Jusik.

"Yes." Unleaning from the rail, Cruin carefully adjusted his white gloves. "Don't bother me with them again until they are certified as competent to talk." Answering the other's salute, he paraded back along the catwalk.

"See?" said Redhead, picking up his feet in time with the guard. He seemed to take an obscure pleasure in keeping in step with the guard. Winking at the nearest prisoner, he let a curl of aromatic smoke trickle from the side of his mouth.

Tutors Fane and Parth sought an interview the following evening. Jusik ushered them in, and Cruin looked up irritably from the report he was writing.

"Well?"

Fane said: "Sir, these prisoners suggest that we share their homes for a while and teach them to converse there."

"How did they suggest that?"

"Mostly by signs," explained Fane.

"And what made you think that so nonsensical a plan had sufficient merit to make it worthy of my attention?"

"There are aspects about which you should be consulted," Fane continued stubbornly. "The manual of procedure and discipline declares that such matters must be placed before the commanding officer whose decision is final."

"Quite right, quite right." He regarded Fane with a little more favor. "What are these matters?"

"Time is important to us, and the quicker these prisoners learn our language the better it will be. Here, their minds are occupied by their predicament. They think too much of their friends and families. In their own homes it would be different, and they could learn at great speed."

"A weak pretext," scoffed Cruin.

"That is not all. By nature they are naive and friendly. I feel that we have little to fear from them. Had they been hostile they would have attacked by now."

"Not necessarily. It is wise to be cautious. The manual of defense emphasizes that fact repeatedly. These creatures may wish first to gain the measure of us before they try to deal with us."

Fane was prompt to snatch the opportunity. "Your point, sir, is also my final one. Here, they are six pairs of eyes and six pairs of ears in the middle of us, and their absence is likely to give cause for alarm in their home town. Were they there complacency would replace that alarm—and *we* would be the eyes and ears!"

"Well put," commented Jusik, momentarily forgetting himself.

"Be silent!" Cruin glared at him. "I do not recall any ruling in the manual pertaining to such a suggestion as this. Let me check up." Grabbing his books, he sought through them. He took a long time about it, gave up, and said: "The only pertinent rule appears to be that in circumstances not specified in the manual the decision is wholly mine, to be made in light of said circumstances providing that they do not conflict with the ruling of any other manual which may be applicable to the situation and providing that my decision does not effectively countermand that or those of any senior ranking officer whose authority extends to the same area." He took a deep breath.

"Yes, sir," said Fane.

"Quite, sir," said Parth.

Cruin frowned heavily. "How far away are these prisoners' homes?"

"One hour's walk." Fane made a persuasive gesture. "If anything did happen to us—which I consider extremely unlikely—one scout could wipe out their little town before they'd time to realize what had happened. One scout, one bomb, one minute!" Dexterously, he added, "At your order, sir."

Cruin preened himself visibly. "I see no reason why we should not take advantage of their stupidity." His eyes asked Jusik what he thought, but that person failed to notice. "Since you two tutors have brought this plan to me, I hereby approve it, and I appoint you to carry it through." He consulted a list which he extracted from a drawer. "Take two psychologists with you—Kalma and Hefni."

"Very well, sir." Impassively, Fane saluted and went out, Parth following.

Staring absently at his half-written report, Cruin fiddled with his pen for a while, glanced up at Jusik, and spat: "At what are you smiling?"

Jusik wiped it from his face, looked solemn.

"Come on. Out with it!"

"I was thinking, sir," replied Jusik, slowly, "that three years in a ship is a very long time."

Slamming his pen on the desk, Cruin stood up. "Has it been any longer for others than for me?"

"For you," said Jusik, daringly but respectfully, "I think it has been longest of all."

"Get out!" shouted Cruin.

He watched the other go, watched the self-closer push the door, waited for its last click. He shifted his gaze to the port, stared hard-eyed into the gathering dusk. His heelbells were silent as he stood unmoving and saw the invisible sun sucking its last rays from the sky.

In short time, ten figures strolled through the twilight toward the distant, tree-topped hill. Four were uniformed; six in drab, shapeless clothes. They went by conversing with many gestures, and one of them laughed. He gnawed his bottom lip as his gaze followed them until they were gone.

The price of rank.

"Step eight: Repel initial attacks in accordance with techniques detailed in manual of defense." Cruin snorted, put up one hand, tidied his orders of merit.

"There have been no attacks," said Jusik.

"I am not unaware of the fact." The commander glowered at him. "I'd have preferred an onslaught. We are ready for them. The sooner they match their strength against ours the sooner they'll learn who's boss now!" He hooked big thumbs in his silver-braided belt. "And besides, it would give the men something to do. I cannot have them everlastingly repeating their drills of procedure. We've been here nine days and nothing has happened." His attention returned to the book. "Step nine: Follow defeat of initial attacks by taking aggressive action as detailed in manual of defense." He gave another snort. "How can one follow something that has not occurred?"

"It is impossible," Jusik ventured.

"Nothing is impossible," Cruin contradicted, harshly. "Step ten: In the unlikely event that intelligent life displays indifference or amity, remain in protective formation while specimens are being tutored, meanwhile employing scout vessels to survey surrounding area to the limit of their flight-duration, using no more than one-fifth of the numbers available at any time."

"That allows us eight or nine scouts on survey," observed Jusik, thoughtfully. "What is our authorized step if they fail to return?"

"Why d'you ask that?"

"Those eight scouts I sent out on your orders forty periods ago are overdue."

Viciously, Commander Cruin thrust away his book. His broad, heavy face was dark red.

"Second Commander Jusik, it was your duty to report this fact to me the moment those vessels became overdue."

"Which I have," said Jusik, imperturbably. "They have a flight-duration of forty periods, as you know. That, sir, made them due a short time ago. They are now late."

Cruin tramped twice across the room, medals clinking, heel-bells jangling. "The answer to nonappearance is immediately to obliterate the areas in which they are held. No half-measures. A salutary lesson."

"Which areas, sir?"

Stopping in mid-stride, Cruin bawled: "*You* ought to know that. Those scouts had properly formulated route orders, didn't they? It's a simple matter to—"

He ceased as a shrill whine passed overhead, lowered to a dull moan in the distance, curved back on a rising note again.

"Number one." Jusik looked at the little timemeter on the wall. "Late, but here. Maybe the others will turn up now."

"Somebody's going to get a sharp lesson if they don't!"

"I'll see what he has to report." Saluting, Jusik hurried through the doorway.

Gazing out of his port, Cruin observed the delinquent scout belly-sliding up to the nearest formation. He chewed steadily at his bottom lip, a slow, persistent chew which showed his thoughts to be wandering around in labyrinths of their own.

Beyond the fringe of dank, dead ash were golden buttercups in the grasses, and a hum of bees, and the gentle rustle of leaves on trees. Four engine-room wranglers of ship number seventeen had found this sanctuary and sprawled flat on their backs in the shade of a big-leafed and blossom-ornamented growth. With eyes closed, their hands plucked idly at surrounding grasses while they maintained a lazy, desultory conversation through which they failed to hear the ring of Cruin's approaching bells.

Standing before them, his complexion florid, he roared: "Get up!"

Shooting to their feet, they stood stiffly shoulder to shoulder, faces expressionless, eyes level, hands at their sides.

"Your names?" He wrote them in his notebook while obediently they repeated them in precise, unemotional voices. "I'll deal with you later," he promised. "March!"

Together, they saluted, marched off with a rhythmic pounding of boots, one-two-three-hup! His angry stare followed them until they reached the shadow of their ship. Not until then did he turn and proceed. Mounting the hill, one cautious hand continually on the cold butt of his gun, he reached the crest, gazed down into the valley he'd just left. In neat, exact positioning, the two star-formations of the ships of Huld were silent and ominous.

His hard, authoritative eyes turned to the other side of the hill. There, the landscape was pastoral. A wooded slope ran down to a little river which meandered into the hazy distance, and on its farther side was a broad patchwork of cultivated fields in which three houses were visible.

Seating himself on a large rock, Cruin loosened his gun in its holster, took a wary look around, extracted a small wad of reports from his pocket and glanced over them for the twentieth time. A faint smell of herbs and resin came to his nostrils as he read.

"I circled this landing place at low altitude and recorded it photographically, taking care to include all the machines standing thereon. Two other machines which were in the air went on their way without attempting to interfere. It then occurred to me that the signals they were making from the ground might be an invitation to land, and I decided to utilize opportunism as recommended in the manual of procedure. Therefore I landed. They conducted my scout vessel to a dispersal point off the runway and made me welcome.''

Something fluted liquidly in a nearby tree. Cruin looked up, his hand automatically seeking his holster. It was only a bird. Skipping parts of the report, he frowned over the concluding words.

''. . . lack of common speech made it difficult for me to refuse, and after the sixth drink during my tour of the town I was suddenly afflicted with a strange paralysis in the legs and collapsed into the arms of my companions. Believing that they had poisoned me by guile, I prepared for death . . . tickled my throat while making jocular remarks . . . I was a little sick.'' Cruin rubbed his chin in puzzlement. ''Not until they were satisfied about my recovery did they take me back to my vessel. They waved their hands at me as I took off. I apologize to my captain for overdue return and plead that it was because of factors beyond my control.''

The fluter came down to Cruin's feet, piped at him plaintively. It cocked its head sidewise as it examined him with bright, beady eyes.

Shifting the sheet he'd been reading, he scanned the next one. It was neatly typewritten, and signed jointly by Parth, Fane, Kalma and Hefni.

''Do not appear fully to appreciate what has occurred . . . seem to view the arrival of a Huldian fleet as just another incident. They have a remarkable self-assurance which is incomprehensible inasmuch as we can find nothing to justify such an attitude. Mastery of them should be so easy that if our homing vessel does not leave too soon it should be possible for it to bear tidings of conquest as well as of mere discovery.''

''Conquest,'' he murmured. It had a mighty imposing sound. A word like that would send a tremendous thrill of excitement throughout the entire world of Huld.

Five before him had sent back ships telling of discovery, but none had gone so far as he, none had traveled so long and wearily, none had been rewarded with a planet so big, lush, desirable—and none had reported the subjection of their finds. One cannot conquer a rocky waste. But this—

In peculiarly accented Huldian, a voice behind him said, brightly: "Good morning!"

He came up fast, his hand sliding to his side, his face hard with authority.

She was laughing at him with her clear green eyes. "Remember me—Marva Meredith?" Her flaming hair was windblown. "You see," she went on, in slow, awkward tones. "I know a little Huldian already. Just a few words."

"Who taught you?" he asked, bluntly.

"Fane and Parth."

"It is your house to which they have gone?"

"Oh, yes. Kalma and Hefni are guesting with Bill Gleeson; Fane and Parth with us. Father brought them to us. They share the welcome room."

"Welcome room?"

"Of course." Perching herself on his rock, she drew up her slender legs, rested her chin on her knees. He noticed that the legs, like her face, were freckled. "Of course. Everyone has a welcome room, haven't they?"

Cruin said nothing.

"Haven't you a welcome room in your home?"

"Home?" His eyes strayed away from hers, sought the fluting bird. It wasn't there. Somehow, his hand had left his holster without realizing it. He was holding his hands together, each nursing the other, clinging, finding company, soothing each other.

Her gaze was on his hands as she said, softly and hesitantly, "You have got a home . . . somewhere . . . haven't you?"

"No."

Lowering her legs, she stood up. "I'm so sorry."

"*You* are sorry for *me*?" His gaze switched back to her. It held incredulity, amazement, a mite of anger. His voice was harsh. "You must be singularly stupid."

"Am I?" she asked, humbly.

"No member of my expedition has a home," he went on. "Every man was carefully selected. Every man passed through a screen, suffered the most exacting tests. Intelligence and technical competence were not enough; each had also to be young, healthy, without ties of any sort. They were chosen for ability to concentrate on the task in hand without indulging morale-lowering sentimentalities about people left behind."

"I don't understand some of your long words," she complained
"And you are speaking far too fast."

He repeated it more slowly and with added emphasis, finishing
"Spaceships undertaking long absence from base cannot be handi
capped by homesick crews. We picked men without home
because they can leave Huld and not care a hoot. They are
pioneers!"

" 'Young, healthy, without ties,' " she quoted. "That makes
them strong?"

"Definitely," he asserted.

"Men especially selected for space. Strong men." Her lashes
hid her eyes as she looked down at her narrow feet. "But now
they are not in space. They are here, on firm ground."

"What of it," he demanded.

"Nothing." Stretching her arms wide, she took a deep breath
then dimpled at him. "Nothing at all."

"You're only a child," he reminded scornfully. "When you
grow older—"

"You'll have more sense," she finished for him, chanting i
in a high, sweet voice. "You'll have more sense, you'll have
more sense. When you grow older you'll have more sense
tra-la-la-lala!"

Gnawing irritatedly at his lip, he walked past her, started
down the hill toward the ships.

"Where are you going?"

"Back!" he snapped.

"Do you like it down there?" Her eyebrows arched in surprise
Stopping ten paces away, he scowled at her. "Is it any of you
business?"

"I didn't mean to be inquisitive," she apologized. "I asked
because . . . because—"

"Because what?"

"I was wondering whether you would care to visit my house."

"Nonsense! Impossible!" He turned to continue downhill.

"Father suggested it. He thought you might like to share a
meal. A fresh one. A change of diet. Something to break the
monotony of your supplies." The wind lifted her crimson hai
and played with it as she regarded him speculatively. "He
consulted Fane and Parth. They said it was an excellent idea."

"They did, did they?" His features seemed molded in iron
"Tell Fane and Parth they are to report to me at sunset." He
paused, added, "Without fail!"

Resuming her seat on the rock, she watched him stride heavily down the slope toward the double star-formation. Her hands were together in her lap, much as he had held his. But hers sought nothing of each other. In complete repose, they merely rested with the ineffable patience of hands as old as time.

Seeing at a glance that he was liverish, Jusik promptly postponed certain suggestions that he had in mind.

"Summon captains Drek and Belthan," Cruin ordered. When the other had gone, he flung his helmet onto the desk, surveyed himself in a mirror. He was still smoothing the tired lines on his face when approaching footsteps sent him officiously behind his desk.

Entering, the two captains saluted, remained rigidly at attention. Cruin studied them irefully while they preserved wooden expressions.

Eventually, he said: "I found four men lounging like undisciplined hoboes outside the safety zone." He stared at Drek. "They were from your vessel." The stare shifted to Belthan. "You are today's commander of the guard. Have either of you anything to say?"

"They were off-duty and free to leave the ship," exclaimed Drek. "They had been warned not to go beyond the perimeter of ash."

"I don't know how they slipped through," said Belthan, in official monotone. "Obviously the guards were lax. The fault is mine."

"It will count against you in your promotion records," Cruin promised. "Punish these four, and the responsible guards, as laid down in the manual of procedure and discipline." He leaned across the desk to survey them more closely. "A repetition will bring ceremonial demotion!"

"Yes, sir," they chorused.

Dismissing them, he glanced at Jusik. "When tutors Fane and Parth report here, send them in to me without delay."

"As you order, sir."

Cruin dropped the glance momentarily, brought it back. "What's the matter with you?"

"Me?" Jusik became self-conscious. "Nothing, sir."

"You lie! One has to live with a person to know him. I've lived on your neck for three years. I know you too well to be deceived. You have something on your mind."

"It's the men," admitted Jusik, resignedly.

"What of them?"

"They are restless."

"Are they? Well, I can devise a cure for that! What's making them restless?"

"Several things, sir."

Cruin waited while Jusik stayed dumb, then roared: "Do I have to prompt you?"

"No, sir," Jusik protested, unwillingly. "It's many things. Inactivity. The substitution of tedious routine. The constant waiting, waiting, waiting right on top of three years of close incarceration. They wait—and nothing happens."

"What else?"

"The sight and knowledge of familiar life just beyond the ash. The realization that Fane and Parth and the others are enjoying it with your consent. The stories told by the scouts about their experiences on landing." His gaze was steady as he went on. "We've now sent out five squadrons of scouts, a total of forty vessels. Only six came back on time. All the rest were late on one plausible pretext or another. The pilots have talked, and shown the men various souvenir photographs and a few gifts. One of them is undergoing punishment for bringing back some bottles of paralysis-mixture. But the damage has been done. Their stories have unsettled the men."

"Anything more?"

"Begging your pardon, sir, there was also the sight of you taking a stroll to the top of the hill. They envied you even that!" He looked squarely at Cruin. "I envied you myself."

"I am the commander," said Cruin.

"Yes, sir." Jusik kept his gaze on him but added nothing more.

If the second commander expected a delayed outburst, he was disappointed. A complicated series of emotions chased each other across his superior's broad, beefy features. Laying back in his chair, Cruin's eyes looked absently through the port while his mind juggled with Jusik's words.

Suddenly, he rasped: "I have observed more, anticipated more and given matters more thought then perhaps you realize. I can see something which you may have failed to perceive. It has caused me some anxiety. Briefly, if we don't keep pace with the march of time we're going to find ourselves in a fix."

"Indeed, sir?"

"I don't wish you to mention this to anyone else: I suspect that we are trapped in a situation bearing no resemblance to any dealt with in the manuals."

"Really, sir?" Jusik licked his lips, felt that his own outspokenness was leading into unexpected paths.

"Consider our present circumstances," Cruin went on. "We are established here and in possession of power sufficient to enslave this planet. Any one of our supply of bombs could blast a portion of this earth stretching from horizon to horizon. But they're of no use unless we apply them effectively. We can't drop them anywhere, haphazardly. If parting with them in so improvident a manner proved unconvincing to our opponents, and failed to smash the hard core of their resistance, we would find ourselves unarmed in a hostile world. No more bombs. None nearer than six long years away, three there and three back. Therefore we must apply our power where it will do the most good." He began to massage his heavy chin. "We don't know where to apply it."

"No, sir," agreed Jusik, pointlessly.

"We've got to determine which cities are the key points of their civilization, which persons are this planet's acknowledged leaders, and where they're located. When we strike, it must be at the nerve-centers. That means we're impotent until we get the necessary information. In turn, that means we've got to establish communication with the aid of tutors." He started plucking at his jaw muscles. "And that takes time!"

"Quite, sir, but—"

"But while time crawls past the men's morale evaporates. This is our twelfth day and already the crews are restless. Tomorrow they'll be more so."

"I have a solution to that, sir, if you will forgive me for offering it," said Jusik, eagerly. "On Huld everyone gets one day's rest in five. They are free to do as they like, go where they like. Now if you promulgated an order permitting the men say one day's liberty in ten, it would mean that no more than ten percent of our strength would be lost on any one day. We could stand that reduction considering our power, especially if more of the others are on protective duty."

"So at last I get what was occupying your mind. It comes out in a swift flow of words." He smiled grimly as the other flushed. "I have thought of it. I am not quite so unimaginative as you may consider me."

"I don't look upon you that way, sir," Jusik protested.

"Never mind. We'll let that pass. To return to this subject of liberty—there lies the trap! There is the very quandary with which no manual deals, the situation for which I can find no officially prescribed formula." Putting a hand on his desk he tapped the polished surface impatiently. "If I refuse these men a little freedom, they will become increasingly restless—naturally. If I permit them the liberty they desire, they will experience contact with life more normal even though alien, and again become more restless—naturally!"

"Permit me to doubt the latter, sir. Our crews are loyal to Huld. Blackest space forbid that it should be otherwise!"

"They were loyal. Probably they are still loyal." Cruin's face quirked as his memory brought forward the words that followed. "They are young, healthy, without ties. In space, that means one thing. Here, another." He came slowly to his feet, big, bulky and imposing. "I *know*!"

Looking at him, Jusik felt that indeed he did know. "Yes, sir," he parroted, obediently.

"Therefore the onus of what to do for the best falls squarely upon me. I must use my initiative. As second commander it is for you to see that my orders are carried out to the letter."

"I know my duty, sir." Jusik's thinly drawn features registered growing uneasiness.

"And it is my final decision that the men must be restrained from contact with our opponents, with no exceptions other than the four technicians operating under my orders. The crews are to be permitted no liberty, no freedom to go beyond the ash. Any form of resentment on their part must be countered immediately and ruthlessly. You will instruct the captains to watch for murmurers in their respective crews and take appropriate action to silence them as soon as found." His jowls lumped, and his eyes were cold as he regarded the other. "All scout-flights are canceled as from now, and all scout-vessels remain grounded. None moves without my personal instructions."

"That is going to deprive us of a lot of information," Jusik observed. "The last flight to the south reported discovery of ten cities completely deserted, and that's got some significance which we ought to—"

"I said the flights are canceled!" Cruin shouted. "If I say the scout-vessels are to be painted pale pink, they will be painted pale pink, thoroughly, completely, from end to end. I am the commander!"

"As you order, sir."

"Finally, you may instruct the captains that their vessels are to be prepared for my inspection at midday tomorrow. That will give the crews something to do."

"Very well, sir."

With a worried salute, Jusik opened the door, glanced out and said: "Here are Fane, Kalma, Parth and Hefni, sir."

"Show them in."

After Cruin had given forcible expression to his views, Fane said: "We appreciate the urgency, sir, and we are doing our best, but it is doubtful whether they will be fluent before another four weeks have passed. They are slow to learn."

"I don't want fluency," Cruin growled. "All they need are enough words to tell us the things we want to know, the things we *must* know before we can get anywhere."

"I said sufficient fluency," Fane reminded. "They communicate mostly by signs even now."

"That flame-headed girl didn't."

"She has been quick," admitted Fane. "Possibly she has an above-normal aptitude for languages. Unfortunately she knows the least in any military sense and therefore is of little use to us."

Cruin's gaze ran over him balefully. His voice became low and menacing. "You have lived with these people many days. I look upon your features and find them different. Why is that?"

"Different?" The four exchanged wondering looks.

"Your faces have lost their lines, their space-gauntness. Your cheeks have become plump, well-colored. Your eyes are no longer tired. They are bright. They hold the self-satisfied expression of a fat *skodar* wallowing in its trough. It is obvious that you have done well for yourselves." He bent forward, his mouth ugly. "Can it be that you are in no great hurry to complete your task?"

They were suitably shocked.

"We have eaten well and slept regularly," Fane said. "We feel better for it. Our physical improvement has enabled us to work so much the harder. In our view, the foe is supporting us unwittingly with his own hospitality, and since the manual of—"

"Hospitality?" Cruin cut in, sharply.

Fane went mentally off-balance as vainly he sought for a less complimentary synonym.

"I give you another week," the commander harshed. "No more. Not one day more. At this time, one week from today, you will report here with the six prisoners adequately tutored to understand my questions and answer them."

"It will be difficult, sir."

"Nothing is difficult. Nothing is impossible. There are no excuses for anything." He studied Fane from beneath forbidding brows. "You have my orders—obey them!"

"Yes, sir."

His hard stare shifted to Kalma and Hefni. "So much for the tutors; now *you*. What have you to tell me? How much have you discovered?"

Blinking nervously, Hefni said: "It is not a lot. The language trouble is—"

"May the Giant Sun burn up and perish the language trouble! How much have you learned while enjoyably larding your bellies?"

Glancing down at his uniform-belt as if suddenly and painfully conscious of its tightness, Hefni recited: "They are exceedingly strange in so far as they appear to be highly civilized in a purely domestic sense but quite primitive in all others. This Meredith family lives in a substantial, well-equipped house. They have every comfort, including a color-television receiver."

"You're dreaming! We are still seeking the secrets of plain television even on Huld. Color is unthinkable."

Kalma chipped in with: "Nevertheless, sir, they have it. We have seen it for ourselves."

"That is so," confirmed Fane.

"Shut up!" Cruin burned him with a glare. "I have finished with you. I am now dealing with these two." His attention returned to the quaking Hefni: "Carry on."

"There is something decidedly queer about them which we've not yet been able to understand. They have no medium of exchange. They barter goods for goods without any regard for the relative values of either. They work when they feel like it. If they don't feel like it, they don't work. Yet, in spite of this, they work most of the time."

"Why?" demanded Cruin, incredulously.

"We asked them. They said that one works to avoid boredom. We cannot comprehend that viewpoint." Hefni made a defeated gesture. "In many places they have small factories which, with their strange, perverted logic, they use as amusement centers. These plants operate only when people turn up to work."

"Eh?" Cruin looked baffled.

"For example, in Williamsville, a small town an hour's walk

beyond the Meredith home, there is a shoe factory. It operates every day. Some days there may be only ten workers there, other days fifty or a hundred, but nobody can remember a time when the place stood idle for lack of one voluntary worker. Meredith's elder daughter, Marva, has worked there three days during our stay with them. We asked her the reason.''

''What did she say?''

''For fun.''

''Fun . . . fun . . . fun?'' Cruin struggled with the concept. ''What does that mean?''

''We don't know,'' Hefni confessed. ''The barrier of speech—''

''Red flames lick up the barrier of speech!'' Cruin bawled. ''Was her attendance compulsory?''

''No, sir.''

''You are certain of that?''

''We are positive. One works in a factory for no other reason than because one feels like it.''

''For what reward?'' topped Cruin, shrewdly.

''Anything or nothing.'' Hefni uttered it like one in a dream. ''One day she brought back a pair of shoes for her mother. We asked if they were her reward for the work she had done. She said they were not, and that someone named George had made them and given them to her. Apparently the rest of the factory's output for that week was shipped to another town where shoes were required. This other town is going to send back a supply of leather, nobody knows how much—and nobody seems to care.''

''Senseless,'' defined Cruin. ''It is downright imbecility.'' He examined Hefni as if suspecting him of inventing confusing data. ''It is impossible for even the most primitive of organizations to operate so haphazardly. Obviously you have seen only part of the picture; the rest has been concealed from you, or you have been too dull-witted to perceive it.''

''I assure you, sir,'' began Hefni.

''Let it pass,'' Cruin cut in. ''Why should I care how they function economically? In the end, they'll work the way *we* want them to!'' He rested his heavy jaw in one hand. ''There are other matters which interest me more. For instance, our scouts have brought in reports of many cities. Some are organized but grossly underpopulated; others are completely deserted. The former have well-constructed landing places with air-machines making use of them. How is it that people so primitive have air-machines?''

''Some make shoes, some make air-machines, some play with

television. They work according to their aptitudes as well as their inclinations.''

''Has this Meredith got an air-machine?''

''No.'' The look of defeat was etched more deeply on Hefni's face. ''If he wanted one he would have his desire inserted in the television supply-and-demand program.''

''Then what?''

''Sooner or later, he'd get one, new or secondhand, either in exchange for something or as a gift.''

''Just by asking for it?''

''Yes.''

Getting up, Cruin strode to and fro across his office. The steel heelplates on his boots clanked on the metal floor in rhythm with the bells. He was ireful, impatient, dissatisfied.

''In all this madness is nothing which tells us anything of their true character or their organization.'' Stopping his stride, he faced Hefni. ''You boasted that *you* were to be the eyes and ears.'' He released a loud snort. ''Blind eyes and deaf ears! Not one word about their numerical strength, not one—''

''Pardon me, sir,'' said Hefni, quickly, ''there are twenty-seven millions of them.''

''Ah!'' Cruin registered sharp interest. ''Only twenty-seven millions? Why, there's a hundred times that number on Huld which has no greater area of land surface.'' He mused a moment. ''Greatly underpopulated. Many cities devoid of a living soul. They have air-machines and other items suggestive of a civilization greater than the one they now enjoy. They operate the remnants of an economic system. You realize what all this means?''

Hefni blinked, made no reply. Kalma looked thoughtful. Fane and Parth remained blank-faced and tight-lipped.

''It means two things,'' Cruin pursued. ''War or disease. One or the other, or perhaps both—and on a large scale. I want information on that. I've got to learn what sort of weapons they employed in their war, how many of them remain available, and where. Or, alternatively, what disease ravished their numbers, its source, and its cure.'' He tapped Hefni's chest to emphasize his words. ''I want to know what they've got hidden away, what they're trying to keep from your knowledge against the time when they can bring it out and use it against us. Above all, I want to know which people will issue orders for their general offensive and where they are located.''

"I understand, sir," said Hefni, doubtfully.

"That's the sort of information I need from your six specimens. I want information, not invitations to meals!" His grin was ugly as he noted Hefni's wince. "If you can get it out of them before they're due here, I shall enter the fact on the credit side of your records. But if I, your commander, have to do your job by extracting it from them myself—" Ominously, he left the sentence unfinished.

Hefni opened his mouth, closed it, glanced nervously at Kalma who stood stiff and dumb at his side.

"You may go," Cruin snapped at the four of them. "You have one week. If you fail me, I shall deem it a front-line offense and deal with it in accordance with the active-service section of the manual of procedure and discipline."

They were pale as they saluted. He watched them file out, his lips curling contemptuously. Going to the port, he gazed into the gathering darkness, saw a pale star winking in the east. Low and far it was—but not so far as Huld.

In the mid-period of the sixteenth day, Commander Cruin strode forth polished and bemedaled, directed his bell-jangling feet toward the hill. A sour-faced guard saluted him at the edge of the ash and made a slovenly job of it.

"Is that the best you can do?" He glared into the other's surly eyes. "Repeat it!"

The guard saluted a fraction more swiftly.

"You're out of practice," Cruin informed. "Probably all the crews are out of practice. We'll find a remedy for that. We'll have a period of saluting drill every day." His glare went slowly up and down the guard's face. "Are you dumb?"

"No, sir."

"Shut up!" roared Cruin. He expanded his chest. "Continue with your patrol."

The guard's optics burned with resentment as he saluted for the third time, turned with the regulation heel-click and marched along the perimeter.

Mounting the hill, Cruin sat on the stone at the top. Alternately he viewed the ships lying in the valley and the opposite scene with its trees, fields and distant houses. The metal helmet with its ornamental wings was heavy upon his head but he did not remove it. In the shadow beneath the projecting visor, his cold eyes brooded over the landscape to one side and the other.

She came eventually. He had been sitting there for one and a

half periods when she came as he had known she would—witho
knowing what weird instinct had made him certain of thi
Certainly, he had no desire to see her—no desire at all.

Through the trees she tripped light-footed, with Sue and Sa
and three other girls of her own age. The newcomers had larg
dark, humorous eyes, their hair was dark, and they were leggy

"Oh, hello!" She paused as she saw him.

"Hello!" echoed Sue, swinging her pigtails.

" 'Lo!" piped Sam, determined not to be left out.

Cruin frowned at them. There was a high gloss on his jac
boots, and his helmet glittered in the sun.

"These are my friends," said Marva, in her alien-accente
Huldian. "Becky, Rita and Joyce."

The three smiled at him.

"I brought them to see the ships."

Cruin said nothing.

"You don't mind them looking at the ships, do you?"

"No," he growled with reluctance.

Lankily but gracefully she seated herself on the grass. Th
others followed suit with the exception of Sam who stood wit
fat legs braced apart sucking his thumb, and solemnly studyin
Cruin's decorated jacket.

"Father was disappointed because you could not visit us."

Cruin made no reply.

"Mother was sorry, too. She's a wonderful cook. She loves
guest."

No reply.

"Would you care to come this evening?"

"No."

"Some other evening?"

"Young lady," he harshed, severely, "I do not pay visits
Nobody pays visits."

She translated this to the others. They laughed so heartily tha
Cruin reddened and stood up.

"What's funny about that?" he demanded.

"Nothing, nothing." Marva was embarrassed. "If I told you
I fear that you would not understand."

"I would not understand." His grim eyes became alert, calcu
lating as they went over her three friends. "I do not think
somehow, that they were laughing at me. Therefore they wer
laughing at what I do not know. They were laughing at some
thing I ought to know but which you do not wish to tell me." H
bent over her, huge and muscular, while she looked up at him

with her great green eyes. "And what remark of mine revealed my amusing ignorance?"

Her steady gaze remained on him while she made no answer. A faint but sweet scent exuded from her hair.

"I said that nobody pays visits," he repeated. "That was the amusing remark—nobody pays visits. And I am not a fool!" Straightening, he turned away. "So I am going to call the rolls!"

He could feel their eyes upon him as he started down the valley. They were silent except for Sam's high-pitched, childish, "Bye!" which he ignored.

Without once looking back, he gained his flagship, mounted its metal ladder, made his way to the office and summoned Jusik.

"Order the captains to call their rolls at once."

"Is something wrong, sir?" inquired Jusik, anxiously.

"Call the rolls!" Cruin bellowed, whipping off his helmet. "Then we'll know whether anything is wrong." Savagely, he flung the helmet onto a wall hook, sat down, mopped his forehead.

Jusik was gone for most of a period. In the end he returned, set-faced, grave.

"I regret to report that eighteen men are absent, sir."

"They laughed," said Cruin, bitterly. "They laughed—because they *knew*!" His knuckles were white as his hands gripped the arms of his chair.

"I beg your pardon, sir?" Jusik's eyebrows lifted.

"How long have they been absent?"

"Eleven of them were on duty this morning."

"That means the other seven have been missing since yesterday?"

"I'm afraid so, sir."

"But no one saw fit to inform me of this fact?"

Jusik fidgeted. "No, sir."

"Have you discovered anything else of which I have not been informed?"

The other fidgeted again, looked pained.

"Out with it, man!"

"It is not the absentees' first offense," Jusik said with difficulty. "Nor their second. Perhaps not their sixth."

"How long has this been going on?" Cruin waited awhile, then bawled: "Come on! You are capable of speech!"

"About ten days, sir."

"How many captains were aware of this and failed to report it?"

"Nine, sir. Four of them await your bidding outside."

"And what of the other five?"

"They . . . they—" Jusik licked his lips.

Cruin arose, his expression dangerous. "You cannot conceal the truth by delaying it."

"They are among the absentees, sir."

"I see!" Cruin stamped to the door, stood by it. "We can take it for granted that others have absented themselves without permission, but were fortunate enough to be here when the rolls were called. That is their good luck. The real total of the disobedient cannot be discovered. They have sneaked away like nocturnal animals, and in the same manner they sneak back. All are guilty of desertion in the face of the enemy. There is one penalty for that."

"Surely, sir, considering the circ—"

"Considering nothing!" Cruin's voice shot up to an enraged shout. "Death! The penalty is death!" Striding to the table, he hammered the books lying upon it. "Summary execution as laid down in the manual of procedure and discipline. Desertion, mutinous conduct, defiance of a superior officer, conspiracy to thwart regulations and defy my orders—all punishable by death!" His voice lowered as swiftly as it had gone up. "Besides, my dear Jusik, if we fail through disintegration attributable to our own deliberate disregard of the manuals, what will be the penalty payable by *us*? What will it be, eh?"

"Death," admitted Jusik. He looked at Cruin. "On Huld, anyway."

"We are on Huld! *This* is Huld! I have claimed this planet in the name of Huld and therefore it is part of it."

"A mere claim, sir, if I may say—"

"Jusik, are *you* with these conspirators in opposing my authority?" Cruin's eyes glinted. His hand lay over his gun.

"Oh, no, sir!" The second commander's features mirrored the emotions conflicting within him. "But permit me to point out, sir, that we are a brotherly band who've been cooped together a long, long time and already have suffered losses getting here as we shall do getting back. One can hardly expect the men to—"

"I expect obedience!" Cruin's hand remained on the gun. "I expect iron discipline and immediate, willing, unquestionable obedience. With those, we conquer. Without them, we fail." He gestured to the door. "Are those captains properly prepared for examination as directed in the manuals?"

"Yes, sir. They are disarmed and under guard."

"Parade them in." Leaning on the edge of his desk, Cruin prepared to pass judgment on his fellows. The minute he waited for them was long, long as any minute he had ever known.

> *There had been scent in her hair.*
> *And her eyes were cool and green.*
> *Iron discipline must be maintained.*
> *The price of power.*

The manual provided an escape. Facing the four captains, he found himself taking advantage of the legal loophole to substitute demotion for the more drastic and final penalty.

Tramping the room before them while they stood in a row, pale-faced and rigid, their tunics unbuttoned, their ceremonial belts missing, the guards impassive on either side of them, he rampaged and swore and sprinkled them with verbal vitriol while his right fist hammered steadily into the palm of his left hand.

"But since you were present at the roll call, and therefore are not technically guilty of desertion, and since you surrendered yourself to my judgment immediately you were called upon to do so, I hereby sentence you to be demoted to the basic rank, the circumstances attending this sentence to be entered in your records." He dismissed them with a curt flourish of his white-gloved hand. "That is all."

They filed out silently.

He looked at Jusik. "Inform the respective lieutenant captains that they are promoted to full captains and now must enter recommendations for their vacated positions. These must be received by me before nightfall."

"As you order, sir."

"Also warn them to prepare to attend a commanding officer's court which will deal with the lower-ranking absentees as and when they reappear. Inform Captain Somir that he is appointed commander of the firing squad which will carry out the decisions of the court immediately they are pronounced."

"Yes, sir." Gaunt and hollow-eyed, Jusik turned with a click of heels and departed.

When the closer had shut the door, Cruin sat at his desk, placed his elbows on its surface, held his face in his hands. If the deserters did not return, they could not be punished. No power, no authority could vent its wrath upon an absent body. The law was impotent if its subjects lacked the essential feature of being present. All the laws of Huld could not put memories of lost men before a firing squad.

It was imperative that he make an example of the offenders. Their sly, furtive trips into the enemy's camp, he suspected, had been repeated often enough to have become a habit. Doubtless by now they were settled wherever they were visiting, sharing homes—welcome rooms—sharing food, company, laughter. Doubtless they had started to regain weight, to lose the space lines on their cheeks and foreheads, and the light in their eyes had begun to burn anew; and they had talked with signs and pictures, played games, tried to suck smoke things, and strolled with girls through the fields and the glades.

A pulse was beating steadily in the thickness of his neck as he stared through the port and waited for some sign that the tripled ring of guards had caught the first on his way in. Down, down, deep down inside him at a depth too great for him to admit that it was there, lay the disloyal hope that none would return.

One deserter would mean the slow, shuffling tread of the squad, the hoarse calls of "Aim!" and "Fire!" and the stepping forward of Somir, gun in hand, to administer the mercy shot.

Damn the manuals.

At the end of the first period after nightfall Jusik burst into the office, saluted, breathed heavily. The glare of the ceiling illumination deepened the lines on his thin features, magnified the bristles on his unshaven chin.

"Sir, I have to report that the men are getting out of control."

"What d'you mean?" Cruin's heavy brows came down as he stared fiercely at the other.

"They know of the recent demotions, of course. They know also that a court will assemble to deal with the absentees." He took another long-drawn breath. "And they also know the penalty these absentees must face."

"So?"

"So more of them have deserted—they've gone to warn the others not to return."

"Ah!" Cruin smiled lopsidedly. "The guards let them walk out, eh? Just like that?"

"Ten of the guards went with them," said Jusik.

"Ten?" Coming up fast, Cruin moved near to the other, studied him searchingly. "How many went altogether?"

"Ninety-seven."

Grabbing his helmet, Cruin slammed it on, pulled the metal

chin strap over his jaw muscles. "More than one complete crew." He examined his gun, shoved it back, strapped on a second one. "At that rate they'll all be gone by morning." He eyed Jusik. "Don't you think so?"

"That's what I'm afraid of, sir."

Cruin patted his shoulder. "The answer, Jusik, is an easy one—we take off immediately."

"Take off?"

"Most certainly. The whole fleet. We'll strike a balanced orbit where it will be impossible for any man to leave. I will then give the situation more thought. Probably we'll make a new landing in some locality where none will be tempted to sneak away because there'll be nowhere to go. A scout can pick up Fane and his party in due course."

"I doubt whether they'll obey orders for departure, sir."

"We'll see, we'll see." He smiled again, hard and craggy. "As you would know if you'd studied the manuals properly, it is not difficult to smash incipient mutiny. All one has to do is remove the ringleaders. No mob is composed of men, as such. It is made up of a few ringleaders and a horde of stupid followers." He patted his guns. "You can always tell a ringleader—invariably he is the first to open his mouth!"

"Yes, sir," mouthed Jusik, with misgivings.

"Sound the call for general assembly."

The flagship's siren wailed dismally in the night. Lights flashed from ship to ship, and startled birds woke up and squawked in the trees beyond the ash.

Slowly, deliberately, impressively, Cruin came down the ladder, faced the audience whose features were a mass of white blobs in the glare of the ships' beams. The captains and lieutenant captains ranged themselves behind him and to either side. Each carried an extra gun.

"After three years of devoted service to Huld," he enunciated pompously, "some men have failed me. It seems that we have weaklings among us, weaklings unable to stand the strain of a few extra days before our triumph. Careless of their duty they disobey orders, fraternize with the enemy, consort with our opponents' females, and try to snatch a few creature comforts at the expense of the many." His hard, accusing eyes went over them. "In due time they will be punished with the utmost severity."

They stared back at him expressionlessly. He could shoot the

ears off a running man at twenty-five yards, and he was waiting
for his target to name itself. So were those at his side.

None spoke.

"Among you may be others equally guilty but not discovered.
They need not congratulate themselves, for they are about to be
deprived of further opportunities to exercise their disloyalty."
His stare kept flickering over them while his hand remained
ready at his side. "We are going to trim the ships and take off,
seeking a balanced orbit. That means lost sleep and plenty of
hard work for which you have your treacherous comrades to
thank." He paused a moment, finished with: "Has anyone anything to say?"

One man holding a thousand.

Silence.

"Prepare for departure," he snapped, and turned his back
upon them.

Captain Somir, now facing him, yelped: "Look out, commander!" and whipped up his gun to fire over Cruin's shoulder.

Cruin made to turn, conscious of a roar behind him, his guns
coming out as he twisted around. He heard no crack from
Somir's weapon, saw no more of his men as their roar cut off
abruptly. There seemed to be an intolerable weight upon his
skull, the grass came up to meet him, he let go his guns and put out
his hands to save himself. Then the hazily dancing lights faded
from his eyesight and all was black.

Deep in his sleep he heard vaguely and uneasily a prolonged
stamping of feet, many dull, elusive sounds as of people shouting far, far away. This went on for a considerable time, and
ended with a series of violent reports that shook the ground
beneath his body.

Someone splashed water over his face.

Sitting up, he held his throbbing head, saw pale fingers of
dawn feeling through the sky to one side. Blinking his aching
eyes to clear them, he perceived Jusik, Somir and eight others.
All were smothered in dirt, their faces bruised, their uniforms
torn and bedraggled.

"They rushed us the moment you turned away from them,"
explained Jusik, morbidly. "A hundred of them in the front.
They rushed us in one united frenzy, and the rest followed.
There were too many for us." He regarded his superior with
red-rimmed optics. "You have been flat all night."

Unsteadily, Cruin got to his feet, teetered to and fro. "How many were killed?"

"None. We fired over their heads. After that—it was too late."

"Over their heads?" Squaring his massive shoulders, Cruin felt a sharp pain in the middle of his back, ignored it. "What are guns for if not to kill?"

"It isn't easy," said Jusik, with the faintest touch of defiance. "Not when they're one's own comrades."

"Do you agree?" The commander's glare challenged the others. They nodded miserably, and Somir said: "There was little time, sir, and if one hesitates, as we did, it becomes—"

"There are no excuses for anything. You had your orders; it was for you to obey them." His hot gaze burned one, then the other. "You are incompetent for your rank. You are both demoted!" His jaw came forward, ugly, aggressive, as he roared: "Get out of my sight!"

They mooched away. Savagely, he climbed the ladder, entered his ship, explored it from end to end. There was not a soul on board. His lips were tight as he reached the tail, found the cause of the earth-rocking detonations. The fuel tanks had been exploded, wrecking the engines and reducing the whole vessel to a useless mass of metal.

Leaving, he inspected the rest of his fleet. Every ship was the same, empty and wrecked beyond possibility of repair. At least the mutineers had been thorough and logical in their sabotage. Until a report-vessel arrived, the home world of Huld had no means of knowing where the expedition had landed. Despite even a systematic and wide-scale search it might well be a thousand years before Huldians found this particular planet again. Effectively the rebels had marooned themselves for the rest of their natural lives and placed themselves beyond reach of Huldian retribution.

Tasting to the full the bitterness of defeat, he squatted on the bottom rung of the twenty-second vessel's ladder, surveyed the double star-formations that represented his ruined armada. Futilely, their guns pointed over surrounding terrain. Twelve of the scouts, he noted, had gone. The others had been rendered as useless as their parent vessels.

Raising his gaze to the hill, he perceived silhouettes against the dawn where Jusik, Somir and the others were walking over the crest, walking away from him, making for the farther valley he had viewed so often. Four children joined them at the top, romped beside them as they proceeded. Slowly the whole group sank from sight under the rising sun.

Returning to the flagship, Cruin packed a patrol sack with personal possessions, strapped it on his shoulders. Without a final glance at the remains of his once-mighty command he set forth away from the sun, in the direction opposite to that taken by the last of his men.

His jack boots were dull, dirty. His orders of merit hung lopsidedly and had a gap where one had been torn off in the fracas. The bell was missing from his right boot; he endured the pad-*ding*, pad-*ding* of its fellow for twenty steps before he unscrewed it and slung it away.

The sack on his back was heavy, but not so heavy as the immense burden upon his mind. Grimly, stubbornly he plodded on, away from the ships, far, far into the morning mists—facing the new world alone.

Three and a half years had bitten deep into the ships of Huld. Still they lay in the valley, arranged with mathematical precision, noses in, tails out, as only authority could place them. But the rust had eaten a quarter of the way through the thickness of their tough shells, and their metal ladders were rotten and treacherous. The field mice and the voles had found refuge beneath them; the birds and spiders had sought sanctuary within them. A lush growth had sprung from encompassing ash, hiding the perimeter for all time.

The man who came by them in the midafternoon rested his pack and studied them silently, from a distance. He was big, burly, with a skin the color of old leather. His deep gray eyes were calm, thoughtful as they observed the thick ivy climbing over the flagship's tail.

Having looked at them for a musing half hour he hoisted his pack and went on, up the hill, over the crest and into the farther valley. Moving easily in his plain, loose-fitting clothes, his pace was deliberate, methodical.

Presently he struck a road, followed it to a stone-built cottage in the garden of which a lithe, dark-haired woman was cutting flowers. Leaning on the gate, he spoke to her. His speech was fluent but strangely accented. His tones were gruff but pleasant.

"Good afternoon."

She stood up, her arms full of gaudy blooms, looked at him with rich, black eyes. "Good afternoon." Her full lips parted with pleasure. "Are you touring? Would you care to guest with us? I am sure that Jusik—my husband—would be delighted to have you. Our welcome room has not been occupied for—"

"I am sorry," he chipped in. "I am seeking the Merediths. Could you direct me?"

"The next house up the lane." Deftly, she caught a falling bloom, held it to her breast. "If their welcome room has a guest, please remember us."

"I will remember," he promised. Eyeing her approvingly, his broad, muscular face lit up with a smile. "Thank you so much."

Shouldering his pack he marched on, conscious of her eyes following him. He reached the gate of the next place, a long, rambling, picturesque house fronted by a flowering garden. A boy was playing by the gate.

Glancing up as the other stopped near him, the boy said: "Are you touring, sir?"

"Sir?" echoed the man. *"Sir?"* His face quirked. "Yes, sonny, I am touring. I'm looking for the Merediths."

"Why, I'm Sam Meredith!" The boy's face flushed with sudden excitement. "You wish to guest with us?"

"If I may."

"Yow-ee!" He fled frantically along the garden path, shrieking at the top of his voice, "Mom, Pop, Marva, Sue—we've got a guest!"

A tall, red-headed man came to the door, pipe in mouth. Coolly, calmly, he surveyed the visitor.

After a little while, the man removed the pipe and said: "I'm Jake Meredith. Please come in." Standing aside, he let the other enter, then called, "Mary, Mary, can you get a meal for a guest?"

"Right away," assured a cheerful voice from the back.

"Come with me." Meredith led the other to the veranda, found him an easy-chair. "Might as well rest while you're waiting. Mary takes time. She isn't satisfied until the legs of the table are near to collapse—and woe betide you if you leave anything."

"It is good of you." Seating himself, the visitor drew a long breath, gazed over the pastoral scene before him.

Taking another chair, Meredith applied a light to his pipe. "Have you seen the mail ship?"

"Yes, it arrived early yesterday. I was lucky enough to view it as it passed overhead."

"You certainly were lucky considering that it comes only once in four years. I've seen it only twice, myself. It came right over this house. An imposing sight."

"Very!" endorsed the visitor, with unusual emphasis. "It looked to me about five miles long, a tremendous creation. Its mass must be many times greater than that of all those alien ships in the valley."

"Many times," agreed Meredith.

The other leaned forward, watching his host. "I often wonder whether those aliens attributed smallness of numbers to war or disease, not thinking of large-scale emigration, nor realizing what it means."

"I doubt whether they cared very much seeing that they burned their boats and settled among us." He pointed with the stem of his pipe. "One of them lives in that cottage down there. Jusik's his name. Nice fellow. He married a local girl eventually. They are very happy."

"I'm sure they are."

They were quiet a long time, then Meredith spoke absently, as if thinking aloud. "They brought with them weapons of considerable might, not knowing that we have a weapon truly invincible." Waving one hand, he indicated the world at large. "It took us thousands of years to learn about the sheer invincibility of an idea. That's what we've got—a way of life, an idea. Nothing can blast that to shreds. Nothing can defeat an idea—except a better one." He put the pipe back in his mouth. "So far, we have failed to find a better one.

"They came at the wrong time," Meredith went on. "Ten thousand years too late." He glanced sidewise at his listener. "Our history covers a long, long day. It was so lurid that it came out in a new edition every minute. But this one's the late night final."

"You philosophize, eh?"

Meredith smiled. "I often sit here to enjoy my silences. I sit here and think. Invariably I end up with the same conclusion."

"What may that be?"

"That if I, personally, were in complete possession of all the visible stars and their multitude of planets I would still be subject to one fundamental limitation"—bending, he tapped his pipe on his heel—"in this respect—that no man can eat more than his belly can hold." He stood up, tall, wide-chested. "Here comes my daughter, Marva. Would you like her to show you your room?"

* * *

Standing inside the welcome room, the visitor surveyed it appreciatively. The comfortable bed, the bright furnishings.

"Like it?" Marva asked.

"Yes, indeed." Facing her, his gray eyes examined her. She was tall, red-haired, green-eyed, and her figure was ripe with the beauty of young womanhood. Pulling slowly at his jaw muscles, he asked: "Do you think that I resemble Cruin?"

"Cruin?" Her finely curved brows crinkled in puzzlement.

"The commander of that alien expedition."

"Oh, him!" Her eyes laughed, and the dimples came into her cheeks. "How absurd! You don't look the least bit like him. He was old and severe. You are *young*—and far more handsome."

"It is kind of you to say so," he murmured. His hands moved aimlessly around in obvious embarrassment. He fidgeted a little under her frank, self-possessed gaze. Finally, he went to his pack, opened it. "It is conventional for the guest to bring his hosts a present." A tinge of pride crept into his voice. "So I have brought one. I made it myself. It took me a long time to learn . . . a long time . . . with these clumsy hands. About three years."

Marva looked at it, raced through the doorway, leaned over the balustrade and called excitedly down the stairs. "Pop, Mom, our guest has a wonderful present for us. A clock. A clock with a little metal bird that calls the time."

Beneath her, feet bustled along the passage and Mary's voice came up saying: "May I see it? Please let me see it." Eagerly, she mounted the stairs.

As he waited for them within the welcome room, his shoulders squared, body erect as if on parade, the clock whirred in Cruin's hands and its little bird solemnly fluted twice.

The hour of triumph.